Acclaim for the Work of
DONALD E. WESTLAKE!

"Dark and delicious."
— *The New York Times*

"[A] book by this guy is cause for happiness."
— *Stephen King*

"Donald Westlake must be one of the best craftsmen
now crafting stories."
— *George F. Will*

"Westlake is a national literary treasure."
— *Booklist*

"Westlake knows precisely how to grab a reader, draw
him or her into the story, and then slowly tighten his grip
until escape is impossible."
— *Washington Post Book World*

"Brilliant."
— *GQ*

"A wonderful read."
— *Playboy*

"Marvelous."
— *Entertainment Weekly*

In the fifth week, they came for him.

It was Friday night. It was too cold now to be autumn anymore, but the snow hadn't started yet. He was walking along the tilted slate squares of sidewalk, past the barren trees and the streetlights; it was just past midnight, and the street was deserted. He was a block from home when the highly polished new black car rolled slowly past him, going in his direction, and crept to a stop a few doors away. The passenger-side door opened, and a man climbed out. He was hard-looking. He stood on the sidewalk with his hands on his hips and squinted at Cole, the squint making the corners of his mouth turn up like the beginning of a snarl.

"Paul Cole?" The man's voice was harsh, but soft, as though there were no strength in it and he had to strain his throat to make any sound at all.

Do I know him? Maybe he knows me from somewhere, and his is one of the faces I've forgotten. But if we already know each other, why did he ask me if I was me?

He moved his head and said, "Yes. I'm Paul Cole."

The man's right hand slipped with surprising speed into his hip pocket, and came out with a wallet, which he flipped open, saying, "Police. Get in the car..."

MEMORY

by **Donald E. Westlake**

A HARD CASE CRIME NOVEL

A HARD CASE CRIME BOOK
(HCC-064)
April 2010

Published by

Dorchester Publishing Co., Inc.
200 Madison Avenue
New York, NY 10016

in collaboration with Winterfall LLC

*This book is a work of fiction. Names, characters, places, and
incidents either are the products of the author's imagination or
are used fictitiously, and any resemblance to actual events or
persons, living or dead, is entirely coincidental.*

ISBN 0-8439-6375-1
ISBN-13 978-0-8439-6375-5

Cover design by Cooley Design Lab

Typeset by Swordsmith Productions

Printed in the United States of America

Visit us on the web at www.HardCaseCrime.com

MEMORY

After the show, they went back to the hotel room, and to bed, for the seventeenth time in three weeks. He had chosen her because, being on the road with him, she was handy; and additionally because she was married, had already clipped the wings of one male, and could therefore demand nothing more from him than he was willing to give. Why she had chosen him he neither knew nor cared.

He was deep in clench-faced sweaty blindness of physical passion when the hotel room door burst open and what could only be the husband stormed in, topcoat flaring behind him like Batman's cloak. He rose up from the mounded woman, smiling idiotically at the enraged face rushing toward him, thinking only *What a cliché!* and so unable to take it seriously. Till the husband reached out one flailing hand and brought it back lifting a chair, the legs pointing at four spots around his head as though to frame him there symmetrically for eternity, and then he scrambled back and away from the woman, his hand slipping on her rubbery breast, and he cried out, "What are you *doing*?"

And the nurse dressed all in white said, "Ah, there you are!" She was smiling, looking down at him, pleased by his presence. Her teeth were wide and shiny, like enamel kitchen cabinets all in a row. The pale lips were an oval smile around them, but then the oval reversed to the comic exaggeration of a frown, and she said, "*Oh*, no. Don't fade away again."

The teeth aren't real, he thought.

There was nothing between the two thoughts, *what are you doing* and *the teeth aren't real*. No transition, no time lapse, no going to sleep and waking up, no explanation.

The nurse had a face of leather, like a cowboy, but with a

soft round nose. She said, "The doctor will want to talk to you. Now don't fade away again."

"I won't," he whispered, because whispering was all he dared until he found out whether or not he was real.

She went away, and his eyes looked at the ceiling, which had no character at all. It was featureless, lifeless, blameless white. He thought, *Something must have happened in between. He must have beat me up, and I must be in a hospital.* But there was no memory to go with the necessity. Not even a memory of time-lapse, such as comes when waking up from sleep. Waking up from sleep, there is the knowledge in the brain that a black form of time has been going on. But this was nothingness and less than nothingness. The four pointed chair legs, and then the nurse, and nothing in between.

A soft decayed face came into his vision, trying to look stern. It wore glasses, in which he could see twin reflections of himself, very small, being nothing but a head on a pillow. This must be the doctor.

It was. He introduced himself as such: "I am Doctor Croft. Are you awake enough to answer questions?"

"Yes."

"Do you have to whisper?"

"I don't know." But he whispered it. He moved his tongue within his mouth, collecting saliva, and swallowed. "I don't have to whisper." His voice was rusty, like something long unused.

"What is your name?"

"Paul Cole. Paul Edwin Cole."

"How old are you?"

His mind slithered, found it: "Twenty-six."

"Where were you born?"

"Troy, New York,"

"What is your father's name?"

"He's deceased." *What a stupid word*, he thought, hearing himself say it. *An Army word. That's where I learned it, when they typed it on the yellow form. Father deceased. Mother deceased.*

But the doctor was not Army material. He persisted. He said, "What *was* his name, then?"

"Robert nomiddleinitial Cole." That was Army, too. NMI.

"And your mother?"

He knew the game now. Deceased was no good here. "Elizabeth Shoreby Cole."

"Is she alive?"

"No, she's— She's dead."

"Your next of kin?"

"*I'm* not dead."

"Who do we notify of your accident?"

"Accident?"

The soft decayed face turned sour. "You were caught, weren't you? That's an accident."

"Why didn't you know my name?"

"I did."

"From my wallet. Then why did you ask me?"

"To see if you knew it." He seemed inclined to explain, to be expansive, though still disapproving. "In head injury cases, particularly after prolonged shock or unconsciousness, we look for memory damage. But you seem all right, at least superficially. Now. Who do we notify?"

"No one."

"You must have a relative."

"It's a rule? I have a married sister. But why tell her? We haven't been in contact in five years."

"What's her name?"

"Ruth Cole."

"You said she was married."

"Oh." He reached for the name, and bumped off it. It was like going down a flight of stairs, not looking, and there is one less step than you think, and your foot starts down for that last step and bumps painfully where there should only be air, and your arms have to pinwheel to keep you from falling, and you drop the newspaper, primary-colored comic pages scattering across the rug. "Her husband's name is Ray, he's got red hair, he—"

"You can't remember his last name?"

"It's been a long while since I've seen them." Cold wetness was on his forehead. Why was the cold wetness there, as though he'd been washed but not dried. He drew a hand out from under the stiff covers and wiped his forehead, and then he felt dizzy and weak, as though he'd only pushed the cold wetness inside his head.

The doctor said, "No matter. I'll talk to you later on."

The face went away, and the face of the nurse with the unreal teeth came back. She was smiling again, idiotically, and he remembered his own idiotic smile when the husband had burst in, and he said, "What's your name?"

"May," she said. "And you're Paul."

"May. All right, why not. Tell me what happened?"

"What happened?" How the oval opening around the teeth could twist and turn, so mobile and cunning. Now it expressed itself puzzled. "Don't you know?"

"He hit me with the chair."

"And we brought you here. And now you're awake again, and just as fine as new."

"Where are the bandages?" He remembered the cold wet forehead, and his hand brushing it, and no bandages there.

"Oh, you have lots of bandages," she said. "Around your head, and—no, higher than that—and all around your chest, because you have broken ribs, too, you know."

He was feeling the tight hard coarse bandaging on the top of his head. It felt white, but not like the ceiling or her teeth. He said, "Tell me, uh…I'm sorry, I've forgotten your name."

"May. In the merry month of May."

"June is a month, too."

"So it is."

"How long have I been unconscious?"

"Fifty-eight hours."

He translated that, frowning, and when he frowned he could feel the bandages, a broad band around his head, and he felt like Civil War wounded, but there were no bandages on his brow. Fifty-eight hours. Two days, and then ten hours. Approximately midnight it had been, of Saturday. Sunday gone by, and Monday gone by, and now it must be ten o'clock Tuesday morning.

With no feeling in his brain of time having passed. It was frightening.

He said, "It's ten o'clock Tuesday morning."

She looked down at a watch with a silver expansion band. "Ten-fifteen," she said.

"I'm not hungry," he said, wondering about it.

"You've been fed intravenously."

"Ah. This is all very expensive, isn't it?"

"Oh, I don't know. Good health is never expensive, *I* say. You're an actor, aren't you?"

"Yes."

"You were with that acting company that was here Saturday night, weren't you? At the Palace Theater."

"Yes."

"I wish I could have gone, but I was on duty. I do love the theater."

"They're gone, aren't they?"

"Gone?" She gazed down at him in innocent astonishment. "Who's gone?"

"The company. The actors. The play."

"Oh, yes. I understand they had to appear somewhere else."

"Yes. Just for one night. Like here."

"That must be a wonderful life."

"Yes. I'm sorry, did I ask you your name?"

"Yes, you did."

"What did you say?"

"May. Remember? The merry month of May."

"Oh, yes."

"Don't worry, now, this must all be confusing to you still."

"That's right."

"I must go now."

"Yes."

Then for a while there was nothing but the blank face of the ceiling.

Troy is a city of steep and stunted hills. Streets and streets of frame houses painted gray and tan. Streets of pockmarked blacktop. Narrow streets. The lights on the movie theater marquees never seem to be getting enough electricity. Down in Albany there are dartboards in all the bars.

The girl who brought him his first hospital meal had the face of an English orphan; pinched, frightened, silent. Her uniform was white and too wide and too heavily starched. It had short sleeves; her elbows were bony and gray.

She cranked the bed so that he was sitting, and wheeled his food in place in front of him. It was on a thick white plate with a red stripe around for decoration, and a small chip out of the edge. On it were two pork chops, mashed potatoes still retaining the shape of the ice-cream scoop, and peas. Two pieces of white bread and a pat of butter were on a smaller plate. A thick squat glass held milk. The knife and fork were heavy, and plain, with the name of the hospital carved on the handles: *Memorial Hospital*.

He didn't feel himself to be hungry, but he ate everything, at a steady pace, and when he was finished he wanted a cigarette. A little later, the English orphan came back, to get the tray, and he asked her for a cigarette. Not looking at him, she said, "No smoking in hospital. Fire law." She cranked the bed down again, and took the tray away. After, he wished he'd thought to tell her to leave him sitting, so he could look at the room.

The next one he saw was male again, with a full and florid face, lined by dissatisfaction. He said, "I am Lieutenant Murray, City Police."

"They tell me I can't smoke here."

"That's right. Fire law. Doctor Croft says you're well enough to answer questions."

He didn't say anything, because he didn't know if it was true or not.

Lieutenant Murray looked down at something—he was

holding a paper or something in his hand, below the line of Cole's vision. He said, "You are Paul Cole, twenty-six years of age, height six feet, weight one hundred fifty-seven pounds, hair black, eyes blue, no scars or marks. Born Troy, New York, current permanent address New York City. Next of kin, sister, married name unknown. That correct?"

The doctor had asked. Lieutenant Murray told. Cole said, "Could you crank the bed up? I can't see you this way."

"I'll get a nurse."

It took a few minutes, but then a nurse—a different one, a new one—cranked the bed up so he was sitting again. It was a private room, small and very clean. There was sky beyond the window. The two chairs—in one of which Lieutenant Murray sat—were covered in green leatherette.

Lieutenant Murray began again, reading everything as before, and now Cole could see that he held a clipboard in his lap, with several forms and sheets of paper on it, with neat black typewriting on the top sheet, the one from which Lieutenant Murray was reading.

When Lieutenant Murray asked him again if that information was all correct, he said, "Yes, it is."

"Remembered your sister's married name yet?"

"No." He frowned, but all he could remember was her husband's red hair. He couldn't remember the husband's name at all, first or last.

"No matter." Lieutenant Murray tossed the clipboard onto the bed, next to his knees. "You won't die."

He smiled faintly, but didn't say anything.

Lieutenant Murray said, "How much do you know about the situation?"

"I'm in a hospital. I guess I was beaten up."

"I guess you were. All right, let me tell you where you stand. You were having intercourse with a married woman. Her husband caught you in the act, and beat the crap out of you. Legally, you have the right to swear out a warrant against him for assault, but legally he has the right to swear out three or four warrants against you. For adultery, for instance. It's illegal in this state, as it is in most states. I can't remember anybody in this state ever going before a judge on it, but there's always a first time."

Cole, watching Lieutenant Murray's mouth, understood that the policeman hated him. There were many reasons why, most of them in Lieutenant Murray's discontented face and harsh voice.

Lieutenant Murray said, "I've talked to the husband. As far as I'm concerned, he had every right to slug you, but he went too far. Unwritten law is a lot of crap. Here's the deal. He doesn't make any complaints against you legally, and you don't make any complaints against him legally. You stay away from him, and you stay away from his wife, and you pay your own bills in the hospital here."

"No."

"What's that?"

"Who put me in a private room?"

"How do I know? Listen, you're being offered a good deal. We could make life rough on you if we wanted. The lady's husband could make life rough on you. And the hotel could make life rough on you. Now, the husband's going to pay for the damage to the hotel room, and you're going to pay your own hospital bill."

"Half. I pay half."

"Nobody's bargaining with you, sonny. It's take it or leave it."

"What happens to the wife?" he said. He felt very mean and angry, all at once, and didn't care why. As though it were the only way to penetrate the fabric of the world enough to be seen.

"What do you mean, what happens to the wife? You stay away from her, that's all you have to do."

"*She* goes home. *He* goes home. I sit here under this ceiling, and you come in and hate me."

"What the hell are you talking about? I'm doing a job, I don't give a damn about you one way or the other."

Cole smiled, and cocked his head to one side. "Would *you* have kicked her out of bed?"

"I'm a happily married man."

"I'll pay half."

Lieutenant Murray got to his feet. "You aren't in New York now," he said. He went away.

You get on the subway at West 4th Street. The D train will take you to Sixth Avenue, and the A train will take you to Eighth Avenue. The token is smaller than a dime, and brass-colored, and has holes in it. The trains are very loud, and the platforms are gray concrete. In the summer it is very hot and in the winter it is very wet. If you go the other way, the trains scream and rush and come up to air in Brooklyn. Fred Crawford lives in Brooklyn, and sometimes has parties.

The doctor came again, and asked more questions, and shined a pencil flash in his eyes. Later, the nurse with the shining teeth came back, and was very jolly, and then two men in starched white jackets came in with a wheeled stretcher and lifted him and set him down on the stretcher, and rolled him out of the room. He felt as though he could walk with no trouble, but they said nothing to him so he said nothing to them.

The corridor ceiling was marked at regular distances by white globes containing light bulbs. He watched them go by, feeling like an artistic traveling shot in a motion picture, and then he was brought into a room where they took x-rays of his head. He said to the technician, "What's wrong?"

"Don't ask me. I just work here."

"Why do they have to take x-rays of my head?"

"Don't ask me. I just work here."

They took him back to the small neat room and put him on the bed again, and left. The bed was cranked down, and all he could look at was the ceiling. He felt lethargic, but with a dull anger, as though he had been cheated in a card game and couldn't understand how it had been done. It wasn't the cheating, it was his own stupidity.

The nurse with the shining teeth came in and cranked the bed up and gave him a copy of the *Saturday Evening Post* that was a year and a half old. He asked her what her name was, and she told him it was May, and smiled brilliantly, but didn't say anything about the merry month.

He looked at the cartoons in the magazine, then read the advertising. While he was reading about death in an insurance company ad Lieutenant Murray came back and said, "He'll pay half."

"Oh. I should have said I wouldn't pay any."

"I advised him to refuse, but he feels responsible."

"He does?"

"Maybe in New York you think adultery is smart, but around here we think it's disgusting."

Lieutenant Murray went away again, and Cole sat there with the magazine closed on his lap. He wondered where the company was now. Tuesday. Where were they booked for Tuesday night? He couldn't remember; all the towns were the same. They came, they played one performance, they went on. The bus was white, with blue lettering on the side, telling everyone this was the National Touring Company of *My Soul To Keep*, which had recently been a Hit on Broadway.

Now Danny Kirkpatrick would move up from his small role to replace him, and the assistant stage manager, Matt Willard, would take Danny's part. And in New York someone would turn the pages of *Player's Guide*, and find a face and form and experience which approximated those of Paul Cole, and someone would be hired, and given a plane ticket, and by next week he would have the part, and Paul Cole himself would be unable to tell whether or not that was him up there on the stage.

The window of sky went dark. When the lighting came on, at the impulse of some unseen hand far away in some dark control room, it was indirect, coming from troughs along the walls, near the ceiling. Like a bar, like a tavern. But the lights were not red and amber and green, they were all white.

His supper was brought to him. Grey slices of beef, covered with brown gravy. Mashed potatoes, still retaining the shape of the ice-cream scoop. Boiled carrots. A thick glass containing milk. He ate it all, and again he wanted a cigarette, but this time he didn't ask.

He fell asleep, and when he awoke the lights were turned off and the bed was cranked down. His chest was itching, but he couldn't scratch it through the bandages. He felt very sad, as though something tremendously important had been lost while he slept, but the feeling was too vague, and he couldn't understand what it was he'd lost. Gradually he sank into sleep again.

2

It was a Monday when they brought his suitcase to him; he had been there thirteen days. He was down at the end of the corridor, in the solarium, looking out past the plants and through the window at the world outside. He stood in a room on the seventh floor, out on the skin of the building. Down below there was a busy street, with a busline on it. Across the road, amid green grounds and autumn-orange trees, was a gray stone building like a monastery, which they'd told him was a teacher's college. The fall semester had just recently started, and sometimes he could see the young girls with red and white scarves around their necks, walking along the gravel paths, embracing their books. There were a few male students, too; they all wore unbuttoned sweaters, and carried a single book in their right hands, and kept their left hands in their trouser pockets, and looked as though they played basketball.

He had gone to college, too, but he didn't think he had played basketball. None of that was very clear now.

On this side there was a curved drive from the street, passing the hospital entrance and then curving back to the street again, leaving a green oval concrete-lined island in the center. There was a large white wooden sign on the island, but he could only see the back of it. He'd asked several times what the front of the sign said, and they had always told him, but he couldn't remember right now. He could ask again, but it embarrassed him to have to keep asking.

There were other male patients in the solarium, sitting around the sofas and reading magazines. He had tried to read magazines at first, but he couldn't concentrate on them. His mind kept wandering away in the middle of a paragraph. He sometimes sat with a copy of the *Saturday*

Evening Post, looking at the cartoons and reading the advertisements. He liked the *Saturday Evening Post* best, because so many of the advertisements were in color. But most of the time, since they'd let him out of bed, he just stood at the window and watched the street. He watched the cars, and the green buses, and the pedestrians, and the young girls across the way.

The nurse with the shining teeth came into the room and called his name, and when he turned she said, "They've brought up your things."

He said, "Thanks, May." He always said her name when he remembered it, and was always irritated by how happy she was at his remembering.

He went down the long corridor to his room, and May said, "When you're ready, Doctor Croft wants to see you. Just go downstairs and ask at the desk. They'll tell you where to find his office."

He thanked her again, and she went away. He went over and stood beside the bed, and looked at his possessions. They were lying on the bed: a suitcase, a small canvas bag, and a large manila envelope.

He opened the envelope first. Inside, there were wallet and watch and Zippo lighter and a stale pack of cigarettes and a ballpoint pen and thirty-five cents in change. Everything that had been in his clothes, he guessed. He picked up the wallet and emptied everything out of it. There was a ten dollar bill, and two five dollar bills, and three one dollar bills. There was a driver's license from the State of New York, with the name Paul Edwin Cole on it, and his sex, and the color of eyes, and date of birth, and weight, and height, and color of hair, and an address: 50 Grove Street, New York, N.Y. There were membership cards for three actors' unions—Actors Equity and SAG and AFTRA. There was a reduced laminated photostat of an Honorable Discharge from the United States Army, which gave his name and rank and serial number. There was a Social Security card. There was a card from the Wittburg Blood Bank that had his blood type as O positive; this card stirred echoes of college, and he thought that once he had sold a pint of blood for money. He felt a sudden intense yearning to know who had received that pint of blood, to meet that person, talk with him, become good friends with him. Then he shook his head, and put everything back in the wallet.

He looked next in the canvas bag. There was a zipper which, when he opened it, made a ragged sound. Inside there was a pair of slipper socks, and some clean underwear, and a paperback novel, and a cardboard box of contraceptives, and a deck of playing cards, and a pair of black shoes in need of a shine. He took all the things out, touching them, feeling them like a blind man seeing with his hands, and spreading them all out on the bed. When they were all out there, spread out, he stood looking at them, counting the objects and thinking about them. Then he put everything back into the canvas bag except the shoes and a set of underwear and socks.

The suitcase had just clothing. There was a pair of brown slacks, neatly folded. There were two belts, all rolled up and held that way with rubber bands. There were white shirts and sport shirts, and a green wool pullover sweater. There were socks rolled into little balls, Army fashion. There were three ties rolled up and stuffed in a row into one of the side pockets. In the other side pocket was a tin of aspirin, and a pair of cufflinks, and two keys connected together with a twist of thick wire. The small key must be for the suitcase, and the large key for 50 Grove Street, New York, N.Y.

When he had touched everything, he stood there dissatisfied. Something was missing, but he didn't know what. His fingers itched for a cigarette; it would help him think.

Looking around the room, befuddled, vague and beginning to grow angry, he noticed a gray suit hanging on the back of the door. He stood studying it, quizzically, and then smiled at it.

He dressed quickly, and filled his pockets with his possessions, and closed up the canvas bag and the suitcase. The gray robe and white nightgown he left on the bed; they belonged to the hospital.

He asked someone where the elevator was, and walked down the corridor. At the end, across from the elevator, was a kind of bazaar counter, like a shooting gallery, but with desks behind it, and nurses, one of whom was May. She smiled and waved to him, and called something he didn't hear, and he nodded gravely. He was distracted because he was making himself remember the doctor's name: Doctor Croft. Doctor Croft. Doctor Croft.

There was a woman in a gray uniform operating the elevator. It was a deep elevator, and some people in back were clustered around an ancient woman in a wheelchair.

He felt very strange, coming down and not remembering going up. He had never seen this lobby before, and he stepped out to it from the elevator slowly, looking at it. A soft impatient voice said, "Excuse me, please," and he moved over for the wheelchair and all the people to go by.

Near the front entrance was a railing, and behind the railing a gleaming wooden desk, and at the desk a woman in a nurse's uniform. He went over there and said, "Doctor Croft's office, please."

"Your name?" She was a narrow, jealous woman.

He told her his name, and she used her telephone, and then gave him directions. There was another corridor to walk along, and then he found the right door, with Doctor Croft's name in gold letters on the glass. He hesitated, and then knocked. A voice called to him to come in, and he pushed open the door and entered.

The room was longish, and very narrow, with a broad window at the far end taking up almost the whole wall. There was a green carpet on the floor, and a gray metal desk, and a black leather sofa, and a black leather chair, and a green metal filing cabinet, and a hat rack. Framed diplomas were on the pale green walls.

Doctor Croft, with his spectacles and his thin frame and his soft decayed face, was standing behind the desk, and a stocky florid man was sitting on the sofa. Cole recognized the stocky florid man, but couldn't remember the circumstances in which he'd known him.

Doctor Croft said, "You remember Lieutenant Murray," and then he did.

He said, "Yes. How do you do?"

"Let's get this over with," said Lieutenant Murray, and looked at his watch.

Doctor Croft said, "Sit down, Paul," and motioned at the leather chair. "This won't take long," he said. "Just leave your luggage on the floor there."

Cole sat in the leather chair. He noticed that Doctor Croft was smoking; there was a filter cigarette burning on the edge of the ashtray on the doctor's desk. He said, "May I have a cigarette? The ones in my clothes were stale."

"Oh. Certainly." The doctor sat down, and took the pack from the handkerchief pocket of his suit jacket. He handed the whole pack over, and pushed a table lighter closer across the desk. The table lighter was gold-colored and Greek in style.

Cole lit a cigarette, and made a face. The smoke was hot and harsh in his throat. He said, "They didn't used to taste like that."

"Oh, of course. You haven't been smoking the last two weeks. You've lost the taste." Doctor Croft nodded and said, "You'll never have a better opportunity to give them up. The nicotine withdrawal is finished now; the rest is just psychological."

"I don't want to give them up."

"Ah. I do; I wish I could." Doctor Croft picked up his cigarette and looked at it. "It's an unhealthy habit," he said, and took a drag. He blew smoke luxuriously, and said, "I suppose you'd like to know about damages, financial and medical, eh?" He smiled without humor. "We'll take the medical damages first," he said. "Your ribs have come along nicely, and if you avoid an excess of physical activity for a few weeks, you'll be all right in that department. As to the head injury, it was superficial, and essentially slight. The x-rays show no brain damage whatsoever. I understand your memory processes are still a bit under par, but that shouldn't be a permanent condition. As it is now, it's too slight even to be termed partial amnesia. You have a bad memory at the moment, that's all. I imagine you'll have trouble remembering phone numbers, addresses, things like that. But it shouldn't last. The condition should clear up with time. Other than that, there are no problems at all." He smiled again. "You're probably the healthiest man in the hospital," he said.

"Good."

"Now, as to financial damages." He flipped open a folder on his desk. "As was explained to you, you couldn't be moved from the private room because the wards were full, but we agreed to charge you at ward rate. Fifteen days at seventeen seventy-five a day, two hundred sixty-six dollars and twenty-five cents. Then there are drugs, and ambulance, and other fees— Here's an itemized list, you can see it for yourself."

Cole took the piece of paper from him. It was thin paper, full of printing and typing. The number in the bottom right hand corner was $488.62. He said, "That's a lot of money."

"Considering what was done for you, not really. Now, as I understand it, you are to pay half of this bill, and the other half will be paid by the gentleman who put you here, is that right?"

Lieutenant Murray said, "That's right."

"Fine," said Doctor Croft. "Your share, then, comes to two hundred forty-four dollars and thirty-one cents." He smiled some more, and opened his desk drawer, and took out an envelope. "Your troupe's manager left with me a check to cover your final pay, and fare back to New York City. The check is in the amount of two hundred thirty-seven dollars and eighty cents. All you have to do—"

"Why have you got the check? Why didn't they give it to me with the rest of my stuff?"

Doctor Croft's smiling face said, "I thought it best to hold it myself, for safekeeping."

Lieutenant Murray said, "We didn't want you to skip."

"Does the check cover it?"

"Not entirely. A balance remains of six dollars and fifty-one cents."

"You've got dough left," said Lieutenant Murray. "You can cover it."

"You looked through my wallet?"

"For identification."

Doctor Croft was extending a pen. "If you'll endorse the check—"

He wrote his name on the back of the check. His signature looked odd to him, large and shaky, with big loops in the l's. He gave the pen back, and the check, and then he gave Doctor Croft a five dollar bill and two one dollar bills, and Doctor Croft gave him back forty-nine cents in change, saying, "I'll take all this to the cashier for you."

"I want a receipt."

"Of course." Doctor Croft took the thin sheet of paper with all the numbers on it and scrawled *Paid* across it. He extended it toward Cole.

Cole said, "Sign your name to it."

Doctor Croft lost his smile. He said, "Are you trying to be smart?"

"No."

"He's one of those smart big city boys," said Lieutenant Murray.

Doctor Croft angrily wrote his name on the paper, and handed it to Cole. Cole folded it and put it away in his wallet.

Lieutenant Murray grunted and heaved himself to his feet. "All right, Cole," he said. "Let's go."

Cole got up and started out, but Doctor Croft said, "Don't forget your luggage." He picked up his suitcase and the canvas bag, and followed Lieutenant Murray out of the hospital to a black car with POLICE written on the doors in block white letters. Lieutenant Murray said, "Get in."

Cole put his suitcase and canvas bag in back, and got into

the front seat next to Lieutenant Murray. He said, "Where are we going?"

"Bus depot. You're leaving town."

"Oh."

They drove away from the hospital, and at the next traffic light Lieutenant Murray started talking. He said, "How much dough you got on you? To the penny."

Cole counted, and said, "Sixteen dollars and eighty-four cents."

"Too bad."

"Why?"

"If it was under ten I could vag you."

"Why do you hate me?"

"I don't hate you. I have contempt for you. Now, listen to me. We're going down to the bus depot, and you're taking a bus out of town. Anywhere you want, just so it's out of town. And you don't ever come back here, or you're in big trouble. You got me?"

"Yes."

They were silent a few blocks, and then Lieutenant Murray said, "Your memory isn't so hot now, huh?"

"I guess not."

"You remember the woman?"

"What woman?"

"The one you were in the rack with."

"Oh." He thought about it seriously, and he could see her face. That was all, nothing else. "I can remember her," he said.

"Was she worth it?"

"What?"

"Getting your head kicked in. Was she worth it?"

"I don't know."

"You mean, that's the part you forgot? Bein' in the rack with her?"

Cole was silent.

Lieutenant Murray laughed. "You paid all this for it, and

you can't even remember it! No, it wasn't worth it, Cole. It's never worth it, Cole."

They stopped in front of a storefront that was used as the bus depot. They went in together, and Cole went over to the old woman at the ticket window and said, "I want to go east. Toward New York City. About seven dollars worth."

"New York City?"

"No. How far east can I go for seven dollars?"

"Seven dollars?"

"Yes."

"Where do you want to go?"

"East. Just east."

She shook her head. "I don't know what you mean."

"If I took a bus to New York, what would the first stop be?"

"Do you want to buy a ticket or not?"

"I want to buy a ticket. If I was going to New York— No. Where does the bus to New York make its first stop?"

"Imlay."

"How much is a ticket to Imlay?"

"Three dollars and forty-nine cents."

"What's the next stop after that?"

"Mister, I don't have time for a lot of silly games. You want a ticket or don't you?"

"I want a ticket to the stop after Imlay."

"You mean Jeffords?"

"That's right, Jeffords. How much is that?"

"Five dollars and sixty-seven cents."

"That's fine. When does the next bus leave?"

"One-oh-eight."

"Thank you." He looked at his watch, and it was twenty minutes to twelve. An hour and a half to wait.

When he paid for the ticket, he had eleven dollars and seventeen cents left. He went over to the one bench, where Lieutenant Murray was sitting, and said, "My bus leaves at one-oh-eight."

"We'll wait here."

"You, too?"

"Me, too. I got to see to it you get out of town. Sit down, Cole."

"I want to buy some cigarettes."

"Machine over there."

He got change from the old woman, and fed thirty cents into the cigarette machine. He'd left the luggage on the floor by the bench, next to where Lieutenant Murray was sitting. Lieutenant Murray looked peaceful and calm, except for the permanent discontent lines on his face.

Cole came back and sat down, opening the pack of cigarettes. Lieutenant Murray said, "Where you going? What town?"

"I don't want to tell you."

"Why the hell not?"

"What do you want to know for? To call the police there, and tell them to give me a bad time?"

"Are you out of your head? What the hell would I do that for?" He was serious.

Cole looked at his face, and saw he didn't know what he was doing. He hated Cole, but he didn't know it. Cole said, "I'm going to a place called Jeffords.

"Jeffords. That's a nice town. You'll like Jeffords."

3

It was dark when the bus made its second stop. The driver called out, "Jeffords!" and opened the door.

Cole got down and stood on the sidewalk, and after a while they got his suitcase and canvas bag out of the side of the bus and gave them to him. He turned away and went walking down the street toward dull traces of neon a few blocks away.

It was a small industrial town, old and cramped, with buckled sidewalks. The evening air was cold, and people on the sidewalks were bundled into heavy jackets. Cole was wearing only his suit; even his sweater was still in the suitcase.

He discovered that the bus depot was on a side street away from the main downtown section, close to the railroad yards. This street was all commercial—plumbers and TV repairmen and tailors and small appliance stores and used furniture stores—with apartments for rent above the shops. There was a stink in the air, like smoldering wet cardboard.

After two blocks, he came to the main street, all of it away to the left. There were a few larger stores, and two movie theaters, and two five-and-dimes, and a couple of small office buildings. This being a Monday evening, only the two movie houses and a couple of restaurants were open.

He stood at the corner, looking that way, and then turned and looked in the other direction, and saw a red neon sign that said HOTEL, half a block away. He went down there.

The hotel was just a big house, made of brick, with bay windows on the front. It was four stories high, and blocky-looking. There was a flight of slate steps up to the entrance.

Inside, there was a very small lobby. Instead of a desk, there was a doorway, with a counter affixed to the bottom half of a Dutch door. A bald man took his three dollars in advance, and gave him a key, and told him it was two flights up. There was neither bellboy nor elevator.

The room was a box. All the woodwork and molding had outlines softened by coat after coat of thick cheap paint. The furniture was stolid and old and functional. The bathroom was at least thirty years old.

He came into the room at ten minutes past seven, and left it again at seven-thirty. He was still wearing the suit, but now he'd replaced the white shirt and tie with a cotton sport shirt and the green sweater. He went out and walked over to the downtown section and went into a restaurant that didn't seem too high class to object to the way he was dressed. He ate supper, and then went out and looked at the two movie marquees, made up his mind, and bought a ticket at the one that was showing a double feature. He saw the last half of one picture, and then all of the second picture, and then all of the first picture, and then the lights went on. There were only four other people left in the theater, and it was twenty-five minutes to twelve.

He was going to go to a bar next, but he decided not to spend the money. He went back to the hotel instead, and when he was in the room he counted his money, and he had five dollars and seven cents.

He hadn't yet started thinking about what he was going to do. He'd been putting it off, thinking about smaller things or nothing at all. But now he stripped to his underwear, and switched off the light, and crawled into bed, and settled himself to think it through.

He had to get back to New York. As close as he could figure, he was now about a thousand miles from New York, but the first thing to do was get back to the city. His life was there, and all his friends were there, and whatever future he had was there.

And there was this memory thing. He didn't think it was getting any worse, but it didn't seem to be getting any better either. If he could get back to the city, back to familiar surroundings, the memory would maybe improve faster.

How to get there. He thought of phoning somebody collect, asking somebody to wire him bus fare. He could do that. But who would he call?

He shifted around in the bed, making its springs squeak. There was a fog in his head, an irritating fog. He could remember faces, he could remember first names, he could remember a few addresses. But nothing complete. Of the people he knew in New York, none of them would come in full and clear, with face and first name and last name and address. He could think of no telephone numbers at all.

They shouldn't have turned me loose, he thought. *They should have kept me at the hospital.*

The window was open a little bit, and that stink of smoldering wet cardboard was in the room. It had been everywhere he'd gone on the street, and in the restaurant, and in the movie house. It distracted him sometimes, the way a persistent noise can distract.

The stink was interrupting his thoughts. He kept trying to remember, trying to put a name to this face, or that face, and it wasn't working. His hands clenched and relaxed at his sides, and his mouth was twisted with strain, but it wouldn't work. He couldn't get them.

He kept trying, and kept trying, and under the covers he was perspiring, but it didn't work at all. The fog was too persistent, it was more like syrup poured into his head, sticking to everything, obscuring all the outlines, like the paint muffling the lines of the moldings in the room, but more softly and more cloyingly.

And what made it worse was that it was ridiculous. It was like being on a crowded street, and your pants have fallen down around your ankles. You bend over and tug at them, but you can't get them back up again because it turns out you're standing on them. You stay in that position, too ashamed to straighten and show your face, and too off-balance to move your feet, and you tug uselessly at your trousers, and they just won't come free. And it's too absurd to be a tragedy. It's even too absurd to be high comedy.

I can't remember my friends.

He could imagine himself going up to a stranger, and asking for help, saying, "I can't remember my friends. I have to get back to New York and see them again, so I can remember who they are."

He tugged and tugged, but the names wouldn't come free.

When he finally fell asleep, it was from exhaustion. He awoke again to a room full of thin sunshine, and the ever-present stink of wet cardboard. He wasn't at all rested. His head ached, and he felt lumpy and awkward.

He washed himself and dressed, and then stood a moment looking at the door. He was all dressed up with no place to go. The door was old wood, aged and varnished a nut brown. It was decorated with knob and bolt and chain and framed house rules. It led generally to the whole world, but particularly to nowhere at all.

He sat down on the bed, and scraped his forehead with the palm of his hand, remembering last night's struggle with names and faces. It was no good, and he knew it. The memory would get stronger again later on, the doctor had said so, but in the meantime what was he supposed to do?

There was only one immediate goal: to get back to New York. It called to him like the womb. There, in New York, *home*, he could crowd himself into a warm dark place and wait for his health to return. Here he was naked, unprotected, out alone on a hostile plain.

He remembered counting his money last night, but he couldn't remember what the figure had been, so he took out the bills and coins, spread them on the bed, and counted them again, and discovered again that he had five dollars and seven cents.

Not enough. Not enough for anything. Enough to pay for this room one more night, and to eat sparingly today, and then tomorrow there would be nothing left of him at all.

When the idea came to him to get a job here in this town, he was at first surprised at it. A job—not a job touring, but a *job*—implied some sort of permanence, and his connection with this town couldn't be more temporary. He wanted nothing more from it than its absence, its replacement by New York.

But it was the only way. He thought about it, turning it over slowly in his mind, and nodded without pleasure, gazing at the door and admitting that it was the only way. He would have to stay here, find a job, and save his money. Once he had enough for bus fare back to New York…

He got to his feet, suddenly with purpose and direction. He left the room and went downstairs, where a younger man, with a sharp guilty defiant face, was standing in the small room behind the Dutch door. Cole went over to him and said, "Where's the Unemployment Insurance office?"

"You planning to stay over?"

"Yes."

"Pay in advance."

"When I come back," said Cole with sudden irritation.

"Checkout time, one o'clock."

Cole looked at his watch, and it was ten-thirty. "When I come back," he said again. "Where's the Unemployment Insurance office?"

"On MacGregor Street."

"Where's that?"

"First street to your left. Turn left, it's in the second block. New building."

"Thank you."

Cole started away, and the clerk said, "Remember. Checkout's one o'clock."

Cole ignored him, feeling angry, and went out to the sidewalk, down the slate steps. He turned left, thinking that he could have paid now and not have to come back by one o'clock, but the clerk had irritated him, and in some obscure way it was a victory not to pay now.

He discovered he had to pass the bus depot to get to the Unemployment Insurance office, and he decided to stop in there first and find out how much money he was going to need. As in the other town, the one he'd left, the bus depot was a small old storefront. There were posters propped in the window of this one for square dances and stock car races.

He went inside, and once again there was a very old woman behind the counter. It was like being in the other town again, and for just a second he was confused, and wondered if his mind had more things wrong with it than the memory, and in reality he was still back in the other town. But the confusion passed, and he came on into the room and over to the desk. There was another old woman, sitting on the bench along the side wall with such stolidity and patience she looked as though she'd grown there, and aside from these two the depot was empty.

Cole said to the old woman, "How much is a ticket to New York?"

"One-way or round trip?"

"One-way."

She looked it up, in a thick small book with flimsy pages, and told him, "Thirty-three forty-two."

"Thank you."

He went back outside, and turned toward the Unemployment Insurance office again. Thirty-three dollars and forty-two cents. It wasn't much. He could earn that in no time.

The Unemployment Insurance office was a squarish one-story building like a truncated block, made of yellow brick and windows. On the glass doors gold lettering read:

DEPARTMENT OF LABOR

DIVISION OF EMPLOYMENT

BUREAU OF UNEMPLOYMENT COMPENSATION

Warren H. McEvoy, *Commissioner*

Cole pushed open one of the doors and went in.

He came first into a long room with a low ceiling from which were suspended fluorescent lights. The right-hand wall was a bank of windows, but the fluorescent lights were all on. There was a railing across the room, near the front, and two long wooden pews facing the railing, but no one was sitting there. Beyond the railing were rows of desks, each one flanked by a filing cabinet on one side and a wooden chair on the other. About half the desks were occupied, by soft-looking thirtyish men in white shirts and dark neckties, or by firm-looking fortyish women in plain unadorned dark dresses or suits. At a few of the desks there were suppli-cants, sitting in the second chair, their left elbows on the desk as they talked. These all wore hunting jackets and held caps in their hands.

One of the women at a desk near the front looked up and noticed him, and made a motion with her arm for him to come forward. He pushed open the gate in the railing and stepped through; the gate was on springs, and snapped back into place after him. He walked through the desks to the one occupied by the woman, and she said, "Sit down." When he was seated, she said, "This is your first visit?"

"Yes. I'm looking for a job."

"Of course." She smiled thinly. "Have you collected un-employment insurance at any time in the last two years?"

"Yes. But not here, in New York."

"I see. And what is your occupation?" She had drawn a sheaf of forms toward herself, and now she picked up a pen.

"Anything at all," he said.

But if she heard him, she made no sign. She said, "I'd better do this from the beginning. Name?"

"Paul Cole."

"C-O-L-E?"

"Yes."

"Social Security number?"

"I don't know. Wait." He got out his wallet, and read his Social Security number to her.

She said, "You should make a point of learning that. What if you lost your card someday, where would you be then?"

"I suppose so," he said.

"Your address?"

He started to reach for his wallet again, to give her his

New York address, but thought better of it, and said, "Wilson Hotel."

"I see. And your last employment?"

"I was an actor. I was on tour with—"

"*Actor*?" She put the pen down, and looked at him severely. "I'm afraid you're barking up the wrong tree," she told him. "There are no openings for actors in this area, which means that you have removed yourself from the labor force. Moving to a location which has no openings for your type of employment is considered removing yourself from the labor force, and you are therefore unavailable for work, and cannot expect to collect unemployment insurance."

"I don't want to collect unemployment insurance, I want "

"I'll fill out these forms if you insist," she said, "but I can tell you right now it won't do any good. You'll be rejected. You'll have to demonstrate that you are making an honest and conscientious search for employment of a type to be found in this locality, and in which, by means of training or experience, you can reasonably expect to be considered acceptable by a potential employer."

"I *want* a job. I want—"

"Protestations are not enough. You will have to bring us definite proof of an active search for employment. A record of job interviews, for instance. In the meantime, there is just no point in my continuing with your application."

"Listen," he said. "Listen to me for a minute."

"I'm being frank with you," she said, and smiled thinly. "I don't know what your experience with the New York office may have been, but here we expect an honest and industrious job search, or you just can't expect to collect."

"I don't *want* to collect. I want a *job*."

"Just *saying* that isn't enough. Can't you understand me? You have to *prove* that you want a job."

"But that's why I came here. It's the Division of Employment—"

"As I told you, there are no openings in this area for actors. Why you came here I have no idea, but you can't expect to remove yourself from the labor force and then rest easy at the public trough."

He didn't say anything for a minute. He was wondering if he could do any better with this woman if his memory weren't hurt; but what did his memory have to do with this? They were just talking at cross-purposes, that's all.

He said, "I want a job. That's why I came here. Don't you have lists of jobs here?"

"As I've told you repeatedly, we have no job openings listed here for actors." She was getting impatient with him, as though he were trying to do something sneaky and was being insultingly obvious about it.

He shook his head and got to his feet. He said, "Where do people go when they want to get jobs? Not acting jobs, just jobs."

"To the tannery," she said promptly.

"The tannery? Is that what makes the stink?"

"We get used to it," she said. She was colder than ever now.

He said, "Do they have any job openings there now?"

"I'm sure I don't know."

"Don't you have a list?"

"The tannery has its own employment department. It doesn't have to list with us."

"That's stupid," he said.

"I beg your pardon?"

"This whole place is stupid."

He went back to the railing and through the gate, and it snapped shut after him. He went back outside, and started to retrace his steps. An elderly man was coming toward him, blinking in the sunlight and holding his mouth open as though he were about to ask for clarification. Cole stopped him and asked for directions to the tannery. The old man told him, at great length, and Cole thanked him and went on.

It was beyond downtown. He walked past the movie theater where he'd gone last night, and down at the next corner there was a brick bridge over a narrow black stream between concrete walls. The stream moved fast, with little white froth bubbles eddying along over the black water.

Beyond the bridge the tannery buildings began. They were old and brick, like pictures he'd seen of New England factories, and they were connected together by thick black pipes high up near the top of the walls. There was wire fencing around all the buildings, and around the parking lots between the buildings. The parking lots were blacktop, with diagonal yellow guidelines, and were only about half full, most of the cars being four years old or more and very dirty.

Cole had to ask directions again, and then at last he found the sign that said *Employment Office*, with an arrow pointing to a concrete walk between two of the buildings. He went down that way and came to a green door that also said Employment Office, and went inside. There were wooden steps to climb, and then a small wooden room and a high counter. A young girl sat at a desk behind the counter, typing on an old Remington. She got to her feet when she saw Cole, and came over to the counter, saying, "Can I help you?"

"I'm looking for a job."

"Oh." She whisked a white form up from under the counter, and picked up a black ballpoint pen. Very quickly she asked him his name and age and Social Security number and address and telephone number and next of kin, but she was slowed down at almost every question, and stopped completely by the last two. He had no telephone number and no next of kin.

"No relatives?"

It was easier to say no than to explain. This girl, like everyone else, asked him a lot of questions about himself, but, like everyone else, she really had no interest in him.

She shrugged faintly, and said, "Skills?"

"What?"

"Skills. Have you ever worked in a tannery before?"

"No."

"Unskilled labor," she said, and wrote something on the form. "What was your most recent job?"

"I was an actor."

"A what? An actor?"

"Yes."

"Why did you leave that employment?"

"I was in the hospital."

"Is your health good now?"

"Yes."

She hesitated, and then looked directly at him. "If you aren't, you might as well say so. You have to have a physical examination before you can be employed here, and if you have any disabilities the doctor will find them."

For unskilled labors, the disabilities would have to be physical. He said, "I'm healthy now."

"All right." She shrugged faintly again, and wrote some more on the form. She had long straight streamers of black hair on her forearms; it made her look like a zebra. Her black hair was untidily upswept onto the top of her head, and her neck was long and thin and pale, with vertical ropes under the flesh at the sides. The top button of her white blouse was open, and the top of her chest was very white and very bony. Her hands were thin and long-fingered, and there were flakes of dead skin, like dandruff, on her knuckles. She was wearing colorless nail polish, which made her hands look as though they were trying not to show hysteria.

She said, "Have you ever been in any trouble with the police?"

"No." He didn't know if the business in the other town was trouble with the police or not, but too many disinterested people had been asking him personal questions. From now on, he would tell them as little as possible. "Name, rank, and serial number," he said.

She looked up from the form. "I beg your pardon?"

"Nothing."

She was willing to forget it. She said, "We may have an opening in the shipping department. Please wait."

He said he would. She went over to a filing cabinet and looked at things in it for a while, and then went over to the desk, carrying a five-by-seven file card, and made a telephone call. She talked softly, and Cole couldn't hear what she was saying. Then she came back and said, "Do you have any limitations as to what hours you can work?"

"No."

"Is the four-to-midnight shift all right?"

"Yes."

"Good. Just take this form," she said, snapping another white form onto the countertop from underneath, "and follow the directions on it." She stapled it to the form she'd filled in before.

"How much does this job pay?"

She seemed surprised. She said, "I really don't know. You'll have to ask at the finance office. That's on your list there."

He picked up the form she was pointing at, and looked at it. It was mimeographed and the reproduction was uneven:

```
JEFFORDS LEATHER WORKS, INC.

    Instructions to New Employees

         Read Carefully!!


Welcome to Jeffords Leather Works, Inc.,
a locally-owned and fully unionized leather
working plant organized in our city in 1868!
And, most particularly, welcome to the Jef-
fords 'family' of employees!
    For your convenience, we have arranged
the 'orientation' of new employees in as
simple and short a manner as possible.
Merely follow the steps outlined below,
and you should have no difficulty of any
kind. All locations are listed on the map.
    Note: You have already completed step
(1).

        - - - - -
```

(1) Go to Employment Office and make your application. (You have already completed this step.)

(2) Go to Finance Office in Building 4. Speak to Mr. Cowley.

(3) Go to Union Steward's Office in Building 1. Speak to Mr. Hamacek.

(4) Go to Doctor's office in Building 6.

(5) Go to _Shipping Dep't_ in Building _3_.

(6) Return to Employment Office in Building 2, and give this form back to the clerk on duty.

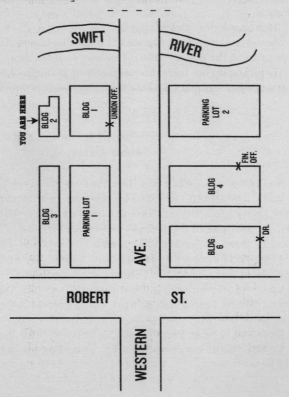

He studied the instructions and the map, then he said, "I have to cross the street four times."

"There's very little traffic this time of day," she said.

He looked at her, to see if she was making fun of him, but she wasn't. She'd thought he meant the traffic would delay him. He didn't say anything else, but went outside and stood in the thin sunshine, looking at the instruction form. He looked at the arrow by the legend *You are here*, and then he gazed around at where he was. The building he'd just left, Building 2, humped squat and square, dirty bricks, behind him. To his right was some scrubby ground, and a concrete wall, on the other side of which must be the Swift River. Ahead of him, not shown on the map, were the railroad yards. To his left was the long low brick shed that was Building 3, the Shipping Dep't, where he would go for step (5).

He turned to his left, went around the corner of the building, and down the concrete walk between Building 2 and Building 3. The wet cardboard stink was much stronger here in the middle of the factory than anywhere else in town. He breathed through his nose because when he opened his mouth the smell became taste.

He passed between Building 1 and Parking Lot 1, and went by the Union Steward's Office. He paused for a second, but the Union Steward's Office was step (3), and he hadn't done step (2) yet, and he was sure they wanted the steps down in order, so he went on, and crossed Western Avenue. He went down between Building 4 and Parking Lot 2, and midway along the brick wall of Building 4 there was a green door. He opened it and went up a half-flight of steps, and on the corridor wall at the top there was sign reading *Finance Office*, with an arrow pointing to the right. He went that way, and found the Finance Office.

It looked like the unemployment insurance office, but older and not so heavily windowed. And instead of fluorescent lights in rows there were big globe lights in rows. But the people looked like the same people, men and women.

Instead of a railing, there was a counter, not quite as high as the one in the Employment Office.

A balding pleasant-faced man with steel-rimmed spectacles and no chin came up and asked if he could be of help. Cole handed him the instruction form and said, "I'm supposed to see Mr. Cowley."

"Ah! You're just joining us, eh?" It seemed to please him. "Come on with me."

Cole went around the end of the counter and followed him. They went down past the rows of desks to a plywood-and-frosted-glass partition, and through the door there, and the balding man said to the man at the desk, "Mr. Cowley, a new employee, Mr. Paul Cole."

"They phoned," said Mr. Cowley. He was a heavyset man with a thick face; he made Cole think of fraternal organizations, the American Legion and the Masons and Kiwanis. He told Cole to sit down in the chair in front of the desk, and then there were more forms to fill out, tax forms and company forms. Cole had to sign his name to two of the forms. Mr. Cowley was dispassionate, doing his job. He looked at Cole when he asked a question, and down at the form when Cole answered it. Most of the forms were filled out in three or more copies, with carbon paper between.

When Mr. Cowley was finished with his forms, he used a paper clip to fasten some of the copies to the instruction form, and then signed his initials on the instruction form, next to the number (2). He gave the instruction form back to Cole, and then stood up and extended his hand, saying, "I'd like to welcome you to Jeffords."

"Thank you." It was meaningless, but Cole shook his hand.

Next, he went to the Union Steward's Office, in Building 1. This was a small office, cut in half by a railing. In front of the railing was a desk with a girl sitting at it, and behind the railing was a desk with a man sitting at it. Cole gave the girl his instruction form, with the Finance Office forms paper clipped to it, and said, "I'm supposed to speak to Mr. Hamacek."

"Just take a seat," she said. She looked as though she

might be related to the girl in the Employment Office.

Cole sat down, and the girl went through the gate in the railing, and it snapped shut after her. She gave Cole's forms to the man at the desk back there, and then went to a filing cabinet and got more forms, and put these on the desk, too.

The man at the desk must have been Mr. Hamacek. He was short and broad and very hairy. He had a leathery face and a thick black moustache and thick black hair. There were black hairs protruding from his nostrils and ears. He was wearing a blue dress shirt and a maroon tie, and he was smoking a pipe as though he'd just recently switched from cigarettes.

Cole had to wait a while for Mr. Hamacek to complete whatever else he was doing, and to look at Cole's forms, and then he glanced over at Cole and motioned for him. His eyes were like black buttons, and very bright. Under the thick moustache, his mouth was thin-lipped and bloodless.

Cole went through the gate and sat down in the chair beside the desk. Mr. Hamacek glanced at his form and said, "Paul Cole? Is that right?"

"Yes."

"Are you a member of atwhee?"

"What?"

"Atwhee. Allied Tannery Workers International. ATWI."

"Oh. No."

"Jeffords is a one hundred percent union shop," Mr. Hamacek said, and paused as though waiting for Cole to make something of it. He seemed defensive. He said, "In order to work here, you have to be a union member. You want to join?"

"I want to work here."

"Then you want to join. Are you a member of any other union or craft guild or similar association?"

"Yes. Actor's Equity and SAG and AFTRA."

"What? What were they? One at a time."

"Actor's Equity," said Cole, and Mr. Hamacek wrote it down. "SAG. That's the Screen Actor's Guild. And—"

"You're an actor?"

"Yes."

"Then what are you doing here?"

"I need money. I want a job."

Mr. Hamacek nodded. "Security," he said. "You're being sensible. There's no security in things like acting, the bohemian life. I didn't know actors had unions, but there's still no security in it. Here, in an established firm, with a strong trade union, you've got a future. Stability and security. What was the other one?"

"What?"

"The other union. You mentioned three."

"Oh. AFTRA. American Federation of Television and Radio Artists."

Mr. Hamacek wrote it down. Then he said, "You'll get your card in about ten days. Now, fill out these forms, and sign at the X's."

Cole took the forms, and the pen Mr. Hamacek gave him, and filled them out. While he was doing it, Mr. Hamacek said, "Dues are five percent of salary, automatically withheld." He signed his initials next to (3) on the instruction form.

After Cole finished filling out the forms, Mr. Hamacek added one of them to the stack of paper clipped to his instruction form, and then he stood up and shook Cole's hand and welcomed him to Jeffords. He told Cole again that he had made a wise move, and then Cole left and crossed Western Avenue again, and crossed Robert Street, and went to Building 6 and into the Doctor's Office.

There was a stout gray-haired woman in a nurse's uniform there. She took his form and told him, "Go through that door and strip. The Doctor will see you in a minute."

He went into the next room. It was small and dim, with a venetian blind closed over the one window. There was a gray leather examining table, and a table with a milk glass top, and a white cabinet with locked doors, and a black kitchen chair. He took his clothes off and hung them on the chair and stood there naked, waiting. Five minutes later the door

opened and a woman started in, carrying papers and looking
preoccupied. She wasn't the nurse, but she was about the
same age and weight. She stopped short and said, "Oh! I *beg*
your pardon!" She backed hurriedly out, and closed the door
so hard it slammed.

Cole felt like crying, but he wasn't sure why. He looked at
his clothing all hung on the black kitchen chair, and wanted
to put it all back on, but he told himself he couldn't do it. He
had to have this job, for money, to get back to New York.

He wanted to sit down, but there was only the one chair,
and his clothing was all on that. The floor was black linoleum,
and cold under his feet.

The doctor came in twenty minutes later, wearing a white
smock. He was a brisk distracted man in his forties, with a
look of impatience to him. He had all of Cole's forms in his
hand. He said, "Sorry to keep you waiting," in a brisk and
meaningless way, and looked at the forms. "You say you've
been hospitalized recently. What was the complaint?"

"I was beaten up."

"Oh. I see." He nodded, and put down the forms, and got
to work. It was a long examination, like the one before the
Army. When it was finished, the doctor said, "Well, you're in
perfect physical shape, if you'd like to know."

"Thank you."

"Get dressed. The nurse will have your forms."

He put his clothes back on and went out to the other
office, and the nurse handed him the forms. There was a
new one under the paper clip with the rest, and another set
of initials on the instruction form.

Cole went to Building 3, the long shed by the railroad
yards, and in through the front door. There was a door
marked *Supply*. He went in there and asked the girl at the
near desk where to find the Shipping Department. She told
him, and it was midway through the building, at the end of a
long corridor, solid double doors with *Shipping Department*
written on them. He went through and found himself in a
long open space, the whole rear half of the building, full of

noise and motion and stacks of boxes. There was a glass-and-wood cubicle to his right. He went over there and inside. It was a small cubicle, crowded with two desks and a row of filing cabinets. One of the desks was unoccupied, and at the other sat a very fat man in a dirty white shirt with the sleeves rolled up, and a black tie. He looked up at Cole and said, "What can I do for you?" His right hand was fidgeting with a pencil stub, and his left hand was fidgeting with a cigar butt that didn't seem to be lit.

Cole held out the stack of forms towards him, and the fat man dropped his pencil and took them. He glanced through them, grunting to himself, and then said, "Yeah. Ellie called. You're Paul Cole, I'm Joe Lampek. You want to start work today?"

"All right."

"Good. Show up here at four o'clock. I'll have a timecard made out on you. You see that door over there?" He pointed to the right, through the glass of the cubicle.

Cole looked that way, and nodded. "Yes."

"That's where you come in. The time clock's right next to it. Look for your card alphabetically. You lose half an hour for every five minutes you're late."

He'd forgotten to ask in the Finance Office about his pay, so he did it now. "How much do I get paid?"

"Straight dollar an hour the first forty hours. Dollar and a half the last two, that's overtime. You work a six day week, Monday through Saturday, four to midnight, with dinner hour at seven-thirty. That's seven work hours a day, forty-three bucks a week."

Cole nodded. He'd only have to work here one week, and he'd have money left over.

Lampek said, "Payday is Friday, and you're paid for the week before. This Friday you don't get anything. Next Friday you get your first pay. Starting today, you'll only have five days in this week, so there won't be any overtime."

"I won't get any money till next week?"

"That's right."

"I don't have any money at all."

Lampek shrugged. "Not my problem," he said. "Take it up with the Employment Office." He scribbled his initials on the instruction form, and handed all the forms back. "Be here at four o'clock."

Cole took the forms, and went out the door next to the time clock, which led him to Parking Lot #1. Building 2, containing the Employment Office, was to his left. He went there, and back into the Employment Office, and put his stack of forms on the counter.

The girl was talking on the telephone. She motioned to him to wait, and kept talking. He stood leaning on the counter, watching the movement of her dry mouth, and after a while she hung up and came back to him. She tried for a real smile and missed, and said, "Well, now. All done?"

"Yes."

She went through the forms, looking them all over, and nodding to herself. When she was done, she said, "That's fine. You're all set."

He said, "They told me I won't get any money till next week."

"That's right. You're paid the Friday after each pay period."

"I don't have any money. I'll need money for food and rent."

"It's possible you'll be able to arrange a loan somewhere. From one of the agencies in town, or from a friend."

"I don't know anybody here."

"Company policy forbids making advance payments."

"Then pay me tomorrow for the work I do tonight."

"As I say, company police forbids making advance payments."

He shook his head. "I don't want an advance payment. Pay me tomorrow for the work I do tonight."

"That would be considered an advance payment, and company police forbids it." She shrugged slightly. "I don't make the rules," she said.

He was going to argue some more, but instead he closed

his mouth and looked at her. It was true what she said, she didn't make the rules. She had no responsibility, she could not be held responsible.

He felt sad again, and felt a mute pity for her, but he didn't know why. He only knew it was cruel to stand here and badger her about her enforcement of rules she hadn't made. He said, meaning it deeply, "I'm sorry."

She looked surprised, and then annoyed, and he realized she thought he was being flippant, because that was supposed to be *her* line. She was supposed to say *I'm sorry*, and he was supposed to answer *That's all right*.

"That's all right," he said. He turned and walked out of the Employment Office. He went back out to Western Avenue and turned left and walked across the small bridge into the downtown section. It seemed to him that the tannery smell was less strong, but then he understood he was beginning to get used to it.

He was very hungry. He stopped in at the restaurant where he'd eaten last night, and spent seventy cents on lunch. Then he went back to the hotel.

He started on by the Dutch door and the young man with the sharp guilty defiant face, the clerk, but the clerk said, "Oh, no you don't! Where do you think you're going?"

Cole didn't understand him. He said, "Up to my room."

"You don't have a room." He pointed. "There's your stuff."

Cole looked, and saw his suitcase and canvas bag on the floor near the door. He said, "What's that for?"

"I told you checkout time was one o'clock." The clerk was making no effort to keep the triumph out of his voice.

Now that the clerk had reminded him, he remembered the conversation this morning. He looked at his watch, and it was quarter after two. He shook his head, and said, "You saw my luggage there. You knew I'd be coming back."

"I told you this morning, checkout time is one o'clock."

"Where's the owner?"

The clerk laughed. "City and County Trust," he said. "Two blocks over."

"The manager, then."

"As far as you're concerned, *I'm* the manager."

There was silence then, while Cole tried to think. He had always been sure of himself, all his life, but this business about his memory was affecting him other ways, making him less sure of anything, less sure of himself. He said, "Why do you have to be like this?"

"We don't want no deadbeats around here."

Cole shook his head. "In this place? What else could you get here? What are you?"

"Just take your stuff and scram. Or, if you want to stay another night, cash in advance."

"The hotel is cheap and shoddy, and you're cheap and shoddy. What can you expect?" But the last sentence was directed at himself.

"If you don't want trouble, buddy, you'll take off right now. Or you want me to call the cops?"

"Don't you feel bad about this?" Cole asked him.

"I'm just doing my job."

"You're like the girl," said Cole, and that ended it as far as he was concerned. He went over and picked up his luggage and went outside and down the slate steps.

It was quarter after two now. He had to be to work at four o'clock. He went along, walking toward downtown, thinking that, and was suddenly afraid that by four o'clock he would have forgotten. If he concentrated on getting a room someplace else, he might forget about the job, and he couldn't let that happen.

The thing to do was go to the bus depot and check his luggage, and then stay near the tannery till four o'clock. After work he could go find a new place to stay. He could probably come back here then, the other clerk would be on duty, but he didn't want to come back to this hotel any more. He'd find someplace else to live; he knew now that he would probably have to stay here two or three weeks.

4

The work was hard, and he enjoyed it for that. He lifted heavy boxes, carried them to a prescribed place, and put them down again. He didn't know what was in the boxes, and he didn't care. For a while, after the dinner hour, they unloaded a railroad boxcar on a siding next to the loading platforms. For that operation, a thing like a conveyor belt was brought out. It consisted of lengths shaped like ladders, but with very many rungs all close together, and with freely-spinning white metal wheels on all the rungs. Six-foot lengths of these were attached together, on legs, with one end in the boxcar and the other end across the loading platform and inside the building itself. The end in the boxcar was slightly higher, so there was an incline. Cole and three others worked in the boxcar, which was full of cardboard cartons about the size of a beer case. Lift a carton, carry it over to the conveyor, set it down, and give it a shove. With the first shove, and the incline, the carton would roll across the open space between boxcar and building, through the wide doorway, and inside, where someone would take it off and put it on the new stack that was abuilding. Cole worked in the boxcar for nearly three hours, and he liked that part best. He enjoyed pushing the cartons along on their journey into the building.

He hadn't forgotten to come to work, though the idea of it had frightened him. Between the time he'd left the hotel and the time he reported to work, he stayed close to the tannery. After spending a quarter to check his luggage in the bus depot, he strolled down to the bridge, and leaned on the brick railing there, looking down at the black water for quite a while. Then he walked all around the tannery buildings, trying to get familiar with the surroundings. He wanted to impress the tannery on his memory, and particularly the building where he was supposed to work.

When his watch told him it was five minutes to four, he went into Building 3 and looked at the cards stacked under the time clock. There was one there with his name on it, and he took it out and stood looking at it, musing. There was no one else around the time clock and when he looked up at it he saw why. It was five minutes slow, and said ten minutes to four. It didn't matter; he struck the card into the slot anyway. The card was punched with the time, and the clock rang a bell. He put the card back where he'd found it, and went over to the cubicle where he'd talked to the fat man, whose name he couldn't now remember. There was only one name he could remember from all the names he'd come across today, and that was Warren H. McEvoy. He remembered that name, but he couldn't remember who it was. The Union Steward, or the man in the Finance Office, or somebody else.

The fat man greeted him warmly, and a few minutes later introduced him to Black Jack Flynn. "Cause there's two Jack Flynns here," he said. "Black Jack and Little Jack."

"No relation," said Black Jack Flynn. He was a huge, muscular man with a smiling face, the kind of man who would drink a lot of beer and shoot darts very well. He was Section Supervisor on the four-to-midnight shift.

Then the work started, and it was hard and pleasurable. Pleasurable both because it forced him to use his body, and because it made no demands on his mind. At seven-thirty, his supper hour came, and while the others opened paper bags or lunch buckets Cole went downtown and had a hamburger and a cup of coffee. That was all he intended to have, but the work had given him an appetite, so he had a piece of apple pie, too. The bill came to sixty-five cents, and he left no tip. On the way back to work he counted his remaining money, and he had three dollars and forty-seven cents.

In a lull after the boxcar had been unloaded, he went to Black Jack Flynn and said, "They tell me I won't get any money till next Friday."

"That's right."

"I don't have any money at all. Three dollars, that's all. How can I get some money, for food and a room?"

"Jesus, buddy, I don't know. You might try Artie Bellman over there. He sometimes loans money, five for four." Flynn pointed him out.

Cole went over to Artie Bellman and said, "Mister Flynn told me you sometime loan money."

"You strapped?" Bellman was short and wiry, with a pinched face. He looked as though he could move very fast.

Cole said, "Yes. I need money for food and a room."

"How much?"

"I won't get any money till next Friday."

"So how much?"

Cole thought about it. Two dollars a day for food, say. Three dollars a day for a room. Ten days till next Friday. "Fifty dollars," he said.

Bellman shook his head. "Too much," he said. "I can let you have thirty. Make it thirty-two."

"All right."

"What you got for security? You got a watch?"

"Yes."

"Let's see it."

Cole took off his watch, and showed it to him. Bellman took it and studied it, dubiously. "I don't think I could get thirty for it," he said, "but what the hell. Let's sign the paper."

Bellman led the way to the office cubicle, and inside. There was no one in here now, and Bellman got a sheet of paper and a pen from one of the desks. "You write it," he said. "It's got to be in your handwriting."

"All right."

"Write, 'IOU forty dollars, to be paid ten dollars a payday.' And sign your name."

"Forty dollars?"

"Five for four. Didn't they tell you? You get thirty-two, you pay back forty."

"Oh." Cole wrote it, and signed it. He was thinking that

he wouldn't be here more than two or three paydays anyway, so Bellman would be lucky to get the money back he was loaning, much less the interest. Cole felt no compunction about it; Bellman was loaning money, but Bellman was a usurer and Cole was feeling the atavistic revulsion toward the usurer. He needed Bellman's money, and was grateful to get it, but wouldn't feel badly about cheating Bellman out of his profit.

Bellman took the paper and put it in his pocket. He already was wearing Cole's watch. He took out his wallet, and gave Cole two tens, one five, and seven ones. "See you payday," he said.

"I won't get any pay this week."

"I know."

Then they went back to work.

When Cole punched the time clock on his way out, his card read 12:02. He put it back in its place, in alphabetical order with the other cards there, and walked out of the building.

His clothing hadn't been right for the work. He'd taken off his tie and suitcoat, but he'd still been working in his white shirt and suit trousers. Tomorrow he would wear his slacks and a sport shirt. And he would buy some bread and cold cuts to keep in his room, and make sandwiches to take to work. It would be cheaper than going out.

He'd forgotten he wasn't staying at the Wilson Hotel any more, but when he started across the intersection where he should turn right to go to the bus depot he suddenly remembered. He stopped in the middle of the street, flushing with embarrassment and anger. He remembered the young clerk now, and the stupid series of events. He shouldn't have let it happen. He was very tired now, after working, and he shouldn't now have to go look for a room.

He turned and walked down to the bus depot, and looked at the locker key to find out what number his locker was. He reclaimed his luggage and then turned to the counter. An elderly man without teeth was sitting on a high stool behind

it, reading a comic book spread open on the counter in front
of him.

Cole said, "Excuse me. Can you tell me where I can find
an inexpensive room at weekly rates?"

"What's that?"

Cole repeated it, a little louder, and the old man said,
"Wilson Hotel."

"No, not there. Someplace else. Is there anything near
the tannery?"

"Everything's near the tannery, sonny. Don't you smell it?"

"Yes."

"Wilson too cheap for you?"

"No. I want something cheap."

"We don't have no YMCA. Try the Belvedere."

Cole got directions to the Belvedere—it was about a block
beyond the Wilson—thanked the old man, and carried his
luggage out to the street. He was very tired now, and as he
walked along, carrying his suitcase and canvas bag, he kept
yawning. He couldn't cover his mouth when he yawned,
because of the luggage he was carrying. He tried ducking
his head instead, but that constricted his jaw when it wanted
to yawn wide, and made his neck and jaw ache, so he just
walked along with his head up, yawning.

He found the Belvedere, and was afraid at first it would
be too expensive, because it had a canopy over the sidewalk,
from the curb to the entrance. But then he saw that the
canopy was very old, and so was the building. It might at one
time have been moderately expensive, but no longer. It was
a decaying pile of stone, looking as though it were settling
back into the earth like an old German castle.

There was a real lobby here, very small, with a real hotel
desk, also very small. A man in a thick moustache and a
yellow suit was on duty, and Cole asked him, "What are your
weekly rates?"

"Single?"

"Yes."

"Kitchen privileges? Telephone? Private bath?"

Cole said no to everything, not paying attention. If it was extra, he didn't want it.

The clerk said, "You can have a single for seventeen-fifty a week. Payment in advance."

"All right."

He gave the clerk Bellman's two tens, and got two singles and two quarters in exchange. The clerk gave him a key, and instructions on finding his room and the communal bathroom. Cole went up the stairs to the third floor, found his room, and went in. It was smaller than the room at the Wilson, and maybe even older. He put down his suitcases, stripped, turned off the light, and went to bed. He had no trouble at all in going to sleep.

There was no sunlight in his room when he woke up; the window faced the wrong way. He got up and dressed and went down the hall to the bathroom to wash. He had no towel, and there was no towel in the bathroom. He used toilet paper to dry his face and hands, which he'd had to wash without soap. He went back to the room and unpacked, putting his belongings in the dresser. He still had the key from the Wilson Hotel, and he was surprised to find it in his pocket, surprised that the young clerk hadn't thought to get it back from him. But the clerk had been thinking too much of his own enjoyment. Cole opened the window and threw the key out. His window faced to the rear; a scrubby lot and, beyond that, the narrow curving Swift River.

He wore his slacks today, and a sport shirt, and the sweater. He put all his money, seventeen dollars and ninety-seven cents, in his pockets, and then he left his room.

He spent money like a miser. He had the cheapest breakfast at the diner, two hotcakes and orange juice and coffee, forty-five cents. Then he did his shopping, buying only what was absolutely necessary. He thought of buying a towel, but decided he could keep on using the toilet paper for the short time he'd be staying in this town. He did buy a cake of soap and a nineteen cent ballpoint pen and a twenty cent pad of lined paper, plus a loaf of bread and a package of cheese and a package of baloney. It all cost him a dollar ninety-three, and he carried his purchases back to his room in a brown paper bag. There were two smaller paper bags inside the big paper bag, and he saved these to carry his dinner in. He put the bread and cheese and baloney on the windowsill, outside the window, put the soap in a dresser drawer, and sat down on the bed with the ballpoint pen and the pad of paper.

The first thing he did was write a note:

GO TO WORK AT TANNERY AT FOUR O'CLOCK
EVERY DAY EXCEPT SUNDAY

He fastened this piece of paper to the nail holding the list of hotel rules to the door, the paper lying over the framed rules. Then he sat down on the edge of the bed again, and started a second sheet of paper.

He was trying to help his memory, get it working again. He thought back to New York, trying to remember the names and the faces and the places. Every scrap he found he would write down, and then later he could go over what he had written and try to add to it. If his memory wouldn't work right inside his head, maybe he could carry an extra memory around with him on pieces of paper.

The first face that came into his mind was narrow and intense, male, with high cheekbones and unkempt black hair. He concentrated and concentrated, and put a name to the face. Nick. Not the last name, that wouldn't come. He thought it started with R, but he wasn't sure.

He wrote the name down. Then he looked at it, his head cocked to one side. It was just a name on a piece of paper, not a memory at all. He could write any name down, and it would mean just as much. He needed something else, something to jog his memory in case he should ever look at this piece of paper and not know the meaning of the name Nick.

Thinking about it, another name came into his head. *The Caricature*. That was a coffee shop in the Village, and he had been there with Nick, once or several times. Or he had been there when Nick had been there. So he wrote

CARICATURE after the name, with a double-headed arrow between the two. He spent a while trying to remember the name of the street the Caricature was on, but he couldn't get it.

He spent a long while sitting on the bed, occasionally writing something else down on the paper, and when he was finished he had a list seven lines long, and on all of the lines at least two names with an arrow between.

When he looked at his wrist, after putting the pen and pad away, he had a sudden feeling of dread, because his watch was gone. It was a dread for more than the loss of the watch; he could lose everything, be reduced to nothingness, and he was helpless.

But then the memory of Artie Bellman came back, and he remembered that Bellman had the watch, and he felt so relieved he had to sit down on the bed again for a while. He sat there with his head bowed and his hands dangling between his knees, and after a while he shook his head. Speaking aloud, he said, "What a sad war. What a slow sad war."

When he thought it was approaching four o'clock, he left the room and went to work.

5

The way they got their pay, they lined up in front of the office cubicle, in alphabetical order, and Joe Lampek handed each man his pay envelope, and then each man in turn signed his name to the sheet of paper on Joe Lampek's clipboard.

Cole had watched them get their pay last Friday, and had felt a biting kind of envy. Because his memory didn't tell him as surely as it should about the past, he had a more pronounced feeling than did most people about the slowness of time; his stay in this town was exaggerated by his perception of time. He felt now, eleven days after arriving here, that he had been in this place, worked in this building, for years, for decades, for a lifetime. And yet, because he kept forgetting the names of his co-workers and the names of the streets and the name of the town itself, he was still a stranger; and wanted, here, to be nothing else.

Now he was watching the second shuffling payline, but this time he was a member of it, standing near the front of the line, behind Artie Bellman. Artie Bellman got his pay envelope, and signed his name, and then it was Cole's turn. Joe Lampek smiled fatly at him, and pointed to where he was supposed to sign, and then he had his own pay envelope. He stepped off to the side and opened it, and shook out into his palm a small folded wad of bills, and some change, and a long ribbon of white paper all folded up. He counted the money, and he had twenty-three dollars and nine cents.

That wasn't right. He was supposed to have *thirty-two* dollars. He turned to Joe Lampek, who was smiling at somebody else now, giving somebody else a brown pay envelope, and he said, "This isn't right."

"What's that?" Joe wasn't mad or irritated, he was alert and curious.

"This isn't right. I'm supposed to have thirty-two dollars, and I've got twenty-three. Somebody made a mistake." He was holding his two hands out toward Joe Lampek, the pay envelope and its contents in his palms.

Joe laughed, and shook his head. "Thirty-two before deductions," he said. "Take a look at your pay slip. That white paper there. Thirty-two before deductions."

With the frightened feeling that somehow he had been tricked, and now he was going to find out about it, he opened the ribbon of white paper. It had printed boxes across it, with printed information above the boxes, and typed information inside the boxes. About half the boxes had typed information inside, all numbers.

The first box was titled *Gross Pay*, and the number inside was $32.00.

The second box was titled *Withholding*, and the number was $4.05.

The fourth box was titled *Social Security Withholding*, and the number was $1.51.

The fifth box was titled *Group Health Insurance*, and the number was $1.35.

The seventh box was titled *Union Dues*, and the number was $2.00.

The last box was titled *Net Pay*, and the number was $23.09.

Joe Lampek said, "Right? You got it now?"

"Yes," said Cole. He was terrified. His week at the Belvedere had been up on Tuesday, and they were letting it ride until tonight because they knew he was employed at the tannery. He had a dollar and some change left; after he paid his room bill he'd only have around seven dollars to last him till next Friday. And next Tuesday his rent would come due again.

How was he going to save money? How was he going to get back to New York?

He turned away, and Artie Bellman was there, smiling. "Hi, there, champ," he said.

"Hello."

Cole started on by, but Artie held his arm, and his smile faded. "Hey, champ," he said. "Aren't you forgetting something?"

Cole was made terrified by the words. Yes, he was forgetting something. But what? He clutched his money tight in his hands, afraid of everything in the world, and said, "What is it? What?"

"You owe me ten bucks, champ. Remember? Ten a payday, four paydays."

Very dimly, he remembered. It had something to do with a watch. He looked at the money crumpled in his fist, and slowly opened his fingers. But he couldn't give Bellman ten dollars; he only had seven dollars over his rent. He said, "I can't give you any money. I didn't get enough."

"That's right, you didn't work a full week. All right, champ, I tell you what I'll do. You pay me the ten, and then I loan you eight, same basis, so you still owe me the ten, and we don't have to renegotiate a new paper. See what I mean? You just give me two bucks, and it's squared away, and you can start paying off next week."

"Two dollars?"

Bellman repeated the arrangement, and this time Cole understood. He gave Bellman the two dollars, and put the rest away carefully in his wallet. He put the white ribbon of paper in his wallet, too, and the nine cents in his side pocket. A few minutes later pay time was finished, and they went to work. At seven-thirty, he ate the two sandwiches he'd brought with him, one baloney and one cheese, and drank some water. Then he went back to work, and at midnight he punched the time clock and walked back to the hotel.

The clerk's name was Ray. Cole had written it down, up in the room, and it helped to have things written down. He found he could visualize the paper sometimes, and see the name he wanted written on it.

He went over to Ray and said, "I've got the money."

"Fine." There wasn't anything wrong with Ray; he was all right. Not overly friendly, but all right.

Cole counted out seventeen dollars and fifty cents, and Ray gave him a receipt. Then Cole said, "I'm going to need to wait next week, too. I didn't get enough money this week, because I didn't work all of last week."

"That's okay," Ray told him. "Just bring it in after work on Friday."

"I will."

Cole went upstairs and counted his money, and he had five dollars and twenty-three cents. He couldn't even start saving for the bus ticket. He put the money away and went over to the dresser and picked up his pad and opened it and started reading the names he'd written.

The first name he saw was:

NICK   CARICATURE

It meant nothing to him.

Nick? Nick? Maybe an artist, somebody who'd made a caricature drawing of Cole one time, or who drew caricatures for a living. Or maybe somebody who'd had his caricature drawn by somebody else.

While he was trying to think of it, trying to make the two words turn something over in his memory, other memories suddenly opened uninvited, and he remembered now that he had borrowed thirty-two dollars from Artie Bellman a week and a half ago, and that he'd given Bellman his watch for security, and that he'd had two or three dollars besides, and that the bus ticket to New York was thirty-three dollars and forty-two cents.

He could have left then. He would have had to leave his watch behind, but what did that matter? Nothing. He could have gotten on the bus and gone straight to New York. Instead, he'd paid rent and bought food and now he didn't have any money at all. He would pay Artie Bellman two dollars a week, and never owe him less than forty dollars. He was in quicksand, already in it up to his waist, and he was noticing it for the first time.

He remembered something else. Somebody—he couldn't put a name or a face or a voice or a time to it—but somebody had said to him once, in a conversation or somewhere, that whatever you lose, you need what you lost in order to find it. If you wear glasses and you lose your glasses, you need your glasses so you can see to look for your glasses. This some-body said he'd had his bike stolen once when he was a kid, and he needed his bike so he could get quickly around the neighborhood and look for his bike.

This was the same situation, the exact same situation. He'd lost a part of his memory, and he needed that part of his memory so he could get quickly back to New York City and find that part of his memory.

He felt such terrible frustration then, he shook his head back and forth and pounded his fists against his knees and made high nasal whining noises that were not exactly crying but were more like the sounds a raccoon makes when a hind leg is in the iron trap.

He saw the pad, lying beside him on the bed, still open and with those two words heading the list. He had three or four pages now, all written in, lines and lines of names and brief notes and isolated facts, all headed by the two words *Nick* and *caricature*, two words which in combination were meaningless now and had been meaningless from the begin-ning of time and would be meaningless always. He pressed his palm down on the pad, and drew his fingers in like a spider closing on a dead fly, and half a dozen pages crum-pled into his fist, ripping loose across the top from the pad. He lifted his hand, the papers crushed and twisted, and threw them at the wastebasket, and they fluttered to the floor.

He got up and went out of the room, leaving the light on.

It was the first time he'd left the hotel except to eat or go to work. He had no money for unnecessary amusements. He stood uncertainly on the sidewalk now, having lost the impetus that had brought him this far. Then he began to walk.

Jeffords was a small lumpy humped-together town, built at a place where the Swift River twisted and corkscrewed and doubled back on itself, so that all over town there were small bridges, and all over town people had the Swift River in their back yards. It was narrow and deep and cold and black, but polluted by the tannery, and fenced or walled-in everywhere it went within the town limits.

The tannery was at the eastern end of town, and the gray stone pile of the Methodist church was at the western end. Between the two crouched the town, with pockmarked streets and grimy houses and squat black fireplugs. Most of the sidewalks away from downtown were squares of slate, jutting up at crazy angles, pushed up by gnarled tree roots from underneath. Some of the sidewalks looked like something in a carnival Fun House, but without the bright paint they would have worn in the carnival.

Cole walked along, wondering how girls could roller skate in this place. He was going nowhere in particular, just walking, having forgotten the emotion that had sent him out here in the first place. He looked at the old cars parked by the high curbs, and the house porches bunched together in rows, and the dirty-looking trees that partially shielded all the streetlights, and he walked up and down over the uneven sidewalks, and from time to time through a living room window he would see somebody asleep in front of the television set. It was around one o'clock; the television would only be showing blue snow.

At one corner he looked to his right and saw the dim glow of red neon. He went that way because he'd seen nothing but houses for blocks, and at the next corner there was a bar called Cole's Tavern. Cole looked at the name on the window, surrounded by the red neon spelling out beer names, and he felt terrified. He clutched his left wrist with his right hand, feeling where the watch had been. Looking at the name of the tavern, he felt such a terrible loneliness and loss that for a minute he was rooted there, unable to move, and the flesh of his face seemed to shrink, drawing his face into a grimace like an Oriental ogre mask.

He turned away, seeking darkness away from the soft red glare, and behind him a voice called out, "Hey! Paul, hey!"

He looked over his shoulder, thinking nevertheless it must be some other Paul they meant, though the street was deserted—but he didn't know anyone here—and then feeling a sudden urge of hope, that by some miracle it was one of the people he knew from New York, for some incomprehensible reason present in Jeffords—and then he saw it was Little Jack Flynn, leaning out from the doorway of the tavern and waving at him.

"Hey! Come on in."

Cole turned all the way around and started back, mumbling something about how late it was. Little Jack Flynn said, "I saw you through the window, why didn't you come in? Come on in." When Cole got to the doorway, Little Jack clapped him on the shoulder. "Have a beer, Paul. Come on."

Little Jack Flynn was the smallest man on the crew, with a hard and wiry body, and a cheerful ugly face. His forehead was low, his ears large, and his black hair a thick unruly mess. He told dirty jokes constantly during work, and kept up a perpetual mock battle with Black Jack Flynn, his homonym, the crew's biggest man. They would spar together during break, Little Jack ducking and weaving and jabbing and calling out bloodthirsty threats while Black Jack shuffled like a bear, grinning and holding him off with big hands.

Cole allowed Little Jack to bring him into the tavern, and he immediately recognized, among the half dozen or so faces at the bar, two other members of the crew, Buddy and Ralph, neither of whose last names he knew or could remember. Little Jack was shouting, "Look who's here!" and Buddy and Ralph were smiling at him in a friendly way, and he found himself smiling back.

The tavern was a large square room, with the bar across the rear wall. There were dim leatherette-and-formica booths on the left wall, and the other walls were lined by machinery;

a shuffleboard along the front, below the window, and to the right a bowling machine, a cigarette machine, and a jukebox. Practically all of the light in the room seemed to come from these bright machines, and the mechanical beer and liquor signs on the backbar.

"Another round!" called Little Jack, and Cole found himself pressed against the bar, Little Jack on his left, Buddy and Ralph on his right. The bartender was a huge bullnecked man with only one arm; Cole watched him with fascination as he drew the beers. He brought them over two at a time, thick fingers entwined between the glasses. The jukebox was playing loudly, an instrumental with a simple repetitive melody over a beat as solid and predictable as the rungs of a ladder, and when they started talking they had to shout over it.

It was as though there had been something curled up inside Cole, as though some small animal had burrowed away into his chest to hide or nurse itself, and all at once it was gone, the pressure had all whistled out of him, and he laughed and became something like his old self again, forgetting that he couldn't remember. They all talked together, about nothing at all but without pause, and from time to time they played teams at the bowling machine, Cole and Little Jack against Buddy and Ralph. For Cole, with so many of his memories gone, this was almost like a revelation of a different kind of life. When one of the others mentioned Artie Bellman, some recent memories crushed back into Cole's mind, depressing him, and he told the others about his money problems, but not about his need to get away. They hadn't asked him about his past, and he felt reticent to tell them about past or future; only the present was relevant here.

Buddy said, "You want to be careful, Paul. Bellman'll bleed you white."

"What can I do?"

"You want to get out of that hotel," Ralph told him. "Seventeen-fifty a week, Jesus, that's way too much."

Little Jack said, "Get yourself a furnished room. Room

and board, maybe. It'll be a hell of a lot cheaper. Get yourself a paper tomorrow and go find yourself a room."

Cole nodded. "All right," he said. "I will."

Shortly afterward, the one-armed bartender, whose name was George, told them it was two o'clock and closing time. They all made a great show of being panic-stricken as they ordered one last round, beating the second hand of the whiskey clock perched on top of the cash register, and a few minutes later they were all out on the sidewalk. Through the window, Cole could see George turning off the lights. His empty left sleeve was folded over onto his stomach and attached to his shirt there with a big safety pin.

The four of them walked together for a few blocks, and Cole had to ask directions to get back to the hotel. When he and Little Jack parted, Little Jack called, "Don't forget. Get a paper tomorrow and go find yourself a room."

"I won't forget," Cole promised. But he was afraid he would forget, so he walked along the cold tilting sidewalks whispering to himself, "Get a paper and find a room, get a paper and find a room."

When he got back to his room in the hotel, he took pen and paper and wrote himself a note. Then he picked up the crumpled sheets of paper on the floor and stood by the dresser, holding the sheets of paper down on the dresser and trying to smooth them out with his other hand. He told himself he shouldn't have got so upset. He looked again at the two names heading the first page, and now he did seem to have a dim memory of a face to go with the name Nick, though what connection that face might have with the word *caricature* he still didn't know.

He read through the rest of his notes. About half of them were meaningful for him, and the other half were just blanks, just gibberish. But that didn't bother him in particular; isolated memories drifted in and out of his mind, and if the blanks had been real memories a week ago that meant they were still in his head somewhere and he could still eventually get them out again.

One other matter did bother him. One of his notes read: "WILL & MARY—BLACKJACK." Another read: "RALPH—SIX-PACK OF BEER UNDER SEAT." Both of these notes stirred memory images for him, but they were the wrong images. *Blackjack* brought to mind only Black Jack Flynn, blotting out any possible chance of seeing Will and Mary behind him, and *Ralph*, particularly with a reference to beer, meant no one but the Ralph he'd been drinking with in the tavern tonight. The stay here in this town was turning into an independent life of its own, with its own memories and images building a wall between him and the earlier memories he was trying to grasp.

"I've got to save the money quick, and get out of here," he told himself, saying it aloud. Then he thought again of the name of the tavern—Cole's—and he smiled at the coincidence, but he still felt a shadow of the irrational fear.

Every night, he counted his money just before going to bed, and tonight he discovered he only had four dollars and eighteen cents. He'd spent three dollars in the bar. How *stupid* could he be! He'd just been paid today, there was no more money for a full week, and he'd spent three dollars in a bar!

He went to bed cursing himself, and it took him a while to get to sleep. When he woke up in the morning he had the feeling he'd had bad dreams, but he couldn't remember them. This was his feeling every morning; bad dreams had come to him during the night, but the memory of them was gone.

He found the note about buying the newspaper, and hurried through his morning toilet, pleased at the thought of finding a cheaper place to live. At the diner where he ate breakfast—a sugar doughnut and a cup of coffee heavy with milk—the clock read quarter past ten. He had till four o'clock to look for a furnished room, and then he'd have to go to work.

The newspaper cost him seven cents, which he paid grudgingly. There were nine furnished rooms listed among the ads in the back of the paper, and three of them offered rooms for nine dollars a week. He asked directions to one of the addresses picked at random, discovered it wasn't more than half a dozen blocks from the tannery, and walked there smiling, the newspaper rolled into a tube and jutting from his hip pocket.

The address was a brown shingle house with an enclosed porch. He rang the bell, and stood on the stoop waiting. After a minute, he saw the inner door open, and then a middle-aged woman in an apron came across the porch and opened the door. She was stout in a firm way, and her gray hair was in the tight ringlets of a home permanent. Her expression was wary and impatient; she looked like someone's overly disciplinary mother.

Cole showed her the newspaper and said he'd come about the furnished room. She gave a slight smile then and told him to come in. There was a straw rug on the porch floor, and a sofa and tables and hassocks. Broad green canvas shades were rolled up bulkily over the windows.

"It's upstairs," she said, leading the way. "It's my older boy's room, he's in the Army. There's no private entrance, does that make any difference?"

"No. I work at the tannery, four in the afternoon to midnight."

"Oh, we'd give you your own key."

The stairs were thickly carpeted. On the way up, Cole got a glimpse of the living room, bulging with maroon over-stuffed furniture and thick carpeting and more hassocks. On the second floor there was a small cramped hallway, with five doors. One of them was open, showing a white tile bathroom with thick yellow towels hanging everywhere, and bottles of shampoo and hair lotion and bath salts and after-shave lined up on the windowsill. There was a soft yellow cover on the toilet seat.

"It's over here," she said. "I'm Mrs. Malloy, by the way."

"Paul Cole." He followed her into the room. It seemed as though there was already somebody living here; college pennants on the walls, personal bric-a-brac on the dresser, clothing hanging in the closet. There were photos stuck into the edge of the mirror over the dresser.

"We'll take Bobby's things out of here, of course."

"That's all right."

"Well, you'll need room for your own things. Where are you staying now, if I may ask?"

"At the Hotel Belvedere. I've only lived here a month."

"You're not from around here?

"No, back east." She looked as though she wanted to ask him more questions about that, so he hurried on, saying, "It's nine dollars a week, is that right?"

"Just for the room. If you want meals, too, we'll have to make different arrangements."

"I don't know about meals. I work funny hours, four to midnight."

"I could make you a nice breakfast when you get up, and pack a lunch for you to take along. You'd have to buy your own dinner, after work."

"How much more?"

"I'd have to talk that over with my husband. Do you know him? Andy Malloy. He's in Building Two."

"I've only worked there a few weeks. I'm in Shipping. Building Three."

"Oh." She looked vaguely around the room. "Well, here it is," she said.

"It's fine."

"We'd want a week's rent in advance, of course. You'd get that back when you left."

"Oh. I don't have any money. I just started working two weeks ago, and I didn't get any pay till yesterday, and I owed some by then." She wasn't happy about that, and he suddenly felt as though important matters hinged on his getting this room, so he said, "Couldn't you check me with the tannery? I really do work there. When I get some money ahead, I can give you the extra week's rent."

"I'll want to call my husband," she said.

"Sure. He can check that I work there."

They went back downstairs, and she told him he could sit in the living room while he waited. "Paul Cole, was it? And what's your supervisor's name?"

"Black Jack Flynn. I guess it's John Flynn. There's two Jack Flynns in the crew, so they call him Black Jack Flynn to tell them apart." He stopped abruptly, feeling that he was talking too much. It was nervousness; he was afraid she wouldn't let him have the room.

He sat on the edge of one of the overstuffed chairs, and waited. There was a dark wood television console in one corner, and it surprised him that anything as modern as a television set could look so old and settled. The whole effect of this house was of a warm neat cave, of a dim safe den lived in by small and fussy creatures who rarely went out into the light.

After a while, Mrs. Malloy came back and Cole got to his feet. She was smiling her small smile again, and said, "My husband says it's all right. And if you want breakfast when you get up, and a lunch packed, that will be another eight dollars a week, or seventeen in all."

Room and board for fifty cents less than what he was paying now just for room. Cole smiled and nodded and said, "Thank you. I'd like that."

"And when would you like to move in?"

"Right now, if I could."

"Well," she said doubtfully, "we have to get Bobby's things out."

"I could help."

"Well, thank you. You'll want to get your things from the hotel."

"Yes."

"Before you go," she said, "there are some points we should discuss. Do sit down."

He sat down, on the edge of the chair again, and she sat on the sofa facing him. "If you wish to entertain," she said, "you may have the use of the porch. The furniture is quite

comfortable out there. We would rather you didn't have
your friends up to your room."

"Oh, sure. That's all right."

"We would also prefer that you not keep alcoholic bever-
ages in your room."

"I won't," he said.

"Bobby's radio is still in his room, and we'll leave it there
if you like," she said, "but we wouldn't want it played after
ten o'clock at night."

He nodded, agreeing with her.

"As to the rest—" She smiled, and spread her hands.
"You may have complete freedom of the house. If you'd like
to watch television with us in the evening, that's perfectly all
right."

"Thank you very much," he said.

She rose, saying, "I'm sure we'll get along just fine."

He thanked her again, and she escorted him to the door,
promising to give him his key when he came back from the
hotel. He walked back downtown, whistling, very happy,
pleased that the sun was shining, though it was cold. He still
had only his sweater and suitcoat, and he was hoping the
real cold would keep away until he'd saved enough money
for the bus ticket.

At the hotel, he packed his suitcase and canvas bag, and
then went downstairs to check out. He told Ray he thought
he should have some money coming back, since he hadn't
stayed the full week, and Ray said, "All right, let's see. You
didn't stay the week, so we'll have to charge you the daily
rate. From Tuesday, checking out today, that's four days,
three dollars, twelve dollars. You get five-fifty back."

Ray filled out a form, and Cole signed it, and then Ray
gave him the five dollars and fifty cents. Feeling even better,
he went back to the house where he'd be living for the next
few weeks. It was on Charter Street, number 542. He
decided to make a note of that, and keep the note in his
wallet.

He'd forgotten the woman's name, but it was on a card

over the doorbell. Malloy. He rang the bell and repeated the name over and over to himself until she came back. Then he said, "Here I am, Mrs. Malloy, came right back." He was proud of being able to say her name.

She had already started clearing her son's possessions out of the room, most of them being transferred to the bedroom of her other son, Tommy. Tommy, she told him, was still in high school, and off with friends today. "You'll like Tommy," she said.

Cole helped her with the moving, carrying armloads of clothing from the closet up to a cardboard closet in the attic. Afterward, they sat in the kitchen together for a while and had coffee and bread with butter. Mrs. Malloy tried discreetly to pump him about his past, but the combination of his reticence and faulty memory defeated her; his answers were vague and unhelpful.

After a while he went upstairs and unpacked, transferring his clothing to the dresser and closet, and stowing his suitcase and canvas bag on the closet shelf. He took a thumbtack from one of the college pennants and fastened his work-note to the back of the door. His other notes, and the blank paper, he stored in the top dresser drawer, and ripped off part of a sheet of paper to write Mrs. Malloy's name and this address on. He put that paper in his wallet, and it made him feel safe. There was an electric alarm clock in the room, so he would know when it was time to go to work, and that made him feel safe, too.

He turned on the radio, but kept the volume low. He found a station that was playing music, and then he lay down on the bed and smiled at the ceiling. He was already thinking of this room as home.

6

His life seemed to be reduced to a series of transitory numbers. Every night just before going to bed he counted his bills and change, and every day he counted the hours. Even his address, 542 Charter Street, was a transitory number. The high points in his life were the paydays, when the numbers reached their highest peak.

After the first week, his pay rose to its normal level. A gross pay of forty-three dollars was hacked away by deductions of ten dollars and eighty-three cents, leaving him thirty-two seventeen. Ten dollars to Artie Bellman, seventeen dollars to Mrs. Malloy, and he had five dollars and seventeen cents for himself. He tried to live on the two meals a day Mrs. Malloy made for him, but sometimes he got too hungry after work and then he'd buy something cheap and filling, like a cupcake and a Coke. He was losing weight, but he didn't seem to be losing strength; the hard work in the Shipping Department had firmed his muscles, and as he went on the work got easier instead of harder.

The Malloys were pleasant people. Mrs. Malloy never gave up her curiosity about his past, but she wasn't insistent about it, and for the rest she seemed willing to let Cole, to a certain extent, take the place of her son Bobby, now off to Texas in Army basic training. This relationship was limited by too many things to become cloying, but from time to time Mrs. Malloy did call him Bobby by mistake, and it always embarrassed both of them. Her husband, Matt, was a hearty industrial peasant, fat from beer but still strong, who wore baggy sweaters his wife had knit for him, and who smoked a stinking thick scraggly old Scottish treeroot of a pipe. Matt was an unreconstructed egalitarian, and since he looked on Paul as a co-worker was perhaps closer to him and friendlier with him than if he'd looked on him as a son. Tommy, the boy still at home, was sixteen, chunky and intense, with deep hungers for which he hadn't yet found any names.

The days took on a sameness. He arose about ten, and went downstairs to find Mrs. Malloy. Usually some murmur met him; the vacuum cleaner in the living room, the radio in the kitchen, the washing machine down in the basement. He would follow the sound, and when he found her he would say good morning, and usually she would say, "Just a minute, Paul. Just let me finish this. Put on the water for the coffee."

He'd put the water on, and then sit in the kitchen and read the paper. Matt Malloy always left it a thick, ill-folded, dog-eared mess, and Cole would arrange it into a neater shape and then read it. He didn't read the national and international news very often, unless an intriguing headline caught his eye, because those stories required continuity, day by day. He liked the comics, and he read the engagement and wedding announcements, and all the columns that weren't political, and while he was reading Mrs. Malloy would be getting his breakfast ready. Almost always she made herself a cup of coffee too, and sat with him while he ate.

After breakfast he watched television, which was game shows and soap operas. Mrs. Malloy came into the living room during the soap operas, but she always left during the game shows, which she disliked. "Something for nothing. You never get something for nothing." And she'd go back to her work.

Cole liked the game shows; they fascinated him. They were mostly just exercises in memory, the remembering of capitals and movie stars and song titles, and he liked to watch the faces of the contestants in those seconds between question and answer when memory was being put to work. He liked the applause that greeted a right answer, and he enjoyed something like a feeling of companionship with a contestant who had just failed.

At three-thirty, he would get ready to leave for work. He

had a heavy jacket to wear now, lined with fiberglass; it belonged to Bobby Malloy and had been loaned to him by Mrs. Malloy. It was a little small on him, but warm.

Work was work, unchanging, and after work he usually went home and to bed. Once or twice a week he would stop on the way home for coffee and a doughnut, and on rare occasions he would go along with Little Jack Flynn and some of the others to Cole's Tavern. He always felt guilty about going to the tavern, because he couldn't spare the money, but he needed the occasional evening of unloosening.

He wasn't saving any money. He couldn't yet, not until Artie Bellman was paid back. His wallet was full of reminder notes to himself now, and one of them was a record of the payments he'd made so far to Bellman. He was afraid that otherwise he would just keep on giving Bellman ten dollars every payday forever, never knowing when the fourth week was reached.

It was an easy life, because there was little to remember. He didn't know if his memory was getting better or worse; he knew that he was still forgetting things, that Mrs. Malloy had given up asking him to remind her to be sure to put butter on the grocery list or start the roast at three o'clock, that every once in a while the name of a co-worker would be lost, that he sometimes did forget the address of the Malloys' house, that there were still mornings when he woke up and didn't remember his job till he saw the note on the door. He could remember the details of his present life better than he could the details of his past life, but that was only natural. And he'd given up the memory list again, this time for good, because the isolated names and facts written on a sheet of paper hadn't been good memory aids at all.

He'd thought it would be difficult to explain to Mrs. Malloy why he had reminder notes tacked up in his room, but when she'd asked him he'd just said, "I have a terrible memory," and she'd accepted it, telling him of her husband's terrible memory; he could never remember birthdays, not even his own, or any other family occasion.

It was an easy life, with a simple pattern to it that didn't strain him overly much, but he never allowed himself to sink into it completely. It was only a transition, and that was all it could be. One night, in his fourth week in town, he happened to be looking in his wallet and he saw his New York State driver's license, and he frowned at it, wondering where it had come from. Then he saw his own name on the license, and an address: 50 Grove St., New York, N. Y. And all at once he remembered why he was here, and that his goal was to return to New York City. It had been out of his mind, completely out of his mind, and he didn't know for how long; just that he had been thinking of this life in Jeffords as permanent, without beginning and without end. New York, his acting career, his old friends, *everything*, had been erased completely from his mind. Not just smudged and misted, but erased. If he hadn't run into a reminder, like this driver's license, he would have stayed here forever.

It terrified him. That night he added a new reminder note to the bedroom door:

50 GROVE ST.—NEW YORK—Look In Wallet

But the note was enough. On seeing it, he didn't have to look in his wallet to find out what it meant. Still, it had been close. He had been on the very edge of losing his identity completely, of falling into the hole between the tick and the tock, of falling out of space and out of time and down into gray mindless emptiness, and not even knowing that anything had happened to him.

"That's what a zombie is," he told himself. "That's what a zombie is."

In the fifth week, they came for him.

It was Friday night. He'd been paid, he'd given the third payment to Artie Bellman, and now he was on his way home. Little Jack and Buddy had wanted him to come along with them, but he never went to the tavern on payday. The idea frightened him, obscurely, though he wouldn't spend very much at the tavern anyway. But he didn't trust himself. He didn't like to carry money with him, more than a few dollars at a time.

It was the end of November. The trees had lost their leaves, and the leaves had been raked and burned, all long since. It was too cold now to be autumn anymore, but the snow hadn't started yet. He was walking along the tilted slate squares of sidewalk, past the barren trees and the street-lights; it was just past midnight, and the street was deserted. He was a block from home when the highly polished new black car rolled slowly past him, going in his direction, and crept to a stop a few doors away. The passenger-side door opened, and a man climbed out. He was hard-looking and chunky, in a baggy suit and a wrinkled shirt and a dark tie. He stood on the sidewalk with his hands on his hips and squinted at Cole, the squint making the corners of his mouth turn up like the beginning of a snarl.

Cole hesitated, not knowing what it was. He looked around, and the street was still deserted, the houses were all dark and silent. A man in a brand new highly polished black car couldn't be meaning to steal his little pay; but what else was this? He stopped, a few feet away from the man, and said, "What do you want?"

"Paul Cole?" The man's voice was harsh, but soft, as though there were no strength in it and he had to strain his throat to make any sound at all.

"What is it?"

"You're Paul Cole?" It was said impatiently; he looked slow-moving but irritable.

Do I know him? He acts as though he doesn't like me, as though he hates me. Maybe he knows me from somewhere, and his is one of the faces I've forgotten. But if we already know each other, why did he ask me if I was me?

His only choice was to admit to the name, and see what happened next. He moved his head and said, "Yes. I'm Paul Cole."

The man nodded, his irritation temporarily satisfied. His right hand slipped with surprising speed into his hip pocket, and came out with a wallet, which he flipped open, saying, "Police."

They were between streetlights, and it was pretty dark here. Cole took a step closer, saying, "I can't see that."

The man held it up higher, being impatient and irritable again, and Cole could now vaguely see an identification card of some sort. The man said, "We're to bring you in."

"What for?"

"They'll tell you when you get there." He stepped over to the car and jerked open the rear door. "Get in."

"But what is it? What do you want?"

"They just told us, bring you in."

"Are you arresting me?"

"Why? What've you done?"

Cole took an involuntary step backward. "I haven't done anything." But he wasn't sure.

"You're just wanted for questioning," the man told him.

"About what?"

"You'll find out when you get there."

The door on the driver's side opened, and the driver got out of the car. He was very tall and very thin, and he was wearing a hat. He looked over the top of the car at Cole, and said, "Get in the car." His voice was flat, and cold, and full of menace.

Cole got into the back seat of the car, and the first man slammed the door after him. The two policemen got into the front seat, and their doors slammed one right after the other, like twin rifle shots. The car pulled away from the curb, and made a U-turn

It smelled of new car. The back seat was firm, the upholstery felt new beneath his palm. The two men in the front seat were dark shapes, a chunky thick-necked shape and a thin, hatted shape. No one said anything, till they stopped in front of the police station, and then the chunky man said, "All right, Cole. Here we are."

The police station was grimy brick. It looked like the

Wilson Hotel, but with green lightglobes flanking the entrance. There were the same slate steps leading up.

Inside, it was all old dark wood and green walls. The thin detective talked to a uniformed policeman behind a high desk, and then Cole was taken down a corridor and ushered into a room. The chunky man said, "Wait here." They closed the door and left him alone.

It was a long narrow room with a high ceiling, and a window high up in one of the short walls. There were exposed pipes running upward in the corners, painted the same flat green as the walls. A single white lightglobe was suspended from the ceiling on a chain, giving the room a stark cold light. The floor was thin wood strips, dark with age and grime, and the furnishings consisted of three armless wooden chairs scattered asymmetrically here and there.

Cole was afraid to smoke, and afraid to sit down. He stood in the room, waiting, and the air felt cold and damp. He was thinking frantically, trying to remember something, remember anything, that would explain this, but he couldn't come up with anything at all.

Oh, God *damn* this memory!

He waited fifteen minutes, and then the door opened and a new one came in. This one was portly, and gray-haired, and smiling. He was short, no more than five-five, and as neatly dressed as a banker. He came in, smiled and nodded, and said, "Sorry to keep you waiting, Paul. Mind if I call you Paul? Sit down, why don't you. The smoking lamp is lit."

Cole sat down, more confused than ever, and lit a cigarette. The chunky man and the thin man had come into the room, too, and had closed the door again.

The smiling man said, "Well, now, Paul, did Blake and O'Hare tell you what it was all about?"

"No."

He smiled some more, and shrugged meaty shoulders. "Ah, it's just as well. May I see your wallet a minute, Paul? Take your money out of it first, all right?"

Cole was the only one seated, and it made him feel uncomfortable, so he stood up to get at his wallet, and then remained standing. He took the bills out and stuffed them in his pocket, and handed the wallet to the smiling man, who took it with dainty pudgy fingers, saying, "Ah, thank you. I didn't introduce myself, did I? Captain Cartwright, that's my name, Captain Cartwright. May I look at your cards?"

"Go ahead."

"Thank you. Do sit down, Paul, I know you have been working hard, you must be tired. This won't take long. Go on, sit down."

Cole sat down. He saw that the thin man had a notebook and pencil in his hands now. The notebook had a soft black leather cover, which he'd folded back. As Captain Cartwright continued to speak, the thin man made jottings in the note-book; it looked as though he were writing in shorthand.

Captain Cartwright said, "What's this? A New York State driver's license, number 2962596. Paul Edwin Cole. Your middle name's Edwin, eh? My first boy's name is Edwin. And the address here, 50 Grove Street, New York City. Grove Street? I thought all the streets in New York were numbered. 42nd Street and Fifth Avenue, and like that."

"Grove Street's in the Village," Cole told him, and suddenly remembered the look of Sheridan Square, the Paper-back Gallery and the Riker's and the florist on the corner; his building was just off the square.

Captain Cartwright managed to smile and frown at the same time. "The Village? What would that be?"

"Greenwich Village."

"Ah! *Greenwich* Village! Is *that* where you lived? Very exciting, I'm told."

"I guess so." Cole was wondering who was Blake and who was O'Hare. He thought the thin man was probably Blake and the chunky man O'Hare.

Captain Cartwright was finished with the driver's license now, and had found his Army discharge. "Well, well! You were in the Army, eh? Serial number US12451995. Honorable Discharge, very good. Did you like the Army?"

"It was all right."

"Of course. But civilian life's better, eh? Particularly in a place like Greenwich Village. Whatever made you decide to leave a place like Greenwich Village and come to our little town?"

"Well...I didn't have any money, I had to get a job, and..." It petered out there, not even the outline of an explanation.

Captain Cartwright frown-smiled again, saying, "No jobs in Greenwich Village? You had to come all the way out here to find a job? Why, it must be a thousand miles."

"Yes, sir."

"Yes, sir? Oh! Oh, you mean yes sir a thousand miles, *I* see!" Captain Cartwright laughed as though someone had just told a good joke. His laughter subsided to his usual smile, and he said, "You don't have any relatives here, do you?"

"No, I don't."

"Nowhere around here?" Captain Cartwright, still smiling, now expressed sympathy. "All back East, eh? Well, well. Curiouser and curiouser, as the fella says. Who *did* say that, Paul, do you remember?"

"Alice, I think. Alice in Wonderland."

"Ah, yes! Alice in Wonderland, of course. Curiouser and curiouser. I like that, don't you? And Greenwich Village, now *that's* supposed to be almost a Wonderland, isn't it? All this free love philosophy, and marijuana parties, and all. I suppose that's exaggerated, though, isn't it?"

"I guess so."

"Yes, I suppose it must be. Still, a kind of Wonderland, really. Now, why would you leave Wonderland, I wonder? *Wonderland I wonder!* Listen to me!" Captain Cartwright chortled. Then all at once he turned serious. His eyes still twinkled, there was still a chuckle trembling at the corners of his mouth, but it was clear he intended his expression now to be serious. He said, "You weren't in any trouble,

Paul, were you? Trouble with a girl, trouble with the police, nothing like that?"

Cole shook his head. "No, sir." But his attention was distracted for a second, as he remembered the easy way he'd answered Captain Cartwright about the quote from Alice. There hadn't been any hesitation, any fumbling awkward search through a foggy memory, nothing at all, just the answer.

"Never any trouble with the police, Paul?"

"No, sir."

Captain Cartwright let his expression relax into a sunny smile. "That's good, Paul!" he said. "I'm glad to hear that. But I still don't quite understand why it is you—tell me now?"

"What?" Cole blinked and looked up, not knowing what had happened. In the middle of Captain Cartwright's question, he'd turned the Captain's voice off completely, not intentionally but effectively, because he'd been thinking about his answer to the question about *curiouser and curiouser*. He'd been asked the question, and the answer had popped right into his mind. Was that the way it worked? If his memory was asked a direct question, out would come answer? But he *did* ask his memory direct questions all the time, and more often than not no answer at all came out. It was just that his memory was erratic; it retained a few odd bits of disconnected and useless information, and Captain Cartwright had happened to touch one of the few remaining buttons that worked.

But in thinking about this, he'd lost the thread of the Captain's question. He said, "I'm sorry, I didn't hear you."

"Didn't *hear* me?" Captain Cartwright smile-frowned, and looked at Blake and O'Hare. "He didn't *hear* me," he said.

The thin one—Blake?—looked at Cole and said, "*I* heard the Captain."

"I'm sorry. I'm tired, I just got off work. My mind was wandering."

Captain Cartwright shrugged and spread his hands. "That's possible, boys," he said, pleasantly, judiciously. "He's answering right along, bright and cheerful, and when we get to the sixty-four thousand dollar question it just happens that his mind starts wandering. Nothing impossible about that, boys." Captain Cartwright smiled broadly, and came a step closer, and leaned forward. He said to Cole, "Would you like me to ask it again?"

"Yes, please."

The chunky man—O'Hare, maybe—said, "He's polite, you notice? He says please."

"Paul's a good boy," Captain Cartwright said, as though defending Cole against an unprovoked attack. "He's tired, that's all. If you lazy bums worked in the shipping department down at the tannery, you'd be tired, too." He nodded triumphantly at Blake and O'Hare, then turned his attention back to Cole. "You ready now, Paul? I'm ready to ask it again, you with me now?"

"Yes, sir."

"There you go, Paul. Now here's what I said, I said, 'How come a smart young man like yourself should leave an exciting place like Greenwich Village to come live in this little dinky town a thousand miles away where you don't even know a soul?' That was more or less what I said, Paul. You get it that time?"

"Yes, sir."

"That's fine, Paul. And what's the answer?"

Cole hesitated, trying to get his thoughts in order. He wanted to answer, but the answer was complicated, more complicated than Captain Cartwright suspected, and he couldn't for a second or two decide where to start. Then Blake, the thin one, said, "Answer the Captain, boy."

Cole said, "I lost my job with the show." Then he shook his head. He'd been flicking his cigarette ashes on the floor, because O'Hare was smoking and that's what he was doing, but now Cole's cigarette was too short to smoke anymore and there weren't any ashtrays in the room. He said, "What can I do with this cigarette?"

"What the hell kind of answer is that?" O'Hare demanded. "You can shove that cigarette up your ass."

"Now, gently, Jimmy, gently," said Captain Cartwright. "You know I don't like that kind of talk. And Paul, you just drop that cigarette on the floor and step on it and forget about it, and then you tell me what in the world you're talking about. You lost your job with *what* show?"

Cole got rid of the cigarette. He said, "Look in the wallet there, you'll see my union cards. I'm an actor."

"An actor, is that right?" Captain Cartwright looked in the wallet some more, and found all three cards. "Well, I'll be," he said. "So many unions? Now, why do you have to be in so many unions?"

"It's for the different kinds of jobs. Equity is legitimate theater, and AFTRA is television and radio work, and SAG is for movies."

"Movies? You've been in the movies, Paul?"

Cole hesitated again, because he didn't know if he'd ever been in any movies or not, but then a phrase—isolated and unexplained, without reference to anything—came into his mind, and he said it: "Industrial films."

"Industrial films. The sort of movie they show at conventions, eh, Paul?" Captain Cartwright's smile got roguish, and he said, "Not the *other* kind of movie they show at conventions, though, eh?"

"No. I'm an actor."

"Then, Paul, I'll be perfectly honest with you, I'm just more surprised and confused than ever. Here you are, an actor, belong to half a dozen different unions, get work in movies and shows, live in Greenwich Village in the heart of New York City, and all at once here you are in this dinky little town, working in the shipping department over to the tannery. Now, Paul, I'm telling you the Lord's truth, I just don't understand that."

"I was with a show," Cole said. "A touring show, and I had an accident. I was in the hospital for a couple of weeks, and the show went on without me."

"Ah, I see! I'm beginning to see the light, Paul. And you

just didn't have the money to get back to New York City, is that it?"

"Yes, sir."

"That's a shame, Paul, that's a truthful shame." Captain Cartwright nodded, looking completely solemn for the first time since he'd come in here. He said, "This touring company didn't carry any insurance or anything, is that it?"

"It wasn't an accident on the job, it was…it was off the job."

"Ah, that must be it. And all the money you had went for the hospital, eh?"

"Yes, sir."

Captain Cartwright nodded thoughtfully. "That certainly does explain it," he said, and it looked as though he were about to smile again, but instead he frowned, saying, "But that wasn't *here*, was it, Paul? I don't remember any touring shows around this town for years and years."

"This is as far east as I could get with the money I had left."

"Ah! Of course! You just came as far as you could, eh? I admire that, Paul, I most certainly do. Now where was this that you were in the hospital?"

"Where?"

"Well, the name of the town, you know."

Cole shook his head. "I don't remember."

"You don't remember? Paul, I should think the name of that town would be emblazoned in your mind, that's what I should think. That was a terrible thing happened to you there. If it was me, *I* wouldn't forget that town in a hurry."

"I didn't pay much attention to the name of it. We just came in, and then I had my, my accident, and then I was in the hospital for a while, and then I left, that's all."

"Well, I guess that's possible," said Captain Cartwright. He nodded, and offered a small smile, and looked at the other two men. "That's certainly possible," he said. "Jimmy, get that plate, will you? Maybe Paul can identify it."

The chunky man, possibly O'Hare, said, "Right away," and went out, closing the door after him.

Captain Cartwright strolled back and forth, his interlaced fingers resting on his paunch, holding Cole's wallet that way. "Acting," he said, testing the word. "Acting, acting. All the world's a stage, eh? That's one I know. Shakespeare. I've done my share of reading. But to be an actor, to live in Greenwich Village, meet all sorts of interesting people, Beatniks and whatnot, that must be something. And now here you are, stuck away in this little hole in the wall. It's really a shame, Paul. No one you could wire for busfare? No family, friends?"

"No, sir."

"Parents dead?"

"Yes, sir."

"I'm sorry to hear that. All alone in the world, a thousand miles from home." Captain Cartwright shook his head solemnly. "I don't envy you, Paul," he said. "I'll be frank with you, I don't envy you. Oh, I might," he said, and flashed his sunny smile just briefly. "I might envy your life in New York, I'll be honest about that, but here and now it's a different story, eh?"

"Yes, sir."

"Jeffords is a good town," said Cartwright, as though all it had lacked was this final commendation. "My home town, Paul. Born and raised here. Oh, I've been away, in the Army and whatnot, but I've always come back home, and I've built my career here, built it around this town. Do you see what I mean?"

"Yes, sir, I guess so."

"I would venture to say I know just about every permanent resident of Jeffords," Captain Cartwright said. "That's something, eh? Over nine thousand men, women, and children, and I venture to say I know them all. Oh, not the youngsters so much, the grade school children, but I'll get to know them as they grown up. Take the Malloys, now. I've known Matt for years, known him for years. I stop in at the union meetings now and again, and he's always there. A very militant man, Matt Malloy, very militant. And a lovely wife, good church-going woman. But of course, you know that yourself. And two fine sons. A fine family all the way around. And then I know the Flynns, Black Jack and Little Jack. You work with them, don't you?"

"Yes, sir."

"And Artie Bellman, there's another one, but a horse of a different color. Loans money at illegal rates, you know. Oh, we know about it, never fear. I like to know everything that happens in Jeffords. And I don't approve of Artie Bellman; he was a wild boy and he's never lost his wildness, and I wouldn't be a bit surprised if he came to a bad end, not a bit surprised. He's been in this very room, you know, in this very room, and more than once. Never anything really serious, just wildness, getting into fights and whatnot. But not one of our leading citizens at all, and never will be. It makes me unhappy to have someone like Artie Bellman here in Jeffords. A bad influence, Paul. If he was a stranger now, like yourself, and carried on the way he does, I'd march him to the town line and boot him across, and don't think I'd be too kindhearted to do it. I'm far too fond of my hometown, Paul, I'll tell you the absolute truth. I'd do it in a minute. But what can I do, he's a local boy, got a family here, as much right to live here as anybody. So all I can do is bring him into this room every now and again, and try to talk to him, try to straighten him out. Not that it ever does any good." Captain Cartwright stood in front of Cole and shook his head. "Don't get yourself involved with him, Paul," he said. "He's not the sort of company you want to keep. And whatever you do, don't borrow money from him. I know there are men on that crew of yours today, right today, who pay Artie Bellman a dollar or two in interest every week on some little loan they made a year ago, and they've never yet paid a penny of the principal. It's a vicious sort of thing to get yourself into, Paul. Steer clear of it. Eh? Will you?"

Cole nodded, as solemn as the Captain. "Yes, sir," he said. And Captain Cartwright burst out laughing. "Paul, you're a wonder!" he cried. He appealed to the thin man, who might have been Blake. "Isn't he something? A first-class actor, I'm willing to bet a week's pay on it. Tell an out-and-out fib like that, and never turn a hair." He beamed at Cole as though he'd invented Cole himself, just this minute. "Why, Paul," he said, "you owe Artie Bellman money right now! You borrowed thirty-two dollars from him, and you've paid him thirty-two back and you still owe him ten. Isn't that so, isn't that the way it is?"

Cole was too flustered to say anything at all. He just looked up at the Captain, and gestured vaguely with his hands.

The Captain waved his hand and said, "Oh, don't be embarrassed about it, Paul, don't bother yourself, I understand the way it was. I said all those things about Artie Bellman, and warned you away from him, and of course you were embarrassed to say you'd already borrowed money from him, of course you were. *I* understand that, Paul." He leaned forward, and closed one eye with a roguish smile, and laid a finger beside his nose. "But didn't I tell you I know everything that happens in Jeffords? Didn't I already tell you that?"

"Yes, sir."

Captain Cartwright straightened, beaming. "Of course I did! Don't ever fib to Captain Cartwright, Paul, don't every try to fib to me, I'll catch you at it every time." He cocked his head to one side, and studied Cole's face, the smile still creasing his own. "Any others, Paul?"

"What?"

"Any other fibs? We've been chatting here for quite a while, Paul, and I must admit that now I know what an accomplished actor you are, I just can't help but wonder. Did you tell me any other little fibs, Paul?"

"No, sir, not at all."

"You don't have to, you know. Not with me. I'm an understanding fellow, Paul, I think you'll find me a very understanding fellow." He waited, as bright and alert as a parrot, and then said, "Is there anything you want to tell me, Paul?

Anything you want to change in your story, anything you want to add?"

"No, sir." Cole had thought, for a split second, of telling the Captain about his memory problem, but he rejected the idea immediately. The faulty memory was a weakness, and something prevented him from exposing a weakness to Captain Cartwright.

O'Hare, if that was the chunky man's name, came back into the room then, carrying a square piece of metal about a foot on a side. It was bright and polished, like a mirror, and the color of an aluminum pen, or automobile chrome. He was holding it by the edges, the way some people handle phonograph records.

"Ah!" said Captain Cartwright. "There it is! Recognize it, Paul?"

Cole looked at the piece of metal, and tried to think if he'd ever seen it before. Maybe he had, and just couldn't remember. But if he had, and Captain Cartwright knew he had, and now he denied it, the Captain would think he was lying again. He shook his head doubtfully, and said, "I don't know. I don't think so."

"Take it," the Captain offered. "Look it over."

Cole took the piece of metal and looked at it. He could see his own face reflected in it. He turned it over, and both sides were alike. It was about a quarter of an inch thick, and absolutely featureless. He studied it, trying to make it click something in his memory, and nothing happened at all. He said, "I'm sorry, sir. If I ever saw it before, I just don't remember."

"Ah, well, that's all right. Take it back, Jimmy."

The chunky man took it back, holding it the same way as before, and the thin man opened the door for him. The chunky man left, and the thin man closed the door again.

Captain Cartwright said, "If it's all right with you, Paul, I'd like to hold onto this discharge of yours for a few days. No problem, of course, you'll get it back in a day or so, but I'd just like to study it a bit more."

"Why?"

Captain Cartwright smiled disarmingly, and shrugged his shoulders. "Just a whim," he said. "I know you plan to go on back to New York City eventually, and— You do plan to go back, don't you?"

"Yes."

"That's what I thought. But still, it won't be for a while, not for a few weeks anyway. You weren't planning on leaving tomorrow, for instance, were you?"

"No. I don't have the money yet."

"Of course not. You have to finish paying Artie Bellman back first, and then you can start putting money aside for your fare, right?"

Cole nodded.

"So there's really no hurry. You'll have this discharge back in plenty of time." He smiled as easily and pleasantly as before, and handed Cole his wallet back, but held the discharge form in his other hand.

Cole took the wallet and looked at it, and out of his confusion and fright felt suddenly again that deep mournful depression that came over him every once in a while these days. He felt like crying, exactly like crying; his eyes stung, but no tears came. Not looking up from the wallet, he said, "Why are you doing this to me?"

"What's that, Paul? I didn't hear you."

"Why are you doing this to me?"

"Doing? Doing what?" Captain Cartwright seemed surprised and bewildered. "Nobody's done anything to you, Paul. We've just had a little chat, that's all, got to know one another. I told you, I like to know everyone in Jeffords, and you've become a resident now, haven't you, at least for a while, so I wanted to get to know you. Now we've met, and we've had a pleasant little chat, and that's all there is to it. We've gotten to know each other, and I want you to feel if there's ever a problem of any kind, any way at all that I can help you, get you situated better in town here, anything at all, you can come to me at any time. I want you to think of me as your friend, Paul, and I mean that sincerely. You ask anyone in town, they'll tell you Captain Cartwright will do anything in his power to help a fellow townsman in trouble, anything in his power, any time at all. I want you to re-member that, Paul."

"But why do it this way? In the middle of the night? And being picked up without anybody explaining anything or telling me anything and just—"

"Now, Paul! I realize you're tired, Paul, but really now. Nobody *explained* anything to you? Haven't I been explaining and explaining, the last half hour here? Isn't that what this is all about?" Captain Cartwright rested a hand on Cole's shoulder. "You're just tired," he said. "Now, we've had a nice chat and all, but it's time for you to get some sleep, and you don't want to stay *here* all night, do you?" He laughed, but the words and the laugh both had something menacing in them, or at least it sounded menacing to Cole. "You just go on home and get your beauty sleep, Paul, and if you want to talk about anything tomorrow, why just come on in, the door is always open. All right, Paul? Good night now."

The Captain smiled and nodded, and strode out of the room, carrying the reduced laminated photostat of Cole's Army discharge paper in his hand. Cole was left with the thin man, who said, "Can you find your own way out?" His face and voice were expressionless.

"Yes," said Cole.

The thin man—was he Blake? Cole wanted to know, but didn't dare ask—the thin man stood waiting by the open door. Cole got to his feet and left the narrow room and walked down the corridor to the front of the building. He glanced back, and the thin man was gone.

Up front, the same uniformed man sat stolid and half-asleep behind the high desk; above his head on the wall was a round white-faced clock, with black numbers and hands and a red sweep second hand. The clock read twenty-five minutes past one. Cole glanced at the uniformed man behind the desk, but there was no reaction to his presence, or to his leaving. He went out of the building and down the slate steps, and stood on the sidewalk a minute, looking at the car in which he'd been driven here.

There were too many things to think about all at once; he couldn't keep them straight in his mind. Why had they picked him up? Why had they kept his Army discharge? What was the metal plate, and *had* he ever seen it before? What did Captain Cartwright really want from him?

He stood thinking, staring at the car parked in front of the station, and then some movement or some instinct made him turn his head. The thin man was standing at the top of the slate steps, by the door, looking down at him. He looked as though what he was was Cold & Merciless Competence. He said, "You're loitering, Cole." His voice was so thin and soft that Cole could barely hear it.

Cole looked up at him and blurted out, "Are you Blake?"

"Move on, Cole," said the thin man.

Cole moved, starting off in the direction from which he'd been brought here, but he didn't know this section of town at all, and before he got to the first corner he knew he was lost. He went on to the corner, and looked back down the block, and there was no one visible around the police station, which was in a cone of fuzzy yellow light by itself, plus the green globes, with darkness all around it.

The only thing to do was move. Sooner or later he would find a store open or someone walking, and he could ask directions. Or he would eventually come to a neighborhood he recognized.

He walked almost at random. It seemed to him that the car that had brought him to the police station had made more right turns than left turns, so in going back it should be just the reverse; from time to time, therefore, he came to a corner and went down the street to his left.

It was as though the town had been chloroformed. Silence, emptiness, darkness. Automobiles were standing here and there in driveways, because all-night parking on the street was illegal. When the automobile was parked back in the

driveway, next to the house, it looked like the rear end of
some snug bear in a warm den, but when the automobile
was just barely onto the driveway, just clearing the sidewalk,
so it was flanked by lawns, it made the whole section look
like part of the construction around a model train layout. As
though Cole could walk across those lawns—which would
crackle like paper, being paper—and look in through those
cellophane windows and see only make believe, no ceilings
and no walls and no furnishings and no reality. As though
Cole himself were one inch tall, crawling slowly across the
table; and what looks like a black and overcast sky above is
only the ceiling of the playroom.

Cole was getting exhausted when he finally saw a light
ahead of him, some light other than the steady march of
streetlights. It was on the other side of the street, a few
blocks away. He hurried toward it, hoping it was some sort
of landmark he would recognize, and when he was within a
block of it he could see it was the bus depot. He smiled with
relief; from here, he could find his way with no trouble at all,
first to the tannery, and then from the tannery on home.

He came closer, and was just about to cross the street to
the depot side when he stopped in his tracks, seeing the
highly polished brand new black car parked in front of the
depot, in the bus zone. It didn't necessarily have anything to
do with him. The car could be there for another reason
entirely. In fact, there was no way they could have known
he'd be coming by here.

But he turned around anyway, and went the other way,
gong around the block and coming out on Western Avenue a
block farther from the tannery. He walked down Western
Avenue, and when he crossed the next intersection he
looked down to his left and saw the black car still parked in
front of the depot. He hurried a bit, and lit a cigarette to
calm his nerves.

From there, it was just walking, with the direction
known. Cole ran the last block, fumbled with the key, and
when he was at last on the dark enclosed porch with the

door shut he suddenly felt so weak he could barely stand. He stumbled across to the porch sofa and sank down on it, breathing in open-mouthed gasps like a man about to faint.

It was beautiful here. Through the windows was the empty street, with a circle of light to the left and a circle of light to the right. No motion, no sound. Around him, the dim bulks of porch furniture. Behind him, the house, solid and silent. Beautiful. It was good to be home.

After a minute he got to his feet and went into the house and up the stairs. He didn't have to strain to be quiet; the whole house was cushioned, soft, muffled. His feet made no sound on the stair carpet.

He closed his bedroom door before turning the light on, and the sudden brightness hurt his eyeballs. Squinting, he read the clock; twenty-five minutes past three. He didn't know how long he'd been held in the bare narrow room at the police station, or how long he'd wandered before finding his direction. Long times, long times.

He undressed quickly, and switched off the light, and climbed into bed. Friday was the day Mrs. Malloy changed the sheets, and the bed was crisp and clean. Beautiful. It seemed to him that everything was beautiful. He closed his eyes, and smiled, and slept.

7

He was not really watching television. He was facing the screen, but he was thinking about Captain Cartwright and last Friday night, wondering again if he should talk to Matt Malloy about it. It was now Monday, two o'clock in the afternoon, and he'd been worrying the question off and on all over the weekend. Captain Cartwright had said he knew Matt Malloy, and it might be that Matt could tell him what Captain Cartwright had wanted him for, but on the other hand Captain Cartwright was a policeman and it might be that Matt wouldn't want Cole to stay on here if he knew Cole had been questioned by the police.

But he couldn't get it out of his mind. Why had they taken him? Why had they done it so nastily? Why had the Captain kept his Army discharge? What was that square of bright metal, and where should he know it from?

It was the square of metal that bothered him most of all. Had he seen it, the Captain had wanted to know, had he seen it? *Had* he? He could remember it now, see it in his mind more clearly than anything else; bright, square, metallic, reflecting his own wondering face. Had he ever seen that piece of metal before? He couldn't guess, he couldn't begin to guess.

So strange. There were so many things lost from his mind, that he wanted back and needed back; and here was one thing he'd prefer not to think about, and it stayed with him doggedly. Portions of the interrogation itself had faded— some of the Captain's questions and his own answers, the names of the other two men, some of the physical look of the room where they'd questioned him—but the fact of it was still clear in his mind. And clearest of all, the square piece of shining metal, reflecting his face.

When the doorbell rang, Mrs. Malloy called from the kitchen, "Answer that, will you, Paul? Please? My hands are in water."

He called that he would, and left the living room, opening the front door and going out on the porch. The venetian blind was shut most of the way over the porch door, so he couldn't see the visitor clearly, just a stocky male shape.

He opened the door, and it was the chunky policeman. The black car was out at the curb, and Cole caught a glimpse of the thin one in it, behind the wheel.

The chunky man held out a card. "You can have this back now," he said.

Cole took it from him, his Army discharge. His mind was full of questions, but too many of them all at once, so he didn't manage to say anything, until the chunky man had already turned away and started back down the stoop. Then, compressing all the questions into a bundle he could get past his lips, he said, "Why?"

The chunky man paused on the bottom step, looking back up at him. "What's that?"

"Why?"

"Why what?"

"Why…why did you do all this?"

The chunky man shrugged. "You got any complaints, talk to the Captain. I just do what I'm told." He turned away again.

And then Cole understood. "Oh," he said. He watched the chunky man go on down the stoop, and a fragment of a phrase passed across his mind: *doun the stair*. He frowned, wondering at it. Doun the stair. Part of a line from a play, he supposed. Odd disconnected bits crossed his mind from time to time, like flotsam from a torpedoed ship.

He watched the chunky man get into the car, and then the car drove away, neither of the detectives looking toward him at all. He stepped back and closed the porch door. He was still holding the Army discharge, and now he studied it, frowning, and wondered for the first time if he should turn himself in at a VA hospital. Maybe what he needed was medical attention.

But he didn't really believe it. What he needed was to be in New York, surrounded by his friends, by the places and purposes and *aura* of his life.

Only a few more weeks. This Friday would be his last payment to Artie Bellman, and then he could start saving his money for the bus ticket.

He put the Army discharge away in its proper place in his wallet, and went back into the house. Mrs. Malloy was coming down the carpeted hall from the kitchen, wiping her hands on a dishtowel, bracelets of detergent suds around her wrists. She said, "Who was it? Nothing important?"

"Just a salesman," he said, lying before thinking about it. "I told him we didn't want any."

"That's good," she said, nodding emphatically. "I never buy from door-to-door salesmen. If I want anything, I can always go to the store for it. And if it isn't right, I can bring it back, which you can't do when somebody just comes to the door." She went on into the living room, saying, "Oh, now, look! *The Silent Heart* is on, and you didn't tell me."

"I'm sorry."

They both sat down in the living room, facing the television set. Mrs. Malloy was somewhat embarrassed about her attachment to the soap operas, and from time to time assured Cole that she didn't take them seriously. But she hated to miss an episode, though the plot movement of the shows was glacial enough for a viewer to watch only once a week and still follow the story threads. Cole liked the soap operas because they were live; he was watching flesh-and-blood actors in a television studio in New York City. There was a notation on his now-abandoned memory list to the effect that he himself had worked on one of the soap operas at one time, though he couldn't now remember anything about it; it had been one of the memories that had returned only once, leaving behind no trace other than the cryptic note in his own handwriting. Still, the soap operas were his only contact with his own former reality; he watched them as a prisoner in a dungeon watches the clouds crossing the rectangle of sky behind his one high window. Sky and clouds might have been only minor parts of his earlier free existence, but now, being the only parts left to him, they have taken on major importance.

Also, he treasured the faint hope that one day he might see a familiar face, some friend of his playing a temporary role on *The Silent Heart* or one of the others. To see the face, to match it to a name on the credits; it would make his past seem even more real.

But today he didn't pay any attention to the screen. He was thinking of what the chunky man had said, and of his own lie to Mrs. Malloy. His decision had been made for him; he would not talk about Captain Cartwright to Matt. He had once again come into contact with those who only work here, and the safest thing to do was get out of their sight as quickly and completely as possible, and say nothing to anyone.

It was over with. It had never happened, that's what his attitude would be. His mouth formed a painful smile; for him, it would be an easy attitude to assume.

8

Artie Bellman didn't come to work on Friday. He had a bad cold. Instead, a young and slender girl with black hair was there to collect the money. "I'm Ann Bellman," she explained. "Artie's sister."

It seemed sometimes as though Artie Bellman were an unofficial part of the management. The way he could freely take over Joe Lampek's office for the purpose of negotiating a loan. The way he openly collected his payments from the men in the payline, standing just behind Joe Lampek. And now his sister was in the building, taking his place, with no questions asked nor comment given.

Ann Bellman looked to be in her late teens. She had her brother's wiriness, and angularity of face, but in her the traits produced an entirely different effect. She was slender, not thin. And her face, a long oval, with prominent cheek-bones and hollow cheeks, had an odd gypsyish beauty. Still, she had the hard look, the same as her brother. It was a look that seemed to tell of large and raggedly dressed families, sagging porches, backyards littered with automotive junk, sloth combined with cunning. Only her eyes expressed something different. They were large, round, soft, doe-brown. As though the hard shell were only there till the world should change, and then another creature would emerge from within.

He gave her the ten dollars, which she stowed away in a deep pocket of her black skirt. He said, "This is my last payment, isn't it?" And was angry at himself for making it a question. It was unsafe to be less than sure.

But she agreed at once. "I've got your paper," she said. "And your watch."

"Oh, my watch." He said it blankly; he no longer remembered any watch.

She'd been wearing it. She took it off now, and gave it to him, and he held it in his hands, studying it. But it had been five weeks since he'd seen it, and he couldn't remember it at all. He put it on his left wrist, and it felt awkward and tight and heavy. The expansion band was pulling at the little hairs on the back of his wrist.

She produced his I.O.U. from the same deep pocket and gave it to him. He would have gone on then, but she was disposed to talk. "How come I never see you around?" she asked.

He shrugged. "I don't go around very much."

"You never come up to Cole's? You ought to, it's named after you."

"I've been there."

"Funny I didn't see you. But I just go there on weekends."

"I don't think I've even been there on a weekend." But he couldn't be sure. Hadn't it been a payday, the first time he'd ever gone there? He thought it might have been, but he didn't know.

"Maybe I'll see you sometime," she said. She smiled suddenly, softening and dignifying her features, and said, "Come on up tonight. Artie always buys a round when a man pays off a paper. Tonight I'll buy it."

"All right," he said. He smiled hesitantly himself, and then felt awkward and foolish, because there wasn't anything else to say. "I guess I'll see you," he said, and started away.

She waved negligently, looking past him at the line of men being paid, waiting for the next one on Artie Bellman's list.

After all the pay had been handed out, they went to work. Cole saw Ann Bellman stand chatting with Joe Lampek a minute, and then she crossed the big room to the door by the time clock, shrugging into a black carcoat as she went.

As well as the black carcoat and the full black wool skirt, she was wearing a dark figured blouse and black flats, but neither stockings nor socks. Cole tried to catch her eye, to wave to her, but she didn't look in his direction. He felt obscurely angry at her for not looking his way, and told himself she was just another like her brother. They were jackals, survival-types.

Because the work was entirely physical, just moving boxes and crates from one place to another place, his mind was free to wander where it wished, and he always spent his worktime in reveries, catching on some fragment of memory and inventing stories about his possible past, or stories about his future once he would have returned to New York. But tonight he thought instead about women.

He could remember women, remember coupling with women, but no definite events came into his mind. No particular face, no one body, no single incident. There was only a general image; darkness, the weight of a sheet across his shoulders, warm breath on his cheek, sweet-slick flesh against his belly, and the pulsing toward crescendo. The image of a woman's body entwined with his own, and humid heat beneath the cover. And, suddenly superceding, an image of an angry fat male face, saying "Was it worth it?"

What time was that? What was the event? Nothing came to him.

But he didn't dwell on it, and face and question receded again. Now that he had begun to think of women, he was surprised that he had *not* thought of them for so long. He didn't think it was a direct result of his injury; he thought, instead, it was because for the last six weeks he'd had other things just as basic to think about. For the last six weeks it had been survival of himself that he'd been thinking about; women were only incidental.

But Ann Bellman had started his mind working on sexual matters again, and he wondered why this one? Why this one, and not that one? He had seen other women in the past weeks, had met them briefly or seen them briefly in passing on the sidewalk, and nothing had turned over in his mind, so why Ann Bellman? She wasn't beautiful. That is, she was beautiful in the way a fox can be beautiful; beautiful of a type, but a type that is not in itself beautiful. She was too slender to have an inviting or provoking figure, and her words and manner were too cheap and matter-of-fact to produce any sensual interest.

It might be because she had invited him to the tavern, had promised to buy him a drink, even though the gesture was meaningless in any personal sense, was merely a business gesture of Artie Bellman's, with his sister for his proxy. It would be too easy to read invitations into it, and make a fool of oneself, particularly for someone who was always alone, as Cole was. He warned himself not to let it happen; she had meant no more nor less than her words had stated.

But should he go? In a way he wanted to, and in a way he was afraid to. He finally compromised by telling himself that he would go if he remembered it by twelve o'clock. Otherwise, he wouldn't go. And there was no way for him to guess the odds beforehand, either way.

During the dinner-hour break, Little Jack Flynn told a very long and detailed story of seduction, with himself as the hero, and claiming that the story was in every respect factual. Cole listened, and Little Jack's story served to add detail to his own composite memory of his relationships with women. It also helped to keep Cole's mind on the one subject, which didn't often happen.

Little Jack's story inspired more like it from other members of the crew, and the storytelling continued past the dinner-break and on through the rest of the evening till quitting time. This had happened other nights, and Cole had only half-listened, while his mind went on with life-fantasies of its own, but tonight he gave the stories his full attention, and fantasized around them, giving the female role every time to Ann Bellman.

It was, he knew, because she had talked to *him*, and she was the first woman to do so since his accident. Clerks who were writing his vital statistics on forms or waitresses who were taking his order for coffee and a doughnut were not talking to *him*; they were all completely impersonal. No matter what the business reasons behind it, Ann Bellman had actually been talking to him, as a person, and it was enough to break him out of his sexual lethargy.

Because of the stories, and his own fantasizing, and his own self-analyses, Ann Bellman and her invitation were still fresh in his mind by midnight, quitting time, but he still hesitated at going. He told himself he couldn't bring all his money with him, it wouldn't be safe. He might lose it, or spend it. He couldn't trust himself. So he could go home first, and put his money in his bedroom, and then decide whether or not to go to the tavern.

It was a cold clear night, but Cole felt flushed and slightly feverish. His cheeks were warm, as he walked toward home, and his hands felt hot, the palms damp. Fragments of the sex stories he'd heard tonight kept crossing his mind, pictorialized with himself and Ann Bellman. The mental pictures were exciting, but they were oddly frightening, too. It was as though some menace hung just out of sight, just beyond the picture edge, ready to leap once his attention was completely diverted. It was only a vague feeling, too slight to be called fear and too dim for him to find its cause, but it was the main reason—coupled with his understanding that Ann Bellman was only fulfilling what she considered a business obligation—for his hesitancy in going to the tavern.

He walked home, worrying it out in his mind, and when he was in this bedroom with the light on and the door closed, he told himself it would be silly to go back out into the cold again tonight. Besides, tomorrow was another workday. So he wouldn't go. Having made the decision, he felt both relieved and sad, safe and lonely.

He undressed, and switched off the light, and went to bed. But he couldn't get to sleep. The sex fantasies kept circling through his head, keeping him awake. He was physically aroused; he was wistful. The house was silent, and the world beyond his slightly open window was silent. Nothing moved nor sounded to break the solitude.

He felt like a skier, about to push off at the top of the jump. Or a racing car driver, hunched over the wheel and waiting for the starter's gun. Or a soldier in a trench, in those seconds before the charge. Poised, static, in the interval just before speed and danger and excitement.

After a while he got up again, and switched on the light, and dressed. He put all but two dollars of his money in the top dresser drawer, and then changed his mind and got a third dollar out to transfer to his wallet. He put on his borrowed jacket, switched off the room light, and went out of the room. The Malloys kept a dim nightlight burning in the hall; it lit his way downstairs. He left the house, and walked to Cole's Tavern.

He got lost for a while, because he'd never traveled the route in this direction before. He'd always gone to the tavern straight from work, and with one or more of the others from the crew. But after a while he saw the light ahead of him, and knew where he was again.

There were a dozen or more people in the tavern, mostly at the bar, with only one booth occupied, and at first he didn't see her, and he was afraid he'd taken too long and she'd gone home. But then her voice called his name, and he saw her in the dimness of the occupied booth, waving at him.

The booth was already full. Buddy and Ralph were sitting on one side, and Ann Bellman was on the other side with Little Jack Flynn. Little Jack had his arm around her shoulders.

He should have known. Of course she was already taken. He'd been thinking she would be alone, but that was foolish. This was her home town, she knew everyone here, she wouldn't be alone. Only Cole was alone.

He came over to the booth, and she said, "There you are. I figured you weren't coming."

"I had to go home first," he said.

"Get a chair. Over there by the jukebox."

He went over and got a chair, and brought it back, and she'd left the booth, was standing at the bar. He put the chair down at the end of the booth and went over next to her at the bar, saying, "What are you doing?"

"Buying you that beer."

He saw that George, the one-armed bartender, was already drawing two beers. He said, "You don't have to buy me a beer. I'll buy you one."

"Okay. Next round. This one's mine."

"No it's not."

But when George brought the beers, she said, "Don't take his money, George," and George took the bill she was holding out.

Cole said, "I'll buy the next round."

"Fine with me."

She got her change, and Cole carried the two glasses back to the booth. He felt depressed now, and the fantasies had all deserted his head. In just a few hours, he'd managed to idealize her somewhat; she didn't look quite as good as the image of her he'd carried in here.

Because he was depressed and disappointed, he didn't have much to say. The others were talking about things that had happened in high school anyway, so there was nothing for him to do but listen. Most of the names they mentioned were strange to him. He drank his beer, pacing his own drinking to hers, so the two glasses were emptied at the same time, and then he bought a round. He thought he should buy a round for the whole table, but he didn't think he could afford it, so he just bought two glasses, and came back to the table feeling somewhat embarrassed about it. But nobody else seemed to think he should have bought them a beer, so he forget about it and sank back into his depression.

Out of the corner of his eye he could see Little Jack's arm around her shoulders, Little Jack's hand squeezing her upper arm. Her arms were very thin, and her flesh was pale, as though she never got any sunlight. She looked as though she'd lived on nothing but Coke and white bread all her life. She was nothing for him to be depressed about, he told himself, but he was depressed about her anyway.

He drank the second beer, and then got up to leave. She broke off the story she was telling—something that had happened at a high school football game, involving a teacher named Mister Bulmer—to look up at him and say, "You going already?"

"I'm pretty tired," he said.

"You be around tomorrow night?"

"I don't know. Maybe."

"Maybe I'll see you," she said.

Little Jack and Buddy and Ralph said good night see you tomorrow, and he left. Walking home, he kept thinking about what she'd said at the end, and wondering about it. She hadn't said a dozen words to him in particular all the time he'd been sitting there, and Little Jack's arm had been around her always, and yet she'd acted at the end there as though she really did want to see him again, wanted him to come back tomorrow night.

It would be a disappointment, he told himself. Another disappointment. She was just being friendly-polite, that was all. There was no point in going back again tomorrow night. Besides, he couldn't afford it.

But he went back anyway. He'd been thinking about it, off and on, all day watching television and all night at work, and at quitting time when Little Jack asked him if he was going up to the tavern he said yes, just for a little while. He'd have one beer, he told himself, just to see, and then he'd go on home.

The tavern was more crowded than he'd ever seen it before, because it was Saturday night. The jukebox seemed louder than usual, and there were three or four couples trying to dance in the middle of the floor, and bumping into each other. They were doing the Twist or something.

Ann was sitting in a booth with another girl, and Cole followed Little Jack over there. Little Jack said, "Sit down, I'll take the first round," and went away before Cole could tell him he was only going to have one beer, so he should buy his own. He shrugged, and decided he'd have two, buy Little Jack a round, and then go home.

He sat down in the booth, facing the two girls, and Ann introduced the other one. Her first name was Edna, but he didn't catch the last name because of the racket from the jukebox. Edna had the thinness and paleness of Ann, but her hair was a dry light brown, and her face was plain, neither ugly nor attractive. Her eyes were a light blue, and she seemed to stare a little bit, as though she should be wearing glasses. Cole, studying her, saw the telltale marks at the sides of her nose; she did wear glasses, but had left them off tonight in an attempt to look more beautiful.

Little Jack came back with four beers, holding them all in a trembling bunch between his two thumbs. He set them down on the table, spilling a little, slid them to their four places like a rapid succession of checker moves, and grabbed Ann to come dance with him.

Cole was left alone with Edna, but it didn't bother him. He didn't know her, so he didn't have to feel as though it was necessary to talk with her. He sipped at his beer gloomily, thinking that he'd be expected to buy four beers when it was his round. It depressed him that he would spend sixty cents, and it depressed him more that sixty cents had to be such a large amount of money to him. He felt like a man grubbing in the dirt for roots to eat, when up on all the slopes happy families were sitting around picnics.

Edna said, "You just moved to town, didn't you?" It was said hesitantly, as though she hadn't wanted to speak at all but had felt she ought to. And she'd had to shout, to be heard over the jukebox. Her voice was a little too high in pitch, so when she shouted it turned shrill.

He said, "About two months ago." Then he drank some more beer, to avoid having to say anything else.

But now he was more aware of the silence, now that

they'd both spoken, and he could see that the silence was embarrassing her, too, much more than him. He felt sorry for her embarrassment, and he managed a smile for her, to let her know the silence was all right.

The smile encouraged her. Either that, or she'd taken all this long to think of something else to say. She said, "Do you like it here?"

"It's all right," he said, but that sounded ungracious. "It's nice," he amended.

"I've never been anyplace else. You're from back East, aren't you?"

"Uh huh." But now he too felt uncomfortable, and felt required to help with the conversation, so he added, "From Troy. That's a town in upstate New York."

"Did you ever go to New York City?"

"I lived there for a while," he said, and was instantly sorry, because he knew that now she would ask him questions about New York City, and what could he say? That he couldn't remember? How stupid that would sound. Grabbing quickly for something else to say, to change the subject before she could begin the questions, he asked, "Do you dance?" And that was no good, either, because he wasn't even sure *he* danced. He thought he knew how, or maybe he'd known how but didn't any more.

But she said, "Not the fast things," and smiled apologetically. "I can dance to the slow songs," she said. "Maybe they'll play one later on."

"Maybe."

"Did you like New York?"

"It was okay."

It started then, the questions about New York City, and he gave vague answers, peppered lightly with the few random facts he could find in his head. After a while Ann and Little Jack came back and sat down, and the conversation shifted to past history again, giving Cole a welcome break. He didn't have to talk, and he didn't have to listen.

He bought his round when the time came, and then just

sat and watched the faces. Little Jack's face showed good-natured humorous competence. Ann's face showed quick eagerness and confidence. Edna's face showed apologetic appreciation and discomfort.

After a while, a slow tune came on the jukebox, and Cole saw Edna looking at him with hopeful expectancy. He didn't understand for a second, and then for a second longer he didn't know what to do. *Could* he dance?

He'd have to try, and hope for the best. He asked her, and she said yes, and they got up from the booth. The tavern was even more crowded now, and there were half a dozen couples moving slowly around the small open space in the middle of the room. Cole took the girl into his arms—the top of her head came about to his ear—and he discovered with relief that he could dance after all. It wasn't a conscious movement; he danced the way he would light a cigarette or tie his shoelaces, with muscle memories rather than mental memories.

She said, "You dance real good."

"You, too," he said, though she wasn't a very good dancer at all; sometimes he had to exert more pressure than was right, in order to get her to follow him. But it was still pleasant to do; pleasant to find himself capable of doing something from the earlier days, and pleasant to be this close to a girl.

Her hair smelled medicinally of a dandruff shampoo, but her body felt amazingly fragile and delicate. She didn't *look* beautiful, but she *felt* beautiful. He smiled softly to himself as they danced, with unaccustomed good humor.

The record ended, and they waited expectantly during the interval of silence, standing close together without touching, but the next record was rock and roll, and Cole felt more irritated at it than he would have expected.

"Oh, dear," she said, and he saw she was embarrassed again.

"Let's do something about it," he said. He took her hand, and led her around the periphery of the dancers to the

jukebox. Her hand was damp, and cool. Feeling reckless—
and feeling foolish to feel reckless over such a trifle—he put
a quarter into the jukebox and punched the buttons for
three slow tunes. "They'll come on sooner or later," he said,
and they went back to the table, where Little Jack had
bought another round.

Time passed unnoticed. They sat at the table for a while,
Cole silent again while the others talked about matters
strange to him, and whenever a slow record played Cole
danced with Edna, and from time to time either Cole or
Little Jack bought more beer. Cole told himself to stop worrying about spending a couple of dollars on a good time; an
occasional good time was as necessary as food and clothing.

But then it was two o'clock, and George the bartender was
telling them they had to go home. They went outside to the
sidewalk and Little Jack said, "See you Monday." His arm was
around Ann's waist. The two of them went walking off.

Cole said, "Shall I walk you home?" He meant *shall*, not
may; he wanted to know if it was expected of him.

But she took it the other way. She smiled a little nervously,
and said, "All right. I live this way."

They walked along in silence, Cole wondering if he should
put his arm around her waist. But he decided he shouldn't;
he'd only met her tonight.

After a block, she started talking about New York again,
but this time not asking questions. She told him about movies
she'd seen which had shown locations in New York, and arti-
cles in magazines about New York. She told him what she
thought New York was, and it seemed that in her mind New
York was an Emerald City for grownups. Cole answered
with monosyllables, knowing her impressions were wrong
but not remembering enough to be able to correct them,
and not even sure that he should correct them if he could.

"I live here," she said finally, pointing to a house like all
the other houses. It was like the Malloys' house, except that
the porch wasn't enclosed.

He walked her up to the stoop, and stopped there, saying,

"It was nice to meet you, Edna. I guess I'll see you there again."

"I guess so," she said, and offered her nervous smile again. "I had a very nice time."

She wasn't going up the stoop. She was just standing there in front of him, smiling up at him, and he knew she expected him to kiss her. He took her into his arms and kissed her, a longish kiss but with closed lips and no real passion. She put her arms around him, the two of them bulky together in their coats, and while he was kissing her he thought she was very frail and trusting and defenseless, and he felt protective toward her, tender toward her.

He released her, and she whispered, "Good night, Paul."

"Do you want to go to the movies tomorrow night?" He said it simultaneously with the thought of it, without reflection; but didn't regret it.

"That'd be fine," she said.

"I'll pick you up at seven o'clock."

"All right."

"Wait," he said, and took out his pencil and the little notebook he carried these days, in which to jot anything he wanted particularly to remember. "You'd better give me the address here, so I won't get lost."

"Three-twelve Lark Street."

He wrote it down, and then he asked her how to get to Charter Street from here, explaining that he was still new in town and didn't know much of it. She told him, and then she went on up onto the porch and into the house and he headed off in the direction she'd pointed out.

Worried thoughts about money were threatening to fill his head, but he held them at bay. "I've got to have some pleasure in life," he told himself. "What am I, a prisoner?"

He went on home, ignoring the worry, feeling relaxed and pleased. Edna was really a very nice girl. He'd been needing somebody anyway.

He didn't think of her in a sexual way at all, didn't even debate his chances for getting anywhere with her sexually. It was simply companionship he was thinking of, somebody to sit next to.

At home, he left himself a note on the bedroom door. PICK UP EDNA AT SEVEN O'CLOCK. ADDRESS IN WALLET. Then he went to bed.

9

He would only have till two o'clock with her, but he wanted to put his money away at home, and change his clothes, and wash his face and hands. Charter Street was only a couple of blocks out of the way, so he decided he could take the time; he went there from the tannery at a steady trot.

It was Edna he was in a hurry to see. He had known her one day shy of two weeks, and in that time he had been with her four times. Twice he had taken her to movies, on two Sundays, and twice he had walked her home from the tavern, on two Saturdays. He kissed her as a matter of course now, and with pleasure. And when they walked together his arm was around her waist.

People knew he had a girl, and they seemed pleased. Ann Bellman acted pleased for Edna's sake, and Little Jack acted pleased for Cole's sake. Mrs. Malloy knew he was going out on dates with a girl these Sunday nights, but she didn't know who the girl was, and she was pleased for her own sake; it increased the slight area of resemblance between Cole and her older son.

Tonight, he felt, was a new plateau in the relationship. Going to the tavern together on Saturday night, and the movies together on Sunday night, were all of a piece, a relationship hardly closer than that with Little Jack Flynn or Matt Malloy. But tonight would be different.

Edna was babysitting. She had a regular job, days, at the five-and-dime on Western Avenue, at the stationery counter, but every once in a while she still babysat for her aunt and uncle, who had friends in a larger city across the state line, and liked to visit them from time to time. "They're never back before two," she'd told him. "They wouldn't like it if you were there, but we don't have to tell them. I'm just doing them a favor anyway, minding their old kids."

Trotting toward home, he wondered just how high this plateau was going to be. Would he go to bed with her tonight? The idea excited him more than he would have thought possible with this particular girl two weeks ago, but he had to admit to himself that it was unlikely. He'd never done more than kiss her goodnight, but that was at least partly because he'd never tried to do any more, and he'd never tried because his instinct had told him it would be a mistake. But tonight? They would be alone in a way they'd never been alone before. They'd never been alone indoors. In the movie or the tavern, there were other people around. They'd only been alone when he'd been walking her home.

Tonight would be the first time he would kiss her without his coat on. And she without her coat on.

It was very cold. His breath misted around his head as he ran. They day before yesterday there'd been slight snow flurries, and a strong wind. There hadn't been enough snow for it to stick to the ground at all, but it was the first real warning of winter. It was the first week of December now; the television was full of commercials for Christmas presents. That was one thing he didn't have to worry about. He'd be back in New York by Christmas.

He got home and hurried up the stairs to his room, where the clock read ten minutes past twelve, so he'd cut five minutes from his usual homecoming time. The first thing he did was get his money out, and sort it on the bed. He had thirty-two dollars and seventeen cents, his usual pay, and he separated it into its three usual stacks; seventeen dollars in one pile, to be given Mrs. Malloy tomorrow, and ten dollars in the second pile, to go with the nine dollars already saved in the dresser drawer, and five dollars and seventeen cents in the third pile, his expense money for the following week.

While he was putting the money away, his glance caught on one of the notes he'd put up on the wall, the one reading: 50 GROVE ST.—NEW YORK—Look In Wallet. He saw that note, and was reminded of why he'd put it there, and nodded to himself. He'd be able to go to New York soon, and it was a good thing, good to be off before he got worse, before he got so bad he forgot all about going, which he now knew was more than possible. At least twice since he'd put that note up it had been used, twice when he'd forgotten all about who and what he really was and what he really wanted from life, twice when he'd fallen into the habit of thinking of himself only as the Paul Cole who worked at the tannery and lived at the Malloy house and went with the girl named Edna. Both times, seeing the note had only confused him, but once he'd looked in his wallet and seen the union cards and the Army Discharge and all the other papers enough memory had come seeping back into his mind to get him once more on an even keel.

But New York was still in the future, and in the interim the note would stand guard. Right now he had other things to think about, and he was in a hurry. He stripped out of his work clothes and put on his suit trousers, then went to the bathroom and hurriedly washed. There was a gnawing in his stomach, part anticipation and part hunger, and he decided the Malloys wouldn't mind if he took a piece of bread or two from the kitchen on his way out.

He put on a clean white shirt, but no tie, and shrugged back into the borrowed coat. He went downstairs without turning any lights on, and felt his way to the kitchen and the refrigerator. Opening the door to turn on the refrigerator light, he used its glow to get two pieces of bread from the breadbox. Then he closed the refrigerator again and went back through the darkness to the front door and outside. He walked along eating the dry bread.

He had the address on a note in his wallet, but he didn't need to refer to it. It was 618 Morton Street. Morton intersected Charter two blocks up, and 618 was in the first block to the left. He'd repeated the address and route to himself so many times that he didn't need the note at all.

There were individual differences in the houses in this

town, differences of color or exterior material, differences between open porch and enclosed porch, dormer attic windows or not, but the basic architectural style was always the same. A rectangular shape, with the short dimension facing the street. A porch, with a four- or five-step stoop. Two stories plus attic, with an A-shaped roof. When it was a one-family house, there was only a porch on the first story, but two-family versions had another porch upstairs, sometimes full-width and sometimes half-width.

618 Morton Street was one-family, with clapboard siding, painted gray, and the porch open. There was a green glider on the porch, and a battered red child's pedal auto. Through the window, Cole could see Edna sitting in the living room, watching a variety show on television.

She'd told him not to ring the bell, it might wake either or both of the children, to rap on the living room window instead, so that's what he did, leaning over the glider to do it. She was startled for a second, and then she looked over and saw him and smiled and waved. She got up and headed for the front door, and he went across the porch to meet her.

She opened the door and let him in, saying, "Boy, it's cold out there, isn't it?"

"Uh huh."

He took off his coat, and they went into the living room. There was a feeling of tension in the air; it was like their first meeting all over again, both of them awkward and ill-at-ease, but she more so than him.

"I better pull the drapes," she said. "In case a neighbor sees you or something."

With the drapes closed over the window, they sat down on the sofa together, both facing the television set.

"This is a good show tonight," she said, artificially, and went on to tell him some of the funny things that had already happened on it. He put his arm around her shoulders, and when a commercial came on he turned his head and kissed her.

For a long time, they didn't say anything at all. They

kissed, or sat with their heads together watching the television screen, and his right hand stroked her arm. Excitement was building very slowly within him, excitement mingled with apprehension, and it took a strong effort of will when at last he tentatively touched her breast.

They were kissing then, and at his touch on her breast she sighed and seemed to melt, to go soft and boneless in his arms. Encouraged, he stroked her breast more boldly, and her arms tightened around him, her right palm moving in a small circle on his back. Her breast was an anonymous soft mound beneath his hand, with the layers of clothing between, obscuring his sense of her body.

There were long intervals, a long time when they were only kissing, and a long time when they were kissing and he was fondling her breast through layers of clothing, and he had tried no further step by one o'clock, when the variety show ended and the television set went silent with blue snow. Only one channel served this town, so she got up from the sofa and went over to switch the set off. When she looked back at him, her face was so soft and happy and trusting and pleased by his presence that he couldn't stand it. He felt suddenly as though it had been a cruelty to touch her breast, and he wanted to apologize to her for it, but he didn't because he was sure she wouldn't understand.

Two standing lamps were lit in the living room, and she switched one off before coming back to the sofa. Her natural shyness was still in her, but her hesitancy and embarrassment were gone. She came back and sat down next to him and leaned forward for his kiss as though they'd been going together like this for years, but also as though in all those years kissing him had never lost its early fascination.

He kissed her, but he kept his hands on her arm and back. She waited, but he didn't move either hand, so she squirmed a little and then took his left hand and placed it on her breast. He closed his eyes, and held her more closely, his mind a confusion of attitudes. The excitement had grown strong in him, but he was feeling guilt too, as though he were lying to her somehow and taking advantage of her. And the apprehension had grown, a prickling across the back of his neck as though something hostile were coming closer, he didn't know what; he wondered if it had anything to do with something in his past.

She was wearing a green pullover sweater. At a point when the excitement was stronger in him than any other feeling, he slid his hand down from her breast to her waist, worked his fingers under the sweater, and slid the hand up again over the electric slickness of her slip, and his fingers curved again around her breast, which felt smaller now, but firmer. She began to tremble when his hand moved under her sweater, and held him more fiercely, and ground her lips against his.

He parted his lips, and his tongue touched tentatively outward, and her mouth opened for him. Their tongues trembled together, and his hand stroked her, and stroked her, and stroked her.

He wanted his hand under the slip, and under the bra, and his fingers explored this way and that way, trying to find an opening somewhere, and failing, so he said the first words either of them had spoken since he'd first kissed her. He whispered, "Take off your sweater."

He couldn't see her face, because their heads were together, his lips by her ear, but he felt her stiffen slightly and she whispered, "I'd better not. What if they come back?"

"It's only quarter after one."

"Paul…"

"I won't hurt you," he promised, not entirely sure himself what he meant, but nevertheless afraid it was a lie.

They separated, he taking his hands off her, and slowly she removed the sweater, keeping her head lowered and not looking at him. Her slip was white, and slick-looking, with thin straps that went up over her shoulders, next to the wider white bra straps. Her shoulders looked thin and hard and pale and cold.

She whispered, "I'm embarrassed to have you see me, Paul. Is it all right if we turn off the light?"

"All right," he said. The one lamp still lit was beside the sofa, on his side; he turned around and switched it off, and then it was pitch black in the room.

"I'm scared," she said, laughing nervously. "Isn't that silly?"

He put his arms around her. "There's nothing to be scared of," he said. The slip had an irritatingly harsh feeling to it, beneath his hands.

She was trembling, just slightly, but when he kissed her the trembling faded away, and she didn't react at all, one way or the other, when he slid the slip straps down her arms and off, and pushed the slip down to her waist. He undid her bra, and removed it, and touched her again, and she sighed again, the way she'd done the first time he touched her. She was very thin; below her breasts her ribs were separate corrugations of her flesh.

He kissed her and caressed her, and the fright seemed to have gone out of her. From time to time she sighed, and her arms were tight around him. When he bent his head to kiss her breast, her right hand stroked his hair, and he thought she was smiling.

But when he put his hand on her leg, she stiffened, pressing her legs tight together, and whispered, "No, Paul. Please." He took his hand away at once, but she seemed to think she had to give him an explanation, because she said, "I don't want to go that far. I'm afraid I wouldn't be able to stop, and we shouldn't do—we shouldn't do anything like that."

"All right. I won't ever try to force you."

"I like you to touch me, Paul, up here. You can do it, I like it. If you want to turn the light on, that's okay."

"Not if you don't want to."

"It's silly to feel that way, isn't it?" She laughed again, briefly and nervously. "To let you touch me, and not let you see me. But I can't help it, I get embarrassed."

"It's all right. I don't want to do anything you don't want."

"I like you an awful lot, Paul. I like you better than anybody else I ever knew."

She thinks I'm going to stay here forever. How can I tell her I'm not going to? That's why I've been feeling bad, because she doesn't know I'll be leaving soon.

Her refusal to let him touch her leg had drained some of the excitement from him, and now this thought drained the rest, and suddenly he didn't want to touch her or kiss her at all anymore. Not because of her, but because of him. He could visualize her sitting there next to him, naked to the waist, her slip all bunched around her middle, hopeful and trusting and shy. He felt as though he'd been playing a cruel practical joke on her.

But to just pull away all of a sudden would hurt her feelings, so he made an excuse. He said, "What time is it?"

"Oh, golly, I don't know!"

"I better check. I'll have to turn the light on for a second."

"Don't look at me!"

"I won't," he promised. He got up from the sofa and felt for the lamp and switched it on, keeping his back to her. Looking at his watch, he said, "It's quarter to two."

"Oh. It's a good thing you thought of it."

"Do you want me to turn the light back off? While you get dressed?"

"Would you? Just for a minute."

"All right."

He switched it off again, and in the darkness heard the rustlings of her. She said, "Isn't this stupid? I don't know what it is, it just embarrasses me. I feel a like a stupid little kid or something."

"Don't worry about it," he said. "There's nothing wrong with being modest."

"But I let you—touch me and all. It's just silly, that's all. I can't find my swea—no, here it is. Just a minute now."

He waited, standing in the pitch darkness next to the lamp, until she said, "There! You can turn it on now."

He switched the light on, and they squinted at each other, he standing and she still sitting on the sofa. Her hair was mussed up, and there were high round spots of color on her cheeks like a toy soldier.

She got to her feet, making final adjustments on her sweater, and saying, "I guess you better go now. They'll be coming home pretty soon."

"I'll see you tomorrow night after work," he said.

"Okay." She smiled happily, and put her hand on his arm as they walked to the door. He kissed her briefly, and put on his coat, and then kissed her again. Then he left, going out into the cold. She stood in the doorway, hugging herself and smiling after him, and when he got out to the sidewalk he waved to her, and then headed home.

What was he going to do about her? He ought to tell her, or stop seeing her, or *something*. It wasn't right just to let it ride like this. Up to now it hadn't bothered him, because going to a movie together or dancing together in a tavern wasn't very much, and didn't imply very much. But tonight had implied worlds. He may not have been the first man ever to touch her breast, what with high school hayrides and such, but he was sure in his mind that he was the first man ever to get even a part of her clothing off.

He shouldn't have done it at all. He shouldn't even have agreed to come here tonight, he should have made some sort of excuse. But the idea had excited him, and he was still strong with the need for *someone*. So he was using her, and it was cruel. And he didn't want to be cruel.

If he just stayed away from her for the rest of the time here, he would hurt her badly, and that was no good. He knew how shy she was, and how unsure of herself. If he stayed away from her now, particularly after tonight, it would be brutal for her.

What he had to do was tell her the truth. Tomorrow night. It would have been better to tell her before this, but the important thing was that she be told. Tomorrow night would do.

He made the turn at Charter Street, and walked toward home. At the farther end of the first block, he saw parked ahead of him a brand new highly polished black car, and he stopped, feeling suddenly frightened. It took him a few seconds to understand the cause for the fright, and then he remembered vaguely a recent time when the police had come for him and questioned him in a long narrow room. Had they come in a car like that one ahead? That must be it.

But why had they questioned him? It had had something to do with a sheet of shiny metal. He could remember holding it in his hands, remember his face reflected in its surface, and one of the policeman asking him if he'd ever seen that piece of metal before.

But what was the piece of metal? He couldn't remember, and he wasn't even sure they'd ever told him or he'd ever known. Whatever it was, he must have satisfied them that he wasn't guilty, because obviously they'd let him go. Had it been a robbery or something? He couldn't remember why they'd picked him up.

He approached the car slowly, wondering if it was after all them again, wanting to ask him more questions, and when he saw that the car was empty he smiled with sudden relief, and lit a cigarette.

He still felt a little shaky, and found himself wishing he was back with Edna again, with his arms around her to drain away the shakiness. He walked on homeward, smiling, thinking about Edna, not thinking about getting back to New York at all.

10

While he was sorting his pay on the bed, he glanced up and saw the note on the wall and realized it didn't make any sense. It said:

50 GROVE ST.—NEW YORK—Look In Wallet

But he didn't have a wallet.

He was just thinking about that tonight, when he got paid, about not having a wallet and so having to carry his pay around loose in his trouser pocket. He remembered thinking about that, and also thinking that he must have had a wallet at some time or another, but a long long while ago. He couldn't even remember it, it was so long ago.

Then why did he have that note up there? If he'd left himself a note in this room about a wallet, then he must have had a wallet at some time while he'd been living in this room, and he'd only been living in this room for how long?

He couldn't remember.

He frowned at that, beginning to be disturbed. Until he'd noticed that note on the wall, he hadn't been worried about anything or even thinking about anything, just going though the normal motions without paying any attention. But now everything was different, now he was starting to be scared.

He looked around the room, and it was full of things he couldn't understand or justify. Not just the note about his nonexistent wallet, but all the other notes as well; why did he have to have notes telling him about his job and his name and the details of his everyday life? And here was the money on his bed, sorted into neat piles, with one of the piles to be added to the little hoard of money in the dresser drawer, but what was that hoard of money for? And how long *had* he lived here? And why couldn't he remember ever having a wallet?

With the money and the pay envelope on the bed was a ribbon of white paper that had come with his pay. He opened it in a distracted way, half-expecting it to be packed with the answers to all his questions, and at the same time realizing it wouldn't have anything to tell him at all.

But it did have two things to tell him: his name, and the date. *Paul Cole.* He not only recognized the name at once, but also recognized that he hadn't remembered it until he'd seen it. And the date, the twelfth of December, seven days from the babysitting evening with Edna.

What was wrong? Why was his mind so leaden? Why didn't he remember anything, or know what anything meant?

How long had it been like this? He slept, he ate, he watched television, he went to work. The world was in constant flux, always either getting lighter or getting darker, and at every shade between night and day he had his simple function to perform, requiring no attention and no memory, and he'd never known anything was wrong.

Now he did. If it wasn't so massive, so total, and yet so vague, he'd be frightened out of his wits, but the wrong was too elusive-pervasive and he was only stunned by it. He sat limp-armed on the bed, thrust out of the mnemonic round of habit, but without strong memories or a sense of identity or place to sustain him. His name was Paul Cole, the date was December twelfth; beyond that he knew nothing.

Well, no. He worked in the tannery, and he'd just been paid, he knew both of those things. This was his room, on the second floor of a house otherwise occupied by a family named Malloy, he knew that. Edna, Little Jack and Black Jack, Ralph, Artie Bellman, and even more, these were all names and faces he knew. It wasn't as though he were drifting in a vacuum.

But it was! What did that note mean?

50 GROVE ST.—NEW YORK—Look In Wallet

The money was for a bus ticket to New York. The fact drifted into his head with the tardiness of someone who hadn't really intended to come at all. The little hoard of money in the dresser drawer was being saved for a bus ticket to New York City.

And thence to 50 Grove St.?

Damn! Where was the wallet? He must have had one, sometime, somewhere, a wallet full of answers, a wallet crammed with statements about himself. But somewhere along the line he had lost it; or it had been stolen from him, and he knew with fatalistic certainty he would never get it back nor ever know what had happened to it.

Curiosity, still sluggish and half-drugged by habit, nevertheless now was stirring, dispelling both the fear and the paralysis of his being wrested from his round of routine. It was curiosity that pulled him finally up off the bed and over to the dresser where, with the money saved in there, he found a note which told him, "Bus ticket, $33.42." There was seventeen dollars in the drawer, and on the bed another ten to be added to this pile. Next week, then. If there was a plan behind all this, and it seemed to him there had to be, then it had to mean he would leave here for New York City next week.

But why? Why go to New York City? He didn't know anybody there, didn't think he'd ever been there in his life. At least, he didn't remember ever having been to New York City.

But he didn't remember *anything*. Not anything back of the present routine, at any rate.

He was supposed to go to New York City, that's all he could be sure of. The reasons for it had once been contained in a wallet, but the wallet was now gone. The only clue he had was the address: 50 Grove St. It was necessary for him to go to 50 Grove St. in New York City, in order to find out why he was supposed to go there.

He shook his head, not liking that. Why should he go running off somewhere without any reason? What was the matter with the life he had here? Was he unhappy here, discontented, ill-treated?

He knew he wasn't. He knew he liked his job, liked the

people he lived with and the people he worked with, liked the girl he went on dates with. Why leave any of this, even for a little while? It was best to let matters lie.

But he couldn't. The thought itself made him suddenly ill, gave him a nervous nausea like the aftermath of a near-accident, the way he might feel right after *not* crashing in an automobile at eighty miles an hour.

He had to go to New York, that was all of it, he had to go there, and it didn't seem to matter whether he understood or not.

Would other people know? Maybe the people around him knew about his trip and could tell him why he was supposed to make it. Maybe Matt Malloy, or Little Jack Flynn, or Edna; maybe he should ask.

But he couldn't do that either, admit to others he didn't know why he was supposed to go to New York. No, more than that; admit to them he didn't know anything about anything, from before.

He didn't even know what he meant by *before*, except he didn't think he had lived here all his life, in this house or in this town. He had come here from somewhere else, though he couldn't remember where or why, and he was supposed now to travel on again, still not knowing why and only by a cryptic note knowing anything of where.

One thing he did know. If he didn't want to be startled again like this he should leave himself a more comprehensive note for next time. He never doubted for a second that there would be a next time, that he would sink into the grayness again, probably by morning, and only another accident would bring him back out of it.

In the same dresser drawer with the money was a large-size pad of paper, and a ballpoint pen. There were also several sheets of paper containing writing, in what he recognized as his own hand, mostly sets of names or objects with arrows between, none of which meant anything to him at all, no more than 50 Grove St. had meant anything to him or the idea of New York City had meant anything to him.

He set the written-on papers aside, and began a new note to himself, actually a letter, without salutation:

I am supposed to go to New York City. The money in the dresser drawer is for my ticket, and I will have enough by next payday. When I get to New York City, I am supposed to go to a place called 50 Grove Street. I don't know why, but maybe I'll find out there.

This note he folded and placed next to the money in the dresser drawer. Then he altered the note on the wall to read "50 GROVE ST.—NEW YORK—Look In Dresser," and he made another note saying the same thing, which he put in his hip pocket, where he would have carried a wallet if he'd owned one.

With all this set, he felt relieved and much safer, as though he'd just dropped anchor after having been adrift on the high sea. He had hacked away at the enormity of his helplessness and the frailty of his plans, reducing them to manageable proportions by writing notes about them. He cleared away the rest of the paper, moved the stacks of money from his bed, and got ready for sleep.

But sleep eluded him a long while, lying there in the darkness. He gazed unseeing upward at the ceiling while emotional remnants fluttered in his mind; fear at the nakedness of his position, curiosity about himself and the world around him, even a kind of heady anticipation about the trip next week.

It never occurred to him that thirty-three dollars and forty-two cents was not the price of a round-trip ticket.

11

He wasn't supposed to come back.

Saturday morning he'd read the notes he'd left himself the night before, and then, just to be sure, he'd stopped at the bus depot on the way to work, and that's where he learned he'd been saving for a one-way ticket. What could that mean except he hadn't intended to come back?

It was frightening, this adventure into the unknown. In many ways it didn't make any sense at all, to go running off to a city he knew nothing about, not even knowing why he was going there. For all he knew, the information in the missing wallet was something telling him to stay away from New York, though that couldn't explain why he was saving money for a bus ticket.

But why leave, why go away from here at all? It wasn't as though he needed somewhere else. Here in this town he had a good job, and a steady girlfriend, and a good place to live, and lots of good friends; who could want anything more than that? In New York City, he had no idea what to expect.

But somehow the thought of staying was even more frightening than the thought of leaving. He didn't understand his feelings himself, but it was as though there were something out there in the world a million times greater than anything he had here in this town, and if he stayed here he'd lose that something forever. It was all as vague as air; he didn't know what the something could be, or if he would ever find it, or even if he would recognize it on seeing it, but the certainty of not finding it, by staying here in town, left him sick with nervous apprehension.

All weekend he lived with his fears and uncertainties, plus one matter more; from the moment on Saturday when he'd learned he was to buy a one-way ticket he had known he would have to tell Edna. It was impossible that she already knew about his plans, or she wouldn't have been so open and total with him. Her behavior implied a permanence he now knew was impossible.

He tried to tell her Saturday night, in the tavern after work, but shyness and embarrassment and a sense of loss stilled his tongue, and afterwards he lay in bed sleepless with a sense of shame. On Sunday evening, as usual, he took her to the movies, and it wasn't until the picture was over and he was walking homeward with her that he finally managed to force himself to speak.

"I've been wanting to tell you something," he began, but from the way her hand tightened on his he knew he'd phrased it badly and she was now anticipating something much more pleasant from him than what he had to say, so he added quietly, "It's bad news, I guess."

"Bad news? What kind of bad news?"

"I'm not going to be staying here very long." He'd said it over and over in his mind all evening, different phrasings, different way of telling her, and this was the sentence he'd finally settled on, so it rolled out of him without hesitation.

"Not staying here? You mean, in town here?"

"That's right."

"Well, where are you going?" From her tone, she didn't really understand him yet.

"New York City."

"You're going all the way to New York *City*?"

"Yes."

"But, but why?"

How to explain to her? He couldn't even explain to himself. He said, "I just have to go, that's all."

"You mean, for a visit?"

He shook his head. "No, I don't think so."

She disengaged her hand from his, but her voice seemed calm as she said, "You mean you're going back for good."

"Back?" He frowned at her phrasing, but it sounded right.

"You *told* me you used to live there."

"Oh. Yes, back, I've got to go back."

"Why?"

He shook his head, feeling more and more miserable. "I don't know," he said. This was the second time she'd asked him why, and this time he'd had to tell her the truth.

But how could she understand the truth? She was walking a little faster now, and her face was wet. She said, "What do you mean, you don't know? Are you trying to make a joke?"

He spread his hands, walking faster and faster to keep up with her, and said, "It isn't a joke. I've got something wrong with me, I don't remember things. All I know is I'm supposed to go to New York. I've got notes in my room, and I've been saving my money for the ticket."

"*Saving* money? You knew about this all along, this isn't something that just came up?"

"I guess so."

"You guess so." She was practically running now, her coattails fluttering around her knees, her face set in harsh lines that made it look bonier and older.

"I wanted to tell you before," he said, "but I couldn't, I was afraid to."

"Afraid I wouldn't let you touch me anymore."

They were about a block from her house now, and he stopped where he was on the sidewalk, feeling ashamed and inadequate. "That wasn't it," he said, but he was only speaking for the last two days. How did he know, from before that? He could remember incidents with her, particularly the baby-sitting episode, but his own plans and purposes were only a blur.

She stopped two paces ahead of him and looked back over her shoulder. "Why did you lead me on?"

"Because I was lonely, I guess."

"Now you want me to feel sorry for you."

"No. No, I don't."

"And this memory thing all of a sudden. You expect me to believe that?"

"It's true, Edna."

She brushed that away with an angry motion, and said, "When are you going?"

"Next week. The end of next week."

"And you won't be coming back."

"I guess not, no."

"And with that convenient memory of yours, you can forget all about me in no time, can't you?"

"I suppose so," he said, feeling painful at having to say it but knowing she would see the lie in anything else he might say. "I'm sorry, Edna," he said.

"You're sorry." Her voice was flat. "What a dirty sneak you are," she said. "What a dirty nasty sneak." Her voice broke on the last word, and she turned away. "Goodbye," she said, her voice muffled, and walked away from him across the tilted squares of sidewalk.

He stood where he was, watching her go. She looked so small and thin and young and frail. He remembered the feel of her ribs against the heel of his hand, when his fingers had been cupping her breast. He remembered her embarrassment at his seeing her undress, and he remembered the moments of awkwardness between them caused by her shyness and nervousness and insecurity.

What good would it be to run after her? He would have to say either *I'll stay* or *Come with me*, and he could do neither. He couldn't stay and he couldn't take her with him, and he only understood in the vaguest way the reasons for both. So if he did run after her, what could he possibly say? "I'm sorry. I didn't ever want to hurt you, and I'm sorry." Useless words. They would only make even larger the words he wasn't saying.

She looked so fragile, walking away from him along the sidewalk. She looked like a child, cruelly hurt. With thin dignity, she was walking straight and even, and she didn't look back. He stood watching after her until she turned at her house and went up the stoop and across the porch, and still she didn't look back. He waited until he couldn't see her any longer, until he knew she'd gone into the house, and then he turned around and walked home.

She was right. I just used her. I did lead her on. That was why I was ashamed to tell her before now, because I knew all along what I was doing to her.

He went on home. The Malloys were all in bed; only the nightlight at the head of the stairs was on. He went upstairs and got ready quickly for bed, and then lay there in the darkness, gazing at the less-dark rectangle of the window. He was feeling again that depression that came over him from time to time, the emotion that brought him so close to crying. He dimly remembered feeling this way before, and not crying, and he didn't cry now.

I wonder if Edna is crying, over there in her own bed. Across the rows of angled roofs, and down, and through her window, and in the corner of her bed she is weeping, muffling the noises with blanket and pillow so her parents won't hear. She is never a pretty girl; sobbing, her face will be ugly. Her body is thin and frail, and under the blankets she is cold.

I'm sorry, he thought, but it didn't do anybody any good.

12

There was no point in working Friday.

The idea had come to him earlier in the week, and he'd been amazed by it; it was a leap of logic he hadn't expected from himself. But once the thought was there, he saw that it was obvious. He was staying here only until he got his next pay, and then he'd be off; he'd told Mrs. Malloy on Tuesday that he'd be leaving this weekend. He'd be paid four o'clock Friday afternoon, and there was no reason in the world why he should work Friday night.

There was only one problem. He wasn't sure exactly what days he was being paid for, didn't know if his pay would include Friday's work, and maybe even Saturday's work too. So the thing to do was just slip away after he was paid, and get aboard the bus, and be off. He'd gone to the bus depot, and there was a New York bus leaving at four-thirty, plenty of time for him to get to the depot from the tannery, even if Joe Lampek was slower than usual in doling out the pay envelopes.

The idea came to him Thursday afternoon, while he was watching television, and he was so pleased by it that he acted on it at once, going upstairs and getting all his money out of the drawer. The full twenty-seven dollars was there. He put ten dollars in his pocket and went back downstairs to the kitchen, where Mrs. Malloy was doing her baking. She baked on Mondays and Thursdays. He said, "I've decided I'll leave right from work Friday night, so I'll give you this week's rent now."

"You're really going, are you?"

"I've got to."

"You want to, Paul."

Yes, that was true. The unknown had a fascination, and so

much was unknown. He knew his life here, but this life faded away in the very near past, and everything beyond it was blank. More than any other reason for leaving here, he was curious about himself.

"We'll miss you, Paul," she was saying. "I only hope our next roomer is half as considerate."

"You'll get somebody else." He made a joke of it, saying, "I'll write you a reference, if you want."

"If you'll write me a postcard sometime, I'll like it even better."

"I will," he lied.

"It's only a week till Christmas. Why not wait till after the first of the year?"

"I can't." Nearly every day he needed the reminder note; to stay here any longer was too dangerous.

"If you must, you must," she said. "Just leave the money on the refrigerator."

He left it there, and went back to watch television some more, burning with impatience. That night he worked twice as hard as usual, trying to burn off some of the excess nervous energy he'd been building up. He worked up a good sweat, but his energy seemed inexhaustible. It didn't even bother him tonight that he was still in Coventry.

As near as he could figure it, Ann Bellman had found out from Edna that something had gone wrong between her and Cole, but apparently Edna hadn't said what it was, that he was leaving. Ann in her turn had talked to Little Jack Flynn, and apparently they'd decided between them that he'd seduced her and, mission accomplished, had now dropped her. Little Jack had come to have a private talk with Cole, to tell him that Edna was a real good kid and nobody should treat her bad. Little Jack had been calm and deliberate and judicial, a strangely solemn attitude for him, and he'd even been diffident a bit about butting in, but Cole's conscience was still bothering him about Edna and he snapped back, losing his temper with a co-worker for the first time since coming to work here. He told Little Jack to mind his own damn business, and Little Jack's face froze and he turned on his heel and went away. That was Tuesday night, and since then no one else on the crew had said a word to Cole. It was obvious that Little Jack had enforced the silence rule, and Cole knew that it was essentially, in a topsy-turvy way, a friendly action. If Little Jack didn't like him, he would have insisted on fighting him. Doing it this way, Little Jack could only be thinking in terms of withholding friendship.

Whatever the motive, the silence rule was complete. It was awkward at first, but Cole got used to it rather quickly. He was used to solitary daydreaming during work anyway, and besides he would be in the company of these people less than a week longer. So it didn't really matter what they thought or did.

Little Jack and the rest of the crew didn't bother him, but Edna still did. He hadn't seen her since Sunday night, and knew he would never see her again, but she bothered him. His sin toward her had been, at the worst, thoughtlessness, but maybe thoughtlessness was the worst sin a human being could commit against another human being. It still stung him, at any rate, and was another source of his nervous energy.

Going home after work Thursday night, he thought of what the next few days would be, if he weren't planning on leaving. Tomorrow night, of course, he would go to the tavern; if he weren't planning on leaving, he wouldn't have to budget his money so tightly. The next night, he would go to the tavern again, and dance with Edna, and walk her home, and kiss her on her front porch, and slip his hand under her coat to touch her breasts. Sunday afternoon, he would sit at the dining room table for dinner with the Malloys, and Sunday night he would take Edna to the movies. Afternoons he would watch television, and nights he would work, and one day would be much like another, all blending in together, with only the Sunday to mark the passage of time.

How easy it would be to slide into that, to join the long

silent throng shuffling toward the grave. For him it would be as easy as breathing; all he'd have to do was rip up a few reminder notes. His memory would do the rest. But the thought of it left him weak with nervousness and fear, and he knew he could never *want* to let it happen.

He was surprised to see, when he reached home, that the living room lights were on. The Malloys were always in bed well before midnight, so he hurried up to the walk, wondering if something was wrong.

Matt Malloy was in the living room, sitting in his easy chair, smoking his twisted treeroot of a pipe. He was wearing slippers and workpants and an undershirt, and on the drum table beside his chair were a quart bottle of beer and two glasses, one of them half-full.

Malloy took his pipe from his mouth and roused himself, as though he'd been dozing or in reverie. "Come on in, Paul," he said. "I been waiting up for you. Have a beer." His voice was a flawed rumble, delivering words slowly and precisely up from his chest.

"What's wrong?" Cole shucked out of his borrowed coat, left it on the newel post, and went on into the living room. Malloy had filled the other glass, and held it out for Cole to take.

"Nothing's wrong. Just want to talk to you. Grab a seat."

Cole sat down on the edge of the sofa, holding the glass in both hands but not yet drinking any of the beer. He could tell nothing from Malloy's expression; he didn't seem especially angry or joyous or sad, not anything in particular, just quiet and perhaps a little solemn. It was just about the same expression he wore whenever he talked about the history of organized labor.

Malloy said, "You're planning on going away."

So that was it. "Yes, I am."

"I'm sorry to hear that, Paul. So's the Mrs. We've both grown what you might call fond of you the last two months. We'll miss you."

"I'll miss you, too."

"I expect you plan to better yourself, I expect that's what's behind it."

"I guess so, in a way."

Malloy picked up his glass and drained it, then refilled it again and that emptied the bottle. He put the bottle on the floor beside his chair. "I don't know exactly how to start," he said. "I feel I want to tell you something, but I don't know exactly how to start."

"My home is back east," Cole told him, in what he knew was a vain effort to duck what was coming.

"In a manner of speaking," said Malloy. "In a manner of speaking, you might say the Earth is your home. Depends on how you look at things." He himself seemed dissatisfied with that; he frowned and shifted position and said, "Let me try to tell you what I mean. Take the Mrs. now, asleep upstairs. Just before you got home, I was sitting here thinking about high school days and the days when I was a young man, before I married. I can think of half a dozen girls I went with then, all different, all of them at one time or another the only girl for me. And maybe a dozen more I never did go with but wanted to. Most of those girls are still right here in town, married and got families of their own. I was thinking about them tonight, just before you come home. How, when all is said and done, it didn't make much difference which of them I married."

Cole frowned at that. Instead of the arguments for staying he'd expected, he was getting a gratuitous look at Matt Malloy's frustrations and failure feelings, and he didn't like it. Especially if Malloy was going to sit there and tell him what was wrong with his wife; Cole liked Mrs. Malloy, she was one of the best people he'd met here.

But Malloy said, "Don't get me wrong, Paul, this isn't nothing against the Mrs. She's a fine woman, and I don't regret for a minute that I married her. But I'm saying it really didn't make much difference if it was her I married or Sarah Cook or Mary Ann Wheeler or which one of them. I'd still be pretty much where I am and who I am. My children would look different, and maybe be a little different—I might have daughters even, instead of sons—but I'd be pretty much the same man. There was one girl, now, Elsie Morlander, if I'd married her I would have most likely stayed in the Army, made a career out of it. But my work wouldn't have been much different from what it is now, and I would have retired after twenty years and come back here anyway, and here I'd be just the same, only maybe working just part-time down to the tannery instead of full-time, and have a bookcase full of books on Army instead of on unions."

Malloy drank some more beer. "I don't know if this makes any sense to you or not," he said. "You're still young, not married yet, not settled into your groove yet, so maybe you just don't know what I'm talking about. But what I'm trying to say, the choices you make in your life, they all seem big and important at the time, but as the years go by they all smooth out and things are pretty much as they would have been anyway. Every once in a while in a man's life, he comes to a crossroads, you might say, a place where he's got to make a decision about his whole future life. But like the fella says, all roads lead to Rome. The scenery might be a little different on each road, but after a while they all come back together again. And then one day you say to yourself, it didn't make a damn bit of difference which way I picked back there. You'll look back at the different girls you went with when you were young, and you'll say to yourself, it didn't matter a particle which one of them I married."

"All decisions aren't like that," said Cole.

"No, they don't *look* it," Malloy told him, "not up close. Like what you're deciding now. Whether you're going to live in this town here or in New York City. It looks like a hell of a difference in that one, don't it? But what is this town but a bunch of jobs and a bunch of neighborhoods and a bunch of people? And what is New York City but a bigger bunch of jobs and a lot more neighborhoods and a great big bunch of people? So twenty-five years from now you'll take the subway to work instead of walking or driving, but how much difference is that? Maybe you'll live in an apartment house instead of a house like this one, but on the inside it's all the same. And a job is a way to make money to pay the bills, so what difference does it make what the job is or where it is? Twenty-five years from now you'll live in a neighborhood and you'll go to a job and your kids'll be growing up, and that's just the way of it. The place you live might be here or New York City or San Francisco, but who you are and what you are and what you've got to look back on will be all the same thing."

Cole shook his head. "I don't think so," he said.

"Because you're young." Malloy smiled and shrugged. "I didn't suppose you'd know what I was talking about," he said, "but I had to go ahead and say it anyway. If you ever want to come back, you just write to me and tell me when you're coming, that's all you have to do."

"Thank you."

"I wish you every bit of luck, Paul." Malloy heaved himself out of the chair. "And now I've got to get off to bed."

"I'll take care of the glasses and the bottle."

"I won't argue about it, I'm tired." He held his hand out. "If I don't see you again before you go, goodbye and good luck."

Cole shook his hand, feeling solemn and a bit sad. But the impatience and the nervous energy overrode all other feelings, and when Matt Malloy went on upstairs to bed nothing of what he'd said remained in Cole's consciousness. He took the two glasses and the empty beer both out to the kitchen, and then he went upstairs and to bed.

Tomorrow night, he thought, and fell asleep smiling.

13

He checked his suitcase and canvas bag at the bus depot, and then went on to the tannery. Mrs. Malloy had insisted he keep the borrowed coat, so he was wearing it the same as usual. He had ten dollars and eight cents in his pockets, and he would be paid thirty-two seventeen. He'd have almost ten dollars left over after he bought the ticket.

When he punched the time clock, the time on the card was exactly four P.M. It occurred to him that he would never punch out again, and this card of his would always be incomplete, like a hole in the world. The idea struck him funny, and he waited in good humor for the payline to form, not caring that he was still getting the silent treatment.

It was only luck that these people didn't know he was leaving. He'd told Edna, and he'd told the Malloys, but apparently neither had told anyone else. If the crew members had known he was leaving, it would have made the silent treatment superfluous and they would have abandoned it, if only to tell him he was a bastard for running out on Edna.

It was about ten after four before the payline got started, but Cole was up near the front of the line and he still had over half an hour to catch his bus anyway. When his turn came he took the pay envelope from Joe Lampek, and headed immediately for the coat rack near the door, where his coat was hung. He paused there long enough to switch the money from envelope to trouser pocket, and to check and be sure it was the same amount as usual. Then he crumpled the empty envelope and the white paper ribbon listing his deductions, threw them on the floor, and shrugged into his coat.

Most of the crew was still on the payline, and not looking in his direction. The others were sitting around on crates,

smoking and talking together. They were excluding him
anyway these days, so none of them noticed when he slipped
through the doorway, shut the door behind himself, and
walked away from the tannery.

Plenty of time, plenty of time. He stopped at a drugstore
on Western Avenue and bought a magazine to look at on the
bus. He selected *Life* because it ran so heavily to pictures; he
had trouble concentrating on reading matter of any kind.

When he got to the bus depot, the clock high on the wall
read exactly four-thirty. There were two pregnant women
sitting on the bench, surround by parcels. They were talking
about their doctors.

Cole bought his ticket and asked if the New York bus was
going to arrive on time. "Don't ask me," said the old man
behind the counter. "It gets here when it gets here. On time
usually, but not always."

He got his suitcase and canvas bag from the locker, and
put them on the floor near the door. He was too keyed up to
sit, but waited standing by the door, looking out through the
plate glass at the street. He chain-smoked, and kept looking
up at the clock.

The bus was right on time. The two pregnant women
glanced at it, and then ignored it, so it was something else
they were waiting for. Cole carried the luggage out to the
sidewalk, and the old man from the ticket counter came out
to put the claim checks on and stow the bags away in the
side of the bus. Cole boarded the bus, and found it nearly
empty. He picked the third seat back on the right-hand side,
and sat there while the bus remained parked at the curb in
front of the depot. That was a lovely moment, a safe and
beautiful feeling, the best of both worlds; to be on the bus,
but the bus not going anywhere.

Then the driver shut the door and hunched over the big
flat steering wheel, and the bus wrenched forward into time.
In that instant, Cole felt a sudden kind of pain, as though in
jolting forward the bus had broken some sort of invisible
cord between Cole and this town, and now both were falling

free of each other, drifting apart like detritus around a spaceship.

Looking out the window, he watched the town go by backwards. He was afraid to be leaving here, afraid to be going into darkness and ignorance, but he couldn't help himself. He had to go.

He'd forgotten the name of the narrow river that snaked through town, but he counted the number of times the bus crossed it and it was three. Shortly after the third time, the houses stopped and were replaced by countryside, barren and brown and wintry.

He sat gazing out the window, the magazine unopened on his lap.

14

Cole awoke to find himself stuffed and folded into his corner of the seat, though the seat next to him was empty. He stretched out his arms and legs, feeling the stiffness in them, and then realized what had awakened him; the bus wasn't moving.

Were they in the city?

He sat upright, and squinted out though the window, but at first he saw only darkness. Then, near the front of the bus, he saw the line of tollbooths, and in the next instant the bus started forward again. He saw the tired-looking man in the gray uniform in the little booth on the way by, and then, looking back, he saw in green neon lettering stretched across the top of the booths, NEW JERSEY TURNPIKE. So they were leaving the turnpike, and wasn't New Jersey very near New York? He leaned his cheek against the cold glass of the window and peered forward, trying to catch a glimpse of the city.

He wondered if he would recognize it, or any part of it. He wondered if he would arrive in New York City and step down from the bus and suddenly know all, who he was and where he was going and why he had had to make this trip. He hoped it would happen that way, but he was afraid it wouldn't.

More toll booths came up now, these for the Lincoln Tunnel. New York must be very close now, very close. His mouth was dry, and he felt he was beginning to shake; a treacherous part of his mind whispered of how pleasant it would be still to be at home.

But that was wrong. Home was not the town left behind him, but the unknown city ahead. Edna had told him he'd once said he came from New York City, and that still did sound right, it did sound as though he must have come from

New York even though New York was now as unknown to
him as the moons of Mars.

In his nervousness he lit a cigarette, and didn't even mind
its taste, though normally he couldn't stand the taste of a
cigarette immediately after waking up. His body was stiff
from sleep, his eyelids were grainy, the palms of his hands
were greasy with sweat, but in his agitation he didn't notice
any of it.

The bus roared through the bright tunnel, and then up
a curving concrete ramp and into the side of a sprawling
building, where it pulled into an angled slot between two
other buses. Cole and the other passengers stepped down
and waited for their luggage, and then all moved away in a
loose mass toward the escalator down to the main level of
the terminal.

Looking down at the main level from above, while riding
down the escalator, he did feel faint intimations of visual
memory, the stirring of belief that he had been in this
building before. When he had been here, under what circumstances, for what purpose, he couldn't tell. But everything he saw he seemed to recognize, as though seeing again
a B-movie he had once sat through fifteen years before.

He knew this building, but he knew it in a strange way,
only as he came across it, without being able to anticipate
what he would come to next. Walking along from the escalator, he couldn't guess what was ahead, but on seeing
the next object—the newsstand in the center of it all, the
Information Booth off to the right, the Walgreen's on the
left—in the instant of seeing it he knew it was right and
correct and in its proper place.

He had been right to come here, to obey that note without
understanding it. Already it was all coming back, memories
and reasons; whatever had gone wrong inside him would soon
be right again.

Still, it was odd he couldn't anticipate, couldn't remember
ahead of time what next his eyes would fall on. It was almost
as though nothing existed until he looked at it, the world had

no existence before he saw it. And would it fade again out of existence behind him?

He spun around, feeling a sudden terror, but the long yellow room full of overcoated travelers was still the same, and still familiar. It was now eleven-forty on Saturday night, and Christmas was next Thursday. Travel had already started to build up; the terminal was almost rush-hour full.

He gazed at it all, feeling sheepish, and then turned back and walked on. He went out through the Eighth Avenue entrance, and stopped there on the sidewalk, for just a moment at a loss.

What now? Faint stirrings of recognition were not enough. He had come here all this way blindly, trusting his unguessable earlier self to have had sensible motives and a workable plan, following through on a scheme he knew practically nothing about, doing it for only emotional reasons. If it had been left to conscious logical decision he would probably still be back in town, but he had been made so disturbed and so upset by the thought of staying that he had had no choice but to go.

And here he was, and what now? He set his suitcase and canvas bag down on the sidewalk, and took his note from his pocket. There was the address: 50 Grove St. That must be where he should go now.

Cabs were milling in front of him, at the curb, unloading old fares and loading new ones. Cole put his hand in his pocket and felt the money there, just under six dollars. He would have to spend some of it on a cab ride, he knew of no other way to find the place he wanted.

He carried his luggage over to where two women were getting out of a cab, and he leaned down to say through the window to the driver, "Do you know where Grove Street is?"

But the driver answered with a question of his own: "In the Village?"

Did that sound right, or did he just want it to sound right? He couldn't be sure. "I don't' know," he said. "Fifty Grove Street, New York City, that's all I know."

The driver shrugged and said, "Sure, the Village. No problem."

No problem. Cole got into the back seat of the cab with all his luggage, and the driver angled out into the snarl of traffic. The back seat of the cab was like a nest, warm and soft and dark, gently rocking as they moved south on the city's broken streets, and once again Cole was surprised that he had come all this long way. All he really wanted was a safe nest somewhere, warm and soft and dark, gently rocking, and hadn't he had that back home? Why had he left? Why had he forced himself to leave?

He was half-dozing, lulled and comforted, when at last the cab jerked to a stop and the driver said, "Fifty Grove. That's it there."

The meter read eighty cents. He gave over a dollar bill and reluctantly told the driver to keep the change, then climbed out to the street and dragged his luggage out after him. The cab jerked into motion again, and away.

This block of Grove Street was very old looking, but not quite quaint. One end of it spilled into a brightly lit open area with a broad main avenue, and the other end receded into a dark narrow area of twisted streets and narrow grimy buildings. Number 50 was just a few doors down from the bright avenue, an old building four stories high. He went in, and saw a row of mailboxes inset in the wall beside the door, and looking, found:

P. Cole, 3-B

He looked at that, and began to smile. He felt as though he'd just taken off a knapsack loaded with rocks, as though the Earth's gravity had suddenly lessened, *P. Cole*. That was *him*, it had to be!

This was home!

So he'd been right all along, right in leaving that town and coming back here. Something had happened to him somewhere, some break in the chain of his existence, but he had struggled through anyway, he had made his way back here, back home, where he could be made whole again. This was the nest he'd been seeking. Everything would be all right now.

There was no elevator. He went up the stairs two at a time, the suitcase and canvas bag dangling from the ends of his arms, and two flights up he found the door marked 3-B. He had two keys in his pocket, one to fit the suitcase and another one, and when he tried the other key it worked at the first turn. He stepped inside, and found the light switch on the wall, then shut the door behind himself and looked at the room. His room.

It was wide and shallow, with a high ceiling. The walls were cream-colored, with rectangular moldings like empty picture frames all the way around, and complicated baroque molding around the top of the walls where they met the ceiling. The molding was all painted too, the same cream color as the walls. There were two windows, widely spaced, in the wall opposite the door.

Between the windows was a broad low bookcase made of planks and bricks. The bricks were stacked up at the ends, with the planks across them to make the shelves. Four layers of brick, and then a plank, and then four more layers of brick and another plank, and four more layers and another plank. The books were mostly paperbacks, but with one section of hardcover books down to the right on the bottom shelf.

There was a sofa against the wall to the far left, a mammoth sagging bulging scraggly surfaced brown Hupmobile of a sofa, with scarred drum tables flanking it on both sides. One of the drum tables was a walnut shade, the other a mahogany shade. The walnut held a porcelain and white table lamp, originally made to grace a lady's vanity, now second-hand.

Everything was second-hand, everything in the room; he could tell it by looking and he could tell it by *feeling*, something too faint for real memory.

On the right-hand wall was the kitchenette, fashioned from a broad narrow closet. The doors had been removed, the closet stuffed with white kitchen appliances in a row, and a bit of linoleum put down on the nearby floor. At the farther end of the same wall was a closed door, and between this closed door and the kitchenette was a wooden-legged formica-topped table all in blue and four brown wooden chairs.

Aside from the square of linoleum, there was a large square of gray broadloom covering a part of the flooring, from the sofa midway across the room to end about where Cole was standing by the door.

To Cole's immediate left was an ancient thick scarred table with uneven legs, and on its surface were radio and turntable and amplifier and a flat stack of LP records. Beyond the table was a scruffy armchair of gray leatherette, and beyond the armchair was an elongated phonograph-system speaker, connected to the equipment on the table and also used as a side-table for the armchair; on its top surface were an ashtray and several glass rings.

To his right, on the other side of the hall door, was an unraveling basket chair, and a floor lamp. Neither this one nor the table lamp on the other side was on now; there was a four-bulb ceiling fixture that looked like a chandelier made by a plumber. The bulbs were bare hundred-watters, and shed a cold light everywhere.

The room was almost devoid of decoration, except for a large square canvas spread-eagled on the wall above and behind the sofa. It was an abstract, and apparently an original, a dilating splatter of white and orange and red and black, meaningless, not even good-looking in itself. Under the glare of the four bright bulbs, it looked naked, like a trickster exposed.

All of this was strange and foreign to him, so unlike his room in the Malloy house, so different from anything he could possibly have imagined, and yet there was a haunting familiarity about this place. Not exactly as though he'd been here before—though he must have been, he'd *lived* here!—but his feeling now was more as though he had once upon a time dreamed this room, without ever expecting to find it in reality.

It was as though he'd been lost in a strange part of town, wandering and wandering, and had suddenly seen a landmark he knew; now the points of the compass will arrange themselves in meaningful pattern, everything will be familiar, the course will all at once become clear. Cole had been wandering, the points of the compass unknown, and here at last was his landmark.

Not that the memories were flooding in; they weren't. That part had remained unchanged, as it had been in the terminal building. He still had no idea what sort of life he had lived in this room, what had happened to change it, what had taken him to a town a thousand miles from here. What skills he might possess, what jobs he might be qualified for, what friends he might have known in the past, all of this was still hidden.

If memory was not returning, still there was recognition, just as at the terminal. He was still recognizing his world in the instant of seeing it. The door to the right, for instance, he knew must lead to a bedroom and bathroom and perhaps some other rooms as well, but what they were and what they looked like he wouldn't know until he went over and saw them.

But it didn't matter. He was home.

He took another step into the room, smiling around at the walls and the furniture, and the door to the right opened, a startled male face looked out at him.

Cole stopped, the smile forgotten on his face. He and the interloper stared at one another, shock on both their faces, and Cole felt exactly like the butt of a practical joke. Somehow, somehow, this had all been arranged, with its tiny false hints of memory and the obscure note about the nonexistent wallet and everything else, all building him toward this crescendo of absurdity; this was not his apartment. P. Cole was someone else, Perry Cole perhaps, or Philip Cole, or Peter Cole, or even another Paul Cole, why not? The tavern was Cole's Tavern, another part of the same joke, so why not?

Then at last the interloper moved, came bustling on through the doorway and shut the door behind himself, saying in a rattling whisper, "Jesus Christ, man, why didn't you warn me? I got a chick in there."

Cole couldn't say a word; he could only stare. The interloper was all flesh, dressed only in white jockey shorts. He was in his middle twenties, a little below average height, with a broad physique. Hair was matted on his chest and tangled on his arms, black and thick. His square broad-nosed face was deeply tanned, and the black hair on his head was a thick mass of curls. He gestured violently but vaguely with his hands, saying, "You shoulda phoned, man. What the hell you think you're doing?"

A name came into Cole's numbed head, a name with no linkages, no application, no associative memories. He said the name, in vague wonder, because his mind was too confused for him to say anything else. He said: "Benny?"

"I'm here, I'm here," he said angrily. Benny was irritated, and panic-stricken, and pleading. He kept gesturing meaninglessly with his hands, and said, "What's the story, for God's sake?"

So this was Benny? Cole looked at him and registered his face, and thought again the name *Benny*. But the name had come into his head like one loose atom in a vacuum, and refused to be combined with anything else. He could accept that this stranger was named Benny, because it was the name the stranger answered to, but he couldn't make this face and this name join in his mind as a fact of memory. So far as he could remember, he had never seen this man before in his life.

But what was he doing here? Cole's name had been on the mailbox downstairs, a key in his possession had unlocked the apartment door. Yes, and more than that, this stranger was behaving in an aggrieved manner but nevertheless a manner that implied Cole's right to be here. So if this was

Cole's apartment—and common sense, after the first instant of panic, told him this had to be his apartment—what was Benny doing here?

Still, how could he be sure of anything, not knowing or remembering? That was why, abruptly, he asked, "This is my place, isn't it?"

But Benny took a different meaning from the words. "I know it is," he said, as though making a reluctant admission. "But if it was the other way around I woulda called first." His hands were still making the excited vacant gestures, and now he glanced back at the closed door, and said, "The least you can do is give me five minutes, man, you know what I mean?"

"What?"

"Go to Riker's, have a cup of coffee. Take a, take a walk around the block or something. Five minutes, that's all I ask, I'll get the beast out of here, okay?"

"You mean, go away again?"

"Five lousy minutes, man." Benny was hopping up and down on the balls of his feet in his agitation, torn amid anger and apology and impatience and worry. "If you'da phoned, she wouldn't of *been* here."

Cole found himself being led slowly out of his apartment again, not understanding it and not believing it, while Benny kept talking away, urgent disjointed phrases repeated over and over again. Till finally Cole was standing in the hall, and Benny handed him his suitcase and canvas bag, said, "Five minutes, man, I swear," and shut the door in Cole's face.

Cole just stood there, facing the door, trying to understand, trying to decide what to do. This *was* his apartment; even beyond the clues of the key that fit and the name on the mailbox, Benny himself had *admitted* this was Cole's apartment. This was where he was supposed to be, the address on the note, the last instruction he had from the past.

What could he do, could he knock on the door now, or open it again with the key, and try to explain things to Benny? He could tell him, "I've got amnesia or something, I don't remember many things, I don't know why you're here or who you are, I don't understand what's going on."

No, no, he couldn't do that, he couldn't tell Benny the truth; no, nor anybody else. What a weakness that was, what helplessness, and to have it here in the middle of a huge city where anyone could take advantage of him and he couldn't defend himself or know what to do about it. Benny was angry with him now, but still in the position of having to ask Cole's cooperation, of having to admit that yes this was Cole's apartment. If Cole let him know the truth, Benny would have the upper hand, he could tell any lie he wanted, he could work it some way so Cole wouldn't even have this apartment any more.

No, it was best to say nothing, to go along with Benny this little bit, to let him have his five minutes.

Five minutes. Where could Cole go, for five minutes? He knew nothing, he knew noplace. He had only the one haven, and others were now moving about in its rooms. Five minutes. It didn't matter where he went, he could go anywhere and nowhere.

One thing he couldn't do, he couldn't go back down those stairs, carrying his luggage, and go walking along the cold pavements. Not when his haven was so close. He looked up and down the hall, not knowing what to do, knowing Benny and the girl would be coming to this door—*his* door, damn them, *his* door—in just a minute or two, and he couldn't still be standing here when they came out.

His eye caught the staircase, continuing on up to the fourth floor and the roof. That was where he would have to go. Not all the way to the roof, just far enough up to be out of sight.

He carried his luggage up the next flight of stairs, and sat on the top step, his suitcase next to him on one side and the canvas bag on the other. Looking down, he could see part of the black composition flooring in the third floor hall, but not his own door. He lit a cigarette, hoping no one would come along during his exile here, and waited.

Everything was silent. There wasn't a sound anywhere, not a sound. Not even a television set or a radio. Not even a baby crying, or a man and wife arguing. He was too high up to hear street sounds; there was nothing. When he moved his foot to ease his stiffness, the scraping of his shoe on the step echoed in the stairwell.

So the sound was very loud and echoing when at last his apartment door did open. He heard it open, and tensed, waiting, and then he heard their voices, hers first:

"The least he could have done was phone you."

"Don't ask me, baby, that's the same thing I told him myself."

"I'm embarrassed, that's what I am. I'm embarrassed."

"Jesus, how do you think I feel? I want us to be so close it's like nothing that ever happened before, and a relationship like that is a delicate thing, you know? If Cole loused it up for us, baby, I'll beat his head in."

"You're sweet."

"Listen, I'll call you, right? Soon as I get a pad."

"All right, Benny."

"I wish I could take you home, but I better stick around and see what's what with Cole." (Upstairs, Cole shook his head violently, but made no sound.)

"That's okay."

Their kiss was loud, too, and then there was the echoing shuffle of her departure; she was wearing tennis shoes or loafers or something like that. The apartment door closed again. The shuffling of the girl's feet faded away down the stairwell.

What now? Benny was still in the apartment, waiting for Cole, and he wouldn't leave no matter how long Cole sat here on the stairs.

The choice was clear. Either he had to go away right now or he had to go down there and face Benny and somehow wrest the apartment from him.

But how? With no memory, no knowledge of Benny or the true situation here, how could he get away with it?

He had to try, that's all there was to it. Somehow, someway, he had to keep Benny from knowing anything was wrong. All he could do was follow Benny's lead, respond to Benny's questions as generally as he could, keep conversations between them down to a minimum until Benny went away.

It was a pretty good plan, and the only one open to him, and if he was careful it might work. Still, he wasn't pleased; this wasn't what he had been expecting, in coming here. He had come here for safety and healing, for security and rebirth. He had come here to have old problems solved, not to have new problems thrust upon him. Arriving here weary, apprehensive, wanting only to rest at the end of his long run, now he was going to have to live some sort of lie for the benefit of an interloper in his home.

But it would end. Sooner or later, Benny too would have to leave, just as his girl had left, and the darkness would have to lift from Cole's mind, and everything would have to be all right again. Sooner or later; it was bound to be.

And it was doing no good to be sitting up here. The sooner he got started, the sooner Benny would be out of there and Cole could begin to rest.

He got to his feet. He felt stiff, his muscles ached, he felt like something made of wood. He carried his luggage back down to the third floor, and tried the doorknob, but the door was locked. He took out his key and unlocked the door for the second time, and re-entered his apartment. Once again the long living room was empty, though this time the light was lit, and this time also the door in the right-hand wall was ajar, and vague sounds of movement came from within.

Cole was weary, exhausted, but tense with the uncertainty of how he would talk with Benny. He dropped his luggage on the floor, shut the hall door, and started to take off his coat. His fingers felt thick and arthritic and fuzzy, fumbling with the zipper. The living room seemed more barren and cold than the last time. He stiffly finished removing the coat, and then went over to the crumbling sofa, moving in a prison shuffle. He sank down onto the sofa, dropping the coat on the cushion beside him. He listened to the faint sounds Benny was making.

After a few minutes, Benny came striding purposefully into the room, and stopped short when he saw Cole sitting on the sofa. He seemed embarrassed, and covered it with a heavy kind of heartiness, shouting, "Hey, there! Why didn't you tell me you were here?" He was wearing khaki Army pants now, and white tennis shoes without socks.

Cole shrugged, not having anything at all to answer. He wondered how long it would take Benny to leave.

But Benny didn't seem to be in any hurry. He said, "You really should of phoned first, man, you know what I mean? You might of screwed it up with that bitch forever."

"I'm sorry," Cole said, because it seemed to him some sort of perfunctory apology would normally be delivered now. "I didn't think."

"Well, I guess it's okay," Benny said, trying unsuccessfully to be gracious. "I got it all squared away with her."

Once again there was no possible response. Cole reached for his cigarettes, to have something to do.

Benny said, "Anyway, it's okay if I rack out on the sofa here a few nights, isn't it? Till I find another place."

Cole stared at him. "Here? You can't stay here."

And now they were both amazed. Benny said, "What the hell? What kind of a way is that to act?"

"You've got to go away," Cole told him; there was no question in his mind. This had nothing to do with making believe for Benny, or anything else. Cole had to have his nest to himself, that's all.

Benny said, "Come *on*, man! You waltz in with no word of warning, you don't give me a chance—"

"You can't stay here."

"Listen, buddy, you sublet this place! You sublet it to me for while you were gone."

"Well, I'm back."

"Yeah? Well, *I* paid the goddamn rent this month!"

"I can't help that."

"What the hell am I supposed to do? I can't go look for a pad till tomorrow."

"Sleep on someone else's sofa."

"You owe me twenty-five bucks, man," Benny told him, angry and cold. "I paid a full month on this place, seventy-five bills, so you owe me one-third. Twenty-five bucks."

"I don't have any money now."

"Yeah, well, tough. You cough up the twenty-five clams, or I don't go anywhere. What the hell you think you're trying to pull?"

Cole said, "I'll pay you when I get some money. But now you've got to go."

"And the hell I do, too."

I'm going to have to fight him, Cole thought, and it didn't matter anymore what Benny thought of him. All that mattered was getting Benny out.

He got to his feet, moving slowly from his weariness, and said, "You've got to go away, Benny."

"Oh, yeah? Who's going to make me?"

Cole walked around him and over to the kitchenette corner, where the formica-topped table and the four kitchen chairs stood. He picked up one of the chairs and held it like a lion-tamer. "You've got to pack your things now," he said.

Benny looked at the chair with wary disbelief and a hardening of his facial muscles. "You'll be sorry for this," he said.

Holding the chair, Cole felt a tingling in his mind, as though some memory of danger or disaster lurked there, trying to come out into the open. He found he was loathing himself for holding the chair—not for wanting Benny out or trying to force Benny out, but simply for the physical act of holding the chair—and a steady repugnance was filling him. All at once, he felt a total sympathy for Benny, understood Benny's feelings at his own unexpected arrival, understood Benny's feelings at thus being shoved out into the night with no home to call his own, and he knew he couldn't do it. With a feeling of great relief, of disaster averted, he put the chair down again. (In his mind, faintly, there was an image of the chair as having eyes in the bottom of its legs. When he had held the chair up, the eyes had been looking at Benny, planning him evil and harm, but now that the chair was put down again the eyes were blinded, shut against the floor.) "Never mind," he muttered, looking away from Benny's wary face. "Stay here tonight."

"That's what I said all along."

"But you've got to leave tomorrow."

"Don't you worry, man."

Cole turned away and went through the doorway on the other side of the kitchen table. At last he would see the rest of the apartment.

A short hall, with a window on the left and a door on the right. A yellow bare bulb hung from a black chain attached to the ceiling, giving a soft light that soothed and smoothed the old walls. Cole pushed open the door on the right and saw a long narrow bathroom with hexagonal white tiles on the floor, square white tiles halfway up the walls, and flat gray paint the rest of the way up. The tub was old-fashioned and old, with rust in the enamel around the drain. There was a copy of *Playboy* on the floor beside the toilet.

Had he know this time, in advance? The hall he had recognized in the instant of seeing it, in the way that was usual with him tonight, but it seemed now that he had anticipated the bathroom by a second or two, that he had seen the bathroom in his mind's eye for just a fraction of time before his hand had turned the knob and pushed open the door for him to see it in reality. But he couldn't be sure; he told himself fatalistically that it was more than likely wishful thinking.

The hall was no more than six or seven feet long, and at the opposite end was another door, open two or three inches. Logic, rather than memory, told him that beyond this door was a bedroom, and the end of the apartment. He stood in the hall a minute longer, testing himself, trying to visualize the bedroom, but he could get no more than faint glimmerings.

Then the door behind him opened and Benny came blundering into the small space. Cole whirled, as angry and embarrassed as if he'd been caught abusing himself, crying, "What do you want? What are you doing here?"

"For Christ's sake, man." Benny took a backward step, startled and aggrieved. "What's got into you? I gotta get my stuff, that's all."

Angry in defeat this time, Cole pushed past him, heading toward the living room again, saying, "Let me know when you're done." He wouldn't go into the bedroom until it was completely and indisputably and finally his.

Benny said more things, but Cole didn't pay attention to them. He paced back and forth in the living room, pausing to light a cigarette, and then pacing again, restless and impatient and irritated. He spied his suitcase and canvas bag on the floor, and his coat over on the sofa, and went and got them, and when Benny came back from the bedroom, his hands full of clothing and magazines, Cole was standing there holding his luggage, the coat slung over one shoulder, the cigarette in the corner of his mouth.

"It's all yours," said Benny, with elaborate sarcasm.

Cole ignored him. Nothing would spoil things for him now. He went past Benny and into the hall, where he set the luggage down and carefully closed the door. There was no key in the lock, but maybe he wouldn't need it. Maybe Benny would keep away for the rest of the night.

He picked up his gear again, and went on into the bedroom. It was a twelve-foot square, scantily furnished. An ancient gray rug covered most of the floor, and the exposed flooring near the walls was scratched and dull and dirty, probably years since its last waxing. The sheets on the double bed were gray and wrinkled, and the blankets were thin and harsh-looking, one green and one rose. There was a small metal bureau painted dark brown, and a small metal desk painted gray, and an antique bedside table of dark wood with gray-white glass circles marring its top, and another wooden kitchen chair like the ones in the living room. The closet door had a mirror on it. There was nothing on the walls here, no paintings or photos or calendars or pennants or anything; into his mind came a picture of his bedroom in the Malloy house.

But this place, bare and austere though it was, contained for him the faint glimmerings of recognition, and he knew he was home. He set his luggage down again, and dropped his coat on the chair, and stood looking around. The presence of Benny in the other room, taciturn and mulish, detracted from his pleasure, but still and all he was home. Now, finally, alone.

And now he could realize just how exhausted he was. He had no plans for tomorrow, no ideas or purposes or goals, but he was too tired to think about it. Tomorrow would be soon enough; right now, he had to sleep. And never mind the gray sheets, tomorrow would be soon enough to take care of them, too.

He undressed. Just before going to bed, he put the kitchen chair against the bedroom door.

15

He awoke slowly, in gradual stages, like surfacing from some deep dark sea. He was conscious at first of himself, his body sprawled in warmth on its side, covered by the warm slight weight of the blankets, and his head burrowed into the pillow, with light a faint awareness only on his left eyelid. He stretched, not yet opening his eyes, and his arms and legs slid out to new and cold areas of the sheets, bringing him closer to wakefulness. He smiled in sleepy content, and rolled onto his back; his eyes were still shut.

He wondered what time it was, where Mrs. Malloy was. Was it Sunday? If it was Sunday, he didn't have to go to work. Maybe he was supposed to take Edna to a movie tonight. No, it was probably a workday.

He opened his eyes, and he wasn't home; he was in a strange room with bare walls.

He sat up, so startled that the backs of his hands started to tingle, that his throat closed, and then in a wash of relief he recognized the room, and remembered the journey, and knew he was home.

Had Benny gone? He cocked his head and listened; nothing, no sound.

He got up from the bed, noticing in the pale daylight that the sheets were really very dirty, gray and limp looking. What kind of person was Benny, anyway? He'd even brought a girl in here, with sheets like that.

Cole's body itched; he went into the bathroom and ran water for a shower. Standing under the water, he let himself relax. All the doings of yesterday had left him passive this morning; he filled his attention with physical details of the present, the feeling of the lukewarm water in the shower, the look of the narrow white bathroom, the sound of the water spraying on his back and into the tub.

Gradually, a curiosity began to grow in him, an almost impersonal desire to know about his past. What sort of person was he, that he called this place home, that he knew such people as Benny, that he lived and worked in New York? What work did he do, for that matter? He knew he was a warehouseman back in that town, but was he a warehouseman in New York? It didn't seem right, didn't seem to fit what he had seen and what he felt.

After his shower, he went back to the bedroom and dressed. He would have to explore in here—and in the living room, too—but only after he was sure Benny was gone. He wanted to learn about himself, but privately, without observers; particularly without Benny.

Was Benny still in the apartment? Had he guessed Cole's weakness?

Cole hesitated a minute or two after he finished dressing, not wanting to go into the living room, afraid Benny hadn't left yet. But it was silly to wait here, he'd have to leave this room sometime. Besides, it was his place, it was home.

He went into the living room and Benny was there, on the far side of the room, next to the crumbling sofa. He was dressed just as he'd been last night, and he was packing a suitcase in a slow and surly manner. He looked over his shoulder at Cole and said, "Well? You still bein' a bastard?"

Cole was surprised. He didn't mind Benny at all this morning, didn't care one way or the other about him. Maybe it was because Benny was packing a suitcase. Cole said, meaning it, "I'm sorry. I was tired last night."

Benny muttered, but didn't say anything out loud, and went back to his slow packing. While he kept up his mumbling and muttering, Cole walked over to the kitchenette, found a jar of instant coffee, and put some water on to boil. Cole understood that Benny craved an argument, perhaps a fight, but was unable to bring himself to do it, was waiting for Cole to make the first aggressive move. This pleased Cole, and reassured him; whoever he had been in the past, he had been dominant over such as Benny. All he had to do was keep Benny from finding out how defenseless he was now, and he'd be all right.

"Hey."

Cole turned, and Benny was standing by the door, wearing an overcoat and a cap, carrying two suitcases and a blue canvas laundry bag. Cole waited; there was nothing for them to say to one another.

But Benny said, "Just remember. You owe me twenty-five bucks."

Oh, that. Cole nodded, and said, "I'll pay you when I get some money."

"You can leave it with Jim. You remember Jim?"

Immediately Cole was afraid of a trap. Did Benny have suspicions after all? Was this somehow a test question? Anything Benny or anyone else might say about Cole's memory would make him instantly alert and wary.

What should he answer? Yes? No? If he remembered everything, would the everything include Jim?

He couldn't chance an answer either way. More brusquely than he'd intended, he said, "I'll get the money to you, don't worry."

"I won't worry," said Benny angrily, but it was hollow defiance. He pulled open the door, picked up his luggage, and stamped out and down the hall, leaving the door open.

Cole closed it, and turned, and looked at what was finally his.

Here was the world: A long narrow living room, a long narrow bathroom, a small square bedroom, a shallow kitchenette. There were closets to be opened, drawers to be looked into, a medicine cabinet to be seen in the bathroom, and high-hung kitchen cabinets to be mapped. There was a whole day of exploration ahead.

Wondering where to start, his eye fell on the record player on the big scarred table in the living room. Music would be good; it would help to fill the empty spaces. The two main rooms of the apartment were badly underfurnished, barren and familiar.

He went over and looked through the records, searching for the kind of music he had always liked on the radio at the Malloys'—soft lushness of strings, ballads hesitantly exposed —but instead he found album after album of aural brass knuckles; shrill-trumpeted big bands, hard cold self-confident male singers with booze-harshened voices, mechanically seductive female singers who seemed to be threatening the microphone with fellatio.

Were these Benny's records? They seemed to suit Benny's personality better than Cole's. Still, he knew in a way too tenuous to be called memory that these were his own records, bought by himself.

"Did I like these?" He asked the question aloud, startling himself. But the records were even more startling. *How much have I changed?* he wondered, and felt a stirring of apprehension. Who had he been?

He selected an instrumental album at last and put it on, turning the bass control full on and the treble control full off. What came out sounded like music from another apartment on another floor; it pleased him.

Now to begin. He picked up his cup of coffee, and went on into the bedroom. The desk in the far corner seemed the best place to begin. It was very small, made of metal, about a yard wide and fifteen inches deep. On its top were a calendar from a liquor store, a coffee cup full of pencils and ballpoint pens, and a telephone. It all seemed very official; looking at it, he wondered if he had operated some sort of business in the past, something from his home. Maybe he'd been an insurance agent or something like that.

He felt almost frightened when he sat down in the chair in front of the desk. Here is where he would begin to learn about himself, begin to find out who Paul Cole was and had been, who he was supposed to be.

He kept hesitating. Would it all be like Benny, and like the phonograph records? His old self had liked those records enough to buy them and to own a phonograph on which to play them. His old self had called Benny friend. Would the things he'd find now be more of the same? And if it was, what could he do then? If the Paul Cole from the past was someone he could no longer like or respect or emulate, what on earth could he do next?

A part of him wanted not to find out, wanted to get up from this desk right now and clear out of here, take a bus back to that town or somewhere else, it didn't matter, anywhere, not worry about any of this, not know about it or care about it or even remember it existed. But his curiosity was too strong. Having found this place, he couldn't leave it without knowing. If it turned out to be all like Benny and the records, there was nothing he could do about it. Time enough then to leave here and take that bus.

So here was the desk. On the left were three shallow drawers and on the right a fairly deep storage well. He started with the drawers first, and in the top left he struck paydirt right away; three thick brown envelopes marked *Income Tax* in pencil. He opened them, and they contained carbon copies of his tax forms for the last three years, and employee's copies of his W-2 forms, and sheafs of receipts.

Here it all was, right here! The first thing to hand, and it was the whole answer at once. He touched the forms with new excitement, all hesitancy gone, going through his find like a detective caught up in the fascination of a complex case, looking for clues to himself.

He was an *actor*.

Was that possible? He frowned, starting at the wall directly in front of him, thinking back to the afternoons in the Malloy living room, watching the soap operas on television. *They* were actors. And was he one of them, after all?

An actor. He didn't know; it seemed neither right nor wrong. In actors on the tiny television screen he had always sensed some inner spark, some magnification from within, like the light of a glowworm; he sensed none of that in himself. And yet, it didn't seem impossible that he *had been* one of these, and the proof of it was here in these papers.

Reading them, he saw that Paul Cole had been in fact moderately successful. Three years ago he had earned just over two thousand dollars from his profession, with an additional fifteen hundred from a temporary office help firm and a furniture moving company. Two years ago his acting income had increased to thirty-two hundred dollars, with a further thousand dollars from the temporary office help firm. And last year he had earned fifty-six hundred dollars from acting, and had needed to do no other work at all.

It was sometimes difficult, with just the employer's name, to figure out exactly what kind of acting job each one had been, but with the help of the deductions page and the receipts he finally filled in most of the blanks. Three years ago he had worked in three off-Broadway plays, none of them lasting more than two months, and had been an extra for two filmed television commercials, and an extra on one live television show. Two years ago there had been another trio of off-Broadway plays, three more filmed television commercials in which he had been an extra, an industrial film for an oil company, and more work on live television; possibly soap opera itself. Wouldn't that be odd, if he had actually played a role in one of those soap operas? But wouldn't Mrs. Malloy have recognized him, then? No; you don't expect to see actors in real life, and unless they're really famous you won't recognize them.

So it was possible he'd acted in soap operas two years ago. And last year; more live television that might be soap operas, and more television commercials, and two months with the national touring company of a Broadway play. And all three years he had spent his summers at the Barn Theater in Cartier Isle, Maine.

When he was finished with all the tax papers, he stopped a while, not searching any farther just yet. This was something to get used to, this idea that he was—had been—an actor. *Was* an actor, still? He couldn't even begin to guess.

That was something he hadn't thought of, that he might no longer work at his occupation of the past. It had never occurred to him that a change in him might mean a change in his suitability to a particular job, because he had been assuming all jobs to be like the one he had handled most recently. But now he didn't know. Maybe it *was* all like Benny and the records, only with the job it wasn't work he didn't like but work he couldn't do.

Still, how did he know, how could he be sure? He was Paul Cole, wasn't he? Something had happened to him— was this what they called amnesia?—something had happened somewhere, and he couldn't remember things any more. But he was still Paul Cole, just the same.

Then the thing to do was learn about himself, learn everything. He shouldn't jump to conclusions from just knowing these few things, he should wait until he knew everything.

He gathered the tax papers into a little pile at one side, and delved into the top drawer of the desk again, looking for more, and came up with another goldmine, the blue address book the telephone company gives its subscribers. He turned the pages and they were full, names and phone numbers, names and phone numbers. Mostly it was just a first name, but now and again there was a full name and even an occasional address, most of the addresses people living outside the New York area, three in California and one in Washington and one in Miami and one at some overseas Army post with only an APO number.

He had known a lot of people.

In the next room, the record ended. He went in and picked another record at random and put it on the turntable. Then he readjusted the base and treble controls till the music sounded the way it was supposed to, and raised the volume so he'd be able to hear it better in the bedroom, If he was going to learn about himself, it included this music. He would have the record player going all the time, till he found out why he had once liked this music.

He spent the next quarter hour practice-dialing. He would pick a phone number from the blue book he'd found, and dial it, leaving the receiver on so he wasn't actually making a call. But in dialing the number, and in thinking about the name that went with that number in his book, he was trying to force his memory to start working. These were numbers he must have dialed often in the past, and names he must have spoken often, people he must have known well. The association of the act of dialing with the knowledge of the person's first name might, he thought, help give him a memory of the voice that went with that name, or some fact or incident about that person.

It did seem to work, just slightly, after a while, but there was no way to be sure. The vague impressions he had of faces and voices might have been real or might just have been his own imaginings, prompted by his desire for memories. After a while he gave it up and went back to searching the desk.

He found a typewritten letter, addressed to "Paul, baby," and full of comment about things that made no sense to him. It was signed "Ray," and seemed to be from one of the people with a California address. There was no date on it, but he got the impression it had been written in the summer. Maybe it was still here because he'd never answered it.

He could see himself answering it now:

"Dear Ray,
Sorry to have taken so long to answer your letter, but I've been lost. If you find me, send me to this address.
Paul, baby"

The middle drawer produced the biggest find yet; a stack of large-size glossy photographs of himself, with a mimeographed resume of his acting credits scotch-taped to the back of each. He read it aloud to himself, lingering over the names of the plays and the theaters and the characters he had portrayed, and then he compared it with his tax forms, going over that ground all over again, seeing it all in a slightly different light now, more pleased than ever at this additional proof of his past existence. And finally he looked at the photo, seeing reflected back at him a face that was his own and yet was not.

He carried one of the photos into the bathroom and stood before the mirror there, holding the photo up beside his head so he could see both in the mirror. Yes it was the same, and yet it was different. What was there missing in the present face that shone in the photographed representation from the past? Something was missing, certainly, something had been lost. Maybe only memory, or self-knowledge. But the face in the photograph was much more confident.

The music came to an end again, and he went in and turned the record over. He stood there a minute while it started to play, frowning as he listened. He didn't like this music very much, it was too loud and cocky, too blatant. Why had he liked it? He couldn't understand the presence of these records, and there was something frightening about that, eerie, as though there were a ghost in the room.

He went back to the bedroom, and searched through the last drawer in the desk, where he found the mail that had accumulated in his absence; bills, and subscription pleas from magazines, and two more personal letters very much like the one from Ray. And under all the mail was a green leatherette folder that proved to contain a checkbook. His name was printed on all the checks, and according to the stubs he now had a balance of sixty-seven dollars and forty-three cents. He smiled at that, and patted the checkbook; worry about money had been hovering all the while in the back of his mind, temporarily shunted away by all these discoveries. Sixty-seven dollars wasn't bad, when he hadn't known he had any at all.

The storage well on the other side of the desk was disappointing, by comparison with the treasures he'd already found. There were the two Manhattan phone books, and some large manila envelopes and a roll of postage stamps, and a stack of typewriter paper. Nothing with personality in it, nothing that was particularly and individually *his*.

He went back to the unpaid bills, which he'd ignored the first time around. He owed a dentist eighty-seven dollars; a panic-stricken dentist, apparently, because there were three bills from him alone. There were gas and electric bills, but no telephone bill; apparently Benny had been paying that one. And there were three payment-overdue notices from his answering service.

Answering service. There'd been something about an answering service in the tax forms, too. Another part of his old life, someone who answered his telephone for him and held his messages. The service's phone number was on their notices to him, so he made his first actual call now, to them.

A woman answered, and Cole said, "This is Paul Cole. Any messages?" The phrase came readily and naturally to him, and he grinned to himself.

The woman asked him to hold on, but when she came back she said, "I'm sorry, Mister Cole, but that service has been discontinued."

Oh. For non-payment, he supposed. He said, "Well, were there any messages up to when it was discontinued?"

"I would have no record here," she said. "The service has been discontinued."

He knew then no matter what he said she would go on making the same reply. He hung up without saying goodbye.

It was the first really depressing event of the day, a part of the past that had been stopped, cut off. He was somehow less Paul Cole without the answering service that had been a natural part of Paul Cole's life, and less capable of being Paul Cole again.

They wanted fifteen dollars from him, so he wrote his first check, and then wrote a note saying, "Please start the service again at once."

In the storage well with the phone books and manila envelopes were some smaller envelopes, and he got one of these and the roll of stamps, and then discovered the booklet, tucked in back, down at the bottom. It was a payment record booklet for the Unemployment Insurance office. He put envelopes and check aside, and studied this booklet, and now the facts of Paul Cole's employment life were complete. In the spaces when he hadn't been working, he had been collecting unemployment insurance. He could follow the weeks, back and forth from tax form and resume to payment booklet, from job to unemployment to job again.

He could start collecting again now. So he'd have a little money coming in, and he'd still be free to spend full time finding himself. He seemed to remember some sort of bad experience at an unemployment insurance office once, but that hadn't been in New York, it had been in the town. He tried for a second to remember the name of that town, but it didn't come readily so he dropped it. That name didn't matter anymore. That had been the interregnum, between Paul Cole and Paul Cole, when he had been X.

He addressed the envelope and put a stamp on it, and put the check and the most recent payment notice into it. He'd go out this afternoon, and he could mail it then.

There was still more to explore, medicine chest in the bathroom, kitchen cabinets, dresser and closet in the bedroom. All contained normal predictable things, nothing specifically and uniquely his, except the contents of a shoebox up on the bedroom closet shelf. It was half full of programs from all the professional productions he had been connected with. He took it to the bed and sat there crosslegged, tailor fashion, and read twice through every word.

He was learning about himself as though he were constructing a jigsaw puzzle. In many ways it was as though he were building up an image of someone else, someone he had never met, with the faint memories that stirred now and then being only particularly vivid imaginings of what that other person's life must have been.

Finally he was finished. He had looked at and touched everything in the apartment. All he could do now was continue to live here, use these things, gradually absorb them once again until they helped rekindle his memory. Right now he *knew* what he had been, at least in part, but he didn't yet remember.

With nothing more to do, he suddenly realized he was ravenous. So far today he'd had only the one cup of coffee. He went back to the kitchenette and opened a can of soup and ate it all. Then he changed his clothes, taking off everything he'd worn here on the bus, putting on all clothing fresh from the apartment. He shrugged into the overcoat he'd found in the closet, and went out to discover his neighborhood.

16

It was like a place where he had lived thirty years ago, and now he was coming back for the first time. Vaguely familiar sights surrounded him, evoking echoes of recognition, muted and clouded by time; except in this case it wasn't time that had smoothed the sands, it was the unknown thing that had happened to him.

His one fear as he walked along was that he would run into someone he had known but would not now recognize. Every stranger that passed him was a potential friend, who might suddenly call out his name and start talking happily to him about incomprehensibilities. Well, if it happened he would try to go along as best he could, making believe everything was all right, hoping he could carry it off. He had a terror of letting any of his old friends know about his present weakness.

It was a cold clear day, crisp, with pale blue sky and high bright sun. The streets were crowded with pedestrians, and cars and taxis jolted by, but Cole had the feeling most of the activity was foreign, that most of the people he saw didn't actually live around here, but were here in the Village because it was Sunday, a part of the weekend, and they didn't have to go to work at their jobs. A vestigial contempt stirred within him, but couldn't gain ground against his conviction that he was even more a stranger here on these sidewalks than they.

He walked for hours, stopping twice for hamburgers and coffee, once on Eighth Street near Sixth Avenue and once on Seventh Avenue near Sheridan Square, not far from his apartment. He was discovering no sudden improvement in his memory, but he hadn't expected it to work that way and so he wasn't disappointed. He would simply fill his senses with the physical facts of his home and former life, and slowly this warming influence might thaw his frozen memory and return him to his earlier condition.

Still, as the afternoon progressed he began to feel his solitude in a way he hadn't anticipated. He wanted to talk about himself, wanted to tell someone all about himself, desired it almost painfully; but at the same time he was still afraid to expose himself to any friends and acquaintances from Before. Walking, walking, he began almost to hope someone would recognize him and force him into conversation and find him out.

He even thought, at one point, of going into a bar to talk with the bartender, but he knew that was a foolish idea. The sympathetic listener behind the bar at the local tavern was a creation of fiction, hardly to be found in any of the tourist traps in Greenwich Village.

There was a church he'd passed two or three times before, and now he was coming to it again. It was a small old church of heavy blocks of dark brown stone, encircled by a fence of tall iron spikes except at the entrance. On impulse, he turned and went up the slate steps and inside.

Within, it had that peculiar quality of some churches, looking larger inside than out. It was dark, lit only by racks of votive candles in red glass containers down front. Cole recognized it as a Roman Catholic church, but didn't know how he knew; there was no memory of his ever having been in this particular church before, nor could he remember in which religious discipline he had been brought up, though he was pretty sure that whatever it was he had abandoned it shortly after going out on his own.

No instinctive rituals came to him as he stood there, no impulse to genuflect or make the sign of the cross. Nor did he know yet exactly why he was here. He had come in, that was all, an impulsive thing. He walked around, noting that the church was completely empty except for himself, looking at the bas reliefs of Christ's execution on the side walls, and the secondary altars to the Virgin Mary and some

male statue—St. Joseph?—flanking the main altar. He walked
around, mildly curious, patient, expecting nothing in particular. He glanced into one of the confessionals, noted that it
made him think of monasteries, and walked on. When he
came near the doors again, he went back out to the afternoon sunlight, which suddenly seemed much brighter than
before.

He stood on the sidewalk a while, indecisive, vaguely trou-
bled. Next to the church, and also contained within the iron
fence, was a two story brick structure of an old-fashioned
residential type, with bay windows on the front. This was
undoubtedly where the priests lived.

He lit a cigarette and considered, and finally understood
that what he wanted was to talk to a priest. He wasn't sure
why, except that a priest was the only dispassionate but willing
listener he could think of.

What could he lose? For the next few days, he would
follow any vagrant notion that came into his head, for who
knew where such a notion might lead? To the center of the
lost landscape perhaps. So he flicked the cigarette away and
went over to the brick house, through the second break in
the fence, and rang the doorbell.

A woman answered, which surprised him, until he realized
she must be the housekeeper. She was a narrow impatient
sharp-faced woman in a faded dress. She asked him what he
wanted, and he said, "I want to talk to a priest."

"Come in," she said. Despite her somewhat hostile appearance, her voice was soft and her manner hurried but
pleasant. She showed him to a small room off the front hallway and assured him someone would be along in a moment
or two. He thanked her and sat down.

It was a strange small room. Two leather armchairs stood
facing one another across a low table containing nothing but
an ashtray. Highly polished small dark tables stood against
the walls, one topped by a leafy plant in a copper pot, one by
a statue of the Infant Jesus in red Imperial robes, one by
little stacks of small square pamphlets. On the walls were a

large painting of the Ascension, a not-so-large portrait of Christ wearing his crown of thorns, and a heavy-looking very large wooden crucifix.

Cole was standing, looking up at this crucifix, noting the minute details of the sculpture of the hanging Christ, when the sliding doors opened and the priest came in, closing the doors again behind himself. He said, "You wanted to talk to a priest?"

He was an old man, short and thin and bent; a gnarled tree. His face was a gathering of lesser features around a long and formless nose, the nose grown blue-white with age. He wore a black gown which was here and there flecked with what looked to be chalk dust, and on his feet—glimpsed beneath the frayed hem of his robe—were old brown bedroom slippers.

Cole looked at him and was unencouraged. He said, "It isn't a religious matter. I don't think—I'm not sure I should even be here at all."

The priest smiled vaguely. "Don't be so certain," he said. "One way or another, nearly everything in life is a religious matter. Come, sit down, we'll talk about it." His voice was frail, windy, the remnants of a voice.

They sat facing one another over the low table, and Cole pointed to the ashtray, saying, "Is it all right if I smoke?"

"Certainly. Relax yourself, be easy." The old priest's elbows rested on the chair arms, his bent-twig fingers interlaced across his stomach. He sat slightly forward in an attitude of alertness.

For some reason, it seemed to Cole this old man was play-acting, being for both their sakes something that each of them expected him to be. But that was probably his own uncertainty, seeing itself reflected in the old man's eyes; blue eyes, faded blue, Virgin Mary blue.

Cole lit his cigarette, and the priest said, "My name is Father Bernardus."

"Cole. Paul Cole." He hesitated, frowning at the ashtray, and said, "I don't know how to start. Where to start?"

"Are you in trouble?"

"I don't know. I suppose I am."

"A young lady? The police?"

"No...no. Nothing like that."

"Well... Begin wherever you like, then. Explain the situation as best you can, and if there are things I don't understand I'll ask you about them."

"All right. What, what it is, something's...happened to me. I used to be an actor, and then this thing, this thing happened to me. I don't remember— No. My memory isn't good any more, that's what it is."

"Memory?" The old priest had a vague and hopeful smile on his face; he was trying hard to understand. "You mean, you have amnesia?"

"I don't know, I don't think so. It isn't, it isn't a sudden break in my memory, it's just that everything sort of fades. People with amnesia remember everything back to when the amnesia started, and nothing before that, isn't that the way it is?"

"I'm sorry, I really don't know anything about amnesia," the old man said, then smiled again, adding, "except, of course, from motion pictures. But I believe it's something like that, yes."

"What I've got is different from that, something else. I remember just bits and pieces of things. My memory is like a sieve, everything runs through it. In a few days, I'll probably forget talking to you."

The priest seemed uncertain at that, as though not knowing whether or not to take offense. Then, setting it aside, he said, "Are you under a doctor's care?"

"No, I'm not."

"Well, you should be." He seemed almost indignant, as though someone had been mistreating Cole. "From what you tell me about yourself, you certainly should have a doctor look at you. Do you live here in the Village?"

"Yes. Over on—" Cole stopped, and felt a sickly smile of embarrassment cutting his face. He squeezed his mind painfully, and the name he wanted popped out. "On Grove Street," he said.

"Is your family there?"

"No, they— Uh. I come from upstate."

"Ah." The priest nodded. "This parish is filled with the rootless young," he said, with some sad satisfaction. "But don't you have any friends, anyone to help you?"

"I haven't talked to anybody since I came back."

"Back?"

Cole realized he'd assumed the priest already knew about all that; as though his own decreased knowledge had proportionately increased everyone else's. "I was away," he explained. "A long way…" He gestured; a far distance. "I had a lot of trouble getting back."

"And you haven't been in touch with your friends?"

"No. I don't remember them, it's been too long, I don't know what to say to them. I want to be better than this before I go see anybody I used to know."

"Well, you really ought to see a doctor. I'd be happy to recommend one for you, make the arrangements— Are you Catholic?"

"I don't know."

"No?" The priest seemed surprised at that, and then, struck by a sudden thought, he said, "Oh! Oh, dear!"

Cole sat watching, wondering, while the priest stared past him at the opposite wall. Cole nervously rolled his cigarette between his fingers, and waited.

"Mm," said the priest thoughtfully. "That brings up the whole question of sin, doesn't it?" Abruptly he smiled at Cole, pleased to see him. "You're quite a theological problem, young man, do you realize that?"

"I am?"

"Yes, of course. Of course! Assuming you are Catholic— or, that is, you *were* Catholic before your accident—and now, not remembering yourself to be Catholic you—oh— you eat meat on Friday, you fail to attend Mass on Sunday, you—oh! Of course! You miss your Easter obligation!" His smile broadened; behind the parchment lips gleamed large, white, square, obviously false teeth. "Do you see the problem?"

"I—no, I'm sorry."

"Well, of course not, you know nothing of Catholic doctrine, the commandments of the Church." He held his hands out, palms up, as though comparing two weights; his palms were blue-white, irrigated with blue veins. "Everything depends," he said, "on whether or not you were a Catholic at the time of your accident. If you were *not*, the problem is still religious but no longer specifically Catholic. You said your name was Cole?"

"Yes."

"Then you're probably not Jewish. You don't look Jewish, though that doesn't necessarily— Still, you're probably some form of Christian, which means you very well *could* have been a Catholic. Have you returned to the home you lived in before the accident?"

"Yes."

"Were there no religious pictures, statues, prayer books? A rosary?

"No. I'm sorry."

"Of course, that doesn't *prove* anything, one way or the other. The rootless young very often drift away temporarily from their parents' religion. On the other hand, if you weren't Catholic, if there weren't some trace of your Catholic past still in your mind, you wouldn't have come here for help, would you?"

Cole spread his hands. "I don't know, I don't know why I came. I just—"

But the priest wasn't interested. "It was memory," he said. "You yourself said your memory isn't really gone, only impaired. Some hint from your past life led you here; you *must* be Catholic."

"Well…"

"Oh, no!" The priest held out placating hands. "Don't worry, don't let it trouble you, I'm not *accusing* you of anything! What is committed in the darkness of ignorance can always be forgiven, washed away in the light of truth. There's time for that, plenty of time. Have no fear for your immortal soul, you won't— For the moment, my interest is purely speculative, purely the simple theological question you raise. If you no longer remember your Catholicism, are you still bound by the rules of the Church? *That* is the question!"

Cole said, "That isn't— The question is, what am I going to do?"

"Well, of course!" The old priest was animated now, his eyes sparkling, his pale hands darting in excited gestures. "What is your course of action? Shall you be treated as a baptized Catholic, with all of the privileges—and yet, all the responsibilities—of that condition, or has your changed physical and mental state created a change in your spiritual state as well? Which sacrament shall I offer you, baptism or holy confession?"

Cole said, "No, that isn't—"

"Good heavens," cried the priest. "Confession! There's *another* problem. Why man, you don't even *remember* your sins; how on earth can you possibly *confess* them?"

Cole brushed his hand in front of his face, like a man who's walked into cobwebs. "I don't care about that," he said. "That isn't what I'm thinking about, I don't care about any of that."

"Of course you don't, that's the whole point! Being lost in the outer darkness, you are unaware of the very *existence* of light. Ignorance remains ignorant of the possibility of knowledge, that is one of the great mysteries of the human condition."

There was nothing here for Cole; he looked pointedly at his watch, saying, "I have to—"

"Of course. We can't go any longer now anyway, I must get advice. You should come back to see me—no. Let me contact you, that would be better, give me a chance to assemble—" Rummaging in unsuspected pockets at the sides of his robe he produced a crumpled small envelope and a ballpoint pen. Clicking the pen with the absorption of a man who's never done such a thing before, he smoothed the envelope on the table and said, "Just let me get your name and address. You said your name was Cole? Paul Cole?"

Regretting having given the name in the first place, Cole now had to nod and say, "Yes, that's right."

"How do you spell that?"

Unhesitating, he said, "K-O-H-L."

"Good. And the address? Grove Street, you said?"

"Yes. One hundred forty-two Grove Street."

"Fine. Your telephone number?"

"I'm sorry. I don't remember it."

"I suppose it's in the book."

"Yes. I think so."

"Well, fine." The priest got to his feet, and Cole followed him. Putting the pen and envelope away, the old man said, "I never fail to be astonished at the complexity of the Almighty." He smiled, patted Cole on the shoulder. "We will help one another," he said. "Come, I'll accompany you to the door."

Walking beside the old man, it occurred to Cole that a doctor had been mentioned earlier, the priest had been going to recommend a doctor, maybe arrange an appointment. In his theological excitement, he'd forgotten all about it. Cole nearly brought it up again now, but held back; he had no desire to prolong conversation with this man.

At the door, the priest said, "You'll be hearing from me, you can be sure of that."

"All right," said Cole. "Goodbye." He turned away from the smiling face, and went down to the street.

The afternoon was ending. The sun had disappeared behind the buildings now, and a colder damper breeze was rushing along the narrow streets. There were fewer pedestrians, fewer cars.

Cole walked toward his apartment, hunching his shoulders within his clothes, wondering why he had expected anything from that visit to the church. The priest had, after all, turned out only to be Benny again, too involved with his own complexities to be of any help to Cole. But what help had Cole expected, what help did he want? He didn't know, couldn't say in words, and maybe that after all was the surest sign that he needed help.

He stopped at a small grocery store on the way, and bought food for dinner.

17

Cole came out of the Unemployment Insurance office feeling bitter and frustrated. In anything he tried to do, there were always necessities he hadn't thought of, and in every contact he made with others of his species there was always a wall of either indifference or self-concentration that couldn't be surmounted.

It had been the same just now, when he had gone in to sign for Unemployment Insurance. He had brought along the payment booklet, but that had turned out to be not enough. They had to know more about him than that. They had to know where he had last worked, and under what circumstances he had left his last employment, and neither of these facts did he know. He had stood in a long line for an hour and ten minutes, and had talked to a snappish stout woman with gray wiry hair for two or three minutes, and now he was back on the street again, having it all to do over again, and facts to learn about himself before he could even re-begin.

Outside, it was a miserable day. A cold slanting rain knifed endlessly from a low gray sky. The Christmas decorations all over midtown Manhattan looked like ancient relics untimely ripped from some rotting attic, hung out in the wet air to finish their decomposition. Surly Christmas shoppers milled aimlessly on the streets, poking one another with black umbrellas. And the subway platform, when Cole went down to it, stank like wet green wool. He stood waiting there for the train; he and all the other waiting people on the platform reminiscent mostly of tired range horses standing in the rain.

The train came and Cole boarded, and found a seat. Mute irritability was on every face, including his own. He rode downtown, and got out at his stop, and walked homeward through the rain, where at first all he did was strip out of his wet clothing and make a cup of instant coffee. He made toast, too, and put one of the blaring records on, and sat a while at the kitchen table in his underwear.

He had the conviction that he didn't belong. This city was two great slabs of concrete, with all the people crawling through the narrow space between them; at least, that was the way it seemed to him now. But he was also convinced that this would all change once he was himself again; in the old days, he must have been adapted to this life. The music was a part of it, and friends like Benny, and an environment that included the subway and the bitter woman in the Unemployment Insurance office. When he was his old self again, all of those things would seem natural to him, and not bother him. Some he would think good, and the rest he would take in his stride. A kind of slow-burning impatience filled him when he thought this way. He wanted to get out of this slough of despond, and soon.

With the coffee and toast in him, with the apartment around him, he gradually warmed, and the present began to look less bleak. He got to his feet after a while, and went into the bedroom, and put on fresh clothing.

The bedroom was already spotted with notes, scotch-taped here and there to the walls. One near the bed told him to wind the clock. One near the door told him not to leave the place unlocked. Another, obsolete now, told him to go to the Unemployment Insurance office this morning, and to look on the desk for the payment book. Another, the result of a sudden thought after he was already in bed last night, reminded him that seventy-five dollars rent was due the first of January, and that twenty-five dollars was owed Benny and must be paid as soon as possible, lest he forget it. And finally, one on the closet door told him to check off each day on the desk calendar, so he would always know the day of the week and the date.

Dressed, surrounded by reassuring familiarity and bolstering notes, Cole sat at the little metal desk and went though his old income tax forms again. It seemed to him that he remembered something about having an agent, an actor's agent. If anyone could give him the information the Unemployment Insurance office needed…

Yes, here it was. Mrs. Helen Arndt. And in the little blue book of telephone numbers, "Helen – CI5-3610."

He hadn't wanted to have to do this, to get in touch with anyone from his old life, but now he had no choice, he needed the money too badly. He'd just have to take the chance. He'd speak to this Mrs. Helen Arndt, and see how the conversation went, and try to see ahead of time the right thing to do.

He dialed, and the phone was answered on the first ring, by a woman with a husky voice saying hello. Cole asked for Mrs. Arndt and the woman said speaking, and Cole gave his name. Her tone suddenly changed. "Paul! Honey, where have you been all these years?"

"Can I come see you this afternoon?"

"Of course, baby. After two-thirty, hear?"

"All right."

"And you'll tell me all your adventures."

"Yes," he said, made wary by that but also somewhat distracted. Her voice had suddenly sounded familiar to him, had sounded like a voice that was no surprise to hear. He tried to put a face to it, but the only thing he got was a dim image of a face below a lavender hat.

"Two-thirty, then," she said, and the conversation was finished.

He immediately made two notes, one with Mrs. Arndt's office address on it, which he put in his pocket, and the other reminding him to go there this afternoon at two-thirty, which he scotch-taped to the front door.

He'd recognized her voice. That was a good sign, that; and if the blurred image in the lavender hat turned out to be meaningful it would be an even better sign. He'd know in less than three hours.

The record on the phonograph came to an end, and he went over and replaced it. This music was still harsh and callous in his ears, but he was determined to adapt to it. Turning away from the phonograph after replacing the record, he glanced across the room at the plank-and-brick bookcase, and it occurred to him to wonder whether the books would be like the records, or if here at last he would find some common ground with his former self. He went over to look, and for the next two hours, he sat on the floor and studied his books.

There were books on acting, plus volumes of plays among the hardcover books on the bottom shelf and anthologies of plays in paperback form, and paperback biographies of current entertainers. Half a shelf was taken up by paperback collections of cartoons, most of a sexual slant, and the rest of that shelf was given over to collections of short stories and paperback editions of bestsellers. There was some science-fiction, too, and a few private eye novels. Finally, there were two or three books on the movies.

Cole looked into almost all the books. Here and there a phrase or chapter title or cartoon would strike a familiar chord, but most of what he saw was strange to him. His old self, of course, had read all these books, contained them all within his mind. So they must still be there in Cole's mind now, part of the knowledge still buried under rubble. Should he reread them all in hopes of the rereading helping to open his memory, or should he wait until other things opened it, when rereading would no longer be necessary? He wasn't sure, and finally decided to let matters take their natural course; if he felt like reading one of these books, he would, but he wouldn't force himself.

At ten past two he left the apartment and walked through the still-falling rain to the subway. The sidewalks were greasy now, the rain beginning to freeze where it landed. Trucks and taxis splashed down Seventh Avenue, most of them with their headlights on though it was still early afternoon. But the cloud layer seemed even lower and darker and thicker than this morning, and the slanting rain was like veils, obscuring everything behind a few feet away.

Mrs. Arndt's office was in a grim building on Eighth Avenue, between 46th and 47th Streets. There was a single elevator, very old-fashioned looking, operated by an old man in a faded flannel shirt and gray workpants. He took Cole up to the third floor, and Cole, walking down the hall amid faint rustlings of recognition, found the office for himself.

HELEN ARNDT
Theatrical Representative

Cole walked in and found himself in a small room shoulder-deep in dark green filing cabinets. In an open space in the center was a small desk and a young red-haired girl who smiled at him and said, "Hi, Paul. Long time no see."

But this wasn't Mrs. Arndt. He knew who she was, this girl, but he couldn't quite get the knowledge out where he could see it. He forced a friendly smile on his face and said, "Hi."

The girl spoke into the cream phone on her desk, and then said to Cole, "Go right on in." The friendly smile was still on both their faces, but Cole was suddenly terrified. He would never be able to keep Mrs. Arndt from finding out. What would she do?

A wooden door that said *Private* on it was on the other side of the desk. Cole went over there, nodded at the girl because he was at a loss for what to say to her, and pushed open the door.

This was Mrs. Arndt, and the second he saw her he recognized her; much more than he had recognized Benny or the girl in the outer office. He recognized Mrs. Arndt the way he had, until now, only recognized places. Looking at her, it seemed to him he knew her as well as he had known his apartment when he'd first walked into it.

She was a stocky middle-aged woman of brassy features, sitting behind a swirling paper-crowded desk. A turquoise hat was on her head, and a long filter cigarette dangled from a corner of her mouth. Her spectacles were horn-rimmed and sequined, designed like a cat-mask, with a thin gold chain draped from the wings down around the back of her neck. The rest of her clothing was dominated by a huge ruffle of white lace at her throat. She said, "*Honey!* Come in, sweets, come in! What have you been *doing* to yourself, you've lost *pounds*."

"Have I?" But he wasn't really paying attention to the words yet. He was recognizing everything, in a rush, her voice and face, her taste in clothing and accessories, her office, her mannerisms. There suddenly popped into his mind the knowledge he was supposed to call her Helen, not Mrs. Arndt.

She was saying, "Sit down, baby, sit down, tell me all about yourself. The last I heard, that little snotnose Gerber told me you were dropped from the troupe, in a hospital somewhere at the edge of the world, and the details were so extremely delicate I would have to wait to hear them from your own lips. Honey, you didn't pick up a dose from one of those cornfed beauties, did you?"

There were too many words coming at him all at once. He recognized and remembered the voice, but what she was saying made no sense to him at all. Gerber? And a hospital? The troupe? None of it meant anything to him.

He was going to have to ask questions, and in order to do that he was going to have to tell her the truth. But somehow the idea, at last faced, and personified in this woman, wasn't so frightening any more. He sat on the edge of the chair facing her desk, and when she finished speaking he said, "I had an accident."

She let him get no farther. An exaggerated expression of concern distorted her face and she leaned forward, elbows mashing papers on the desk. "Honey, you look ghastly, do you know that? What on earth *happened* to you? Tell me all."

He spread his hands and shook his head. "I don't know very much. I guess I had some kind of accident or something, you said I was in the hospital."

"That's what I was *told*, honey."

"Well, whatever it was, it did something to my memory. I don't remember things anymore. Maybe it's a kind of amnesia, I don't know."

"Amnesia? In real life? Not *total* amnesia, surely."

"Everything in my past is just fuzzy, that's all. I don't know how to explain it exactly."

"You remembered *me*, honey. Here you are." She said it as though explaining something that was not only obvious, but was also the solution to all his problems.

"I remember you now," he said. "Your face and your voice. But I don't remember any other time I ever talked to you. And I didn't come here because I remembered you, but because I found your name on my income tax forms and in my phone book."

"Good heavens. I don't know if I ought to be insulted or compassionate. *Everything* is gone?"

"Just clouded over."

"You've been exposed to the Shadow, poor lamb. Never mind, it was just an allusion. How long have you been back in town?"

"Two days."

"But good heavens, sweetie, all this must have happened months ago! Where in the world have you been all this time? Just wandering, dazed and alone, not even knowing your own name?"

"I was working in a place. I didn't have much money, so I had to get a job and save up for a bus ticket."

"But honey, for heaven's sake, why didn't you *call* me? You could have called collect, you know that. I would have wired you money instanter."

"I didn't remember," he said.

"Oh, dear." A slow surprise was coming over her features. "Oh, for the love of God. You just didn't remember anybody, did you?"

"Not clear enough."

"Oh, honey, there are just ramifications and ramifications of this thing, aren't there? Honeybunch, how can I get you work? I mean, if you can't memorize lines, baby, you can't *act*."

Cole frowned. Was he going to act, to be an actor? If that was what he'd been and what he was supposed to be, then he would. Some day Mrs. Malloy would switch on the television set, and there he'd be, playing a part in a soap opera.

That hadn't occurred to him before. Of *course* he would act, that was a vital part of being Paul Cole. Even though the prospect was inconceivable to him right now, even though he had no idea of how to be an actor or how he had ever been an actor, he still knew he would one day soon be acting again.

The phonograph records, and the friends like Benny, and the books, and the apartment, all were only tassels and fringes at the perimeter of Paul Cole, the trappings around the outer edge. But *acting*, that was the core.

But now Helen Arndt had said if his memory was bad he couldn't act. He frowned, and shook his head, and said, "I think it's going to get better. It ought to get better."

"It *has* to, sweetie. Maybe I can get you a job as an extra here and there, you know the sort of thing you used to do… Or do you? No, I see you don't. It's all gone, isn't it?"

"I guess so."

Her eyes were bright, and she studied him now with a strange faraway smile on her face. "Do you know what you are, honey?" she asked. "You're a virgin all over again. Aren't you? Do you remember any of your women? I bet you don't."

Her words made him think of Edna, back in the town, but he knew Edna wasn't what Helen Arndt meant, because he had never gone to bed with Edna. Had he? No, he hadn't. For the rest, she was right, and he nodded reluctantly, feeling the topic was wrong under these circumstances.

"I knew I was right," she said. Her gaze roamed him, and the faraway smile was fixed on her face. "You're a brand new virgin, that's what you are. Some girl's going to have to teach you everything all over again."

She was making him uncomfortable, and he couldn't

remember why he'd come here in the first place. He knew he hadn't intended to see his agent or anyone else until he was in better shape, but something had made it necessary...

She was snapping her fingers at him, in a humorous manner, and saying, "Hello? Are you there?"

"I'm sorry," he said. "I was thinking about something else."

"What I asked you," she said, "was your financial condition. How are you fixed at the moment?"

Then he remembered. "Oh," he said. "I'm going to collect unemployment insurance."

"Good. Got a little cash to carry you in the meantime?"

"Yes."

"And have you been to see a doctor here in town?"

"No, I haven't."

"Well, you certainly should. Here, let me give you my doctor's name and address." She rummaged amid the papers on her desk, and found a memo pad and a wickedly sharpened pencil. As she wrote she said, "Would you like me to call him now, make an appointment for you?"

"Not now. I don't think so, thank you."

She paused in her writing and studied him again, this time critically. "You're altogether different," she said. "Do you know that?"

"I suppose I am, yes."

"Much quieter, much less sure of yourself. You were always a brash self-confident boy. You knew you had talent, you knew you had looks, and you knew you had a future. I don't know whether I like you better this way or not." She shrugged, and suddenly smiled meaninglessly, and finished writing the doctor's address. She ripped the top sheet off and extended it to him, saying, "You call him now, you hear me? I'll be in touch with him, and if you don't go see him I'll know about it."

He took the paper and stored it carefully in his pocket. "I'll call him," he said, not sure yet whether he would or not.

He felt a reluctance to rely on anyone but himself, but at the same time he longed for outside help.

"You're living alone, aren't you?"

He nodded.

"I don't suppose you're eating properly," she said. "Don't eat at home, will you do that for me, honey? Eat in restaurants."

He shrugged, not seeing the point. "All right," he said, to be polite.

"If you're broke any time, I can always feed you. Do you have my home address? Do you remember it?"

"No, I don't."

So she wrote again on the memo pad, and when she handed him this second slip of paper there was a sad humor on her face. "Everything's gone, isn't it?" she said. "Honey, you're depressing the hell out of me, do you know that? No, never mind. Was there anything special you wanted? I'll see what I can do for jobs for you. Extras or walk-on, that's about it until your memory comes back. Is there anything else?"

"There was something…" Lowering his head, he massaged his brow, trying to get it back again, and in this position the payment book in his inside coat pocket pressed against his chest, causing him to remember. "I've got it," he said. "I want to collect unemployment insurance, but they want to know about my employment for the last year, and I don't know it."

"Oh, that's easy enough. Just a sec." She picked up the phone and pressed a button, then said, "Cindy, bring me Paul Cole's folder, will you? That's a good girl." She hung up, and smiled brilliantly at Cole again. "Won't take long at all," she said.

Talking to himself as much as to her, he said, "I don't know about the other job, either. I worked in a tannery, to get the money to come home. I don't remember the name of it, or exactly how long I worked there."

"Honey, honey, you're just a babe in the woods. Don't

you say a word about that tannery, not in the unemployment insurance office. You're an *actor*, sweetie, and you don't tell them about any kind of job but *acting* jobs. Because it's only an acting job you'll take, do you see what I mean? If you mention any sort of factory work, they'll try to put you to work in a factory the very first thing."

"Oh." The near-miss frightened him; it hadn't occurred to him to hide his tannery job.

She said, "You left your last employment because you fell ill, but now you're available for employment again. Can you remember that, sweetie? Want me to write it out for you?"

"No, I'll remember it."

"And I'll back you up on it," she said. "Just tell them you've been to your agent again, and I'm out looking for work for you. And you're completely healthy, baby, remember that. If they ask you if you're still sick at all, you tell them no."

"All right."

The red-haired girl brought in the folder then, put it on the messy desk, and smiled and winked at Cole on the way out. Cole gave her a weak smile in return.

When he left five minutes later, he had a list of his acting jobs for the last year, and he had promised to call Helen Arndt to tell her if he could go to her place for dinner Friday night.

Now he had exposed himself to someone from his past, and it surprised him how much relief he had felt in doing it. Still, he wasn't sure it had been the best thing to do; something dark and sly had opened behind Helen Arndt's eyes after he'd told her, when she was talking about him being a virgin again. His original plan might have been best all along; hide from the old friends, the old ties, and if forced into contact with them avoid letting them learn the truth.

He walked crosstown through the rain to the unemployment insurance office.

18

The voice said, "Look at this. This is your life."

Hands were holding out to him a square of shiny metal, very thin and about a foot square. He said, "I never saw it before," but in his heart he knew he had seen it somewhere.

The voice said, "You *must* remember, or you will die."

"But I can't remember," he said. The square of metal began to grow, getting larger and larger but never any thicker, always staying just as thin, getting larger and larger till it was a mammoth wall, stretching away on either side to infinity and looming up into incredible heights of darkness over his head.

The voice said, "If you don't remember, you'll never get on the other side."

As the huge square of metal began very slowly to topple over on him, he cowered, and then he turned and tried to run away, but the slab of metal was too huge, it was miles long and toppling so slowly over onto him, he couldn't even run halfway to safety before it would land on him. He ran and screamed, and ran and screamed, and the slab of metal lowered with a grinding rushing noise like horses' hoofs.

He sat up in bed, terrified, gasping for breath. The sheets and blankets were twined around his legs, imprisoning him. He kicked himself free, as though life itself depended on his speed now, and lunged up onto hands and knees on the disheveled bed, looking wildly around. But even as he was doing all this, the terror was fading, and the dream was fading with it.

When he lifted his hands to rub his face, he saw that they were shaking. He looked around, disoriented for a second, and then found the night table, containing his cigarettes. He crawled across the bed, got a harsh-tasting cigarette going, and then, too late, tried to remember the dream. He frowned, furrowing his forehead, but couldn't remember a single image of it, though he had the feeling one of the characters in it had been the girl back in that town. After a minute the name came to him: Edna. He thought Edna had had something to do with the dream.

"What am I dreaming about her for?" He said it with a kind of impatient irritation, not only because of the fact, but because he was talking to himself out loud again, a habit he was trying with no success to break.

He sat up in bed, frowning and smoking, trying to ignore the uneasiness that still remained with him even though the details of the dream had vanished, and trying also to keep from vocalizing his thoughts. The electric clock he'd bought the day before yesterday—forgetting to read all the notes strewn around the room before going to bed at night, he would also forget to wind the clock—read twenty minutes past ten, which meant he had slept too long. His head was thick, and his nerves stayed jumpy from the terror with which he'd awakened.

Hunger pangs forced him to put out the half-smoked cigarette and get up from the bed. He padded nude to the living room, where he put water on for coffee, and thence into the bathroom for his morning toilet. He was brushing his teeth when the kettle started whistling, and he walked out with the toothbrush stuck at an angle into his mouth. He made the coffee, and then went back and finished in the bathroom.

The mornings were developing forms of habit now, and what bothered him was that these habits, this routine that was developing, might differ in significant respects from whatever his routine had been here in the old days. Any new habit that was a departure from old habits would only interfere with his struggle to return to that old self. Still, routines and habits developed naturally, and there was nothing he could do about them.

For instance. He always started the record player going

immediately after coming out of the bathroom, and this was only natural. He was trying to fill himself with those records, readapt himself to the person who had bought those records, so the earlier in the day he started listening to them the better. So he started them playing right after he came out of the bathroom, then carried his cup of instant coffee into the bedroom and got dressed.

Normally, the coffee was finished by the time he was dressed, and next he would go carefully around the room, reading all the notes, and checking off one more day on the desk calendar. Then he would go back to the living room and put on the bacon. Bacon and scrambled eggs, toast, and a second cup of coffee, this was his inevitable breakfast, every morning.

But this morning his pattern was disrupted by the ringing of the telephone.

He looked at the phone with dislike. It had only rung twice before, both times being Helen Arndt inviting him to her apartment for dinner. Something dark and greedy in her manner repelled him, and he made up excuses both times.

If this were her again, what would he say this time? Not yet knowing, and trying already to find a sensible-sounding excuse, he picked up the phone and said hello.

It wasn't Helen Arndt. A male voice said, "Merry Christmas, you son of a bitch. Why didn't you call?"

Oh, God. A friend. But the voice meant nothing to him, rang no bells at all. He said, noncommittally, "Hello."

"Don't you know who this is, you silly bastard?"

"No, I don't. I'm sorry..."

"It's Nick, you clown. Where the hell you been keeping yourself?"

Nick. He got an image, a piece of paper and written on it NICK   CARICATURE. His mind slithered off, away from the problem of *who is Nick*, wasting itself on the problem of *What is that piece of paper*, and he said, "Oh. Hi. I've just been around, I guess. Around the apartment."

"You know who's pissed off at you, you silly bastard?

Benny is, that's who. That's the only way I knew you were back, I heard him pissing and moaning."

"Oh, yeah? Because I made him leave here, I guess."

"Threw him out in the street, the son of a bitch. The best thing that ever happened to him. What are you doing?"

"Eating breakfast."

"You gonna be in today?"

Cole knew what the question meant. This stranger/friend, this Nick, wanted to come over and see him. He thought desperately for a way out, and his eye fell on the unemployment insurance payment book on his desk. He said, "No, I've got to go up to the unemployment insurance office."

"On Christmas Day? You gone loco, you silly bastard?"

"Oh. I forgot. It—it must be tomorrow."

"What'd I, wake you up?"

"Yeah, I guess so."

"Well, look alert. Today's Thursday, clown, the twenty-fifth day of December. If you'll hark a minute, you'll hear the herald angels singing. Hear them?"

"I just forgot, that's all."

"Make me a cup of coffee, I'll be right over."

The phone went dead, and Cole said into it, reluctantly, "All right." Then he cradled it, finished his coffee, and put on his shirt. He went on with his routine, but distractedly, thinking about his impending visitor. Nick. Caricature.

Meaningless.

He was eating breakfast, fifteen minutes later, when there was a sharp paradiddle of knuckles on the hall door. He went over reluctantly, and opened it, and felt an overwhelming sense of relief when he recognized the face smiling there. Nick, of *course*!

This was even stranger than the recognition of Helen Arndt the other day. He looked at Nick and immediately felt he knew him the way he'd know somebody like Little Jack Flynn. Not with the details, the memories of specific incidents and occurrences with this person, but just as surely and confidently as though those memories were there.

"Hello there, you silly bastard," said Nick, and lunged into the apartment, looking around. "What the hell you been doing with yourself?"

"I set you a place," Cole told him. "You want some eggs?"

Nick spun around to frown worriedly at Cole. "What's the matter, clown? Somebody die?"

"No. I'll tell you about it. Sit down there. You want some eggs?"

In a garbled Cockney accent, Nick said, "Ye fair gi' me the creeps. Ye'r fey, ye'r."

Cole went over to the kitchenette and got a second cup of instant coffee. He repeated his question about the eggs and this time Nick shook his head, but continued to watch Cole worriedly. He seemed to be wanting to make some sort of joke, but not sure he should.

Cole wasted more time at the kitchenette, stalling the moment when he would have to sit down and begin to talk with this new person. He understood that Nick was his friend—much more than that Benny, much more sensibly the sort of person he could conceive of as a friend—and he knew that meant he was going to have to tell Nick the truth. He had promised himself after the interview with Helen Arndt he wouldn't weaken again, and he had thought at the time it was a promise he could keep.

But he couldn't continue alone indefinitely. If he was going to tread carefully back into his old footsteps, he would need an ally, someone to tell him when he was on or off the path. Nick didn't seem to have the self-centered impatience of Benny, nor the greedy self-interest of Helen Arndt. Besides, Cole felt easy in his mind about this one, sure they could still be friends in this altered present. So maybe this was the ally he'd been needing.

Nick sipped at his coffee and said, "If you're putting me on, you son of a bitch, I'll kill you. If you're trying some goddamn characterization out on me, I'll break your silly neck."

Cole shook his head. "I'll tell you everything I remember," he said.

He told the story again, and Nick listened silently, squinting a bit as though he could see Cole better that way, and as though in seeing Cole better he would be able to hear and understand his words better. When Cole was finished—with the little bit he remembered, it didn't take long to tell—Nick asked a few questions which didn't get very helpful answers, the way everybody did at this point, and then for a minute or two they sat in silence at the table, Nick nibbling monkey-like at his coffee.

Cole got up and started clearing the dishes from table to sink, and Nick said, "You ought to see a doctor." His tone and facial range were completely different now; with solemnity, his voice deepened and his thin face became hollowed and large-eyed.

Cole shrugged. "It should get better," he said. "In fact, I think it has. I didn't remember you until just now, when you came in."

"Do you remember what happened to start it?"

Cole shook his head. "Only what Helen Arndt said, about me being in a hospital. But I don't remember it."

Nick said, "So maybe it isn't getting better, maybe it's getting worse. If it got worse, how could you tell?"

Cole smiled wanly. "If it got worse, I wouldn't know my own name."

"Then you better see a doctor."

"I suppose so."

Nick lit himself a cigarette, and said, "Why didn't you come around? You've been home almost a week now."

"I didn't remember anybody. I told you, I didn't even remember you until you walked in here."

Nick shook his head. "No good," he said. "You could of gone out and walked around the street. Walked into a few coffee shops. You would of run into somebody you knew, sooner or later. Don't you have my telephone number around here someplace?"

"I guess so," Cole said, guiltily thinking of the little blue book of phone numbers.

"You could of used it, just to see what would happen. You could of asked Helen to put you in touch with me, or some of your other friends. Hell, when I called up this morning, you tried to give me some phony excuse you weren't going to be here."

"I forgot it was Christmas."

"Sure. You've been hiding out, that's what you've been doing. The only reason you went to see Helen was because you had to, you told me so yourself. You're a silly ass bastard, you know that?"

Cole shrugged, not knowing what to say.

But Nick persisted. "Why, Paul?" he asked. "What silly ass idea you got in your head?"

"I don't know. I didn't want to see anybody till I was better, I guess."

"Brilliant. Old go-it-alone Cole, huh?"

"I guess so."

"Won't see a doctor, won't see your friends, won't do anything but sit around here and wait for your idiot mind to go out like a candle."

"I'll see a doctor," Cole promised. He was embarrassed now, with an obscure feeling of having been ungrateful about something, of having hurt Nick's feelings some way.

Nick said, "Tomorrow. Go tomorrow."

"I can't tomorrow."

"Why not?"

"I don't have enough money. I don't even have enough to pay the rent next week, and the unemployment insurance people don't pay any money for the first week you're out of work." That had been another unpleasant interview. He had asked the woman in the unemployment insurance office how they expected him to survive for the two weeks until his thirty-seven dollars a week started being paid to him, and she told him flatly that was none of her concern, had him sign the yellow form, and dismissed him simply by turning her attention to the next person in line.

Nick shook his head with mock sadness that seemed to

cover real irritation. "You're a lulu, you silly bastard," he said. "You go away, and you tell him to bill you. Helen'll give you a recommendation, won't she?"

"I guess so."

"So go tomorrow. Right?"

Cole nodded. "All right, I will."

Nick stood up and stuck the cigarette in the corner of his mouth. "Get your coat on," he said.

"Where we going?"

"Around. See who's doing. Lot of people gone home for the holidays, but there's still some around."

"Nick, I don't think I ought to—"

"Just put your coat on, clown. You don't think at all, period."

"Maybe I ought to," said Cole. He felt excited at the prospect, and frightened of it, too, like a man getting out of prison after twenty-five years.

They put on their coats and went out. The weather was good for Christmas Day this year, clear and cold, and few pedestrians were moving on the sidewalks. Nick led the way; they crossed Sheridan Square and headed east.

The first coffee shop they entered was nearly empty; a few solitary people sat at tables reading books or just stirring coffee. Nick looked around and said, "Nobody here. Come on."

"Let's have a cup of coffee here anyway." Fear was beginning to overcome excitement now; who were his friends, what were they like, what would they think of him once they knew the truth?

But Nick said, impatiently, "Come on, clown. We're not here for coffee." He pushed his way back out to the sidewalk, and Cole had no choice but to follow him.

At the second coffee shop, Nick recognized a group of four people at a table near the rear. He shouted, "Hola!" and advanced, waving his arms. They all shouted back, and shouted also, "Hey, Paul! When'd you get back?"

Two more chairs were dragged over to the table, and they

sat down. Nick said, "You'll have to excuse Paul, he's had an accident."

They all started asking questions, and Cole stammered, "Let Nick tell it. You tell them, Nick."

"Sure." Nick seemed to take a proprietary air in him, or maybe a showman's air, displaying an unusual exhibit. He told the story Cole had told him, and told it much better.

While Nick was talking, Cole studied the faces of the four people at the table, seeing if he remembered them. Two were named Ed and Frances, he knew that. He remembered their faces, and could put first names to them, but could remember nothing more about them at all. The other two he knew were married, but even their names escaped him. He had the feeling he'd been to their apartment, probably more than once, at parties in their apartment.

Nick had finished telling the story, and all four of them were offering him sympathy and looking at him with fascination and curiosity, as though they'd never seen him before. Nick turned to him and said, "You remember these people?"

"You're Ed and Frances," he said, pointing. "But that's all I remember. And I remember you two are married—"

They laughed, and the man said, "I'm glad of that. Just keep it in mind."

"I've been to parties at your house, haven't I?"

"Check. But you don't remember our names?"

Cole shook his head. "I'm sorry."

The man named Ed said, "Are you two putting us on?"

"Honest to God," Nick said. "I thought it was a gag at first, too, but it isn't. It's straight poop."

"I'm Fred Crawford," said the other man. "You remember now?"

"You live in Brooklyn."

"Sure. You remember my wife's name?"

Cole felt embarrassed, as though to admit ignorance would be insulting. He frowned, concentrating, trying to remember.

The girl said, "It's Mattie." She said it as though she felt sorry for him.

He nodded. "That's right, Mattie."

"*She* knows it," said Fred, and they all laughed.

Nick said, "We can't stick around. I want Paul to go see everybody, everybody we can find."

"Lot of people gone home for the holidays," said Ed.

"There's still some left."

Fred Crawford said, "Hey, Paul. We're having a New Year's Eve party. You coming?"

"I'd get lost."

"Nick'll bring you, won't you?"

"Sure," said Nick. He grinned and said, "You're my date, baby."

Cole tried to laugh, too, to get into the spirit of it, but he was too self-conscious. All of these people were so sure of themselves, so solidly placed. He felt like a bubble, floating, doomed to disappear with a pop any second.

Nick got to his feet, saying, "See you later. Come on, Paul."

Cole rose and said, "Glad to have met you," because he was self-conscious. They all laughed at that, except Mattie, who looked embarrassed and pitying. In confusion, Cole turned away and hurried after Nick out of the place, knowing it was going to go on like this all day.

But it would help. That was the only reason he'd put up with it; it would help.

19

The girl named Rita was walking homeward with him, but he didn't know yet whether she would be coming up to his apartment or not. He wasn't even sure whether he wanted her to come up or not.

In a whispered conference in the men's room at the East Side coffee shop where he and Nick had wound up a little after midnight, and where they'd run into Rita and three other people, Nick had told him that Rita and the old Paul Cole had been going together for about six months prior to Cole's going off with the touring company. Cole then had hemmed and hawed, but there hadn't been any roundabout way to ask it, so finally he'd just blurted the question out: "Did we sleep together?"

"Beats me. Maybe."

All in all, in their wandering throughout the day and half the night, they'd met fifteen or twenty people who had known the old Paul Cole, ranging from party acquaintances to close friends. As with the first group, Nick had in each instance taken over the task of explaining Cole's memory problem, always with that bit of flair in his manner, a hint of fanfare in his voice.

There'd been nearly as many reactions as people. Some had seemed sincerely concerned about him, wishing him well. Some had acted awkward and uncomfortable in his presence, after hearing about him. And some had found a kind of rough humor in his condition, making jokes he sometimes understood. Half a dozen times Cole had been on the verge of bolting, of running flat out across the sidewalks and home, of locking the door behind him and crawling into bed to cower there in misery, ignoring any ringing of phones or knocking at doors, until the memory of tonight would have faded and disappeared. But each time he had restrained himself with the same argument: Meeting these people again, talking with them, moving through these surroundings, all would help him regain his memory.

And it did seem to be working. Through conversations he had learned much about himself, adding to the information he had gleaned from constant reading and re-reading of the tax forms and resume and the other treasures in the desk at home. He had learned tonight about the tour he had been on when he'd had his accident, though he hadn't met anyone who had been along on that tour or could tell him specifically what sort of accident it had been. But slowly the parts of Paul Cole were being made known to him, and this accretion of knowledge made the uneasiness and the self-consciousness and the nervousness all more than worthwhile.

As to the people, most of the ones he'd met tonight he did recognize, and even here and there caught sight of a faint visual memory glimmering down at the end of a long tunnel in his mind. Exposing himself to his past this way was agitating his brain, forcing his memory to start to work again, and that was all to the good. He understood now why it had been so necessary for him to leave that town; if he had stayed there, his memory might never have gotten well. He was only lucky he'd obeyed the urge to come here, even though at the time he hadn't understood it.

Not that his memory was well now, not at all. Only a few faint memories had been sluggishly stirred so far, and some of the people he had re-met tonight he didn't remember or recognize at all, including this girl Rita, whose arm was now linked with his as they walked westward across Eighth Street toward his apartment. Her face, her voice, her words and mannerisms, all were as foreign to him as though she had just this night been created. Yet Nick had said this stranger had been his girl for six months, and it was possible they had gone to bed together.

There was an eerie feeling in it, to be walking with a girl who was such an unknown quantity to him, yet who knew him, perhaps, as much as any woman knows any man. It was like the eeriness of dreams where one walks naked through crowds.

He wished Nick had come along. But Nick had winked and grinned and pushed him toward the door, saying, "I'll see you around, you silly bastard. Go for a walk with Rita, go on."

She did all the talking, now. She would mention someone's name, and say something about what he or she was doing right now, and then try to remind him of the person by telling anecdotes from the past. A few times the anecdotes rang small bells in his memory and he'd say, "I remember now. A short fat girl," or something like that. But most of the time there was no memory at all, and nothing for him to say, and for the last few blocks Rita's chatter faded away and they walked silently together.

She was, all in all, a beautiful girl, a natural beauty. Twenty or twenty-one, with gleaming black hair and large dark eyes and a clear soft milk-white complexion. Her features were regular and cleanly drawn, and if they contained any flaw at all it was not in the features themselves but in her expression, which, because she was tired and because she'd been drinking, was somewhat loose and vague.

They stopped at last in front of his building, and stood looking at one another, while he belatedly began to wonder whether or not he should ask her upstairs. If only he knew just what their relationship used to be, but he didn't.

She broke the silence, saying, "You're not a bit like you used to be, you know that?"

"I don't know very much about what I used to be."

"You going to change back?"

"I guess so. I hope so."

"It's cold out here. Let's go on up and have a cup of coffee."

"All right," he said. "Good." He was relieved to have the

problem decided for him, though it still didn't answer the
main question.

He unlocked the street door, and they started up the
stairs together. She took his hand and led the way, a step
ahead of him, and he followed, frowning. It was stupid not
to remember her. Her of all people, it was stupid.

He felt her hand warm and moist in his as she led him
up the stairs. Her coat was unbuttoned, with a black wool
sweater beneath; looking up at her, he saw the fullness of
her breast defined by the black wool, and all at once a scene
came into his mind, a full memory, of himself and a girl on a
sofa, his hand touching the girl's small breast beneath a
brown wool sweater.

He frowned at the memory; it was from the wrong world.
That town had no meaning for him anymore, no purpose in
his thoughts. Memories of it were wasteful, consuming space
needed for more meaningful memories of more meaningful
times. And why should he think of Edna now, anyway, why
should he even remember her name? He could see her
clearly, could hear her frail voice and list the whole catalog
of her nervous mannerisms. Compared with this girl Rita—
No, there was no comparison. Not in looks, not in personality, not in anything. And particularly not in meaning. It was
important for him to remember Rita, necessary for him to
remember her, but remembering Edna could only be a
barren luxury.

Nevertheless, Edna remained in his mind. That one scene,
the single time they had been alone together when Edna
was babysitting, the whole length of that evening coming to
him compressed and clear, more clear in his mind than the
coffee shop he'd just walked from with Rita. It was like a
strip of movie film spliced into a circle, running over and
over on the projector of his mind. The touch of her, the
sound of her voice, the awkward period of darkness when
she had insisted on the lights being out, and the even more
awkward time after the light was on again, all circling and
circling in his mind, blotting out any possibility of thinking

about Rita, of trying to find some way to unlock the memories of his old relationship with her. .

He tried to concentrate on physical movement, hoping to defeat the persistent memory. He concentrated on climbing the stairs, on holding Rita's hand, on looking up at her breast. He concentrated fiercely on unlocking the apartment door and going in and switching on the lights. But nothing did any good.

Rita looked around and said, "Boy! I never saw it *this* clean."

"I didn't used to clean the place?"

"What a talent for understatement. I'll make the coffee."

"All right," he said, suddenly remembering the notes stuck to the walls all over the bedroom. He couldn't let her see those notes, he'd have to make some excuse to go in there and take them all down. Then he reflected that he had no assurance yet that she had even been in his bedroom, much less that she would eventually be in there tonight. Still, he didn't want to take the chance. And doing something, doing anything at all, should help to distract from the persistent memory of Edna.

He said, "Shall I play a record?"

"Sure."

He put a record on, turning the volume low, and said, "I'm going to go put my slippers on."

"Be my guest," she said, and smiled at him. But because he wanted so badly to understand every nuance of her smile, he couldn't understand its meaning at all.

He went into the bedroom and switched on the light, and traveled around the room taking his notes down. He stuffed them all into the top desk drawer, and then surveyed the room. It seemed empty. It seemed like a room in a balloon. "I'll put it all back tomorrow," he promised, and went back to the living room, where the water was just boiling for the instant coffee.

They sat across from one another at the kitchen table and she said, "Paul, I don't get it. Either you've got amnesia or you don't, that's all I ever heard of. But you've got something in the middle, right? Like, it's worse than a cold but not as bad as pneumonia, is that it?"

"Yes, I guess so. I'm in the middle."

"Mm." She shrugged, and drank some coffee, and rummaged cigarettes out of her skirt pocket. Her skirt was black, too, and very full, and she was wearing a black leotard. The only departure from black was on her feet; she wore brown loafers.

He lit her cigarette for her, then held the match up while he got out a cigarette of his own. He lit it, and then abruptly she said, "What do you remember about me?"

He looked at her. She sat hunched forward, her forearms on the table, wrists crossed and hands dangling down out of sight into her lap. She was watching him closely, but trying to look as though the question was a casual one.

Before, back in the coffee shop, he had lied and told her he remembered her vaguely, more out of politeness than for any other reason. Now he tried to decide what answer to give her, and tried also to dredge up some specific memory he could tell her about, but the Edna scene was still circling and circling, breaking into his uneasy concentration, making it difficult for him to think at all, impossible to think about Rita. Finally, he said, "Just what you look like, I guess. I can't remember anything in particular."

She thought that over for a while, and he saw her glance toward the bedroom door and then quickly away from it again. She said, "You don't remember anything—nothing we *did* together? Like, go to the movies or something, I mean."

He shook his head. "Nothing at all. I'm sorry. I'd lie to you, but you'd catch me at it right away."

She gave a nervous laugh and said, too brightly, "You don't even remember kissing me or anything? What a femme fatale, huh?"

"I'm sorry," he said, thinking, *She's turning into Edna.* But that wasn't it; it was just that he couldn't get Edna out of his head. And why not? There was no emotion involved in the scene grinding and grinding through his head, no love or even fondness, nothing but embarrassment and a depressing feeling of pity. It was a mournful scene to him, neither erotic nor pleasant.

Rita was sipping her coffee again, the too-bright smile gone. She set the cup down and studied him, vertical frown lines appearing between her brows. "I never heard of anything like it," she said. "I don't know what the hell to say to you."

"Maybe you could tell me about myself," he said. "Or about yourself."

She got to her feet, as though movement of some kind were absolutely necessary for her now. "If you're putting me on," she said, a little wildly, "I'll slit your throat."

"I'm not putting you on. I'm telling you the truth."

"You got any scars?"

"I don't know. I don't think so. It would be on my head someplace." He rubbed the top of his head, but felt nothing like a scar.

"You know what?" She was pacing back and forth now, away from the table to the middle of the room and back, smoking her cigarette with quick puffs and hugging herself with her right arm. "You know what I feel like right now?" she asked. Her voice was more brittle than before.

He shook his head.

"Every time my father comes down from Rome," she said. "Two, three times a year, down he comes, and he comes into my apartment and he brings a bottle of bubble bath for my roommate, and I cook him dinner. You know the scene? We got a hundred bottles of bubble bath in the closet, you know? Who the hell uses bubble bath anymore? And we sit around, the three of us, and we talk a lot of crap, and then he takes us to a Broadway musical, and then he goes back to Rome. Two, three times a year. And that's what I feel like right now, just exactly like the way I feel when my father's in town."

"I'm sorry," he said.

"Why did I ever get involved with you? Will you tell me that?"

"I don't know."

"Paul, will you *do* something? You sit there like you're *dead*, for God's sake."

"I don't know what to do."

She came over and stood looking at him, and then, her voice much softer, she said, "It's real, isn't it? They scraped you out."

"It's supposed to get better. Pretty soon, after I'm here for a while, it's supposed to get better."

"You poor bastard. It isn't your fault, is it? I'm sorry I got mad."

"I wish I could remember you," he said, meaning it. But Edna was still there in the middle of his mind.

"I've got to use the john," she said, abruptly, and walked away from him. He sat at the table and finished his coffee and started a new cigarette. He felt weary, and irritated because of the unnecessary memory crowding his head, and impatient because today he had finally been pushed all the way into his old world and he wanted to assimilate it quickly and fully.

What had Rita been to him?

When she came back he said, "I've got to ask you a question."

"You've got to ask me a million questions," she said. Her good humor was back. She was the same now as she'd been in the coffee shop, and on the walk here. She said, "You want more coffee?"

"No. It's a tough question to ask."

"Oh, shit." She plopped down into the chair across from him and said, "Can't you wait till your memory comes back?"

"I don't think so."

"All right." She sighed, and shook her head. "We did," she said. "That's what you want to know, right? So that's the answer. We did."

"Here?"

"Why do you *do* this to me?" She was all upset again, but

this time stayed in the chair. "Why do you make me feel so goddamn cheap?"

"I want to remember. You're a beautiful girl. I guess I must have liked you a lot."

"Don't, will you? Do you mind just cutting it out?"

"I don't know what to say. Everything I say is wrong."

"It's no good. Give me a light."

He lit her cigarette for her, and she said, "You just make me too uncomfortable, that's all. You know what I had in my head? I was going to come home here with you, and take you into bed and we'd make it, and like magic you'd be all better again. Your memory would come back like a light bulb, right in the middle of the whole thing. That's what I was thinking. Like some crummy one-act play, you know? Or don't you remember any of that either?"

"Any of what?"

"Class. Acting class. Robin Kirk."

He shook his head. "No."

"No," she echoed. "Nothing. It wouldn't work. We'd fumble around, and you wouldn't remember a damn thing."

"Were we going to get married?"

She seemed startled. Wide-eyed, she said, "You never saw me cry in your life, baby, whether you remember or not. You want to make me cry now?"

"You mean we were?"

"No, I do not mean we were. I mean we not were, that's what I mean." She got to her feet so abruptly the chair tipped over with a crash. She made a strangled sound of rage and kicked at the chair legs. "You're like my goddamn *father!* What the hell do you think I am, anyway?"

"Rita. Please…"

"You're a stranger to me, God damn you! You think I'd go to bed with a complete *stranger?* What do you think I am?"

The record had ended, and suddenly he became aware of it. He got to his feet and went over to change it. A shushing sound was coming from the speaker, and the needle was

wavering as the record went around and around, like Edna
going around and around in his head. If he could only get
that damn session with Edna out of his head, maybe he
could say something right to Rita.

He turned the record over, started it playing, and went
back to the table. Rita had put the chair back on its legs, and
was standing next to it. She said, "I better take off now." She
was much more subdued than at any time before this.

He said, "Couldn't we have another cup of coffee?"

"What's the point? You're not good for me and I'm not
good for you. What I wish, I wish you'd waited till you got
your memory back before you came around, because this
way it's just all screwed up. I mean completely."

"It should come back soon," he said, to reassure her.

But she shook her head. "Forget it, it's no good. Right
now you're some guy I never saw before in my life. You
could come to me tomorrow and say, 'Look, Ma, I'm cured,'
but it wouldn't do any good. I'd look at you and I'd see this
guy I never saw before that makes me feel so lousy rotten,
and I'd just be all turned off. I'm sorry, Paul, I guess it's
selfish and snotnose but I can't help it."

"I didn't mean to hurt you."

"I know you didn't." She was evading his eyes. She went
around him and over to the basket chair, where she'd tossed
her coat. Her back to him, she put the coat on and buttoned
it up.

He said, "Can I call you sometime?"

"I wish you wouldn't."

"Rita—"

"Just shut up, that's all." She moved with choppy strides
to the door and went out. She shut the door after her.

He stood looking at the door, and now, when it was too
late, the Edna scene began to fade. A heavy depression was
oozing in in its place, like a weight on his chest. He went
over to the sofa and sat down and stared across the room at
the kitchen table where the two of them had tried to talk
together. The depression was strong in him, making the

room lights seem dimmer, the room seem longer and taller. It was the feeling that came on him every once in a while, like the need to cry, but without tears. The music stated itself with brassy assurance, raucous with optimism.

After a while, when the weight of the depression lessened somewhat, he got to his feet and turned the record player off and went on into the bedroom. He started to undress, but the room seemed wrong to him somehow, and then he remembered the notes. He got them out of the desk drawer and put them all back up again, but when he was finished the room didn't look as reassuring as it always had before. The notes looked like false courage.

He went to bed, and lay thinking uneasily of Rita for a while, and finally fell into fitful sleep. In his sleep, he dreamed of a square of shiny metal. Edna was on the other side of it, and for some reason it was important that he get to her, but there was no way to do it. Everywhere he turned, the square of shiny metal was in front of him, blocking his way.

When he woke up in the morning, he remembered he'd had bad dreams, but couldn't remember the details of them.

20

The days passed glacially, and slowly a routine of living emerged, a pattern of movement and rest within which waiting was bearable, though sometimes he startled himself out of reverie with the realization that he had been forgetting what he was waiting for. Rebirth, it was, nothing less. He thought of himself sometimes as a kind of double image as seen through binoculars, two Paul Coles somewhat overlapping but neither substantial, so that a watcher could see through him. When the binoculars were adjusted, when the two images were brought together and matched, he would be himself again. In the meantime, what else was there to do but wait, and what else could he do while waiting but mark out the perimeter of the small circle he trod?

His day usually began at ten or eleven in the morning, when he awoke and got out of bed and padded to the living room to start the record player; he had grown used to the music without growing to like it, another of the danger signs that preyed on him when he was depressed. With the music playing, he next made the round of his walls, reading all his notes, old and new, sometimes reading them aloud slowly, the better to impress them on his mind. Then he dressed, and made himself breakfast. The living room always seemed unusually large and barren during breakfast, with him sitting hunched alone in a corner of it, mechanically putting bacon and fried egg in his mouth, looking around, half-listening to the strident music. He had his first cup of instant coffee at breakfast, and kept drinking more coffee all day long.

After breakfast, the routine was that he cleaned the apartment, thoroughly, every day. Every day he swept, every day he dusted, every day he polished the furniture and made the bed and cleaned the two sinks and the bathtub and the toilet and washed the windows. He knew that most of this was unnecessary, but what else was there for him to do? An integral part of his plan was that he would keep himself surrounded by reminders of his past, which meant he couldn't take any non-acting job, so practically all of his time was spent alone here in the apartment, and he had to be able to occupy himself some way. He couldn't read the books in the bookcase; he'd tried that and he lost the thread of everything, couldn't stumble through two pages of a book without being baffled by what he was reading. There was no television set, and it wasn't enough to sit and listen to the record player, it didn't distract his mind and body sufficiently. Physical labor was what made the time move, the purposeful moving of his arms, his legs, his back muscles. So every day he cleaned the apartment until it shone.

The work in the apartment always reminded him of the job he'd had in that town. Most of that time had faded away now, like the times before it, but bits and pieces still remained. Edna, intact. The name of the family he'd stayed with: Malloy. A name without a face: Black Jack Flynn. A bar run by a bartender with one arm. The job he'd had, in a tannery, loading and unloading freight cars. He could remember the physical feeling of that job much more clearly than any of its details, or the details of the place where the job had been done, and he remembered it as a pleasant physical feeling, the thing he was striving for every day when he cleaned the apartment; the easiness of mind that comes from physical toil.

By the time he was finishing his cleaning, it was always late afternoon, and time for the day's second meal. He never knew what to call that meal; it was too late for lunch and too early for dinner. Whatever it was, his work always gave him an appetite for it. TV dinners he had, or cans of beef stew, with a lot of bread and butter and two or three cups of coffee. The emptiness of the living room never bothered him as much at this meal as at breakfast; he ate more rapidly, and with more concentration, and with more pleasure.

In the evenings, he walked. He walked around the Village, looking in shop windows, stopping in coffee shops for fifteen minutes or half an hour, wandering through bookstores looking at the titles of all the books, roaming up and down and back and forth in the area between 14th Street and Canal Street, Hudson Street and Fifth Avenue, like a steel marble in a pinball game, back and forth from border to border, always in motion, never getting anywhere, under glass. He sometimes saw people he recognized—or, more often, who recognized him—but the meetings were usually short, and full of silences, and he was relieved at their termination. Nick came around from time to time, and seemed to make more of an effort than anyone else to relate to this new Paul Cole; Cole liked him, was gladdened by his presence, was pleased that not all his old friends were Bennys.

Late at night, well past midnight, he would return to the apartment, and read all his notes again, and add any new ones that occurred to him, and go to bed. In the night dark dreams would twist him like wires, but in the morning he could never remember their images; only sometimes the feeling that Edna had been concerned in them, and always the knowledge that the dreams had been bad.

The Monday after Christmas and after the bad scene with Rita, Cole awoke to find that today was to be a departure from routine. First he ran across the note that reminded him to cross off the date on the calendar, and the calendar told him today was Monday, and then another note reminded him he was to report to the Unemployment Insurance office on Monday, at one-thirty in the afternoon.

He smiled with pleasure at that, like an invalid who's been promised an outing. He reset his alarm clock for twelve-thirty, so he wouldn't forget to leave the apartment on time, and then returned to the normal routine, washing and dressing and feeding himself and then cleaning the apartment.

Reveries filled his mind as he worked around the apartment. In fantasy, his memory had already returned, and he had been reunited with his real self. That self, of course, was only magnificent. Graceful, polished, witty, self-confident, surrounded by friends, fulfilling the promise of his early years by going on to the heights as an actor. Smiling, mumbling snatches of dialogue to himself, he scrubbed the windows and the toilet and the tub.

The alarm clanged out when he was deep in fantasy, shocking him. For just a second he was completely disoriented, thinking, *It was only a dream! I never lost my memory at all!* A great happiness flooded through him. Fantasy and reality ran together like the view through a rain-wet window, and then the world righted itself again, and he remembered the note about the Unemployment Insurance office.

He changed his clothes, putting on his gray suit and a dark figured tie, taking time to polish his shoes. It was a good thing he'd remembered about the unemployment insurance; he had less than forty dollars left, and had to pay seventy-five dollars rent on Wednesday.

It was a heavy overcast day outside, the sky low with dirty clouds. Cole hunched inside his topcoat and hurried along the narrow sidewalks to the subway entrance. His pockets were full of notes, telling him the address he was to go to, and how to get there, and what line to stand on.

The Unemployment Insurance office, when he got to it, was crowded and damp. Long lines stretched back along a cigarette butt-strewn floor from the high counter. Cole found his line, and waited in silence, self-contained, paying no attention to the people standing around him, aware only vaguely of their similarity to the men he'd worked with in that town.

In twenty-five minutes, he reached the head of the line, and handed his booklet to the woman behind the counter. She was about forty, with dry and kinky black hair and a blotchy face. She had shaved off her eyebrows and drawn two thin arched black lines on her forehead to take their place. She stamped his booklet, and asked him questions while she filled out a square yellow form. Her voice was flat and metallic.

"Were you employed at all last week?"

"No, ma'am."

"Did you seek employment?"

"Yes, ma'am."

"Are you available for employment?"

"Yes, ma'am."

He answered her metallic questions, and then she slapped his booklet back on the counter: "That's all."

He looked at the booklet, and at her face. "What about the money?"

"What? Next, please."

"The money, I'm supposed to get money."

"They mail it to you. Next, please."

"Wait a second, wait a second."

A stocky man in a mackinaw was trying to push past him, but Cole clung to the counter, trying to catch the woman's eyes. She refused to look at him, but he spoke to her anyway. "When will I get it? Tomorrow?"

Then she did look at him, grimacing in irritation. "What's the matter with you? Do you mind telling me? You're holding up the line."

"I just want to know when I'll get my money."

"Next week. Now, step aside."

"Next week?"

"You don't get paid for the first week, that's waiting period. Next week you'll get your full four days' credit."

"But I've got to pay rent."

The stocky man said, "Sing us your troubles some other time, pal, I forgot my violin."

"I've got to pay my rent," Cole insisted.

"Not my problem, pal," said the stocky man. "My problem, now, my problem is you're holding up the line."

The woman said, "Next, please," and reached her hand way over the counter to take the stocky man's booklet. Cole looked at the two of them, the stocky man and the woman, and as far as either of them knew he wasn't there anymore. The woman was asking her metallic questions again, and the stocky man was giving his metallic answers. Neither was looking at the other.

Cole took a step back, feeling frightened, and backed into the people standing on the next line. "Excuse me. I'm sorry, excuse me." Clutching his booklet, he turned away, hurrying down the gauntlet between the lines, bumping into people who didn't even bother to turn around and look after him. He rushed out to the street, and turned the wrong way, going down the block away from the subway. When he realized his mistake, he was embarrassed to let everyone know about it by turning around and retracing his steps—besides, he didn't want to have to go past the Unemployment Insurance office again, where the stocky man might just be coming out—so instead he walked all the way around the block, and then to the subway.

Riding downtown, he began to worry, as his self-consciousness wore off. He hadn't worried very much about money before this, expecting that he'd have just enough to survive on if he was careful, and for the moment he couldn't want or expect any more than that, but now, with money he'd counted on suddenly and inexplicably being withheld, money began all at once to loom in importance.

He would have to get a job now. Yes, any kind of a job, maybe with a moving company or in a factory somewhere, any kind of job at all. The idea appealed to him in a guilty way; it would give him something more or less meaningful to do, it would fill his days without the makework of constantly cleaning the apartment. But at the same time he was afraid; it would be like a confession of defeat. As long as he was still struggling to find his old self, he didn't dare expose himself to *anything* that would have been foreign to the old Paul Cole, had no right to fill himself with useless confusing new memories that could only hamper his regaining the old.

But what else was there to do? He had to pay his rent, had to buy food, had to stay alive until the Unemployment Insurance money started to come in.

He couldn't make up his mind. He almost missed his

subway stop, but jumped to the platform just as the doors were closing, and walked home through the gray air. He went into the apartment and looked at his watch, and it was twenty minutes to three.

Pawn the watch. Yes. He looked at it again, remembering the existence of pawn shops, the idea of selling property to get cash. Of course, pawn the watch.

And anything else? He looked around the living room, and saw again the painting on the wall over the sofa. Could that be valuable? It was an original, not a print, done, he remembered vaguely, by a friend of his. No, he couldn't expect to get anything for that. Besides, he wouldn't even know how to go about selling it.

The books, what about the books? He couldn't read them now, so they were useless to him. He supposed he already had read most of them or all of them in the past, so once his memory returned he still wouldn't need them, because he would then remember their contents.

He went to the bedroom and got the telephone book and looked up used book stores. Yes, there they were, and most of the addresses were on Fourth Avenue, all clustered together. He called one of them at random, and the man said yes, they did buy used books, and his store was located between 10th and 11th Streets. The other bookstores in the phone book had addresses similar to that one, so they would all be close together. He could even shop around and get the best price.

He was pleased now, and excited. He was doing for himself, working his own way out of a dilemma. He hurried back to the living room and got two large paper grocery bags he'd been saving for rubbish, and sat on the floor in front of the bookcase to select his books.

Not the paperbacks, he couldn't expect more than what— half-price?—about ten or fifteen cents each for those. But the hardcovers, particularly the thick ones. No, all of them, all of them, he could carry them all. And if he could get, say, a dollar apiece for them—why not? most of them had cost three or four dollars new—then that would be… He counted the hardcover books, and he had twenty-seven of them. Twenty-seven dollars. All right, it would help, it would certainly help.

He loaded them into the bags, and there was a little room left over in one of the bags, so he stuffed some of the higher-priced paperbacks to fill it out. These paperbacks were marked at ninety-five cents or a dollar forty-five, prices like that; surely he could get a quarter each for them. Six in the bag, six more in his coat and trouser pockets. Another three dollars, plus twenty-seven dollars; thirty dollars. And if he could get another twenty-five for his watch, wouldn't that be enough? Fifty-five dollars. Plus forty he already had. He could pay his rent and have twenty dollars left over to live on till the Unemployment Insurance money came.

He picked up the two bags, and found them surprisingly heavy. Books weigh a lot; he was surprised. They hadn't seemed to weigh much when he'd handled them one at a time.

He left the apartment and went downstairs and out again to the gray air. He started walking east, over to Eighth Street. The bags of books got heavier and heavier, and before he was halfway down Eighth Street to Fifth Avenue he had to stop and rest, setting the bags on an automobile fender. The exertion was making him sweat, and the perspiration on his forehead was cold as ice in the cold air. He wiped it off, and wiped it off, but more kept coming out; and he was panting, dragging cold air into his lungs too fast and too frequently, so that his throat ached.

After a few minutes, he gathered up the bags again and started forward. He reached Fifth Avenue, crossed it, and walked another block to University Place before he had to stop again and rest. Then there was a long long block from University Place to Broadway, and he rested again. The next block was short, and then he was at Fourth Avenue. He turned left, and walked uptown, and two blocks up he came to the first of the bookstores.

There was a cluttered desk just inside the door, and

behind it sat an elderly man in ragged clothes. Cole stood in front of him, holding the two bags in his arms, and said, "I want to sell some books."

The elderly man grunted, and then just sat there.

Cole didn't know what to do. His arms ached from elbow to shoulder; all he wanted was to put the bags down somewhere. He said, "You buy books, don't you?"

"Let's see 'em."

"Where do I put them down?"

"Floor."

Cole went around to the side of the desk, where the elderly man would be able to see the books, and went through contortions trying to get the bags down onto the floor. He finally did it by going down on one knee, and two paperbacks slid out of the top of one of the bags.

The elderly man said, "All paperbound in that one?"

"No, mostly hardcover. I've got some more…" He pulled the extra paperbacks out of his pockets, put them on the floor, and started unloading the bags, stacking the books up on the floor.

The elderly man watched, and when Cole was done, he said, "Ten dollars."

"Ten? Is that all?"

"You got nothing there. Plays? They're a dead item, nobody wants last year's plays."

"They ought to be worth more than that."

The elderly man shrugged. "Try around," he said. "Try next door. Two or three more up the next block. You won't get a better price."

Cole knelt on the floor and looked at the stacks of books and the empty bags. To load the books into the bags again, to somehow pick them up from the floor, to go through the same motions again in another store, and then another store… "All right," he said. "Ten dollars."

The elderly man opened the center drawer of his desk. It was full of crumpled bills. He found a ten and handed it to Cole, who stood up and carefully put the bill away in his wallet. There was nothing to say, and the elderly man wasn't looking at him anymore, so he went back outside, and turned downtown again. Walking away from the store, he began to regret having sold the books. His old self had valued them, had kept them after reading, had constructed a bookcase to store them in. And to only get ten dollars for them, that was terrible. But he couldn't have carried them anymore, that was the main reason he'd sold them.

He'd meant to pawn his watch, too; now it was more necessary than ever. He walked slowly westward, looking for a pawnshop, but that was no way to go about it. There might not be any in this neighborhood at all. He went into a bar and asked the bartender, who told him there was a pawnshop on University Place, and gave him directions to get there.

It was three blocks. The store was on a corner, with heavy mesh screening over its windows, and a ragtag jumble of goods on display. Inside there was a low-ceilinged crowded darkness, with narrow aisles between dusty display cases. The store was very hot, but somehow damp.

Cole had expected an old man, like the man in the book store, but the man who came expectantly toward him was young, no more than thirty, wearing a business suit. He could have looked like any sort of clerical worker, except for his glasses; the frames were orange, and the lenses as thick and distorted as soda bottle bottoms. He came forward with a small smile playing about the edges of his lips, and as he moved his hands washed each other.

"Yes? Buy or sell? Buy or sell?"

"I want to pawn my watch."

"Your watch." He still smiled, but he seemed disappointed. "Well," he said, like a sigh. "Let's have a look at it."

Cole took it off and showed it to him. The man took it, fingered it, listened to it tick, looked at the back of it for inscriptions, tugged at the expansion band a bit, and said, "Five dollars."

"Oh, no. I need more than that, no, never mind."

Cole had reached out to take the watch, but the man ignored his hand, and kept the watch himself, touching it all over with his fingers. "You want to pawn? Not sell? Pawn? Five dollars. What if you never come back, never claim the merchandise? What then, eh? Come here."

He still had the watch, so Cole had no choice; he followed him deeper into the store, to a far wall, where the man waved his arms and said, "See?"

Nails studded a large green rectangle of wall, and watches hung from all the nails, two or three watches per nail. Many of them had expansion bands, catching what little light there was, reflecting it back in muted glitters.

The man said, "What do I need with another watch? You pawn it, you don't claim it, what then? If you wanted to sell, now, that would be a different story."

Cole didn't understand what he meant, but he said, "What would you give me if I sold it?"

"Well, now." He went through the same inspection all over again, Cole's watch turning and turning in his fingers. His head was cocked to one side, and behind the thick lenses his eyes were slowly and steadily blinking. He said, "Mmm. Twelve-fifty. Yes."

"All right," Cole nodded. "All right, I'll sell it, then."

"That's a different story." The man whisked his arm out, and Cole's watch was hung on one of the nails, where it swayed a bit, and then stopped.

Cole followed him again, around the end of a display case to a narrow crowded counter. The man had papers to fill out, had to have Cole's name and address, and then he gave Cole a crisp new ten dollar bill, two crisp new singles, and a shiny half dollar. "A pleasure to do business with you. Anything you want, buy or sell, always be happy to deal with you."

Going out, Cole passed the wall of watches. He stopped and studied them a minute, but he couldn't find his own; there were too many of them there, all crowded in together.

He saw the man peering at him, white circles of light on

his lenses, so he gave up looking for the watch, and left the shop. He walked homeward, adding up numbers in his head; forty dollars, and ten dollars, and twelve dollars and fifty cents. But the numbers didn't yet add up to seventy-five, so he would have to find something else to sell. In different places, though. He didn't want to meet either of these people again.

He went back to the apartment, and felt such relief at being safely indoors again that he decided not to try to sell anything else until tomorrow. It was nearly four o'clock anyway; if he went back out, he'd be caught in the rush hour.

Something looked funny, looked wrong. He frowned at the living room a minute, and then realized what it was: the bookcase. It was only a little more than half full now, and it had been almost completely full before. His world was such a narrow one now, so ritualized and so dependent on physical symbols of the past, that this dislocation bothered him all out of proportion to its actual effect on the appearance of the room. After he hung up his coat, he knelt in front of the bookcase and switched the books around, moving handfuls of them this way and that, trying to give it more of the proper appearance. He could get it to seem more full, but still it wasn't right; there had been hardcover books on the lower right before, and now there were paperbacks there. But there was nothing he could do about that.

Having rearranged the books and put a record on, it seemed natural to continue around the room, straightening up, cleaning. His routine had been disrupted today, by the trip to the Unemployment Insurance office and the time spent selling the books and watch, so the apartment wasn't even half cleaned yet. Soon he was back in the normal pattern again, scrubbing and dusting, whispering dialogue to himself.

21

On New Year's Eve, he went to Fred Crawford's party. Nick came by for him around eight o'clock, and had to remind him he'd been invited. Fred Crawford lived in Brooklyn, so they rode the subway endlessly southward from the Village. Because of the noise of the subway, they couldn't talk together during the trip, and Cole sat silent and apprehensive, wondering if going to this party was a mistake.

Today had been strange from the beginning. It had started, while he was still eating breakfast, with another call from Helen Arndt. This time she didn't ask him to come to her apartment for dinner; instead, she wanted to know why he hadn't yet got in touch with the doctor she'd recommended. He said that he'd forgotten about it, he'd lost the doctor's name and phone number, he was sorry, and she gave him the name and address and phone number again. He promised to call the doctor at once, and make an appointment, without intending to at all. What did he need from a doctor? More, what could a doctor do for him? He needed time, that was all, time and to be surrounded by the familiar. But he couldn't explain that to Helen Arndt.

Then she called again, two hours later. She was mock-severe with him, play-acting at being the overly protective type. She told him she had checked again with the doctor, and learned that Cole still hadn't called, and so she'd made an appointment with him for this very afternoon, at three-thirty. "Now, you go," she said. "You hear me, sweetie?"

"All right. I will."

"I'm serious about this, honey. You go see that doctor, or you're in trouble with me."

That he didn't want. Helen Arndt was his agent, his one remaining contact with the reality of his professional life. The last thing in the world he wanted was to alienate her. So he promised again to go to the doctor, and this time he meant it.

With the aid of a special note, and the alarm clock, he remembered to leave the apartment in time, and to keep the appointment with the doctor, who turned out to be a tall heavyset man with gray hair and tortoiseshell glasses and a permanent secret smile. His name was Bertram Edgarton, and his manner was cultish, an outer phlegm implying an inner activity of computer-like speed and power.

He asked no questions, beyond the initial request for Cole to state his problem. Cole stated it, in his usual fumbling way, because no matter how often he explained what had happened to him and what he was like now the words and the facts never came easy for him. He had to search the same compartments for the same fragmentary answers every time.

People usually helped this process by asking questions, helping him in his search for particular answers, but Doctor Edgarton was silent, sitting as heavy in his chair behind the desk as if he had grown there, his flecked eyes on Cole's face. Cole bumbled and fumbled, trying first to explain his condition, and then to explain why he hadn't sought medical help before, and then he was just trying to fill the silences. But soon he was repeating himself, and then contradicting himself, and finally he just stopped and sat looking sullenly at the doctor, who at last roused up and said that X-rays would have to be taken. He made a brief phone call, and gave Cole a slip of paper containing an address and a date and a time. "After the X-rays," he said, "we'll see."

Riding along in the screaming subway now, he wondered what good the X-rays would do, what good the doctor could possibly do. X-rays, a rich doctor; it would cost money. The doctor had told him not to worry about paying yet, but still, he would have to pay sometime. Yesterday he'd sold his suitcase and a summer suit and a pair of shoes to make up the money for his rent; he had less than three dollars in cash, so money was much on his mind.

Nick rapped his knee, and motioned that theirs was the next stop. Cole nodded and stood and groped to the door. The car was full enough to have several standees, and since this was New Year's Eve it seemed that most of these people must also be on their way to parties, but their faces were closed and stolid and indrawn, no different from the rush-hour faces on their way to work.

Cole's face was reflected dimly in the glass of the door, and studying it he saw that he too bore the same expression. He tried a smile, his face close to the door so no one else could see it, but it felt strained and looked ghoulish. He turned away, and looked at the advertising posters instead.

The train shuddered to a stop, the doors slid back away from each other, and Cole stepped out onto the platform. Nick motioned, saying, "This way," and they walked together to the end of the platform where the concrete stairs were. Beside them, the train jolted forward, and then rushed away as though racing a deadline to the junkyard.

When the noise of the train was gone, Nick said, "Most of the crowd you met already. I mean met again, since you've been back. If there's anybody there you didn't meet, they'll know about your memory so you won't have to go through that all over again."

"Good."

They went up the stairs to the street, and paused there to light cigarettes. Too casually, Nick said, "Rita'll be there."

Cole shook his head. Rita was something he had done stupidly, but he had no idea yet what the right thing or the bright thing would have been. In his mind was the idea that when he was his old self again he would not only know what he should have done last Thursday night, but also how to make up for it. He wanted to see her again—a note about her was now prominent in his bedroom—but not yet, not while he was still stupid.

Nick had taken a step away from the subway entrance, but Cole hadn't moved, and now Nick looked back at him, saying, "What's the matter?"

"Maybe I'm not ready for a party."

"What are you talking about?"

"I'm not sure—"

"Rita, huh?" Nick looked around the intersection, and pointed across the street. "Let's have a cup of coffee."

"All right." Any delay was welcome.

The store was diagonally across the street. This was a dim and musty neighborhood, the streetlights yellowish, not strong enough to show anything clearly. The intersection was occupied at the corners by a dry cleaner, a bar, a small clothing store, and the candy store they were walking toward, with squat brick row houses radiating away in four directions.

Three high school boys in dark clothing, looking angry and morose, stood on the sidewalk in front of the candy store, watching Cole and Nick with a kind of bitter hopelessness. Cole and Nick passed them, and went on inside.

The magazine rack was to the left, the phone booths in back, the counter on the right. They sat down at the counter, and Nick asked the thin old man behind it for two coffees. Nick paid, and for a minute they sat in silence, till Nick said, "Something went wrong with you and Rita, huh?"

"Yes."

"You want to talk about it, or no?"

"I don't understand it, that's all. We didn't know each other, and we made each other nervous. She said she didn't want to see me anymore."

"You make a pass?"

"No."

"Maybe you should of."

"I don't know."

Nick stirred his coffee, frowning thoughtfully. Then he shook his head and said, "You're a real problem, Paul. You're a first-rate clown."

"I'm sorry."

"Say that again and I'll get you lost in Jersey someplace." Nick drank coffee, and put the cup back down on the saucer too hard. It made a sharp noise, and coffee slopped over onto Nick's fingers. He cursed, and dried his hand with a paper napkin. Watching himself, watching his hands, he said, "Forget that. That Jersey crack. That wasn't fair."

"I feel the same way sometimes," Cole told him. "Impatient. I get so impatient with me I want to throw me away and start all over again."

"We're all clowns," said Nick. "All God's chillun been nuffin but clowns." He swung around on the stool to face Cole. "There'll be sixteen, eighteen people there," he said. "They got a four-room apartment. You want to keep away from Rita, it's the easiest thing in the world. Same if she wants to keep away from you. She's got to know you're coming, so if she really doesn't want to see you again she just won't show up."

"Maybe."

"Maybe shmaybe. You got troubles enough, you silly bastard, without making up extras." Nick was getting more and more impatient with him.

Cole shrugged. "I guess so."

"That's all you ever say, damn you. I guess so, I suppose so, I'm sorry, I don't know. Get with it, will you?"

"All right. I'll get with it."

"Good man. Drink your coffee."

"I don't want it."

"Then let's go."

They left, and passed the three high-schoolers again, and Nick led the way down the street to the right. "It's two blocks down," he said.

They walked in more relaxed silence now, Cole feeling relieved about the Rita problem. It hadn't been solved, but Nick had assured him it could be evaded, which was just as good. They crossed one intersection, and then Cole said, "What's his name again?"

"Who?"

"This guy, at the party. The one whose house it is."

"Oh. Fred. Fred Crawford. You met him last week, remember? Christmas Day. First guy we ran into."

Cole nodded, remembering. "Tall, blond hair. He's got kind of a paunch, but he's thin."

"That's the one."

"Tell me about him."

Nick hesitated, and then said, "You first. Tell me what you remember."

"I don't remember anything."

"You aren't even trying."

Cole stopped, and frowned as though he were in pain. "I don't know what's the matter with me," he said. "It's like I don't have the energy."

"Force yourself. Tell me about Fred Crawford."

They stood facing each other on the sidewalk. Slowly, Cole said, "I remember what he looks like. I just told you that."

Nick nodded. "Right. What else?"

"He's married?"

"You asking or telling?"

"I'm trying to remember her. Red hair?"

"That's up to you."

"Well, let me know when I'm right, for God's sake."

Nick shook his head. "This isn't Twenty Questions," he said.

Cole shook his head like a boxer shaking off a daze. "I'm really trying, Nick, I really am."

"Good."

"His wife has red hair. She's—she's short and kind of heavy. Wait a second, she's pregnant."

"That was a year ago."

"They've got a baby?" Nick didn't say anything, and Cole spread his hands vaguely. "I don't remember the baby," he said. "I don't know if it's a boy or a girl."

"Never mind the baby. What about Fred?"

"What else? He's a salesman, he tried to sell me something. A camera? Something like that. But how come I know him? I don't know. I heard him sing one time, I remember him singing, he opened his mouth like opera singers do, that big O they make." Cole turned, walked in a small circle on the sidewalk, and stopped where he'd started. "That's all," he said. "Maybe I'll remember more when I see him. That happens sometimes, I remember more about a person when I see him."

"You saw Fred last week."

"That's right, I remember that. I guess I knew more about him then, I forgot some of it."

"Okay," said Nick. His manner had been hard, but now it was gentle. "Okay, you did pretty good. Come on, we'll walk and I'll give you the rest."

Cole fell into step with him. "I guess I need somebody to keep pushing me," he said.

"I'll tell the world. Fred's a singer. He gets work sometimes with choruses, on television or making records, and in the meantime he works in a camera store in Manhattan. Their kid is a boy, and his name is Bruce, and I guess he's about a year old now. His wife was in Robin Kirk's class for a while, but she dropped out."

"Robin Kirk. Acting teacher?"

"Good man."

"Rita told me, I think. I remembered the name from that, but I don't know what he looks like or anything. Is he going to be at the party?"

"Not Robin." Nick said it as though the idea was inconceivable, but didn't add any explanation.

They walked for a few seconds in silence, and then Cole said, "Was I still in his class?"

"Not for a couple of years."

"Oh."

"It might be a good idea to go audit the class a couple of times. It's a part of your past, it might open up a few more memories."

"All right, I will. You mean just go there."

"Yeah. Here's the house here."

It was in the middle of a block of two-story row houses, with exterior steps to the second story, up to a shallow porch that ran across the face of the row from one end of the block to another, like a catwalk, with low brick railings to separate it into a rectangle per house. Going up the steps, Cole whispered, "Have I ever been here before?"

"Sure." Nick was ahead, and he looked back and down at Cole, grinning happily. "You remember it, huh?"

"No."

Nick went on up the steps, shaking his head. When Cole got to the top, Nick had already rung the bell. Nick said, "Now I know what a tragicomedy is," and the door opened. A short red-haired girl with soft-looking breasts was there, smiling at them, telling them she was glad they could make it. Behind her, a room was full of people blocking light, talking together, and smoke rising toward a low ceiling.

Cole said, "Mattie," because in seeing her he suddenly remembered her name, and that she was the wife of Fred Crawford, and that their child, named Bruce, was an ugly baby with red hair, looking, as infants do, as though he'd been left underwater too long.

Everybody was pleased that Cole had remembered Mattie's name, particularly Cole, and they stepped into the party in high good spirits.

The Crawfords' living room was long and narrow and underfurnished. An anemically modern sofa, composed of a thin wooden plank and two blue-covered foam rubber cushions, was the largest and most substantial piece of furniture in the room. Two benches served dual purposes; half covered by a square yellow cushion for seating space, and half bare, holding lamp and ashtray, the lamps with long tubular shades. Four kitchen chairs had been brought into the living room to give more of the guests a chance to sit down, but these were unoccupied, most people preferring to stand in tight talkative clusters.

Cole didn't see Rita in his first scanning of the room, and

felt relieved. He hoped she wasn't here, and wouldn't be coming. Several people noticed him, and waved, and he waved back. Nick said, "I'll get us drinks," and went off to the kitchen, which was next to the living room at the front of the house. Mattie, with a vague smile, had already drifted away, deeper into the room.

Feeling shy and exposed, because he knew these people now only slightly while they knew everything about him there was to know, he pushed one of the kitchen chairs into a corner and sat there, content to watch and listen without becoming involved. Nick found him after a while, and pushed an ice-cube clinking drink into his hand. He murmured something about a chick, winked at Cole in a distracted way, and went away again. Cole sat in the kitchen chair and sipped at his drink, and watched and listened.

He never left the chair. From time to time, Nick or Mattie or Fred Crawford would bring him a fresh drink, and stand by his chair to chat with him for a minute or two before hurrying off again. These brief chats were like duty visits to a friend in the hospital, and Cole choked on gratitude, being silent and morose when one of them tried to talk with him. Mattie and Fred, of course, had the whole party to concern themselves with, and Nick seemed mainly to be trying to seduce a girl who had come to the party with another man, though whether Nick was serious about it or just killing time Cole couldn't tell.

At one time or another, nearly everyone at the party came by to talk with Cole, curiosity and sympathy glittering on their faces. Cole tried to rouse himself from his apathy, and pay attention and detect individual reactions to him, but the struggle was too hard. He was bowed down by the feeling that he was a freak, a curiosity; in the eyes that turned from time to time to look at him he saw no acknowledgement that he was still a person. Rita was there; he saw her after a while, and occasionally caught further glimpses of her, but he never saw her look in his direction.

One time when Nick was standing near him, having just

brought him a fresh drink, he said, "Are the parties always like this?"

"Like what?"

Cole shrugged. "Talking and everything."

"Sure. Nothing coming back?"

"Just little bits, like always. Edna would like this."

"What?"

"She'd be thrilled, you know it?"

Nick was frowning at him. "Who?"

"Edna," said Cole, as though it were obvious, and suddenly realized what he was doing. The plane of reality had shifted, this world and the stopgap world were bleeding together, obscuring what few outlines did exist. It was the alcohol doing it, so it was a temporary thing, but it frightened him just the same.

Nick was saying, "Edna who? What are you talking about?"

She'd sit here the way I'm doing, he thought, but he said, "Nothing. I made a mistake."

"You okay, Paul?"

"I'm fine. The booze is getting me, that's all."

"New Year's Eve comes but once a year." Nick grinned and winked. "Be seeing you, buddy."

A little while later a girl came over, pulling a kitchen chair with her, and sat down in front of him. She said, "Hi."

"Hi," he said, trying to remember her. She was pixieish, small and well-built, and slightly drunken in a high and happy way. He couldn't get a name for her at all.

She said, "You're the amnesia boy, right?"

"That's right. I don't remember your name."

She laughed. "Doesn't surprise me at all. You never met me before."

"Oh."

"I came with Bobby Loomis. You remember him?"

"I'm not sure."

She wave negligently. "That's him over there, trying to put the make on our hostess. He's a shmo."

"Oh."

"You really got this amnesia, huh?"

He nodded. He thought her manner was probably offensive, but he wasn't offended. He was like the self-conscious man on roller skates; knowing for *sure* that everybody is staring at him, he doesn't have to worry about people staring at him anymore. This girl openly displayed the attitude he felt hidden behind the eyes of all the others here, so he was more relaxed and comfortable with her. He said, "Yes, I've really got it."

"Did you try a blow on the head?"

"A what?"

"Like in the books. One blow on the head, blackout. Another blow on the head, and it all comes back."

"I don't think this is the same thing."

"Oh." She shrugged carelessly. "Just a suggestion. Anyway, it isn't really amnesia, is it? You can remember *some* things. If I told you my name, you'd remember it, wouldn't you?"

"For a while."

"Just for a while?" She pouted. "For how long?"

"A few days, maybe. Maybe not even tomorrow morning."

"What if I did something terrible? If I took off all my clothes, or spilled my drink on your head, or set fire to the house."

He smiled faintly. "I guess I'd remember it a couple days longer," he said.

"Well, my name is Judy Fitzgibbons. You got it?"

He nodded.

"Then say it."

"Judy Fitzgibbons."

She looked thoughtfully at her drink. He told her, "Don't do it."

She laughed again, and said, "I'm just teasing." But he knew she'd been thinking about it seriously. She studied his face, and said, "What would you do if I did?"

"Hit you, I guess."

"Then Bobby Loomis would come over and hit *you*."

There was an aura of brittle danger about her. He was beginning to feel tense again, in a different way, and he wished he'd been able to bring Edna along. He'd wished that before, because she would be so fascinated by this party, but now he wished it because she would be a defense against this girl.

I've got to stop thinking about that time. That's stupid, wasteful.

The girl was saying, "You know, you're lucky in a way."

"I am?"

"Being able to forget things. Not having all sorts of old problems around to make you depressed."

"I never thought of it that way," he said.

"Oh, well." She sighed offhandedly. "Would you get me a new drink? Vodka and water, just tap water."

"All right."

He took her glass and his own and pushed through the press to the kitchen. The party had reached that inevitable stage where the guests were gradually shifting from the living room to the kitchen; at the moment, they were about evenly divided between the two rooms. Moving through and around the talking clusters, Cole made two fresh drinks, adding ice cubes to both from a bowl of them in the refrigerator. He carried them back, gave one to the girl, and sat down again. It was the first time he'd left the chair since coming to the party, and no one had paid any attention to him. He'd been here long enough, he decided, for his curiosity value to have waned.

The girl said, "I've been thinking about that. About having a really terrible terrible memory. I mean, you can remember enough to get around, can't you? You always know who you are and where you live and like that."

He nodded.

"And I guess you can leave notes around for anything important you want to remember, like parties and going to work and all."

"I do."

"You do? There, you see? And I figured it out!" She seemed very pleased with herself all of a sudden. "How do you like that," she said, more to herself than to him.

There was nothing for him to say. He sipped at his drink instead, wishing she'd go back to Bobby Loomis.

But she said, with a kind of negligent wistfulness, "I bet that would be wonderful, I really do. There are just all *sorts* of things I'd sooner forget, and don't you ask what sorts of things they are."

"I won't."

"I actually envy you, do you know that?"

"You shouldn't," he said. Into his mind came an image of metal, square and shiny, but it was gone again before he could understand it.

She said, "Do you remember my name?" There was a challenging smile on her face, and her eyes were bright.

He felt a moment of panic, and then the last name came to him and he said, "Fitzgibbons."

"Straight A. And what's my first name?"

It was gone, hidden in the shadows behind the name Edna. Or *was* it Edna? He tried to think if he had remarked on a coincidence when she'd told him her name, but he couldn't be sure.

"Well?" The aura of danger was around her again, like a faintly shimmering yellow-green light.

He took the plunge. "Edna?"

"Wrong," she said, very coldly. "F minus." She got to her feet. "The name is *Judy*, my friend. Judy Fitzgibbons. And you won't forget it."

He saw the sudden tension in her, and understood it, and jumped up from the chair, slapping at her forearm as her hand came around with the drink. Glass and all shot out of her hand, missing him and crashing into the wall. Her face winced into a grimace of pain but she didn't cry out; her right hand clutched her left forearm where he'd hit her.

"Cut it out!" he said, trying to keep his voice low but meaningful.

Instead, she tried to slap him, backhanded, and in warding the blow off, he hit her other forearm. She jumped at him then, and he pushed her off, shoving out with both hands high on her chest. She staggered backwards, running into one of the clusters that hadn't yet moved to the kitchen, and a bull roaring made Cole look off to the right, where he saw the chunky young man identified as Bobby Loomis running toward him with cocked fists and enraged face. Because most of the partygoers were in the kitchen now, there was clear floor between them, nothing in the way to hinder Loomis or slow him down.

Cole saw him coming, and a feeling almost like pleasure came over him. For a week now, a throbbing rage had been building in him, without his recognizing it as more than the depression and frustration and impatience that made up his normal state, but all at once it was on the surface. The insoluble stupidity with Rita, the aimlessness and lack of progress of his days, the impassive cruelty of the doctor, the guilty curiosity of the partygoers who had looked on him like a fetus in a jar, all fused and found animation in the angry red-faced boob blundering toward him.

The body remembered where the mind forgot; somewhere, Cole had learned at least the rudiments of boxing. Without conscious thought, he turned his left side toward Loomis, cocked his right fist at his chest, and stuck out his left. Loomis came in charging, arms out as though to wrap him in a bearhug; Cole jabbed him three times in the face and moved to his left. His right feinted, and his left jabbed out over Loomis' belatedly protective hands to scrape cheekbone. His right foot came forward, his body angled left, and his right crossed to Loomis' midsection. Loomis, who hadn't stopped his blundering forward motion, staggered over Cole's chair and ran into the wall.

Cole felt good. He felt like a bedridden invalid suddenly healthy and able to walk around again, like a man carrying a heavy sack suddenly relieved of the load. He felt taller, lighter, more sure of himself. He waited, shifting on the balls of his feet, for Loomis to come at him again.

The chair had gone over, and Loomis' feet were entangled with it. He seemed groggy, too, and in coming back off the wall almost sprawled onto his face. But he got his balance back, and spun around, and let his weight rest on the wall, back to the wall now and enraged face glaring at Cole.

There was silence everywhere now; the party guests had been struck dumb. The fight was still less than half a minute old, and no one yet had recovered sufficiently from surprise to try to stop it. The guests weren't in Cole's mind at all now. Nothing was there now but this unexpected physical well-being, and the desire to smash that pig face to ruin.

Loomis picked up the chair.

Cole saw it, saw the intent expression on Loomis' face and then the chair being lifted, the legs pointing at the corners of a square around his head, and a cold terror filled him, draining him of everything, of purpose and understanding and strength. A shrill shriek ran endlessly from his mouth, and he went down on his knees, down on his face, crouched in a tight ball on the floor with his ineffective arms crossed over the back of his head.

In the pit of his terror he heard angry voices and crashing, and he drew himself in smaller and tighter. Something hit him in the side, half-rolling him over, and he saw struggling above him, his angle of view making them monstrous, two men: Loomis and Fred Crawford. And beyond them Nick's face, looking down at him with total disgust, his mouth moving as he said words Cole couldn't hear. Cole rolled onto his face again, and cowered there.

After a while, people were talking in his ear but he wouldn't listen to them and wouldn't move. When their hands touched him, he trembled, and bit his tongue to keep from screaming. If they thought he was dead, they'd leave him alone.

But they picked him up, and carried him somewhere. His

eyes were closed, he was still curled in on himself; it was as though they were carrying a large medicine ball wearing clothes. They put him on something soft, and then they left him alone. The terror in him ruptured, and he fainted.

When he came out of it, he was in darkness, lying on a bed. A drone of voice came from somewhere, and down beyond his feet a thin line of light outlined a door. He came awake remembering nothing, in total confusion that quickly became fear. He didn't know where he was, or what the drone of voices meant. Was he in a hospital?

But his shoes were on. All his clothing was on. His left hand ached slightly, particularly the first knuckle of his middle finger. His whole body felt cramped, as though he'd been sleeping sitting up.

What should he do? There was a feeling of danger, but he didn't know what it meant. Those talking people, he didn't know whether they were a danger to him or not, and he didn't dare risk going out to them. He lay on the bed, trying to understand what had happened, remembering only his own apartment and knowing only that he wasn't there.

He lay there about ten minutes before the door opened and a male silhouette came in and said, "You awake?" It was Fred Crawford's voice.

Fred Crawford. It all came back then, the party and the fight, but ending with his facing Loomis, who was against the wall. Had Loomis knocked him out? His memory stopped with himself facing Loomis, who was against the wall.

He said, "I'm awake. Did he knock me out?"

"No. He went after you with a chair, and you passed out." Crawford came farther into the room. "How do you feel?" His voice was neither friendly nor unfriendly, and not particularly curious, perfunctory.

"All right, I guess." But at mention of the chair he had felt a wave of weakness go through his body, as though he'd faint. He pushed away from thought of the chair. "What time is it?"

"Little after one. You missed the New Year."

"Oh."

"You want a cigarette?"

"Yes, please."

"Okay if I turn on the light?"

"Sure."

"Watch your eyes."

The light came on, a blinding ceiling fixture, and Cole squinted away from it. When he could see again, Crawford was holding out a lit cigarette to him. Cole took it and thanked him, and sat up.

He was in the Crawfords' bedroom, underfurnished like the rest of the apartment. It contained this double bed on which he lay, with neither headboard nor footboard, and a bulky scarred dresser with a mirror, and a small plastic radio on the floor beside the bed. There were venetian blinds on the window, but no curtains or drapes.

"I'm sorry it happened. Did anything get broken?"

"A glass, that's all. Don't worry about it, it wasn't your fault. Loomis got thrown out."

"What about the girl?"

Crawford looked puzzled. "What girl?"

Cole shook his head. "Never mind. It doesn't matter."

"You okay?"

"I guess so. Where's Nick?"

"He left. Took Angie home."

"Oh. He was mad at me, wasn't he?"

Crawford shrugged. "You want a cup of coffee?"

"Yes, please."

"Wait, I'll get it for you."

Crawford left, shutting the door behind him. Cole patted his pockets, found his cigarettes, and lit one. Crawford didn't want him to go out with the other guests, but that was all right; Cole didn't want to go out there either.

It was Mattie who brought the coffee. "You all better now?"

"I'm sorry about the fight. I didn't mean it to happen."

"It wasn't your fault, Paul," she said. She was smiling brightly, but she looked uneasy. "It was Fred's idea to invite that idiot, and this is the absolute last time."

Cole got up from the bed, feeling faint pins-and-needles sensations in his legs. He took the coffee cup from Mattie and said, "Nick's sore at me, isn't he?"

"That's just his way. When you're all better, you two'll be friends again."

"I guess so."

"Well...I'd better get back to my guests." She closed the door behind her when she left.

Cole drank the coffee, and smoked his cigarette, and walked across the room, walking off the shakiness and nervousness in his body. When coffee and cigarette were both finished, it was time to leave the room.

He went down the narrow hall, which split at the end, opening onto both the kitchen and the living room. Fred Crawford intercepted him at the living room entrance, saying, "I'll take the cup. You okay now?"

"I'm fine. Thanks a lot."

"That's okay. Can you find the subway?"

It took him a second to realize what Fred meant, and then he understood that he, too, was to be thrown out, but gently, because of his condition. He wished he could say that he could find the subway, that he needed no help, but if he left here alone he knew he would get himself hopelessly lost. He didn't even know the name of the subway. Hating this helplessness, this dependence on people who would prefer not to be his keeper, he nevertheless said, "I don't think I can. I'm sorry."

"That's all right, I'll walk you. Wait there, I'll get rid of this cup and get your coat."

Cole waited. He could see into the living room, and into the kitchen. The party had thinned out a little, but was still noisy and animated. He saw Rita, talking with a tall thin man, but he didn't see the other girl, the one who had started the trouble. No one in either room seemed to notice him.

Crawford came back, with his coat, and Cole shrugged into it. Crawford led the way through the living room, which was somewhat less populated than the kitchen. He opened the front door, and started out, and when Cole moved after him someone plucked at his sleeve. He looked around and it was the girl who'd started the trouble.

She looked more drunk now, and somehow bitter. Challengingly she said, "What's my name?" She said it like a demand for a password; give the countersign and you can come in.

He shook his head, not wanting to think about her or be involved any further with her. He pulled his arm away, and went out the front door. He went down the steps to where Crawford was waiting impatiently on the sidewalk, and behind him the girl came out on the narrow porch and shouted down, "What's my name? What's my name?"

Crawford was looking up at her in bewilderment. Cole brushed by him and walked away down the block, remembering which direction he had come from, walking with his hands in his pockets and his shoulders hunched to keep his coat collar up and around his neck.

Behind him, the girl was screaming with increasing urgency, "*What's my name? What's my name?*"

Crawford caught up with him and said, "What the hell is that all about?"

"Nothing. She's crazy."

"She's something."

Behind them, the girl kept screaming.

22

He was impaled on dreams, dark shadows and sharp stab-
bings and great white squares of gleaming metal while he
slept at night, pointless rambling fantasies of an unknowable
past and an unguessable future while he worked around the
apartment by day.

He had sold the rest of the books, all the paperbacks, carrying them on two trips crosstown to Fourth Avenue, selling
each load in a different store, getting eighteen dollars for
them. The empty bookcase scraped at his mind, and he
filled it again, with anything, with the records from the
table, with dishes from the kitchen cabinet, with odds and
ends from the desk drawers. Empty, it ached at him like a
sore that wouldn't heal, and it would be even worse if he just
dismantled the bookcase and left a great blank empty space
along the wall. Filled with bits and pieces from all over the
apartment, there was a comfortable deceptive look to it,
counterfeiting the original closely enough to give him ease
of mind.

Nick came around no more. No one called, not even
Helen Arndt. Sometimes, following the instructions on one
of his notes, he called his answering service, but there were
never any messages, and he knew now that when this current paid-up period was finished he would let the service
lapse.

He had left the apartment only twice since Wednesday,
when he had sold the rest of the books, and those were the
only times he had spoken to anyone, in the short empty conversations with the terse man who had bought them. He was
closing in on himself, closing in. How could he get better
this way, living like a hermit? But every time he tried to

enter his old life, he destroyed a part of it. With Rita, with Nick, with all the people at the party, all the people he'd met in his first week of wandering. They didn't think of him now as they had thought of him in the past, as Paul Cole, their friend and the actor. They thought of him now as that silent stumbling freak, plodding his small apologetic circle.

Where was the *memory*? He'd been back now over two weeks, and there was practically no improvement. His memory was still bad, and his physical contacts with his past had deteriorated. Even the apartment no longer looked as it had when he'd first come back to it; the books all gone, notes on all the walls. Surely, with his incessant cleaning, there were other differences as well, subtler but just as damaging.

On Sunday, four days after the party, he could take it no longer. He had to get out, had to break free of this stupid circle. For one day at least, he had to refuse to clean the apartment, had to go outside, had to move about the world, had to alter the inevitability of his days.

The routine was so strong in him that he felt a nervousness, an unease, when he left the apartment immediately after breakfast instead of getting out the cleaning tools. He went down to a gray overcast day, and began to walk.

The Village was in its Sunday morning hush, the streets nearly empty. Cole walked along, smoking, looking at the old buildings, enjoying the walk for its own sake and very nearly forgetting what trouble he'd had driving himself out here.

After a while he stumbled across Minetta Lane, that tiny L-shaped side street in the heart of the Village. The street attracted him, pleased him; it made him feel buoyant merely to walk back and forth on its narrow sidewalk. He spent nearly half an hour there, with only an occasional hurrying pedestrian to interrupt him, and finally emerged on Macdougal Street refreshed and happy. Macdougal, the self-conscious center of the bohemian Village, made him nervous, and he hurried north out of that section as quickly as he could, coming to Washington Square Park, another oasis of calm, where he strolled back and forth amid the families and policemen until hunger pangs told him it was time to go back to the apartment.

He left the park on the wrong side, but didn't realize it till he'd walked three or four blocks and made at least one turning. Gradually it came to him that the quality of the streets had changed, that he was no longer in the neighborhood he'd been limiting himself to. Warehouses and display rooms and office buildings crowded together here, and even on Sunday there were trucks parked along the curb.

When at last he realized his mistake, he tried to reverse direction, but that only made things worse. He walked and walked, this way and that, while panic grew in him, and the sudden sure knowledge that he could get just as brutally, just as totally, lost only a few blocks from home as if he were a thousand miles away.

All the policemen seemed to be in the park. It was twenty minutes before Cole saw one walking ahead of him on the sidewalk. He could have asked directions of some passing pedestrian, but some self-consciousness had made him wait till he could find a cop.

He hurried to catch up to this one, and said, "Excuse me. Pardon me, I'm looking for Grove Street."

"Grove Street?" He was middle-aged, very tall and somewhat overweight, with an expression of wary coldness. He said, "Over in the Village?"

"Yes. That's right, the Village."

"You want to go that way," the policeman said, pointing. "The Village is over that way."

"Thank you very much."

Cole hurried on in the direction the policeman had indicated, and after several blocks he began to recognize buildings, intersections, signs. He had to ask directions once more, this time of a young woman wheeling a baby in a stroller, and eventually found Grove Street and home. He was trembling with nervous anticipation as he raced up the stairs and unlocked his apartment door, and once inside, the door safely shut behind him, he felt as relieved as if he'd just crossed no-man's land at the height of a battle.

Ten minutes later, stripped to the waist, he was scrubbing the bathroom floor.

23

It was an impressive building, with a broad façade of glass and chrome, and a doorman in a maroon uniform piped with gold. Cole was awed a bit by it; the first time, he went on past, peering in at the entrance from the corner of his eye, bashful about approaching the doorman directly, and still not sure that it was wise for him to be here at all.

This was Thursday evening, four days after his walk through the Village, and that he was here now at all, slinking guiltily past Helen Arndt's apartment building, was, in essence, an outgrowth of the same impulse that had sent him on the walk; the knowledge that it was wrong and dangerous for him to reduce himself to a hermit in the apartment. If he didn't want to shrink, to wither, to become even worse off than he was now, he had to get out sometimes, see people, do things, *move*.

But what was there to do, where was there to go, who was there to see? Not Rita, not Nick, not Fred or Mattie Crawford, not any of the people he had met in that week between Christmas and New Year's. If staying in the apartment was bad for him, what was the alternative, other than more futile attempts to maintain contact with the friends of his past?

There was another choice, of course; he could break off from the old Paul Cole completely, start building an entirely new and different life. He could get a job, make friends among people who hadn't known him in the past—he'd been able to make friends in that town, hadn't he?—gradually build up a whole life that would give his every movement meaning in the immediate present, but at the same time cut

off the last remote chance of finding meaning in the past or
in the future. But that black road he couldn't permit himself
to travel.

So every path was closed. He couldn't mingle with the
people of his past life, he couldn't establish new relationships
that had no bearing on that past life, and he couldn't just sit
in the apartment and rot.

Still, one thing was clear. He needed to be out of the
apartment sometimes, around other people sometimes, with
something to occupy his mind sometimes; otherwise, survival itself was impossible. But who and where and what?
Day by day, who and where and what.

Monday, the day after his walk, was easy; that was the day
he went to the Unemployment Insurance office. By leaving
earlier than was necessary, by strolling along and window-
shopping on the way, by stopping in for coffee and a danish
afterwards, he managed to make the trip last over three
hours; it was twenty to four before he returned to the apartment. But once he was back, that was an end to it. There was
nowhere else to go, nothing else to do. He thought for a
while of going to a movie after dinner, but rejected the idea.
Nick had told him the kind of movie the old Paul Cole had
liked, Italian social dramas and English comedies, and he
had already tried both and learned that both were now too
subtle and complex for him to follow. It was better not to go
at all than to sit with no comprehension, mocking himself
with what he had once been.

Tuesday, again, there was something already determined
for him to do; it was the day of his X-rays. He had a note
about it prominent on the bedroom wall, and Doctor Edgarton's nurse phoned a little before noon to remind him, just in
case. He went to the address, a squat yellow brick building
on 53rd Street off Second Avenue, where a succession of
white-garbed people, male and female, handled him with
impersonal dispatch, maneuvering him this way and that
like an automobile on an assembly line. As always, being
surrounded by people who were not aware of him as a

person made him nervous and sullen; toward the end he was being dense and uncooperative, and he was relieved when at last it was finished and he could go back out to the street again. Walking to the subway, he passed a movie house where a musical was playing. On sudden impulse he bought a ticket and went in. He sat through it twice, enjoying himself more than any other time he could remember. From instant to instant there was never anything he had to fix in his mind, only a series of brightly colored movements to watch and pleasant sounds to hear. But afterward, riding home on the subway, he regretted having done it; movies of that type had been foreign to his old self. He couldn't go to see movies like that anymore.

Wednesday, there was nothing to do. He fretted around the apartment a while after breakfast, but then he reassured himself, telling himself that even in the old days he must have stayed home from time to time. And the apartment hadn't been cleaned now in three days. With anticipatory pleasure, he got out the cleaning gear.

But then Thursday, another blank day. He told himself he'd work on the apartment only until the mail came; his first unemployment insurance check hadn't come yet, and was due this week, so would in all probability be here today. When it came, he would take it to the bank and cash it, and then do some shopping; his food was getting low.

But there was no mail for him at all. He looked through the slots of the other mailboxes, and saw that the mailman had been here already, so there was nothing to do but go back upstairs, and go on with the routine, until, unexpectedly, the phone rang.

It hadn't rung in...how long? Well, the nurse had phoned him Tuesday, but other than that, how long had it been? He couldn't remember.

Nor could he guess who it might be. Nick? Nick hadn't been in touch with him in over a week, not since the night of the party. Or maybe it was Rita, to tell him they might take a second chance at getting to know one another again.

He hurried to the bedroom, drying his soapy hands on his trousers, and picked up the phone.

It was Helen Arndt: "Sweetie, don't you ever call your answering service?"

"My… Oh, I forgot." It had been days since he'd even bothered to call there; they never had any messages for him.

"I called *Tuesday*, honey, and when you weren't home I left a message with your service. You know, there's no sense paying them if you don't call them from time to time."

"I know. I forgot to call. I never get any messages anyway."

"You poor dear, you sound frightful. What on earth is wrong?"

"I don't know, I'm just depressed, I guess."

"Honey, I want you to come see me, hear? You come right over tonight, and I'll give you a great big steak, and we'll talk. Now, I won't take no for an answer."

A couple of times before she had extended similar invitations, and he had made excuses, but not this time. He needed a reason to leave the apartment, and she was giving him one. "I won't say no," he told her.

"Well, now, that's more like it. Have you got my home address?"

"I don't think so."

"Well, get pencil and paper."

"Got it."

"Three-twelve East 63rd. Have you got that?"

"Three-twelve East 63rd."

"Fine. The man at the door will tell you the apartment number. Eight o'clock?"

"All right, eight o'clock."

"Shall I call a little later, and remind you?"

"No, I'll remember."

"You're sure, now."

"Yes, I'll remember. Eight o'clock. Three-twelve East 63rd."

"That's a dear boy. A steak smothered in mushrooms. I'll see you then."

"Yes."

He hung up, and wrote himself a note, and tacked it to the hall door. There was a slight feeling of unease—he was still a bit afraid of Helen Arndt, unsure of her—but it was overridden by his pleasure at the prospect of getting out of the apartment.

Now, a few minutes after eight, he had passed her building, and had walked down to the next corner. He stood there irresolutely for a minute, tempted to give it up, to forget the whole thing and go right back home again. But that would be stupid; he had come this far. Besides, why should he feel so uneasy about her? She was the only one from his past who hadn't, one way or another, broken off relations with him since he'd come back.

All right. It was the doorman intimidating him, and that was even more foolish than being afraid of Helen Arndt. All right. The thing to do was get it over with.

He was smoking. He took one last drag on the cigarette, threw it into the gutter, and walked back to three-twelve. Inside the glass doors the doorman lounged against a little desk affair built into one of the walls, with a telephone on it and rows of pigeonholes above it. He saw Cole, hesitated a second as Cole moved toward the door, then sprang forward and pulled the door open.

Cole stepped in and said, "Mrs. Arndt."

"Yes, sir. Your name, please, sir?"

"Paul Cole."

"One moment, please."

Cole waited, while the doorman talked briefly on the phone. The doorman's attitude had been odd; a strange cold mixture of firmness and servility. If Cole turned out to be an expected and admissible guest, the doorman would not have acted in an offensive manner. On the other hand, if Cole turned out to be an attempted gate-crasher who was to be ousted, the doorman would not have lost his dignity by affording him a courtesy he did not deserve. It was a very odd middle ground of demeanor; Cole wondered at it, how long it had taken him to find the exact note to strike. It was too bad this doorman couldn't treat each person differently, as an individual, but of course there was no way that could be done.

The doorman replaced the phone receiver and said, "Yes, sir. That's apartment 7-H. Use the rear elevator, please, sir." He pressed a button on his little desk, and a faint buzzing sound told Cole he could now push open the inner glass door.

Beyond the doorman's domain was a broad low-ceilinged foyer with cream-colored walls and pale blue carpeting. Mobiles of bright metal hung unmoving in the corners; one of them included a square of shiny metal.

Cole stopped in his tracks. He stared at that mobile, disturbed by it, frightened by it, and not sure why. Was this something from his past, something he should know? He moved closer to the mobile, studying it, seeing himself reflected in miniature within the hanging flat square of shiny metal. What did this mean? He reached out, tentatively, and touched the cold surface of the square; the mobile trembled, giving off faint tinkling sounds, as though from a garden far away.

"The rear elevator, sir."

Cole turned his head. The doorman was standing in the inner doorway, watching him noncommittally. Cole said, "I'm looking at this. I'm not lost."

"Yes, sir." To the surprise of both of them, the doorman had been outfaced; he retired to his own area, the glass door closing slowly and silently.

But Cole was lost. This mobile...no, not the whole mobile, just this one piece of it. It reminded him of his dreams. He was still having bad dreams every night, sometimes woke once or twice to darkness, contorted and gasping on the bed as though in his dreams he had been fighting monsters. But the content of the dreams always eluded him upon awaking.

Why should this thin square of metal remind him of his dream? It was flat, thin, featureless, about a foot square, highly polished. It reflected his own face with a slight and subtle distortion that made him seem to be in the midst of writhing out of human shape. There were two small holes in it, at top and bottom, through which ran the wires that held it in its place within the mobile.

In the past, he supposed, he had been to Helen Arndt's apartment once or several times. He might have seen this mobile then, noticed this particular square. But what meaning could it have? What connection with his dreams? His impression had been, whenever any smoke or odor of a dream was left in his mind by morning, that Edna somehow figured in the dreams; what possible connection was there between this square of metal in the foyer of Helen Arndt's apartment building and Edna, the girl from that forgotten town? Or was it that this piece of metal here was only a reminder of some *other* piece of metal? But what, and with what meaning?

He felt the doorman still watching him warily through the glass. There was no answer here; he could stand here all night and find only questions. He turned away from the mobile and crossed the foyer.

At the opposite end were two elevators, and between them a broad low-ceilinged hallway. He walked down the hallway, which had mirrored walls, and at the far end were two more elevators, facing one another. He pushed the button beside one, and the door immediately slid open. He boarded, and poised his finger over the panel inside.

What was the apartment number? *No!* He *wasn't* going back to ask the doorman again! What *was* it, what *was* it, what *was* it?

Seven, seven. It was seven, seven, seven…seven H.

He pushed the button with 7 on it, and the elevator door slid shut again.

There was no sensation of riding, no sensation of movement at all. He simply stood a while in the cubicle of the elevator, and then the door slid back again, and he was on the seventh floor. He stepped from the elevator to a smallish room done in shades of green, with a mirror on one wall, and an ornate antique table bearing a vase filled with flowers. The room smelled of flowers, like a mortician's.

There were two doors in the wall opposite the elevators, and one door in each side wall. The door to the left was marked H. He rang the bell, and after a minute the door opened, and Helen Arndt was smiling at him, saying, "You made it. Come in, come in, you must be starved."

"I guess I'm late."

She closed the door after him, saying, "Don't think a thing of it. Honey, give me your coat, and we'll go right on in and eat. Your timing couldn't be better, dinner is just this minute ready."

She took his coat and said, "I won't be a minute," and went away. He stood uncertainly, looking around.

He had entered on a kind of low balcony with a wall on the right and a metal railing on the left. Beyond the railing, two or three feet lower than this level, was the living room, a long sprawling affair dotted with intricate antique chairs and dark-wood tables and cabinets and small Persian rugs scattered over a gleaming hardwood floor, with closed French doors at the far end. A few feet away from Cole, the railing ended, and four broad steps led down to the living room. Beyond that, at the balcony level, an archway led deeper into the apartment.

In a minute, Helen was back, coming through the archway. She was wearing something loose-fitting, not quite a dress and not quite a robe, very Oriental in feeling. She seemed heavier than in the suit she'd been wearing at the office that day, but at the same time she seemed somewhat younger. He guessed her age to be somewhere in the middle forties.

She held her hand out to him. "Come along, honey, let's tie on the feedbag."

He wasn't pleased that she had taken his hand, but he could do nothing but accept it. She led him through another room, a smaller version of the living room, and then into the dining room, an oblong rectangle dominated by a long heavy table with two gleaming place settings opposite each other at the far end. Crystal-filled breakfronts and candelabra-topped serving tables flanked the walls. A hefty woman of about thirty was fussing with the place settings, moving a knife a little this way, a bowl a little that way.

Helen said, "All right, Ruth," and the maid smiled briefly and left the room, going through a swinging door at the far end.

Helen said, "Sit down, honey. Right over there."

Cole's discomfort was steadily growing. The doorman, the low-ceilinged foyer, the silent elevator, the furnishings of this place, the maid, the heavy cordiality of Helen Arndt... and the square of shiny metal. Sitting down, he said, "I've been here before, haven't I?"

"Well, of course!" Sitting across from him, she smiled possessively. "Does it all look familiar?"

"No, but down—"

The maid came in, with two small glasses of tomato juice. She left again, and Helen raised her glass, saying jokingly, "Cheers."

"Oh. Cheers."

From then on, throughout the meal, there was little chance to talk. He wanted to ask her about that mobile downstairs, though now he was pretty sure it wasn't the mobile itself that disturbed him but something else from his past that the mobile was reminiscent of, but he would have to wait till after dinner. The maid was constantly in and out, bringing and taking plates, and Helen was chatting about the current theatrical season, about which Cole knew nothing.

The meal was delicious, but his discomfort kept him from enjoying it properly. He didn't like being waited on— he wasn't in a restaurant now—and whenever he glanced across at Helen her eyes were gleaming at him. The expression in her eyes bore no connection with the idle chatter coming from her mouth.

There was a complex sort of pastry sculptured with
berries for dessert, and when it was finished Helen told the
maid, "We'll have our coffee in the living room."

"Yes, ma'am."

"Come along, Paul."

She took his hand again, as she preceded him to the
living room. On one side, two long sofas were angled
together in a V, with a triangular coffee table between
them, and this is where they sat, each on a sofa. The maid
brought in a serving tray, holding a rococo coffee pot and
sugar bowl and creamer and demitasse cups. Helen poured,
and the moment was full of incongruities; the movements
and symbols implied tea and yet they were drinking coffee;
they implied an attitude of restraint and serenity contra-
dicted by Helen's feral eyes and loose-fitting Oriental gown.
Helen said, "That's all, Ruth," and the maid went away for
the final time.

"Now. Tell me about yourself. What have you been doing
the last few weeks?"

"Not very much. I'm collecting unemployment insurance."

"And your memory's just the same as ever. What did
Doctor Edgarton say?"

"I had X-rays a couple of days ago. He said we'd find out
after that."

"I have utter faith in that man. Just put yourself totally in
his hands."

"I will."

They talked a while longer, but the conversation never
became easy and relaxed. Mostly, she asked him questions
about his activities; some things he told her and some things
he hid. He told her about Nick and the party and the fight,
but not about Rita. Even when he was making full answers
of her questions, he was slow and hesitant, with little gaps
and silence between his words.

They finished their coffee, and the conversation, fal-
tering to begin with, died away. They sat looking at one
another a while, Helen half-smiling, her legs tucked up

under her on the sofa, her hands at ease in her lap. Cole was acutely embarrassed; the apartment seemed full of echoing silences. Somewhere, in some cubicle, the maid was still present. All he could think to talk about was the bad weather they'd been having lately, and even silence was better than that.

It was Helen who finally broke the silence, getting to her feet in a solid and graceless movement, saying, "Would you like to see my view? Come along."

He went with her, across the living room to the French doors. She pulled two of them open—the movement was reminiscent of her earlier pouring of the coffee—and stepped out onto a narrow empty terrace. "In the summer I have furniture out here, and plants along there. Look."

They stood at the brick railing and Cole looked out at her view. The terrace faced south; he looked over the roofs of a few low buildings, then past and among other tall apartment buildings like this one, and far away there was a red and yellow glow that must be midtown.

"On a clear day," she said, laughing, "you can see Central Park, way down to the right there." She suddenly embraced his arm, pressing herself against him. "Brrr, it's cold! No time of year for terraces. Come on back in."

She released his arm, but took his hand again, and they went back inside. She shut the doors and laughed in a forced and artificial way. "No Eskimo blood in me! Do you remember how to make a highball, dear?"

"I don't know, I'm not sure."

"Come along. I'll make the first, and you watch how it's done."

She led him to an anonymous piece of furniture against a side wall. It was mahogany, very broad, about four feet high, with squarish doors on the front. More than anything else, it looked like a TV-radio-phonograph console. But it turned out to be a bar; she opened doors and revealed ranks of bottles, ranks of glasses, and a small refrigerated compartment for ice cubes. "I like ginger ale," she said, "but you never did. You liked vichy water. So here's some specially for you. Now. Pay attention, honey, from now on this is your job."

He paid attention. She told him what she was doing as she was doing it, and it wasn't complicated at all. Into a glass she put ice cubes and whiskey and mixer, that was all. Ginger ale for herself, soda water for him. She handed him his glass with a flourish, and they went back to the V of sofas again.

This time she sat next time him on the same sofa, though a foot or two away. She sipped at her drink, then put it down on the coffee table and said, "You're awfully quiet, sweetie. Cat got your tongue?"

Cole was quiet because his embarrassment and discomfort hadn't lessened at all. They had, in fact, increased, when she'd grabbed his arm out on the terrace. But now he *had* to say something, so he cleared his throat and said, "I guess I just don't have anything to talk about."

She shook her head, a sad smile on her lips. "I hope you break out of this pretty soon, sweets," she said. "I've got a lot invested in you. I mean, aside from humanitarian considerations, of course."

"Invested?" He frowned, not knowing what she meant; did he owe her money?

"It's like talking to a babe in the woods. Honey, you're beginning to make me feel absolutely ancient. The first thing you know, I'll start mothering you, which would be embarrassing for you and ridiculous for me. I'm not the mother type. Drink your nice drinky, it'll help you relax."

He obediently swallowed some of the highball, and she said, "I'll tell you what I mean by invested. Most of my clients aren't wee beginners, you know. At this very moment, I have twelve clients performing on Broadway." She looked at her watch, and nodded. "Yes, at this very moment. Beginning act three, most of them. And then there's television, and motion pictures, and God knows what all. My client list is first-rate, honey, believe me."

"Then why were you my agent?"

"That's what I'm going to tell you. Every once in a while,

dear, I take on a newcomer, such as you. It's a calculated risk, a speculation. If I'm right about you, and you eventually make it very big, you should be more than grateful to me, and it should be very difficult for some other nasty agent to steal you away from me. You see? In the early years, I handle you at a loss, but if you turn out to be a winner, then it all comes back with interest."

"I didn't know that."

"I don't suppose," she said, "you've brought in even a thousand dollars in commissions yet, and I've spent at least twice that on you, in phone calls and lunches and God knows what all."

He finished his drink and gazed gloomily across the room. "I wish my memory would come back," he said.

"Of course you do!" She rested a hand on his arm. "Don't get feeling bad, honey, I wasn't trying to depress you. Your memory will come back, don't you worry."

"I wish it would hurry."

"Make us fresh drinks, why don't you?"

He made the fresh drinks, remembering how to do it, and irritated at being pleased by remembering, and when he was seated again on the sofa she said, "Have you seen Robin Kirk at all?"

"Robin Kirk?" He remembered the name vaguely, from somewhere. Nick had mentioned it, or maybe Rita, he wasn't sure.

"Your teacher," she said. "Acting teacher. You haven't been in his class for a year or more, but I'm sure he'd be glad to see you again. He might even be able to help you."

"I'd forgotten about him."

"You go see him. I tell you what, I'll call him tomorrow and tell him about you. All right?"

"All right, sure." He smiled for the first time since coming into this apartment: here was something to do. At least one more day when he'd be able to escape the routine, get out of the apartment. He'd go see his old acting teacher, yes.

She patted his knee. "We're all rooting for you, honey," she said. "Doctor Edgarton, and Robin, and me. We're all in your corner." She smiled at him and squeezed his knee.

His pleasure was scattered by confusion; he wasn't sure what was expected of him. Did she want him to go to bed with her? He'd been avoiding even thinking the thought, because if that was what she wanted he had no idea what to do about it. He didn't want to go to bed with her, he was sure of that much, but how could he avoid it without getting her mad at him?

But then she took her hand from his knee, and leaned back on the sofa, and began to talk again. She started to tell him stories about her other clients; clients she had stolen from other agents, clients other agents had stolen from her, clients who had gotten in trouble with Equity or with the law or with each other, clients who had been—like Cole— speculative gambles taken on before their subsequent rise to success, clients who drank too much, clients who played around too much. From time to time she told him to drink up, or to go make fresh drinks, and then on she would go with the stories. There were no uncomfortable pauses now, because she didn't wait for him to add anything to the conversation, and all he had to do was sit and listen.

For a while, even just listening was difficult, because with the thought of sex in his mind had come the memory of Edna. He was alone with Helen now just as he had been alone with Edna, the two of them sitting together on a couch in a living room, alone, but other than that there was no similarity between the occasions at all. With Edna he had *wanted* sex. And would Helen, under any circumstance at all, shyly ask to have the lights turned out?

Thinking about Edna always irritated him. He felt angry and impatient with himself whenever that girl came back in this mind, and she was forever returning. Sometimes, cleaning the apartment, he would suddenly realize that his fantasies about his past and future had somehow altered into fan-

tasies about Edna. Sometimes, seeing a good-looking girl on
the street or the subway, he would find himself thinking
about Edna, remembering that evening alone with her and
the other evenings when he'd walked her home and necked
with her a while on her front porch. Everything else from
that time was fading and fading; all but Edna. It infuriated
him. What did he care about Edna? Nothing. Why should
his mind, with so many things of more importance to exert
itself over, constantly fill itself with useless imaginings about
that girl from the one meaningless period of his life?

It was his irritation over the presence of Edna in his mind
once again, and a desire to wash her away into oblivion, that
made him down the highballs faster, and make the fresh
ones increasingly strong. And it did, after a while, begin to
work; the memories of Edna faded slowly from his mind,
and he found that he was concentrating with unusual lucidity
on Helen's stories. He was enjoying the stories, too, and
enjoying being here. He was relaxing, after having been so
tense for so long, and he couldn't remember ever having felt
so pleasant and so content.

Helen's stories, as time went on, began to change slightly,
to alter, to become steadily more sexual. Her expression, of
face and wording, were becoming…roguish. Her hand was
more frequently on his knee.

He didn't care. He wasn't aroused at all, felt no stirrings
of desire; his only feeling was contentment. A slight loss of
equilibrium when he made the frequent trips for fresh drinks
didn't bother him; he found it funny.

He was beginning to lose the thread of her conversation.
His concentration, which had seemed to get clearer and
stronger than ever for a while, had now dwindled away completely. But he laughed whenever she laughed; not merely
to be polite, but because he felt like laughing.

Time seemed to rush by, faster and faster. She told him,
at one point, that her twelve clients currently acting on
Broadway were all taking their curtain calls right about now.

Later—he didn't know how much later, maybe a few seconds or maybe a few weeks—she cleaned close to him, her shoulder against his arm, and winked at him as she told him her twelve clients were undoubtedly all in their trundle bed by now. "Or somebody's trundle bed," she said, and winked again, and squeezed his knee. He laughed, because she was smiling, and because he felt like laughing.

A while later, a physical problem came along to mar his contentment. He tried to ignore it a while, but it just got worse, so finally he turned his head and whispered, "Bathroom."

"Gotta go wee-wee?"

He nodded solemnly. She nodded to him, and looked judicious, and said, "Come, I'll show you the way." She spoke with exaggerated care.

He had trouble getting to his feet, which struck them both funny. They laughed, leaning on each other, and moved across the living room. Cole murmured to himself, "I'm pretty drunk." He nodded; he didn't mind being drunk at all. There was no longer anything to worry about.

She said, "What? You said something, honey?"

"I'm drunk."

"Lord, so am I."

They moved from room to room, Helen switching on lights as they went, till they came to a bedroom, a huge square room dominated by a double bed covered with a purple quilt. She pointed unsteadily at a door beyond the bed. "Right through there. All the comforts of home."

"Thank you." He made a comic bow, and smiled blearily.

All at once she embraced him, folding her arms around him and kissing him hungrily. He smiled through the kiss, thinking it was funny, and closed his arms around her because he was afraid of losing his balance.

"Hurry back. You hear?" Her voice was a husky whisper.

"Yes, ma'am."

He made it around the bed and through the door to the

bathroom. He found the light switch beside the doorway, clicked it on, and shut the door.

He was longer than he'd expected to be, because his coordination was bad. The light was very strong in the bathroom, reflecting from coral tiles all around him. As he stood there, he felt the first twinges of a headache, and squinted. But he still wasn't thinking clearly.

When he came back to the bedroom, she was supine on the bed, limbs spread out, fast asleep. He stood looking down at her, trying to understand why she was asleep, and trying to decide what he was supposed to do now.

He should go home, probably. He was very very drunk, and he knew it. And so was she; she'd passed out. So he ought to go home.

He sat on the side of the bed and leaned over her and mumbled, "Good night, I had a very nice time."

She stirred, and smiled, and murmured. Still more asleep than awake, she raised her arms in a slow and fuzzy movement, but the weight of her arms was too much for her; her hands slid down his chest and fell again to her side.

He felt very friendly toward her, very comfortable. He patted her cheek gently. "A very nice time," he repeated. Then he got up from the bed.

His sense of direction was gone. He wandered around the apartment a while, through all the rooms she had lit on their way to the bedroom, and discovered his coat by accident, draped over a chair in a small room containing a television set and several bookcases. He struggled into the coat, and lumbered on, and found the living room, and from there the front door. He rode down in the elevator, and walked along the mirror-lined hallway, stopping halfway to look at himself and grin. He had lipstick smeared across his face. He rubbed at it with his fingers, but didn't do much good. He gave his reflection an exaggerated shrug, and a salute, and moved on.

In the foyer, his eyes fell on the mobile, and the square of

268   DONALD E. WESTLAKE

shiny metal. A sudden rage filled him and he shouted,
"Bastard! Rotten bastard!" He ran across the foyer and
slapped at the gleaming square, and the mobile rattled and
clanged and trembled.

The doorman came, indignantly, and threw him out.

24

Across the street, something had been torn down, just recently, along the whole length of the block. Behind a temporary fence constructed of green and gray doors, tilting drunkenly, black machines and men in yellow helmets moved minutely across a plain of pulverized brick.

It was Friday, the afternoon after the evening with Helen Arndt, and Cole was on Varick Street in lower Manhattan, a street of warehouse lofts and squat old office buildings. He was on his way to see Robin Kirk, his old acting teacher.

Helen had called this morning a little after eleven. There had been an artificial brightness to her voice, and she had talked jokingly about how drunk they got together last night, and seemed somehow to be asking questions with direct statements, as though she wanted him to tell her something about last night, but he couldn't understand what. "We'll have to get together again soon, honey," she said. "And this time I guess I better not get quite so drunk. I don't want to miss anything." And she laughed, a brittle sound.

"I've got a real headache myself today," he said, not knowing what else to say.

They talked—aimlessly, it seemed to Cole—about the evening a while longer, and then she suddenly became brisk, saying, "I called Robin Kirk for you. Remember? I said I would."

"My old teacher."

"That's right. Good boy, you remembered. He said you can come by any time at all. This afternoon, if you want."

Another chance to get out of the apartment. "That'd be fine."

"He knows about your accident, so you won't have to explain anything."

"Fine."

She gave him the address and told him to be there around three; that was when Kirk's afternoon class started.

He left the apartment at two-thirty, stopping on the way to check the mailbox, and found in it a notice from the Screen Actors' Guild to the effect that he was overdue in his annual dues payment. They would give him thirty days to pay, or he could consider himself no longer a member of the union. When he saw that notice, it seemed to him as though he could feel the moorings begin to slip, as though somehow he were drifting farther and farther away from his goal rather than toward it, as though, in spite of himself, he was methodically closing off and boarding up every room and alley of his former life.

Kirk had to be able to help, that's all there was to it.

Well, here he was. He'd been walking south on Varick Street from the subway stop, looking at the house numbers, and now he knew the address should be in this block someplace, where across the street something had just recently been torn down. He looked over there, squinting in the cold sunlight—his head still ached a little—and he was angered by the machines and the men, as though they were doing their work simply to annoy him. How could he begin to remember, if they kept tearing things down? In every neighborhood he'd been to it was the same; empty buildings with the white-X'ed windows that meant they were marked for demolition, raw rust-colored holes between buildings where something had just been stripped away, steel frameworks for new buildings rising behind board fences like monkey bars for giants, as though in some enormous auditorium it was intermission and here on stage the set was being changed.

The address he wanted was in the middle of the block, on the side that hadn't yet been torn down. It was a narrower building than its neighbors, made of stone, five stories high. The first floor was a store, the display windows painted green, and with rubbish stacked in the entranceway. The windows on the upper stories were all blank and uncurtained and covered with dust.

There was a door beside the green display window. Cole pushed it open and climbed steep stairs to the third floor, where a piece of shirt cardboard tacked to a door bore the message: ROBIN KIRK STUDIO. It had been carefully lettered with a ruler, the letters filled in with a ballpoint pen.

Nothing yet had stirred Cole's sluggish memory, not the street nor the building nor the stairwell nor this sign. He opened the door and stepped into a long dim room, and still there was no feeling that he had ever been here before.

The room filled most of the third floor, unpartitioned, with grimy windows at front and back. Wooden folding chairs in rows faced the back, where a table and two chairs stood on a raised platform. There was little light anywhere except at the platform, which was lit by two standing photographer's spots at the side of the room.

The class had already begun. A dozen boys and girls in bulky sweaters and dark slacks sat near the front, down by the platform. On the platform was standing a fortyish man of medium height, wearing gray slacks and a tweed jacket with leather elbow patches. His face was not handsome but strong, lined and firm like the face of a man who spends most of his time outdoors. His brown hair was thick, and wavy, and a little too full and too long, distracting slightly from the masculinity of his face.

Cole recognized him at once; this was Robin Kirk. Images came to him of Robin Kirk on a platform, lecturing, or in discussion in a bar booth, or listening with frowning concentration as they walked together through Washington Square Park. But not this room, this was still alien; he wondered why.

Kirk was talking about emotion: "No matter how many people there are on stage, I don't care if it's tragedy or comedy or whatever, one character is always the focal point of emotion. It may shift a dozen times in the same scene, or it may stay with one character throughout a play, but there is always just one character toward whom all emotion is directed, and a part of your job is to determine which character. Who is the emotional center of this scene, and when does it shift to some other character? The amateur plays every line as though the emotional focal point was himself, but the professional knows better."

A pinched-faced girl with a black ponytail had come to the back of the room where Cole was standing, and now she whispered, "Are you going to audit this class?"

Audit meant watch, he'd learned that already from Nick. He said, "Yes."

"That's four dollars," she whispered.

"I have to pay?"

"Yes, of course."

He gave her a five dollar bill, and she whispered to him that she would bring him his change later. She had a clipboard with her, and asked him his name; when he told her, she wrote it down, and then slid silently back to the front of the room again.

Cole was irritated at having to pay; he couldn't remember anything about auditing, or that visitors to the class had to pay. He moved forward and took a seat in the last row of chairs, and watched with a feeling of mistrustfulness.

Kirk finished his lecture on emotion, and said, "Now we'll go to work. Greta? Robert? Is your scene ready?"

It wasn't. They offered excuses, too low for Cole to hear, and Kirk was obviously angry. He and the two students bickered a while, and Cole began to wonder if it was all right to smoke. He looked at the students, and then saw one of the boys smoking, so it must be all right. He lit a cigarette, and continued to watch.

The second couple Kirk chose did have their scene ready. Kirk left the platform, going over to sit at the end of the first row, and the students took his place. They were a short and stocky girl with wild black hair and beautiful brown eyes and a prominent jaw, and a tall gangly boy with a shock of carrot-colored hair and a bony nervous face. The boy announced the scene: "*The Cocktail Party*, by T. S. Eliot. Act Two. Celia and Reilly."

The two arranged the table and two chairs, and explained to the audience that the table was a desk. They sat on opposite sides of it, and began to talk. The boy's voice was a growl, unnatural and intense, much deeper than the voice with which he'd announced what they were going to do, and the girl's voice was quietly pleasant, with a hit of the rasp it would assume later in life, and slight indications of the Bronx accent she had almost completely cured herself of.

The talk they did seemed rambling and self-conscious. The boy, particularly, gestured with great wide winglike swooping motions, striving for too much emotional impact in every word. The two of them up there were like little girls walking in their mothers' high heels. Cole watched, knowing it was bad without any hint in his own mind about how to make it good, and the sense of the words drifted by him untasted.

The couple on the platform finally finished, to scattered and perfunctory applause from their classmates, and returned flustered to their seats. Kirk took over the platform again and led a discussion about what the two performers had done wrong. Each student in turn criticized the performance, and with each in turn Kirk either agreed or disagreed, but in either case amplified the student's remarks. And this part, too, stirred faint memories in Cole.

Next came the improvisation. Kirk called up two of the girls and told them they were a first-grade teacher and the mother of an unruly child whom the teacher had slapped that day. The mother had come to argue about the slapping of her child. Kirk gave them this information, and then went and sat down again in the front row.

The improvisation was even more like children play-acting in their mothers' shoes, except that the girls on the platform lacked the unselfconsciousness of children. They ranted at each other, mouthing cliché-filled dialogue and gesturing far too broadly with their hands. When it was done, there was another round of criticism led by Kirk. He wanted to know which of the girls was the emotional center at the beginning of the scene, and if the center shifted at any time, and if the girls had seemed to be aware of the emotional center throughout the scene. No one could seem to agree on where the emotional center lay, and the class ended on a note of incompleteness. Kirk told Greta and Robert they had damn well better have their scene ready next time, and dismissed the group.

Cole waited at the back of the room as the students filed out, talking together enthusiastically but quietly. At the far end of the room, Kirk sat down in one of the chairs on the platform, lit a cigarette, and rested an arm on the table. He looked tired.

When there were only the two of them left, Cole got to his feet. His chair scraped against the floor slightly as he did so, and Kirk looked up, squinting against the lights aimed at the platform. He called, "Hello?" And then, "Paul? Is that you?"

"Yes." Cole walked forward, down the aisle through the uneven rows of chairs.

Kirk didn't get up. Watching Cole come forward, he said, "Helen told me you might be around. She told me what happened to you."

Cole stopped at the edge of the platform. "I remember you," he said, "and the class. But I don't remember this place."

"This is new. We used to meet up on Carmine Street. In the basement, remember?"

"No, I'm sorry. I'd have to see it, I guess."

"It's torn down. They're putting up one of their ugly co-ops. Beehives for drones, society's cattle. Come up here and sit down."

Cole took the other chair; the table was between them. Kirk's face, seen up close, looked weaker and more tired, lined not by strength but by exhaustion. Kirk studied him a minute and said, "You're changed. The arrogance is gone."

"Was I arrogant?"

"In a good way. You were sure of yourself, proud of yourself." Kirk shrugged carelessly. "You had reason to be."

"I guess I'm not sure of myself anymore."

Kirk motioned disgustedly at the empty chairs. "Did you see what I've got this time? Not a spark in a carload. Drones with big ideas, killing time on their way from their parents' homes to their childrens' homes. I keep waiting for one of them to show me something, but they never will." He made a face and shook his head. "Do you know how many reasons there've been since you? Two. In three years, just two of them."

"Reasons? I don't know what you mean."

"You forget that?" Kirk grinned sardonically and looked out at the empty room. "You're a walking symbol of man's futility now, aren't you?"

"I'm sorry, Mister Kirk—" at least he'd remembered that much, that no one was ever permitted to call this man by his first name, but only *Mister Kirk* "—I don't remember very many things."

"You've been to a doctor?"

"I had my X-rays the other day. I don't remember what you mean about reasons, would you tell me again? If you tell me, maybe I'll remember it."

Instead of answering, Kirk got to his feet and walked to the edge of the platform, where he stood gazing down the length of the room to the dimness at the far end. After a minute, he said, "You make me uncomfortable now, Paul. Helen said she thought I might be able to do something for you, help you some way, but I don't know. There's an atmosphere of hopelessness around you, like a cloud. You come near me, and I begin to wonder what use I am. Then you ask me about my reasons, and that in a way is pretty comic."

Kirk stepped down off the platform and began to walk this way and that amid the rows of chairs. His hands were in his hip pockets, bunching up his coat-tail, and he talked as he wandered, not looking at Cole as he talked but gazing upward at the ceiling. His voice was unnaturally loud, as though he were addressing an assembly.

He said, "I am an acting teacher. Robin Kirk, professor of dramaturgy, instructor of the hopeful, tutor to tomorrow's stars, keeper of the flame, confidence man. You saw my present crop, my pitiful pupils? Not a one of these, not a single solitary one of these, will ever be an actor of the slightest talent or integrity or meaning. Not a one. But they pay me four dollars an hour to tell them they have talent, and I do it. Simply by letting them sit in this room, simply by taking their money, I tell them they have talent and promise and a brilliant future." He stopped, and looked suddenly over at Cole. "Did Marcia charge you for auditing?"

"Yes."

"She shouldn't have, I'll give you your money back." He turned away again, and roamed some more. "You'll get your money back," he told the ceiling, "though you're the one who's an actor. The rest don't get their money back ever, not even when they give up their idiotic dreams and go home where they belong. Four dollars an hour, one hour a week, thirty-two students in three classes, one hundred twenty-eight dollars a week. It keeps me alive, it keeps me alive. One hundred twenty-eight dollars a week keeps me alive. But I'll tell you something," he called to the ceiling. "If the only justification I had for keeping alive was to go on lying to those stupid drones for more money to keep alive to keep lying, I'd stop it, I'd *stop* the cycle and lie down in the gutter and die. I've got to have a better reason for living than living itself, and I do have one, and you are it, Paul Cole, you and the others, less than a dozen over the years, two in the three years since you."

Cole sat watching him, listening, trying to understand and through understanding to remember. Kirk's voice was getting louder and louder, and in his ramblings back and forth amid the chairs he was moving farther and farther away into the dim opposite end of the room. Except for the one question about money, he hadn't looked at Cole at all.

"Every once in a while," he called, walking around and around, "through that door over there comes an *actor*. Every once in a while, every once in a great great while. Not one of these pale idiots who *wants* to be an actor, can you think of anything more foolish? It's like wanting to fly, isn't it, you can or you can't and that's an end to it, wanting has nothing to do with it. You can even want *not* to fly, but if you've got the wings you'll fly, one way or another, and wanting has nothing to do with *that*."

He stopped again. He was now very near the door, standing facing it with his hands on his hips in a belligerent way. He talked now at the door, but loudly enough for Cole to hear him, with a slight echo in the words. "These young fools come in here with their feeble desires and chip away at my *life!* Like woodpeckers. What sort of a useless stupid appendix of the emotions is desire, what has desire ever done for anybody but turn him into an embarrassing fool? How can you *want* to be an actor? You are or you aren't, and ninety-nine percent of them coming through the door are *not*. But then there's the one who is."

Kirk's voice had lowered on the last sentence, so that Cole could barely hear him, and now he turned back and came walking straight toward the platform, looking directly at Cole now as he spoke: "That's what I live for, Paul, that's the reason for my existence. I sit here and wait and wait and wait, and every once in a while an actor comes through that door back there, a boy or a girl who's been an actor from the minute he was born, whether he knew it or not. They come to me, and I give them the rudiments, I give them the terms for what they already know how to do, and I give them freely from my own poor store of contacts in the theatrical world, and I watch them discover themselves, discover their own powers and the gulf that yawns between them and the poor fools sitting around them in class, and I start another scrapbook with another name at the clipping service. Did I ever tell you about the scrapbooks? I keep them on all my birds, on all the rare ones with wings; I have one for you. I'm a *midwife*, Paul, I'm a *teacher*. What do you think a teacher is?"

Kirk waited, but Cole could think of nothing to say, and shook his head.

But Kirk didn't answer the question; instead, he said, "There've been damn few of them, Paul, but they're my reasons for existence, my only only reasons. And you were one of them, I saw it in you from the very first day and saw it grow in you, the way it always does." He was standing at the edge of the platform, staring intently at Cole. "God help me," he said, "I don't see it there now."

"It will come back," Cole told him shakily. "When I get my memory back, I'll be my old self again."

"Make it soon." Kirk turned away, glaring out over the empty chairs again, and then looked back at Cole. "Will you try something?"

"What?"

"An improvisation. You remember how they work?"

"I saw one today."

"That isn't how they work." Kirk shook his head in disgust. "That's how they *don't* work. Will you try one with me? We'll see if Helen's right."

It was important to Kirk, so Cole felt he ought to try. He nodded reluctantly and said, "I don't know if I can, but I'll try."

"Good." Kirk moved suddenly with speed and determination. He came up on the platform and grabbed the chair he'd been sitting in before and carried it away, to put it over in a corner. He came back and made sketching gestures in the air. "A jail cell," he said. "Death row. Tonight at midnight they electrocute you. Your cot there, and this table and chair. A window high in the wall there, door of bars over here. I the attendant bringing you your last meal. *I* am the one guilty of the murder for which you are to die tonight, and you know it. You can't prove it, and no one will believe you, and you've given up trying to convince people. We will be alone together for just a minute now, as I bring the tray in. You won't try to attack me, because you know there are half a dozen guards just down the corridor. All right?"

Cole frowned, trying to absorb the information, which was like pieces of foam rubber. What was he supposed to do? Doubtfully, he said, "All right."

"Take a minute," Kirk told him. "Get into the character."

Cole sat pensive at the table, trying to think about it, but he could get no clue. It wasn't real. Was this supposed to have happened sometime? But it didn't make sense. Why would the attendant come into the cell alone? Why should he kill anybody, why should he be in jail? The thought of jail was frightening, with an image like quicksand. Bars, and cold rooms, and sneering faces, and squares of bright metal. What was he supposed to do?

Kirk had stepped down off the platform. Now he said, "Begin." He held up his hands, as though carrying an imaginary tray, and came up on the platform again. He said, "Your dinner. Everything like you ordered." There was a sly look on his face now, and some sort of faint accent in his words. He set the imaginary tray down on the table and stood looking at Cole.

Cole knew he was now supposed to say something, but what? He poked at the bits and pieces Kirk had told him, and finally said, "You killed—" Who? Panic filled him for just an instant, followed by annoyance. When he couldn't even remember himself, why should he ensnarl himself in sketchy absurdities? He gestured vaguely, and said "—him?" He shook his head. "Who did you kill? I don't know."

Kirk waved his hands in exasperation. "What difference does it make? Make up any details you need, I'll follow along. We'll start again." He went back down off the platform. "You ready?"

"Yes."

Kirk began the scene again, same movements and same

words and same attitude. This time, he had barely finished his speech when Cole said, "You killed him."

"Now, don't start that again."

"I—" Cole looked around miserably, and found nothing to say.

Kirk snapped out of character again and said, "You aren't *trying*, Paul. You've got to *feel* the character. He's going to die, *tonight*, for a crime he didn't commit, and the guilty one is standing there in front of him. Can't you *feel* it?"

Cole tried to feel it, but he couldn't. There was too much discomfort and worry and doubt in his real self; he couldn't believe in the condemned man at all. He shook his head and said, "I'm sorry."

"Switch the characters? I'll be the condemned man, you be the attendant, it might be easier for you."

"I'll try," said Cole.

They switched places. Kirk sat down at the chair, and slumped, his whole body registering despair. Cole went down off the platform, and did as Kirk had done. He carried an imaginary tray onto the platform and said, "Your dinner. Everything like you ordered." He tried to say it the way Kirk had done, but it sounded flat to his ears, just words droned out in a monotone.

Kirk raised his head laboriously, as though it weighed a ton. "Oh," he said. "It's you." Bitterness and despair and the cold remnants of anger were mixed in his tone and expression.

Cole put the imaginary tray down on the table, and straightened, wondering what to say next. Now was he supposed to be a murderer, and Kirk was supposed to be someone convicted of a murder that Cole had done. What would a murderer say to Kirk now? Cole had no idea, and he shook his head, giving up. "I'm sorry," he said.

But Kirk thought it was part of the improvisation. Wearily he said, "You're sorry. Tomorrow you'll be here, and I'll be nothing."

"I don't know what to do," said Cole.

"You mean you don't have the courage to do what you know you should do." Kirk glanced up at him again, and then frowned. "Are you in character or not?"

"I guess I'm not. It just isn't working."

"You can't feel these people at all? You can't *feel* the grimy damp atmosphere of the cell, the…the *guilt* between these two men? You can't feel any of it?"

Cole shook his head.

Kirk got to his feet and took out his cigarettes. His expression was irritated, his movements quick and impatient. He lit the cigarette and said, "What did you come back here for?" His voice was cold now, unfriendly.

"I thought it would help. Everywhere I go I remember more things."

"How long have you been back in town?"

"I don't know. I'm not sure."

"You don't know."

"Since before Christmas. A few days before Christmas, I think."

"Two weeks? Three weeks?"

"I guess so."

"You've see your friends? Your neighborhood? Your apartment?"

"Yes."

"And now you've seen me. And I've given you a basic exercise." Kirk was glaring at him, spitting out his words. "And what's the result? Is it all coming back in a flood?"

"No, not in a flood."

"Not at all. There's nothing in you now. What did you come back here for, to bring me pain?"

"No. No, I—"

"I can't talk to you any more now. I have people to see. I'm sorry you can't stay here, but I have to lock up when I leave."

"I'm sorry I couldn't do it."

"That's all right, it's not your fault." But the words were said with mechanical rapidity; Kirk was already starting for the door.

Cole followed him. It was like Rita again, but this time he didn't entirely blame himself. Kirk knew what had happened to him, why should he expect him to be the same? Why treat him like this? Why so cold and bitter?

Kirk held the door for him, and then closed and locked it. Cole had already started down the stairs, but moving slowly, hoping Kirk would get over his irritation. They went down the stairwell together in silence, and out to the late afternoon sun and the bitter cold of the street. Kirk said, brusquely, "I wish you a speedy recovery. Goodbye, Paul." He turned and strode away, his hands in his overcoat pockets.

Cole stood a while on the sidewalk, watching the movement of the wreckers across the street. The machines made grinding clanking noises, and the men shouted to one another. The sun was bright, making Cole squint, but the air was like ice and smelled of snow.

Kirk hadn't given him his four dollars back after all.

Cole walked slowly northward, toward the subway station. None of it, back there in the big room where Kirk held his classes, none of it had been real. It was all like the condemned man and the jail cell, fantasy and make-believe. The students were not students, but were either hopeless misfits who couldn't learn or natural actors who didn't need to learn. The teacher was not a teacher, but simply a spectator of failures and successes, grubbing a living out of the one and justifying it with the other, but influencing neither. And the subject of their gatherings in that room was itself fantasy and make-believe, level after level.

What did Kirk know? What, at bottom, did that fantastic man know? Nothing. He had left in rudeness and contempt, and why? Was it because Cole was no longer as good an actor as Kirk? No. It was because Cole was no longer wearing the coat-tails Kirk wanted to ride. That was it, pure and simple, nothing more to be said.

Except that Kirk was wrong. Knowing nothing, having nothing, being nothing, offering nothing, it should be no surprise that Kirk was wrong. He looked at Cole now and he didn't see the bright young arrogant Cole of three years ago, and in the simple illogic of his mind he concluded at once that that earlier Cole was gone forever.

Well, he's not. He's still in here, he's inside my head. He's an actor, he's a man with a vocation, a man with a talent, a man with a future. He's down inside here, and he'll come back out without your help, as strong and as full as ever. You haven't discouraged me, damn you, all you've done is strengthened me. So what do you think of that?

He walked along with rapid strides, though there was no particular place he had to go. But the physical movement of hard walking helped to bolster him, helped to keep him thinking confident and defiant thoughts, to ignore the doubts nibbling in around the edges.

25

But the feeling of belligerent self-assurance he had taken away with him from the meeting with Robin Kirk couldn't last, not without further sustenance. The periods of black depression came and went, like a slow and heavy pulse. When they came on him they drained him of all strength and all purpose, left him slumped and morose and sorrowful. He very often felt like crying at these times, and sometimes thought crying would help, would work some darkness out of his system, but the tears never came.

Helen Arndt phoned the next day, Saturday, to hear how the meeting had gone with Robin Kirk, and he was embarrassed to have to tell her it had gone badly. But she cheered him up—or tried to—saying, "Don't take it to heart, honey, that's just Robin's way. He's as emotional as if he had talent."

She asked him, too, if he would like to come over for dinner again that night, but he claimed a prior engagement, people he was supposed to meet at a Village bar, with whom he was to talk about his past. The excuse had been readied in his head for two days; he was terrified of going up to that apartment again. It embarrassed him and made him feel foolish to have a woman so obviously lusting for him, and now that she seemed to believe they had already had relations together once, he knew any subsequent time alone with her would be uncomfortable in the extreme.

His spate of traveling and visiting seemed to have come to a close, and reluctantly but inevitably he slipped once more into his routine. The first unemployment insurance check had been waiting for him on Friday when he'd returned from seeing Robin Kirk, and on Monday he cashed it at the bank. He had kept two dollars in his checking account there in order to keep the account open, and he now added twenty-eight dollars of the thirty-eight dollar unemployment insurance check to it, keeping the rest for groceries and cigarettes. The trip to the bank, and to the supermarket on Seventh Avenue, were his only journeys away from the apartment; from then on he stayed at home, working aimlessly in his two rooms and half-listening to his records. No one came by, no one telephoned. The two times he remembered to check with his answering service, there were no messages.

At night, the dreams. Sometimes now he did have vague visual memories of the dreams after awakening; the square of shiny metal was prominent, full of menace, and sometimes he seemed to remember having seen Edna's face. Edna also still came into his waking mind from time to time, as clearly and as uselessly as ever, but he'd given up trying to exorcise her; the unfaded memory of her was just one of the vagaries of his mind that he could do nothing about. Once his full memory was restored, the part of his past that had involved Edna would sink to its proper insignificance.

On Wednesday, six days after the phone had last rung, it suddenly commenced a flurry of activity; two calls the same morning. The first came while he was scrubbing the tiled bathroom floor, and for just a second he couldn't think what was making the noise. Then he hurriedly dried his hands and ran to answer the ringing, and a male voice said, "Paul Cole, please."

"Speaking."

"This is Doctor Edgarton."

The name meant nothing. Cautiously, Cole said, "Yes?"

There was a short silence on the line, and then the doctor said, "Oh! Of course, you don't remember. You came to see me two weeks ago about your head injury. Your memory problem."

"Oh. Yes, that's right. I'm sorry, I didn't remember the name."

"That's quite all right, I should have realized. I have your

X-rays. Could you come down this afternoon? Say, three-thirty?"

"What time is it now?"

"Just after ten."

"Yes, I can come down."

"Do you have the address?"

"I don't know, I'm not sure…"

"I'll give it to you again, anyway, to be on the safe side."

Cole got a pencil and a sheet of paper from the desk drawer and wrote down the address the doctor gave him. He promised again to be there at three-thirty, and hung up.

Almost immediately, the phone rang again. Cole stared at it, not believing it. Twice in a row? Could it be the doctor again, with something else to tell him?

But it was Helen Arndt. "I finally got you something, honey," she announced, immediately after his hello. "A job. If you think you can handle it, of course. It isn't much, but you'll make a hundred or so, and it is work, a fresh start for you. It's one line, all right?"

She couldn't have known it, but his answer all depended upon the timing of her call. If she had phoned during one of the times when he was feeling depressed and defeated, when the curt dismissal of Robin Kirk was smarting in him and seemed somehow justified to him, he would have refused the job, certain he couldn't handle it. But her call had come right after the silence of his days had already been broken, and this combination of calls made him full of confidence in himself. He *would* get better. He'd been home less than a month, and it would take a little time, that was all. That was all.

He said, "I ought to be able to remember one line. What is it, a play?"

"No, baby, television. A drama special, you know the type? It's one of those live-on-tape things."

"All right, I'll do it."

"Sturdy boy. Do you have a pencil?"

There were pencil and paper right in front of him, the

paper already written on. He turned it over to the blank side, picked up the pencil and said, "I'm ready."

"The studio is in the Bronx, God alone knows why." She gave him the address, and said, "Now, you're to be there next Monday, the nineteenth. Write that down, baby."

"I will."

"Monday, the nineteenth of January. Ten A.M. Bring two or three suits with you."

"All right."

"Honey, you want me to call you Monday morning? To remind you."

"No, that's all right, I'll leave myself a note."

"You've got an answering service, haven't you? Have them call you, so you don't oversleep. All right, honey?"

"All right, I will."

"How is it coming? Any improvement?"

"I don't know. Maybe a little, I'm not sure."

"You poor boy, you don't know how I feel for you. Listen, come on up this evening, we'll have steak again and everything, same as last time. But not quite so much to drink, eh?"

"Oh, uh...I'm supposed to go, I've got a date tonight already. I'm sorry, I...It's a girl named Rita, I don't know if you know her."

"Sweetie, where's your sense? Don't come flaunting your other women in my face. For Heaven's sake, honey."

"Oh, I'm sorry, I..."

She laughed, as though it were a joke, but there was something brittle in her laughter. "Never mind, honey," she said. "We'll make it Monday. You can tell me all about your first day back on the job."

There was no way out of that. He nodded reluctantly, though she couldn't see him, and said, "All right."

"Good boy. Be good tonight."

"I will."

He hung up, relieved that the conversation was finished, and sat a while longer at the desk, looking at the note he'd written. He had a job. A job in his profession, by God. He was going to act, he was going at last to do what Paul Cole was born to do.

He immediately put the note up on the wall, so he wouldn't miss the opportunity. He had forgotten all about the address on the other side, forgotten he was supposed to go see the doctor this afternoon.

The prospect of work so exhilarated him that he couldn't stay around the apartment. He put on his coat and went out, to find the first real snowstorm of the season just getting underway. Snow angled down in white regiments, battalions. It was like looking at the world through a misted window and a shredded white curtain. Cole walked through this, enjoying the fact of snow the way children do, and when he saw a theater marquee that offered two musical comedies at once he bought a ticket without a qualm. At four o'clock, when the doctor began phoning his apartment, Cole was sitting warm and happy in a theater on Sixth Avenue, bright pictures on the wall in front of him and white snow building on the roof.

26

When the doorbell rang, Cole was washing underwear in the bathroom sink. It was Friday, two days since he'd heard about the acting job and forgotten to go to the doctor's office, and already it seemed to him as though the unchanging round of his days had remained static almost forever. The ringing of his doorbell startled him the way some people are startled by bulletins on television.

He approached the door warily, drying his hands on a towel, and before he was halfway there the bell jangled again, prodded by an imperious thumb. He dropped the towel on a kitchen chair, crossed the room, and at last opened the door.

It was Helen Arndt, looking stern; her expression terrified him. Then he realized it was not to be taken seriously, she was only imitating sternness, for apparently humorous reasons.

Still, it was strong make-believe. When she came into the apartment, her high heels beat purposefully on the floor. Heavily girdled, fur coat hanging open, she was encased in a dark green suit like a medieval knight in his armor. Only the little chartreuse hat perched atilt atop her head belied the general effect; otherwise, she was as solid and intimidating as a battleship.

Once in his living room, she took a stance, right arm pushing fur coat back to put right fist on cocked right hip. "All right, sweetie," she said, her voice continuing the mock-severity of her manner, "what you need is a nurse. So here I am. Put on your coat."

Cole hadn't yet closed the hall door. He said, "What? What's wrong?"

"Remember Doctor Edgarton? The one I made you go see?"

Yes, he did. And dimly now it seemed to him he'd heard from or of the doctor more recently, but he couldn't be sure. He said, "I remember him."

"He phoned you Wednesday. Just before I did, apparently. You remember me calling you Wednesday?"

"About the job." Of course he remembered that. He read the note about it three or four times a day.

"You were supposed," she told him, ignoring his right answer, "to see the doctor Wednesday afternoon. No, you don't remember that at all, I can see it in your face." She sighed, a burlesque sigh of long-suffering martyrdom. "Well, it's not your fault, it's just the way things are."

"I was supposed to—"

"This time," she interrupted, "he did it right. He phoned *me*. Helen is to bring little Paul to see the nice doctor. All right?"

"I'm sorry if I did something wrong. I don't remember—"

"Oh, sweetie, stop that. Nobody blames you for anything. We want to help you, that's all. Now, go put on your coat like a dear boy, I have a cab waiting."

"I'll have to change my clothes, I've got these old things on."

She made a show of looking to Heaven for understanding and aid. "Then," she said, "all I can do is sit here and wait. Do hurry dear, won't you?"

"All right. I'll be right back."

There was no graceful way to leave the room. He left by fits and starts, in an excess of awkwardness, finally backing out like a chastised student leaving the principal's office. In the bedroom, he hurriedly changed to a suit and white shirt and tie, and put on his overcoat, then hurried back to the living room.

She greeted him with, "Pots in the bookcase? Is this another manifestation, sweetie, or shouldn't I mention it?"

He looked helplessly at the bookcase, full of odds and

ends, everything but books. He could see how odd it looked
to anyone else, but how in the world could he explain it? He
shrugged helplessly, and said nothing.

She waved a hand negligently. "It hardly matters. Come
along, I can hear the meter ticking all the way up here."

On the way downstairs, she took his arm and smiled brilliantly at him.

Two days had elapsed since the storm. Though the sun
was shining today, it was a weak and pallid brightness, and
there was now a permanent clamminess in the air. The sidewalks had been cleared of snow, but were wet with puddles
and gray slush, and flanked by the low dirty ramparts of
snow that had been pushed aside. Grime streaked every
passing vehicle, and the buildings seemed darker in color,
and older, and smaller. The interior of the cab smelled of
wet leather.

This was the first time Cole had ridden in a cab since the
night he'd come back to New York. This time, he was plagued
by feelings of discomfort. Helen Arndt, seated so close beside him, made him uncomfortable to begin with, but also
there was the ticking meter, which read over a dollar when
Cole entered the cab and which seemed intent on reaching
two dollars before they reached their destination. It seemed
to him that he should pay for this ride, but he couldn't really
afford the money, and in a way it wasn't fair to ask him
to pay. Left to his own devices, he would have taken the
subway.

No. Left to his own devices, he wouldn't have gotten to
the doctor's office at all. So maybe it was fair to ask him to
pay, whether he could afford it or not.

Still, when at the end of the trip Helen insisted on paying,
Cole didn't try particularly hard to dissuade her.

The doctor's office was on East 67th Street, between Park
and Lexington. It was a broad tall old apartment building,
with four separate doctors' offices on the first floor, each
with its own entrance. When they went in, Helen motioned
him to sit down while she went over to the glass hole in the

wall to talk with the nurse. Cole sat on a green leatherette sofa and looked around at the hunting prints on the paneled walls. He'd been here once before, a little more than two weeks ago, but he hardly remembered the place. Through the door in the opposite wall must be the doctor's office, but Cole couldn't visualize it. He must have gone through that door last time.

Generally, he'd grown used to such signs of his malady, and didn't brood on them. But here in this waiting room he did brood, like a patient in a dentist's outer office prodding with his tongue his aching tooth.

At least there were no other patients waiting.

Helen came over and sat down beside him, saying, "She says in just a minute." Even though they were alone, she spoke just barely above a whisper.

Cole roused himself, in an effort to be polite. "Thank you for bringing me. I would have gone on forgetting."

She petted his hand and gave him again the brilliant smile. "I take a special interest in you, Paul, you know that."

There was nothing to say. Cole smiled awkwardly, and looked away from Helen's bright eyes.

The nurse leaned out of her cubicle across the way to say, "You may go in now." She had a harsh British accent, as though she'd lost her original accent and was trying to re-create it from memory.

Helen took his hand again, saying, "I'll come in with you for just a minute."

"All right."

She continued to hold his hand as they crossed the room, but let go just as they entered the doctor's office.

Doctor Edgarton was again behind his desk, behind his tortoiseshell glasses, behind his faint and secret smile. He hesitated, then rose behind the desk and said, "Helen. How nice to see you again."

"Well, I brought him for you."

"So you have." He directed the smile at Cole. "You forgot me, I see."

"I'm sorry, I—"

"There's really nothing to apologize for, Paul. I know that, if anyone does. Sit down, why don't you? Take this chair here."

Helen said, "Shall I wait outside?" Clearly, she wanted to stay.

Cole didn't want her around now; the thought of her presence while he talked with the doctor made him tense. So he felt relief when the doctor said, "Really, Helen, you'd do better not to wait at all. This session may take some little time."

"Oh." She glanced at Cole, and away. "Well, I'll get back to the office, then."

Smiling his secretive smile, the doctor said, "Good idea, very good."

To Cole, Helen said, "You must call me. Promise?"

He nodded. "All right. I will."

"And do *not* forget the job on Monday."

"No, I won't. I've got notes up."

"Fine. Well, I must be off. Goodbye, Doctor."

Behind the desk, he smiled and bowed. "A pleasure to have seen you again."

Helen seemed to hesitate, her smile doubtful, then left, closing the door behind her. The doctor sat down behind his desk and turned his smile on Cole, saying, "A fine woman, Helen. A trifle…acquisitive. But a good friend, a good friend."

"Yes."

The doctor picked up a long slender yellow pencil and tapped it against a cream-colored folder on his desk. "Your X-rays," he said.

Cole looked at the folder. In there were photographs of the inside of his head, photographs of the city in which he used to live and at the gates of which he now was camped.

"The X-rays," the doctor went on, "were helpful, somewhat helpful. But more is needed."

"Whatever you say, Doctor."

"Yes." He reached for a slip of paper. "I have some questions first, this won't take long. I'm going to ask you about symptoms, current symptoms. Do you have frequent headaches?"

"No."

"Any headaches at all?"

"No. None at all."

"Fainting spells?"

"No."

"Do you get drunk easily? More easily than normal?"

"I don't think so. I don't know for sure."

"Do you find you are very irritable at times, excitable, prone to sudden rages?"

"I get irritable sometimes, because I can't remember things."

"Of course. Do you have trouble getting sleep at night?"

"Not much."

"Is your sleep untroubled?"

"I have bad dreams. But I can't remember them when I wake up."

"I see. Do you really want to remember your past?"

"What? I've *got* to."

"Of course, but do you *want* to?"

"Yes."

The doctor paused, tapping his pencil on the desk, and then said, "Would you take a truth serum?"

"A what?"

"I want to try narcoanalysis on you. Sodium amytal. It may open your memory a bit, at least temporarily, and it may tell us how much of your memory loss is physical and how much is subconsciously desired. If any. Will you do it?"

"If it's going to help…"

"I don't know if anything is going to help. What has happened to you is something called concussion. I can't tell you, no one can tell you, if the condition is going to improve at all, or if so when. Since the concussion must have taken place a few months ago at least, I can tell you for sure that you won't die from it, but that's all we can be sure of. Your memory may come back, or it may get worse, or it may remain just as it is now. I can't be sure, or even advise you to any great extent, except to caution you to get enough sleep always and to limit your intake of alcohol, and of course to tell me of any change in your physical condition. In the meantime, all I can do is observe you and try to find out if there are any other factors at work in your memory loss in addition to the concussion."

"It may never get better."

"I'm sorry to have to tell you that, but it is a possibility."

Cole sat shaking his head, trying to fit this new fact in with everything he'd done in the last few months, the possibility that he had been struggling all along for an unattainable goal.

The doctor took off his glasses. Without them he seemed more human, more compassionate, but also more fallible. He said, "If the thought of self-destruction is occurring to you now, or if it occurs to you in the future, cast it firmly aside. You are far from totally disabled. If your memory doesn't improve, you will always have to make special provisions for it, leaving notes in conspicuous places and so on, avoiding any occupation which demands a lot of travel, but other than that your life can be full and productive as anyone's."

Cole touched his fingers to his temple, and said, "But I'm an actor."

The doctor shook his head. "No, you're not. Not now. I'm sorry to be this blunt with you, but these are facts you'll have to face sooner or later anyway. Memory is the actor's one basic tool. He needs it to learn his role, for one thing. For another, from what I understand of the acting method popular today, it requires the actor to simulate a particular emotion by recalling an actual incident in his own past in which he felt that emotion in reality. In essence, you have no past to draw upon."

"But—they said…"

"Who said? What did they say?"

"All the people I've met since I came back. They said I was an actor, a real actor. I had a, a vocation, to be an actor. It's what I'm supposed to be."

"If your memory comes back, it's most likely what you will be. But only if, and I wouldn't depend on it too heavily if I were you."

Cole shook his head, rejecting the words.

The doctor got to his feet. "Will you take the truth serum? That's a misnomer, truth serum, but we won't go into that. Will you take it?"

"Yes. All right."

"Then come along."

The doctor took him to another room, where there was a high gray leather cot. Cole lay on this, suitcoat off and left shirtsleeve rolled up, and the doctor injected the needle into his arm. A plastic tube led from the needle to an inverted bottle, like a blood plasma bottle, but the fluid in this was almost colorless, with only a faint rose cast to it.

The doctor talked all the time now, explaining what he was doing every step of the way, a complete reversal of his earlier role as silent listener. Cole wondered at it, trying to understand, and the doctor's voice droned on, and drowsiness came down on Cole's mind, like green shutters slowly closing, leaving only the thinnest crack of light, in which the doctor's voice throbbed like the sea.

"Can you hear me, Paul?"

The question was abrupt, and louder than the droning that had come before it, but Cole didn't mind. He said, "Yes."

"Will you tell me your name?"

"Paul Edwin Cole."

"You were hit on the head, weren't you?"

A twinge of nervousness came and went. "Yes."

"What hit you?"

Cole thought about that. The question intrigued him, and he searched around in his mind for the answer. He was surprised when he didn't find it. "I don't know," he said, the surprise in his voice.

"Were you in an automobile?"

"I don't—I don't know."

"Did someone hit you? Were you hit by a person, Paul?"

The twinge of nervousness flickered again, and his hands moved slightly.

"Lie perfectly still, Paul. Don't move your hands."

"All right." He didn't mind at all; it was easier to lie still anyway.

"Were you hit by a person?"

"I'm not sure," he said. That whole compartment was blank; he was still surprised that it was. He knew he'd been hit on the head, but nothing about it at all.

"Are your parents living, Paul?"

"No, they're not."

"Neither of them?"

"No."

"When did they die?"

Another surprised "I don't remember."

"Do you remember their funerals?"

"A little bit."

"Which funeral do you remember, your mother or your father?"

"I don't know which one. It was in the spring, and the grass was wet."

"Did you get along with your parents?"

"I guess so."

"You aren't sure?"

"I don't remember."

"Were you happy in the sixth grade?"

"The sixth grade?"

"Do you remember the sixth grade? What was your teacher's name?"

"No, I don't remember."

"Do you remember what she looked like?"

"No."

"What about high school? Were you happy in high school?"

"I guess so."

"Tell me what you remember about high school."

"Long corridors. Books with shiny paper."

"What was the name of your high school?"

This time, it was frightening. He reached for the name and it wasn't there. He reached and reached, and picked up a different fact instead: "The colors were garnet and gray."

"What colors?"

"The school colors. Garnet and gray. Garnet is dark red, like maroon."

"Do you want to remember high school, Paul?"

"Yes, sure."

"Do you want to remember your mother and father."

"Yes, I don't know—I don't know why I can't."

"Because you were hit on the head."

"But I can't remember!" He was becoming agitated, more frightened. He felt as though he were sinking.

"All right, now, Paul, take it easy. Just rest a minute."

There was silence for a while, and the agitation went away, and left him feeling relaxed and pleasant. His eyes were open, and he could see the ceiling and a window. The room was dim; it was like being underwater. He found himself smiling.

The doctor's voice came back: "What did you do this morning, Paul?"

"I cleaned the apartment."

"What did you do yesterday afternoon?"

"I went for a walk."

"What did you do New Year's Eve?"

"I went to a party. In Brooklyn."

"What was your host's name?"

"Crawford."

"What was Crawford's first name?"

"I don't know."

"Did you ever know?"

"Yes."

"Would you like to know again?"

"Yes, I would."

"Crawford's first name is Harry. Now you know it. Is that right, is it Harry?"

"Harry? Is it?"

"I asked you, Paul."

"I don't know. Harry? I don't think it's Harry."

"All right. Where were you Christmas Eve?"

"Nick came over, and we went out to meet people, and I met Rita."

"Is Rita your girl?"

"She used to be."

"She isn't any more?"

"I made her feel bad. Because I couldn't remember her."

"Did you want to remember her?"

"Yes."

"Would you like to marry her?"

"No."

"Does she want to marry you?"

"No."

"Where were you two months ago, Paul?"

"In the town."

"What town?"

"Where I was working to get the money to come to New York."

"You were stranded in a town?"

"Yes."

"This is after you were hit on the head."

"Yes, that's right."

"Where did you work?"

"In a tannery."

"What did you do there?"

"I loaded and unloaded freight cars."

"Did you like that?"

"Yes."

"Did you like it better than acting?"

He felt a slight tension again, and frowned. "It's a different thing," he said.

"In what way, a different thing?"

"I liked it because it filled the day."

"Then why do you like acting?"

"It's what I do." The tension was resolved; he relaxed again.

"You still want to be an actor?"

"I *am* an actor."

"But do you want to be an actor?"

"Yes."

"You're sure."

"Yes."

"What was the name of the town where you were stranded?"

"I don't remember."

"You have bad dreams, don't you?"

"Yes."

"What are they about?"

"Sometimes, Edna. Sometimes, the square of shiny metal."

"Just a minute. Edna. The square of shiny metal. What square of shiny metal?"

"They want to know if I ever saw it before."

"Who?"

"They." He shook his head. "I'm getting cold."

"I'll turn the heat up. How large is this square of shiny metal?"

"All sizes. Sometimes it's little and I can hold it in my hands. Sometimes it's a wall and I can't climb over it."

"But you want to climb over it?"

"Yes."

"And someone wants to know if you ever saw it before. Did you ever see it before?"

"I don't know! I don't know!"

"Paul! Stop that!"

He subsided. He'd been thrashing, and now his left arm

hurt. Slowly the pain went away, slowly his upset lessened, and he relaxed again.

The doctor said, "Tell me about Edna."

"I took her to the movies sometimes."

"When you were in high school?"

"No. In the town."

"Oh, in the town. You knew Edna in the town, when you were working in the tannery."

"Yes."

"Was she your girl?"

"Yes."

"Did she want to marry you?"

"Yes."

"Did you want to marry her?"

"Yes."

"Then why didn't you?"

Cole frowned. The answers had been easy and obvious, yes and yes. He hadn't had to think about them, and he hadn't been surprised by them. But now he was surprised. He said, "Because I was coming to New York."

"Couldn't Edna come to New York?"

"I didn't think of it that way."

"What way did you think of it?"

"Just to get out of that town, and come back. Not that it meant anything."

"Didn't you know you were in love with Edna?"

"No."

"When did you find out?"

"I don't know. Right now, I guess."

"Well, well. You mean you didn't know that before?"

"No."

"Now that you know, are you going to ask her to marry you?"

"I don't know." There was confusion in his mind, and a heavy grating shifting, like great blocks of granite grinding away under pressure.

"Are you glad to know this now, that you love Edna?"

"I don't know. I guess so." It seemed as though the ceiling was getting lower; he wasn't at ease anymore; this wasn't calm and pleasant anymore.

"Were you trying to hide your feelings about Edna from yourself?"

"No. I didn't know about it."

"I see. Do you remember about the square of shiny metal now?"

"Remember what?" Trailing strands of fright touched him, making him quiver.

"What does the square of shiny metal mean?"

"I don't know."

"Why do you dream about it?"

"It frightens me."

"Why does it frighten you?"

"I don't know. I wish they'd take it away."

"Who?"

"The men!"

"What men?"

"*I don't know!*"

"Is it your father, Paul? Is he the one with the square of shiny metal?"

"No. No."

"Is it Edna's father?"

He was calm again now, these questions were meaningless. "No."

"Well, never mind. Would you like to work in the tannery again?"

"Yes."

"What about your acting career?"

He frowned, not understanding the question. "What?"

"Do you still want to be an actor?"

"Yes, sure."

"Which do you want most, the job in the tannery or to be an actor?"

"It isn't the same thing. I can't answer that, it isn't the same thing."

"Yes, of course. You're right. Tell me, Paul, do you think your memory will come back?"

Something cold blew across the side of his neck; there was somberness in his chest. "I don't know," he said. But then, because it didn't matter really what he revealed, he said, "I don't think so."

"Why don't you think so?"

It was an effort to breathe. He said, "Because good things don't happen."

"Never, Paul?"

"Sometimes they do."

"All right, Paul, I guess that's enough for now. You're going to take a nap now, and when you wake up we can talk some more."

"All right."

The doctor did something with the needle in Cole's arm, and the green shutters closed all the way.

27

When he awoke, he was still on the leather cot, but now he was alone in the room. He sat up and stretched, feeling physically good, rested and relaxed. It was like waking from a summer afternoon nap under a tree; he even felt thirsty, the way you do when you take a nap outdoors in the summertime.

He remembered everything the doctor had asked him, everything he had answered. A lot of foolishness about mothers and fathers, high school and all that. The doctor was trying to make him fit some sort of psychological cutout, that's all it was. But he remembered his answers, too, and he knew he didn't fit that cutout; the doctor must know that now, too. Still, it hadn't occurred to him before that he might be having trouble with his memory because he wanted to forget his past, and he was glad to have the question raised and answered all at once. By the things he'd said, while under the influence of the truth serum, his memory problem was proved to be entirely physical. Not even in his subconscious was there any desire to hide from his past. He wanted his memory back, and he knew that even more surely now than he'd known it before.

Then there were the other things, the questions that had bothered him when they were being asked, and that bothered him again now as he remembered them. The square of shiny metal, that filled his dreams and shadowed his days; even in his subconscious he didn't know what it was. But it was important, that he knew; otherwise, why would it bother him so? It seemed at times as though that square of shiny metal was the last clue, the one missing piece of information that would unlock his memory for good and all. But whatever it was, the knowledge about it wasn't contained in his head, not anywhere that he could find it.

Whatever you lose, you need what you lost to help you find what you lost. In the pattern in his head, it seemed that he had to know about the square of shiny metal in order to get his memory back, but he would have to get his memory back before he could know about the square of shiny metal. Except that he couldn't really be sure that the square of shiny metal meant anything at all; it was just a feeling he had, tinged with fear and a sense of something looming over him.

And there was one more question that had been raised. Edna.

Was *that* why he couldn't get her out of his head, why she had confused his mind that time when he was with Rita? Of everything he had seen and known and been occupied by in that town, only Edna remained with any clarity at all in his mind. Because he was in love with her?

But that was nonsense, it had to be. She was awkward, nervous, shy, a frail and bony bundle of jitters, plainfaced and dull. She had no sophistication, and only what passes among the uncritical for an education. She was not beautiful, she was not smart, she was not strong, she had no connection with his past or his interests or any part of his world.

He knew what it was. He felt guilty about her, because of the way he'd treated her there at the end. And he did feel a sort of protective tenderness toward her, as being someone possibly even less equipped to cope with reality than he was in his present state. And he supposed he still had some residue in him of the small cramped lust he had felt toward her in their few unsatisfactory sessions together. Guilt, and tenderness, and a trace of physical desire; he had mixed the ingredients inside his head, and somehow had convinced himself all unknowingly that the resultant mixture was love.

Well, it wasn't. It was guilt, and it was tenderness, and it was the dregs of lust, but it was not love. It was not love because it *couldn't* be love. Where did love for Edna fit in with any of his desires and any of his potential? Nowhere. Nowhere.

It would be absurd to think of *marrying* Edna. To begin with, he was in no condition to marry *anyone* now. And besides, what about after his memory came back? On the day his memory was full and strong again inside his head, he would look at Edna and she would be nothing to him but boredom and embarrassment; even guilt and tenderness and lust would be washed away.

And the memory *would* come back. Some of the doctor's questions had tipped him over into a feeling of depression there toward the end, so when the doctor had asked him if he thought he would get his memory back he had said no, but that hadn't been a true statement of his feelings, truth serum or no. That had been the voice of his depression, that was all, and his depression couldn't be relied on to produce any sort of coherent or intelligent response to anything.

Why shouldn't his memory come back? Its loss was purely and entirely a physical matter, that he knew for sure now, and the doctor himself had admitted that in concussion cases there was no telling what might happen. The doctor couldn't say for sure one way or the other whether his memory would come back or not; he couldn't even *guess*.

It was only partial amnesia, after all. It wasn't as though his brain had been wiped clean, it hadn't been. He recognized places from his past life, and people; he remembered incidents. There were still some threads of memory uncut, so there was no reason to believe he couldn't pull those threads and eventually drag the rest of his memory out into the light as well.

This was Friday. On Monday he would go to his first acting job since coming back to New York. That very fact in itself, the very motions of going through the actions of his profession, might be all he would need to give his memory that first strong jolt that would set it rolling and trundling down out of the darkness and into the light.

The door opened, and he looked up, startled, to see the doctor peering in at him. The doctor said, "Ah, you're awake. Come on in here."

"All right." He got up from the cot and went over through the doorway into the office. The lights were on in here, and the world behind the window was dark. The doctor had gone over to his desk and seated himself there, watching Cole in waiting silence.

Cole said, "Can I get a glass of water someplace?"

"Through there, there's a sink. You might want to throw some cold water on your face, too."

"I think I will."

He crossed the office diagonally to the other door, and went through into a small dim room full of glass-fronted cabinets. He switched on the light, and saw marked bottles in rows in the cabinets, and some machines on wheels, and a sink with a drinking glass standing on it between the faucets. He drank some water, scrubbed his face, and dried face and hands with paper towels from the dispenser above the sink. Then he went back to the office, and at the doctor's gesture, sat down in front of the desk.

"Well." The doctor was smiling slightly, but his eyes were watchful. "Do you remember what we talked about?"

"Yes."

"What do you think about it all?"

"I don't agree with all of it."

"Oh? What exactly don't you agree with?"

"About my memory not coming back, and about Edna. It's just as good a chance my memory will come back as not, isn't it?"

The doctor spread his hands. "I would guess it's a smaller chance," he said, "but it would only be a guess. Based on the fact that your memory hasn't started to improve at all as yet, and it's been some time since the accident took place. I'll grant you, that doesn't mean your memory won't improve at some future date, but my guess is it won't."

"I'd rather guess the other way."

"By all means. I think you should. You mentioned the girl, Edna?"

"Yes. I told you I was in love with her, but that isn't right. I feel guilty about her, because of the way I walked out on her, and I guess I feel sorry for her, because she's…because of what she's like. She's very nervous, and self-conscious."

"I see. Guilt and pity, not love."

"And, sex a little bit, too, I guess."

The doctor nodded. "And now," he said, "about this matter of the square of shiny metal."

"I don't know what that is. I dream about it sometimes, but I just don't know what it is."

"It seemed to agitate you at the time. Do you feel agitated now?"

"No," Cole said truthfully. "I feel…relaxed."

The doctor smiled. He remained silent, watching Cole, but Cole was on to that trick, and said nothing. They both waited, watching one another, and at last the doctor sighed and roused himself, shifting position in his chair, looking away from Cole. "Well," he said. "We seem to have gone as far as we can today. But I'll want you to come back."

"All right."

"We want to watch for any change in your physical condition, any new symptoms of any kind, no matter how remote they may seem from our primary concern."

"All right."

The doctor glanced around his desk, turning his head this way and that, as though looking for something. "Well, now," he said. "My nurse has gone for the day, so I'll have to make out a receipt for you myself. Two office visits, sixteen dollars."

Cole brought out his checkbook. He made out a check, and traded it for a receipt. Then the doctor said, "I'll want to see you again relatively soon. In two weeks, say. Let me get my appointment book."

Cole waited while the doctor went to the other office. He returned with a black-bound ledger, resettled himself at his desk, and began turning the pages. "Let me see. January thirty? Yes. Excellent. That's a Friday again, two weeks from today. All right?"

"I guess so."

"I'll give you a note, so you won't forget. Do you keep a diary?"

"A diary? No."

"You should. Write in it the memorable things that happen to you each day, and jot down on the appropriate days such appointments as this one, so when that day comes around you'll open the book, and there's the reminder waiting for you."

"That's a good idea," said Cole, pleased by it. "I never thought of that."

"It might help." The doctor smiled. "At least keep you from missing appointments," he said. He extended a card across the desk. "Here's a reminder about our next. January thirtieth, three-thirty in the afternoon. If there's any change in the meantime, of course, you'll contact me at once. My number's on the card there." He got to his feet, smiling more broadly than before, and said, "I wish you the very best of luck, Paul, and I hope your optimism proves to be more prophetic than my gloom."

"Thank you."

Cole left, to find it was seven o'clock in the evening, and the air was, if anything, even colder and damper than when he'd come here this afternoon. He walked to the subway and rode it home, and stopped in at a bookstore on Sheridan Square to buy a diary. When he got home, his first entry in the diary was for next Monday, telling him about the acting job, and his second entry was on January thirtieth, reminding him of his next appointment with the doctor.

28

It would have been impossible for him to miss getting to his acting job. He had reminders everywhere; a note on the bedroom door, another on the wall over the desk, another on a wall in the bathroom, yet another on the hall door in the living room, all in addition to the reminder note in his diary and the fact that he'd asked his answering service to phone him at eight o'clock that morning, so he'd be sure to get up on time. And then, as though all of that weren't enough, the telephone rang again at five minutes past nine, and it was Helen Arndt.

"I'm glad I caught you before you left, sweetie," she said, right away. "You remember about the job today, don't you?"

"Yes, sure. I left notes up."

"Good boy. There's something I forgot to tell you last week, and it's very important. Can you remember something very very important for just today?"

"I think so," he said. He couldn't keep a trace of coldness out of his voice; her manner was too condescending.

She said, "Here's the story, honey. The way I got you this job without an audition is because of Herbie Lang. Does the name ring a bell?"

"Herbie Lang? No, I'm sorry, I don't think so."

"He hired you once before, when you were on *Silent Heart*. You remember being on *Silent Heart*, baby? The soaper."

"I know I was on it," he said, which he knew was begging the question—he *knew* he'd been on that show, from his tax forms and resume, but he didn't *remember* being on it—but her maternal condescension was irritating him, he couldn't help it.

"Well, that's where Herbie knows you from. So he knows your work, he knows you're very very good, and you got the job without an audition. But the point, honey, the point is that I didn't say anything about your little problem, do you follow me?"

"He doesn't know about my memory?"

"Not a bit, honey. You don't get jobs by announcing to one and all that your memory's gone. I didn't say anything about it, and you shouldn't say anything about it either."

"All right. I won't." He hadn't intended to, anyway, but for a different reason; it was too complicated to try to explain about his memory to everybody he saw.

"But you don't remember Herbie," she said. "That, my boy, is a problem."

"I'll probably remember him when I see him."

"Let's not take a chance on it. I'll describe him, and when you see him there, you make the first move. Go right on up to him and say how are you, Mr. Lang—you call him Mr. Lang, honey—and you thank him for the job, and let him take it from there. If he talks about the soaper, you can fake it, can't you? You were in a trial scene, as I remember. I think you were a policeman guarding the defendant, something like that."

"All right."

"Now, here's what he looks like. Short, shorter than you, of course, maybe five foot six or seven. Very young, in his twenties somewhere, but prematurely balding, you know the way? A receding hairline, a very very high forehead. It shines under those lights they have."

"All right."

"He wears glasses, with very black hornrims, and he has a round chubby sort of face, smiling to beat the band. Some people say he's gay as a jay, and some people say he's just uncommitted, and I say he ought to make up his mind pretty soon, he's been married two years now. There. Do you think you'll recognize him?"

"I think so. Short, balding, young, black hornrim glasses,

round face, always smiling. Herbie Lang, and I call him Mister Lang."

"Good boy. Now, so far as I know, there won't be anyone else there you know, but if there is just fake it. You are an actor, after all, isn't that right?"

"Right," he said, more forcefully than he'd intended. But this was confirmation of his reason for existence, his reason for struggling against the dullness of his days and the sluggishness of his memory and the pessimism of the doctor. His irritation with her was forgotten; she was his agent, and he was an actor. The fact of that relationship was enough to bolster him.

"Give me a call when it's finished, sweetie," she said. "Let me know how it works out. And don't forget about tonight. Be there about eight."

"All right, I will."

He hung up, suddenly remembering his agreement to go see her this evening, and a pall was cast on his pleasure. He'd been nervous before Helen's call, and then for a minute he had been calm and relaxed, almost like a professional, and now he was nervous again. Not because of the job this time, but because of the evening that was supposed to follow it.

All right, never mind that for now. One thing at a time. Take care of the job, and then see what could be done to get through this evening.

It was time to leave. He got an extra suit out of the closet and folded it carefully into his canvas bag; they'd said they wanted him to bring two suits, and he was wearing the other. He put on his overcoat, checked his pockets to be sure he had everything he needed, read the notes on the wall to be sure he wasn't forgetting anything else he was supposed to do today, and at last he was ready to leave. He hefted his canvas bag, grinned uneasily around the apartment—he felt uncomfortable these days if he had to go out before the place was cleaned from one end to the other—and finally he did leave, locking the door behind him.

He had a subway map, and he'd bought maps and street guides to Manhattan and Brooklyn and the Bronx, and last night he'd mapped out his route to the studio; it was with him now, folded and in his pocket, carefully drawn on a sheet of writing paper. He took it from his pocket as he walked toward the subway, refreshing his memory, and then stuffed it back again.

It was a clear day, the first in nearly a week. The sun was very high and very pale, and the sky was such a pale blue as to be almost white, but at least there were no low-hanging greasy-looking clouds, and the dank cold of the last few days had been replaced by a drier breeze whistling down from the north. It was an invigorating day, and he took that to be a good sign.

The trip was no trouble at all. He had only the one subway transfer to make, at Columbus Circle, where he picked up the train to the Bronx. It was only a three block walk from the subway station in the Bronx to the studio, and he got there ten minutes early.

The building was an old neighborhood motion picture theater, converted to television work. Boards had been put over the faces of the old marquee, and painted white, and given the legend in black: FINE ARTS STUDIOS. The building was of old brick, very grimy and ancient looking, and the row of doors leading to the lobby were gray with grime and dust.

Cole pushed through one of the doors and crossed the small lobby to another row of doors, these of wood. He went through, and found himself in a large echoing room. The movie theater seats had been removed, and so had the railing behind the last row. Movie theater floors slant downward toward the rear wall, where the screen is located, but here both slant and screen had been removed. The floor had been filled in and straightened to the level of the lobby all the way to the rear wall, and now consisted of wooden planking which rang with a somewhat hollow sound whenever people walked on it. Pipes traversed the ceiling, in a complex kind of tic-tac-toe board, with heavy spotlights suspended from them and cables wound snakelike around them. In the far right corner squatted a bulky bank of electronic equipment. Flimsy looking sets and odd pieces of furniture made little island groupings here and there around the floor, and Cole counted four television cameras standing around waiting, untended now. A group of people were clustered around a large table to the left, which was covered by a sloppy mass of papers and cardboard coffee containers and wadded napkins. Not knowing what else to do, Cole started toward them, and suddenly one of the people there spied him and came walking rapidly toward him, arms outstretched, shouting out, "Comrade!"

It was a short man. He had a receding hairline, and a round face, and hornrim glasses, and he was smiling. He came hurrying forward, and grasped Cole's right hand in both of his and pumped it effusively, saying, "Good to see you again, comrade, good to see you again."

"Mister Lang," said Cole. He said it as a statement, as a greeting, but he meant it as a question.

Apparently the answer was yes. Lang pumped his hand a few seconds longer, and then released it and grabbed his elbow instead, saying, "Get right on into makeup, comrade, today's the day we beat every speed record, depend on it. We're liable to use you before lunch, what do you think of that?"

Lang was propelling him toward a door to the left; the room it led to must be next to the lobby. Cole went along willingly, carrying his canvas bag, and Lang said, "It's good to see you again, comrade, it really is. It's been too long." He winked, and smiled broadly, and patted Cole cheerfully on the back, and left him at the doorway, calling, "See you later, comrade."

Cole went on into the room, and at first glance it looked like a barber shop, full of barber chairs. But they weren't exactly barber chairs, and the man in the white jacket who began at once to order him around wasn't exactly a barber.

He was a short and narrow-faced man, with moles on his forehead and thick dry-looking black hair. He bundled Cole out of his overcoat and suitcoat and tie and shirt, told him to sit down in one of the chairs, and said, "Right. Who are you?"

"Paul Cole."

"Paul Cole?" The man seemed baffled. "What the hell—? *No*, no, I mean in the goddamn *show*! How do I make you up if I don't know who you are in the show? What's the matter with you, you never done this before?"

"I didn't know what you meant. Nobody told me who I am in the show."

"Well, shit. That's what I say, shit. How they expect me to get anything done around this goddamn place? Shit in a bucket, that's what I say. Don't you move, you. You stay right there in that chair."

"All right."

The makeup man hurried out of the room, and Cole heard a sudden spate of shouting echo around the big room outside, and then the makeup man came bustling back in, looking indignant and harried. "You're Condemned Man," he said brusquely, and turned to the counter where the makeup was.

Condemned Man? Cole started half out of his chair, looking around wildly, as though someone were playing some sort of joke on him in very bad taste. Condemned Man? Was Robin Kirk out there? Was this some sort of joke they were pulling on him, Helen Arndt and Robin Kirk in on it together? Condemned Man!

The makeup man turned back, his hands full of tubes of makeup. He stared at Cole, still half out of the chair, and said, "Where you think you're going? You think I got all day? You think you're the only one I got to do?"

Cole stared at him. "Is this a joke?"

"What? What the hell you talking about?"

Cole was trembling now, but not from nervousness; he was trembling with anger. His hands gripped the arms of the chair, squeezing tight so the knuckles stood out white and knobby. He said, "You better tell me. Is this Robin Kirk?"

"What are you, a nut? Is that what you are, you're a nut?"

The makeup man wasn't part of any joke; that much came through clearly to Cole, and he subsided, sitting back down in the chair. "I don't know," he said, feeling as though he ought to try to explain. "It's some kind of coincidence or something."

"Don't tell me your troubles, you, I got troubles of my own. No talking now, I got to do your face."

Cole leaned his head back on the rest, and the makeup man went to work on him. The creams he smeared on Cole's face were cooling, helping to relax him further. But still, it was unnerving. Condemned Man! Sitting there, thinking of it, the coincidental connection with that improvisation of Robin Kirk's, he began to feel more and more apprehensive. He hadn't been able to do that improvisation, that bit of make believe about a condemned man in Robin Kirk's loft, but he'd ignored the implications of that failure. Was it all gone, whatever talent or ability he had had? Then what would happen this morning, when it came his turn to step in front of the television camera?

No, this was going to be different. That improvisation had been nonsensical, a piece of fantasy without beginning or end, without rhyme or reason. It had meant nothing, and it had proved nothing. This was different, this was *work*. There was an actual play, a complete and total play, not some excerpt wrested foolishly out to be performed for no reason, not some spur-of-the-moment invention without depth or purpose. And besides, what had stopped him in the improvisation? Lines, that was all. He hadn't had anything to say, there were no lines prepared. But here, today, he would have his line. One line to speak, and that was all, and it was already written down for him, with its proper place in the sequence of a planned and purposeful play. There was no reason why he couldn't do it, no reason at all.

And as for the coincidence, what of it? Condemned men weren't exactly rare in fiction; they were stock enough for

Robin Kirk to have thought of one. So the coincidence didn't mean a thing. It was a coincidence, and nothing more.

The makeup man was finishing his face as two more men came into the room. He looked at them and said, "One minute. Be with you in one minute, don't go nowhere." And then, under his breath, "So I got to work alone? When that son of a bitch gets here, I swear to Christ—" He stepped back, studied Cole critically, and finally nodded. "All right," he said. "You're done. They want your hands done, come back. If they don't say nothing, you don't say nothing."

"All right. Thank you."

But the makeup man was already snapping at one of the others to come sit in the chair.

Cole put his shirt and suitcoat on and went outside and headed toward the group of people still clustered around the big table, and once again Herbie Lang came scurrying toward him, beaming, arms outstretched, shouting, "Comrade! You look perfect! Absolutely beautiful! Come along, come along." He grabbed Cole's elbow again, and guided him over to the table and to a woman in a beige tweed suit. "Karen. Karen. One second."

She turned around, glancing with irritation at Lang and noncommittally at Cole. "Who's this?"

"Condemned Man. All right? Beautiful makeup job?"

"Gray suit," she said. "I don't like the gray suit, that light a gray. Condemned Man, it ought to be darker, more somber." She turned her head. "Harvey?"

A gaunt tall man came over, carrying a cardboard coffee container. "Something wrong?" He said it in a long-suffering way, as though he'd always known something would go wrong now, at this exact moment in time.

She gestured loosely at Cole. "Condemned Man," she said. "The gray suit. Is it too light or is it too light?"

The gaunt man studied Cole and nodded. "Too light," he said.

"That's what I thought," said the woman. To Cole she said, "Did you bring another suit?"

"Yes, it's in my—"

"What color?"

"Darker than this."

"Go try it on."

Lang had his elbow again. "Come along, comrade," he said gaily. "I'll show you the dressing room. Where's your suit?"

"In my bag, in the makeup room there."

"Oh. I'd better not go in there, Ralphy's peeohed at me. You see the stairs over there?"

"Yes."

"Up them, and first door to your right. Got it?"

Cole nodded.

"Good, kimosabe." Lang patted him on the back again, and hurried off.

When Cole went into the makeup room the makeup man spun around to glare at him, saying, "The hands? Is that it, the goddamn hands?"

Everyone was nervous, the makeup man and Lang and the woman and the gaunt man, all of them, exuding nervousness from every pore. Cole's own equilibrium was held only tenuously, and all this nervousness around him was having a bad effect on him. He pointed at his canvas bag, unable to say anything, and his hand was shaking.

"Shit," said the makeup man, and went back to work.

Cole picked up his bag and carried it upstairs and through the first door on the right. This was a barren room, with pale green walls. A row of wall lockers was stretched across the opposite wall, with a wooden bench in front of them. A middle-aged man was getting laboriously into some sort of police uniform. He nodded to Cole, but didn't say anything, so Cole only nodded back.

Cole changed quickly, and put his first suit in the canvas bag. Then he looked around, wondering where to leave the bag, and the middle-aged man said, "Just stick it in one of the lockers. Nobody'll take it."

"Thank you."

"Don't mention it."

Cole went back downstairs, and this time it was the woman who caught him first. She stopped him and stood peering at him a minute, and then nodded emphatically. "Much better," she said. "Much much better. Come along, we need Harvey's okay."

He went with her to find the gaunt man, who was now standing broodingly in an office set in the middle of the room, gazing unhappily at the desk. The woman attracted his attention and asked him if Cole's new suit weren't much better, and he said deliberately that it was. The woman was pleased, and told Cole, "All right then, you find yourself a seat over there and we'll call you when we're ready. Be careful you don't smudge your makeup now, we'll be ready to use you very soon."

Cole went over where she'd pointed, to the side wall, where he found some folding chairs set up against the wall. The middle-aged man was there, in his police uniform, and another man in a police uniform, and two others in business suits. Cole sat down near them, but not with them, and waited. To his right, the other four men chatted together; out on the floor, men in shirt sleeves wrestled the television cameras around and shouted to one another and pointed up at the ceiling and spoke into headsets and hurried this way and that. Other men, in work shirts, carried pieces of furniture around, or stood in small groups talking together and smoking cigarettes.

The waiting began to bother him after a while. He'd gotten over his first shock at hearing the part he was supposed to play, and he had stopped being bothered as much by the nervous motion going on all around, but as the time went by the very fact of waiting began to prey on him. There was hustle and bustle everywhere, and the woman had told him they would be ready to use him very soon, so he was expecting to be called any second, but the time went by and went by and went by, and nothing happened.

From his position here, on the side wall, he could see

the control room, a concrete block affair built up on the balcony, with broad soundproof windows overlooking the whole work area. Through the windows he could get dim glimpses of men in white shirts, their heads bobbing back and forth; they were in semi-darkness up there, with faint red and green lights playing on them, reminding him of aquariums.

An hour went by, and a second hour, and no one had come near him, and then all of a sudden Herbie Lang came trotting over, smiling as broadly as ever. Lang spoke to them as a group, to Cole and the other four men, saying, "Well, comrades, it won't be long now. We've had our little problems, you know how it is, but we're all squared away now and we'll be ready to use you right after lunch. Take a lunch break now, be back at one-thirty. Check? Check." He hurried away again.

The other men got to their feet, grumbling together, and started off in a body toward the doors. Cole trailed after them, not knowing what else to do, but then he realized they weren't paying any attention to him and didn't consider him a part of their group, and he hung back, embarrassed at having tried to attach himself to them like a fifth wheel. He moved with deliberate slowness, letting them get farther and farther ahead, so that they'd already gone out the street door when he pushed through one of the doors into the lobby. They went off to the right; when he reached the street, he turned left.

He had to go all the way back to the subway entrance before he found a luncheonette, and then he stood for a second on the sidewalk, gazing at the concrete steps down to the subway, feeling in himself a desire to keep on going, to go down those steps and into a subway car and ride all the way back home. Everything was depressing him today, everything. The name of the character he was to play, and the tension crackling around the big shots in the studio, and his complete isolation from the other actors with minor roles, all of it surrounding him with premonitions of danger and trouble, of the presence of threats to himself that he could neither anticipate nor understand.

He told himself angrily that it was just the cycle affecting him, just one of his normal depressions coming over him, and what a hell of a time it had picked to come back. This was the most important event since his accident; the day on which he was starting again to live his old life. What he had been doing so far was not living his old life, it was living a kind of interregnum in the *area* of his old life, and that wasn't the same thing at all. Today was a new beginning, the first real step in the return to normalcy; he couldn't let any depression or any gloomy premonitions ruin this for him.

He went into the luncheonette and sat down at the counter. There were middle-aged women, shoppers surrounded by brown paper bags, eating lunch in two of the booths, and a few men in work clothing were sitting at the counter. A youngster in his late teens, pale and thin, came over to serve him, and Cole asked for hamburger and coffee. The counterman looked at him somewhat oddly, but didn't say anything. He went away and put the hamburger on, and Cole watched him, wondering why he'd been given such a funny look. But there wasn't any explanation.

He got his food and started to eat, and after he took his first sip of coffee he saw a dark red smear on the cup, the kind women leave with their lipstick. He stared at it, and suddenly remembered the makeup. He was in full makeup; his whole face covered with an orange-like grease, black and white and gray lines streaked this way and that across his forehead and cheeks, dark red on his lips.

No wonder the counterman had stared at him. He remembered now that the other actors had gone off to the right; there must be a lunch counter nearby in that direction, where the actors from that studio always took their lunches, and where the sight of a face covered by makeup wouldn't be uncommon. But no one came here from the studio; in here he was only some kind of insane freak.

He couldn't eat any more. He dragged a dollar bill from

his wallet and dropped it on the counter and hurried back out to the sunlight. He practically ran now, wanting desperately to be back in the studio. He averted his face whenever he passed another pedestrian.

Back in the studio, there was still activity, but only the stagehands were still there. No actors were present, and none of the people in white shirts. He looked up at the control booth, and it was empty, too. He walked back over to the folding chairs and sat down to wait.

After a while, people began to come back into the studio, and the noise built up again, and the tension, and the scurrying. The four other actors came in, strolling across the floor in a casual manner, talking together and smoking cigarettes. They sat down near him, and continued to talk. The middle-aged man Cole had seen up in the dressing room nodded at him in a friendly way, but made no effort to include him in the conversation.

The afternoon dragged on just as the morning had, and finally at three-thirty the woman in the tweed suit came over, bustling, nervous, tense, and said, "All right, we're ready for your scene now."

Cole and the others followed her across the room, through and between the various sets. It was like going through a maze, with the black pipes across the ceiling far above, and the feeling of great immensity in the room because in among the sets it was impossible to see the far walls any more.

They stopped at a courtroom set. It was just the front end of a courtroom, and looked thin and fragile. There was a judge's bench on a paint-stained platform, and a wooden railing, and two long tables backed by wooden armchairs, and just the first two spectator pews behind that. Other people were already there, actors and others. An actor dressed up like a judge was up in his place, and other actors were sitting at the two long tables. Herbie Lang was standing to one side, arms folded across his chest, a strained smile on his face. The gaunt man was walking back and forth, studying the set and actors in a fatalistic way. There were two men with clipboards, just standing around. And there was a stocky gray-haired man with a harried expression on his face, who turned out to be the director.

It was the director who positioned them, taking each actor in turn by both elbows and backing up, as though actors were things that had to be dragged into place. When he came to Cole, he maneuvered him over to one of the long tables and sat him in the chair on the end, next to a tall distinguished-looking actor whose face Cole found vaguely familiar.

Once everyone was in place, the director came around to each one, telling him what he was to do in this scene. One of the young men with clipboards followed him this time, and the director occasionally consulted with him briefly. When they got to Cole, the director said, "You're who? Condemned Man? Is that right?"

Cole nodded. "Yes. Condemned Man."

"Very good. Your cue is—" He consulted with the young man carrying the clipboard. "Your cue is, 'Hanged by the neck till you're dead.' No, that isn't right!" He consulted again, and said, "That's what I thought. That's your *speech* cue. First things first. Your *first* cue is, 'The prisoner will rise.' Then you stand up and face the judge. He pronounces sentence, blah blah blah, and then your cue is, 'Hanged by the neck till you're dead.' Shouldn't that be, 'Hanged by the neck until dead'? Somebody? Somebody?" He was looking around frantically, and three or four people hurried over. They talked together, checking with the clipboard, and finally straightened it out. The director said, "Yes, that's right. That's what I thought. 'Hanged by the neck until dead.' You got that?" He turned and shouted the last to the actor who was playing the judge.

The actor nodded and repeated the line back to him.

The director said, "Good. If you're going to do this right, let's do it right. Now. You, Condemned Man. You're already standing. The line is, 'Hanged by the neck until dead.' Then you, and you—" pointing to the two men in police uniforms

"—you take his arms, like so. Got that?" He demonstrated, grabbing Cole's arm. "You start to exit that way. You go over there, that way." He started off in the direction indicated, and stopped a few paces away. "And when you get here, you, Condemned Man, you twist out of their grasp and you make a lunge toward the judge's bench, like so—" He demonstrated, leaping forward. "And you shout out your line. Shout it out, now, really shout it out, don't worry about volume, that's the sound man's job. You got that? You know your line?"

"I haven't got it yet," said Cole.

"What? Why not? Herbie?"

"Right here, comrade commissar," cried Lang. He hurried over and said, "I'll give it to him right now, right this minute. Paul? It's, 'I don't want to die!' Simple, comrade?"

"I don't want to die."

"Right!" Lang beamed, and hurried back to the sidelines.

"He should have had his line," said the director. He studied Cole mistrustfully. "You've got it now?"

"I don't want to die."

"All right. And shout it out, really shout it out. Then you two, you grab him again, and you hustle him on out. Check?"

Cole nodded, and the two actors playing policemen nodded. The director nodded back at them, and went to talk to the people sitting in the two spectator pens, who would make believe they were the audience at the trial.

Cole went over it and over it, wanting to be sure he had it exactly right. Stand up, start to be led off, turn back and jump at the judge's bench, shout out, "I don't want to die!", be grabbed again, and be hustled off. It was just a short bit, and it was completely laid out for him; not like that nonsense at Robin Kirk's. He knew in advance everything he was supposed to do, and that made all the difference in the world. Of course he could do this, why not? Confidence began to grow in him, dispelling the depression he'd been feeling most of the day.

"People! People!"

The director was in the middle of the set, clapping his hands and calling to attract their attention. He said, "Everyone set now? You new people, court officers, Condemned Man, spectators, you know your jobs? Questions? Problems? Nothing? All right, then, good, then we'll have our runthrough. This is dry, this is just the runthrough. Arnold? *Arnold*?" He was looking far away, and shouting. "Are these damn mikes hooked up or aren't they? Arnold!"

A man wearing a headset like those worn by switchboard operators came over, trailing cables. "He can hear you, Bruce," he said.

"Well, why didn't you say so? Arnold, are you set?"

"He's set, Bruce."

"All right, then. Remember, people, this is dry. Charlotte, begin any time, dear."

The scene started. Cole tried at first to pay attention to the things that were being said, so he would know what the play was about, or at least what this scene was about, but his main attention was riveted on the details of his own part. His confidence was still a frail thing, and he didn't want any possibility at all that he would make a mistake.

A television camera began to roll toward him from the left, the three lenses pointing directly at him. He looked at it, watching it come toward him, wondering if this meant his line was coming up soon.

"Hold it! Hold it, people!" It was the director, running into the set. He stood there and looked off at the distance again, shouting, "What's the matter, Arnold?"

The man with the headset came on, and pointed at Cole without looking at him. "He's looking at the camera," he said. "The camera's on him, and he's looking at it."

"What? For the love of God!" The director came hurrying over, looking frantic. "Listen," he shouted at Cole. "Listen, you, this is a dry run but that doesn't mean you look at the *camera!* You're supposed to be *acting!* The judge is about to pronounce sentence on you, man, goddamn it, look at *him!*"

"I'm sorry," said Cole. Under the makeup, he felt himself blushing. He should have known better than to look at the camera, memory or no memory; he just hadn't been thinking, that was all.

"Start reacting to the *dialogue*," the director told him. "Don't sit there like a bump on a log. Am I right?"

"Yes. I'm sorry."

"All right, then. George, take it from where you were."

The director and the man with the headset both backed off the set, in opposite directions, and the scene went on again. Cole now watched the judge, staring at him intently. He tried again to listen to the dialogue, so he could react to it, but out of the corner of his eye he was aware of the television camera staring at him, and it took all his concentration to keep from turning his head and looking at it.

"The prisoner will rise."

He was just a second late, and then the echo of the line came back to him and he remembered that that was his cue. He stood up hastily, feeling awkward, the chair scraping loudly on the floor. He suddenly felt very nervous, very exposed. Not only the television camera was looking at him now. All around him people were sitting down, but *he* was standing up, looming up above them like a stick, and they were all looking at him. All around the perimeter of the set, people were standing and looking at him. He was embarrassed, terrified; sweat broke out on his forehead.

The judge had stopped speaking, the two actors in police uniform had grabbed his arms and were starting to push him to walk, but he hadn't heard the line. He hadn't heard anything. He let them push him, and his mouth was dry, his mind a complete blank. They moved across the floor, and from behind him someone shouted, "What are you waiting for? Cut, cut, hold it, you've gone too far! Condemned Man, you're out of the picture, for the love of God. Come back here."

Cole and the other two actors went back. Cole was facing them now, the ranks of people watching him. The director came dashing out, showing him again where he was supposed to turn, how he was supposed to leap, what he was supposed to shout. "You got it now?"

Cole cleared his throat, licked his dry lips. "Yes," he said. His voice was hoarse. "I'm sorry, I guess I forgot."

"Take it from the line again, take it from the line again. Look at the time, it's ten minutes to four! Let's get this show on the *road!*"

He was standing alone again, by the table, facing the actor who was playing the judge. More than ever he felt embarrassed and exposed, more than ever he felt their eyes on him, because now he had made two mistakes. His mouth trembled, and he repeated over and over in his head, "I don't want to die, I don't want to die, I don't want to die."

The two actors took his arms again, led him out across the floor, where everyone could see him. But this time he had to do it, he had to. He twisted away from them, despairing, turning back to leap toward the judge's bench, but he was clumsy with fright and embarrassment; his feet tangled up and he sprawled on the floor, skinning the heels of his hands. "Oh, my God," he muttered, "oh, my God." He scrambled to his feet, shaking so badly he could barely stand, and made a tottering step toward the bench. "I don't want to—" he wasn't shouting "—*I don't want to die!*"

Hands grabbed at him, trying to pull him away, and he fought loose, shouting, "Oh, let me alone! Let me alone, let me alone!"

"*Now* what?" The director was there again, face red with rage. "What is the *matter* with you? Who hired this man, who hired him? Herbie? Is this one of *your* little jokes?"

Cole could hear them through a great roaring in his ears, see them through a rose red hue. He was trembling, shaken; he wasn't sure he could go on standing.

Herbie Lang was standing there, smiling at him in brilliant hatred. "What's the matter, comrade?" he was asking. "Off your feed?"

"Is this an actor or a jackass?" demanded the director.

"Will you tell me that, Herbie? Is this an actor or a jackass?"

Cole said, "I'm going to faint." But he had no strength, he could only whisper it, and no one heard him. The other two actors weren't holding him anymore, and he felt himself swaying.

The director's face was inches from his, distorted with rage. "Now, listen, you!"

Cole leaned backward, away from the face, and lost his balance, and crashed over backwards, the rose red roaring swooping down on him like a funnel and everything turned off.

When he opened his eyes, he thought they'd been closed only a few seconds, but he wasn't even on the set any more. He was lying on a cot somewhere; when he sat up he saw that he was in the back of the makeup room. The makeup man was packing his gear, paying no attention to Cole.

The memory of what had just happened was strong in Cole's mind, making him wince in embarrassment and shame. He'd done everything wrong, everything, and then to top it all he'd fainted.

He had to go back. He didn't want to go back, he didn't want to go through all that again, but he had to. He had to prove to *himself* that he could do it, and he had to prove to *them* that he could do it.

He felt weak, and shaky, as though all his nerves were untied and hanging loose, but he forced himself to sit up. As he was getting unsteadily to his feet, Herbie Lang came into the room. He smiled like knives. To the makeup man he said, "Out."

"I got things to—"

"Out, comrade. Schnell."

The makeup man, grumbling, turned away and went out of the room.

Lang came over, the smile still scarring his face. "Well, well, tovarisch," he said. "That was quite a little scene."

"I'm sorry, I don't know what happened. It won't happen again, I know it won't."

"Oh, so do I, Nikolai, so do I. You don't do that to Herbie Lang twice, believe you me you don't."

"I didn't mean to—"

"What you meant and what you didn't mean, Nikolai, are matters of no interest to yours truly. I just want you to know that if there's ever anything I can do to you, any little bamboo shoot I can stick under your fingernails, I'll be more than happy to oblige. Pack up your apples, little man, your job is finished here."

"I can do it, something just—"

"It's done, Luchibka. Someone else leaped into the breach. So just toodle off. And do me a favor, will you? Hold your breath till the check comes. Will you do that for me, Nikolai?"

"But I didn't—"

"Of course you didn't, tovarisch, I know that." Lang's smile stretched and stretched; his teeth were square and white. "And the next time we need a little match girl, you'll be the *first* to know." Lang bowed with heavy irony, and turned around and walked out.

Cole sat down again on the cot. He felt bruised all over, and naked, and weak. The makeup man came in, grumbling, and went back to his work, not looking at Cole at all.

Cole didn't want to leave this room. He felt as though outside that door a semi-circle of people was waiting, a whole crowd of people just standing there, watching the door and waiting for him to come out; not to do anything to him or say anything to him, but just to stand there and look at him.

The makeup man said, "You gotta get out of here, you. You can't hang around here."

"All right." Cole got heavily to his feet.

"Come over here," said the makeup man. "Take that shit off your face."

Cole went over and the makeup man gave him a box of Kleenex and a jar of cold cream. There was a mirror on the wall, and Cole watched himself in it as he smeared the cold cream on. His eyes seemed set deeper into his skull than usual; there was a look of dry horror around his face. When he wiped the cold cream and makeup off, his flesh seemed pale and pasty. He watched the movements of his hands, trying not to meet his own gaze in the mirror, and hurried to finish the job. Then he got his overcoat from the hook where he'd hung it this morning, when all the world had still seemed possible, and left the theater.

He was a block away when he remembered the canvas bag and the other suit, still up in the dressing room. But he couldn't go back there again, not for anything in this world. He trudged on to the subway.

29

When the phone rang in the middle of the afternoon, he was washing the living room windows.

He almost didn't answer it, knowing what it had to be. But it kept ringing and ringing, with shrill insistence, and finally he padded obediently to its call, and, as he'd known it would be, it was Helen Arndt.

He hadn't gone to her place last night, hadn't even thought of it. After getting the verbal slicing from the smiling man—Herbie Something—he had gone straight home, to sulk and cower and try to build up his never-strong and now demolished confidence. In the evening he'd gone out and bought himself a fifth of store-brand whisky in a liquor store near Sheridan Square, had brought it home, and had drunk all but an ounce or two, neat, splashing it into a glass and then drinking it down, warm and undiluted.

He had been trying to make himself drunk, and in that much of his desire he had succeeded. But he'd wanted to be drunk only so he wouldn't feel so rotten about the day's defeat, and in that desire he had been thwarted; he was a mournful drunk. He sat in the dark living room, with only a little spill of light from the bedroom to see by, and he dwelled in agony on the events of the afternoon. The phone rang once, but he made no move to answer it, and sometime after midnight he fell into an uneasy and fitful sleep, in which the dreams to which he'd almost become accustomed by now suddenly reached new heights of ferociousness and whirlpool terror.

This morning, badly hung over, he had sunk without reluctance, almost with relief, back into the routine, just as though he had never tried to fight his way out of it.

But the outside world was insistent, ringing and ringing

at his mind, until finally he had to answer, and to hear Helen
Arndt's voice in his ear.

She was noncommittal, impersonal: "I wondered why
you didn't show up last night, but now I know. Herbie Lang
just called."

"Oh."

"You weren't ready, were you?"

"I thought I was. I guess I made a mistake."

"I guess you did. Don't get me wrong, sweetie, but this
isn't something you can just play around with, this isn't
make-believe. Herbie Lang is a very nasty little man when
he wants to be. He's perfectly capable of taking it out on my
other clients."

"I'm sorry. I tried to do it, I really did."

"I'm sure of that, honey, but look at the position you've
put *me* in. I mean, after all."

A sudden agitation shook him, and he shouted, "Your
position? What about *my* position? Why is it always everybody else's position, your position and Rita's position and
Kirk's position and *everybody's* position, why isn't it *my*
position sometimes?"

"Now, don't get huffy, baby."

"Don't call me baby, don't call me honey or sweetie or any
of that, don't do it anymore."

"Now, slow down there, my friend."

He shook his head desperately and said, "I'm sorry, I didn't
mean that, I'm just all loused up."

"I'd say so."

"I'm really sorry."

"Honey, have you thought about seeing a psychiatrist? I
mean, I don't want to tell you your business, but from what
Herbie says of the way you carried on yesterday…" She let
the sentence drift off.

"No," he said. "I don't need a psychiatrist. I don't need…
I don't want all this. I don't know what I want."

"You know I'm in your corner, honey, but there are limits.
Before I try to find anything else for you, I want to be sure

you're all right. I'll want to see you in something first. Do
you understand me, dear?"

"Yes, you're right. I shouldn't have tried it before I got
my memory back, that was all."

"You let me know when you're ready, dear. Let me know
when you're in a production somewhere."

"Yes. All right."

"Good luck to you," she said briskly, and broke the connection.

He hung up, and went back to work on the windows, and
he didn't understand the implications of what Helen had
said to him until hours later, until he was sitting at the kitchen
table, eating a TV dinner and drinking instant coffee, with
night outside the gleaming windows, and then all at once it
occurred to him what she had really been saying.

She had dropped him. She was no longer his agent. "Let
me know when you're in a production somewhere," she had
said, and what did that mean? It meant that his next job he
would have to get himself, on his own, without an agent.

He remembered this much from the dim past: The first
necessary goal of the young actor is to be accepted by an
agent. No matter how hard the struggle after that, it is
nothing in comparison to the struggle preceding it. The unagented actor gets no television, no movies, no Broadway,
and damn little off-Broadway. The unagented actor will take
any part in any medium for any pay or no pay at all, if only an
agent or two will be in the audience.

It was all going, all crumbling away like an island being
swallowed by the sea, eroding like river banks in the spring
floods. Rita, avoiding him. Nick, impatient with him. Kirk,
irritated by him. Helen, through with him. His vocation,
impossible for him to handle. On his desk, propped up
against the wall, was the notice from the Screen Actors'
Guild demanding an amount of money he couldn't possibly
pay.

The next day, Wednesday, a similar demand for back
dues came from Actors' Equity. That was the same day his

paid-up time with the answering service was done, and he didn't renew.

What was left? Of everything that Paul Cole had ever done or ever been in this towering city, what was now left? The apartment. Only the apartment, now antiseptically clean in a way that the old Paul Cole wouldn't recognize, and littered with notes and reminders that the old Paul Cole wouldn't need.

He stayed in. No one phoned, no one knocked at his door. He didn't bother to wear a shirt, or shoes. He shaved, but only from habit. From Monday to Friday he stayed in the apartment, making his narrow little round by day, trampled by the monsters of his dreams by night. Edna. The square of shiny metal. "Have you ever seen this before?" "Help! Paul, help me!"

Edna. The afternoon in the doctor's office came into his mind unbidden, time after time. Of course he wished that Edna were with him now, why not? What did that prove? She would console him and comfort him, she would be someone he could talk with and be with without the self-consciousness and without the danger of destroying yet another part of the past. It would be pleasant to have Edna here with him now, but it would be unfair to *her*. Once his memory came back, she would be out of place here, she would be as unhappy here then as he was now.

And it *would* come back, it *would*.

But he couldn't make himself believe in the scaffoldings of confidence he was trying to erect. An oceanic lethargy weighted his limbs and dragged at his mind; he shuffled through the days, worried and distraught and weary, unable to push himself into any concentration, any thought or any action.

Early Friday afternoon, he came to himself with a start, realizing that he had spent the entire day so far in a blank. Not once all day had he had any thought beyond the motions of eating and washing and housecleaning. Not once had he thought of any person, not once had he thought about what had happened to him or what he could do in the future. He had been mindless today, the routine taking on its own reason. Early in the afternoon he came to himself and realized: *I'd forgotten who I was!*

He had to break out of this. He'd been as purposeless as an animal, he'd *die* this way. He'd even forgotten to go to the unemployment insurance office. There'd be a check in the mail today, for last week, but none next Friday. No money, no agent, no friends, no past, no future, no hope.

How small the apartment was! The gray walls leaned inward ever so slightly, and the windows looked out at brick walls which themselves were edging slowly closer and closer. The ceiling was low, really, very very low, and dark with dirt. The notes tacked to the walls fluttered as he moved by them, making a small rustling sound, the only sound in the apartment; he played the records no more.

Out, he had to get out of here! Away...

He fled the apartment, and downstairs in the mailbox was the check from the unemployment insurance people, as he'd expected. He went out, shivering in the cold air, and hurried through the streets to the bank, getting there just before closing and cashing the check, keeping all thirty-eight dollars, putting none in the checking account.

From the time he left the apartment till the time he walked out of the bank with the cash in his pocket, he had been moving at last with a purpose, no matter how slight or unimportant that purpose was. But at least he'd had a *reason* to do something. The purpose had been to cash the check; now it was cashed.

He wandered. He was afraid to go back to the apartment, actually afraid, as though within the apartment lurked some miasma, some green gas that would fill him and enfold him and reduce him to pulp. The coffee shops and bars and theaters where his former friends were to be found were mostly eastward from where he was, between Fifth and Seventh Avenues, so he wandered westward instead. He roamed up and down and around the narrow streets, the twisted Bagdad of streets south and west of Sheridan Square. He crossed Hudson Street into the West Village, where he hadn't gone before, and strolled this way and that, stopping in an Italian grocery to buy a fresh pack of cigarettes, and then going on.

In the next block on his right, there was a dirty red brick building with garage doors across the front and a big green sign with white lettering above the doors. It looked vaguely familiar, the first even remotely familiar sight he'd seen in half an hour or more.

He stepped out to the curb so he could read the sign better, and squinted up at it in the failing light of late afternoon: CASALE BROS. MOVING & TRUCKING.

Why was that familiar? Then he remembered; he'd seen that name on a form somewhere. On his tax forms? Maybe, he wasn't sure. On some form somewhere, more than likely the tax forms.

He must have worked there, in the old days, between acting jobs.

All at once he laughed aloud. Between acting jobs! By God, if he was ever between acting jobs in his life it was *now!* He was between acting jobs like nobody's business!

Why not? Get him out of the apartment, get him doing some sensible physical labor for a little decent money, and it wouldn't even be a break with the past, because he'd *worked* here in the past! Here was one part of his past he could touch all he wanted, and it would *never* crumble in his hands!

He hurried down to the far end of the building, past the shut green garage doors, to the smaller door, the entrance to the office. He went in, and it was a small crowded room with girlie calendars all over the walls and a rolltop desk littered with pink and yellow sheets of onionskin paper. A short stocky man with thick black hair—black hair growing out of his ears, out of his nostrils, on the backs of his hands, a prickly stubble of black beard darkening his jaw—was sitting at the desk in his shirt sleeves, one pencil in his hand and another stuck behind his ear. He looked up when Cole came in and said, "Yeah?"

"My name's Cole. Paul Cole. I worked for you part-time a couple of years ago. I was wondering if you could use me again."

The stocky man squinted at him, and drummed his pencil point on some papers. Then he said, "Cole? An actor?"

"That's right."

"I didn't recognize you. You look different."

"I guess I am different." Cole grinned, trying to make a joke of it.

The stocky man nodded. "I remember you," he said. "Sure, I can use you. When do you want to start?"

"Any time."

"Tomorrow?"

"All right, fine."

"Nine A.M., check?"

"Check," said Cole.

He left there, walking purposefully once again, headed back to the apartment. The apartment had no fears for him now, it couldn't trap him. He had things to do. The apartment could only trap those who were meaningless and purposeless, those who had nothing to do, no reason for existing.

As soon as he got home, he went to work. First, he made a tour of the walls, ripping down all the notes that no longer had any purpose, notes about Nick and Rita and Helen and the job he'd failed on Monday, and when he was done the walls were almost bare again. Then he made up some new notes. One, on his pillow, reminded him to set the alarm for eight o'clock before going to bed. A second, over the desk, reminded him that he had a job with the moving company. A third, for his pocket, gave the name and address of the moving company, which he found on an old W-2 form.

He'd been right in telling the doctor he'd like to work in that tannery again. Physical labor, filling the day and using the body and easing the mind, was the best prescription in the world for while he awaited the return of his memory.

When he was done with the rearrangements in the apartment, he felt a restlessness, a new energy. He went out again, and walked a while, and at one intersection he saw a block away to his right the lights of a movie marquee. He walked down that way, and the theater was showing a double feature, two Technicolor musical comedies. He bought a ticket and went in.

He sat through until the last showing was finished, at five minutes before midnight. He enjoyed it all, the singing and the laughing, the bright music and the bright colors, and the sense of freedom. He wasn't forcing himself to do what he could not do, or scuttle around after this former friends, or listen to music he didn't like, or go to movies he couldn't understand. It was as though he'd been a prisoner within the old Paul Cole and now he was no longer a prisoner.

He was starving when he left the theater, so he stopped at a Riker's for hamburgers and coffee, and then he went home and set the alarm for eight in the morning, and went to bed. He fell asleep relaxed and happy, sure there would be no bad dreams tonight, but they assaulted him just the same, gnawing and clawing at him, sticking razors into his brain, and he awoke twice during the night in shaking terror, sweat-soaked, both times with the conviction that something critical had been told him which he had not understood.

And Edna.

And the square of shiny metal.

30

When he awoke he knew at once that it was Sunday and that he wouldn't be working today, and he thought, I'm taking Edna to the movies. Then he remembered where he was, and that yesterday he had worked not at the tannery but on the moving van, and he got mad at himself for the stupid thought, and got angrily out of bed.

He'd made it to his new job yesterday morning exactly on time. The boss had assigned him to a big rattling truck with a red cab and a black body. The driver's name was Marty, and the other helper's name was Jack; they were both professional movers, doing this full time and not waiting for any other career to suddenly flower in some other corner of their lives.

It had been fun working on the truck. That was the only word for it, fun. Their first job, they'd driven over to Fifth Avenue and 12th Street, to one of the apartment hotels over there, and unloaded four rooms of furniture from a seventh floor suite, taking everything down the big square open-sided slow-moving freight elevator at the back, and out the rear door to where the truck was double parked on 12th Street. The party was two elderly ladies and two small brown dogs with silky hair in their eyes. The furniture was all bent and twisted, gnarled and gleaming antiques padded with green felt. The two ladies twittered like birds, afraid everything was going to be broken; they stood around in the way, each of them holding a little dog to her breast. But they got everything out okay, and loaded onto the truck, and the two ladies went off in a cab, and the truck snorted through traffic uptown to West 73rd Street, Marty driving hard and screaming out the window all the time, Jack telling dirty jokes or how he'd screwed companies out of money in the past.

After that first job, they did a short haul, taking three rooms of furniture from East Seventh Street near Third Avenue over to Minetta Lane. The party that time was a young couple with a baby; the wife reminded Cole a little of Edna, but somewhat prettier.

They ate lunch at a White Rose on Fourth Avenue, and then they spent the afternoon in Brooklyn, moving a bachelor from Manhattan Beach to Bay Ridge. He had thousands of books and phonograph records all packed away in grocery cartons, and he kept making jokes about girls and offering cans of beer.

After work, Cole went with Marty and Jack to a bar on West 14th Street, over near Ninth Avenue. As far as he could tell, he'd never been there before; it didn't look like the kind of place the old Paul Cole would have gone to. Nor his friends, either. There was a shuffleboard in the back of the place, and the three of them played for beers until three o'clock, when the place closed. Then he'd gone home and to bed and to sleep. The dreams had come—the dreams were always there waiting for him—but they hadn't been as vicious as usual.

Now it was Sunday, nearly noon, and he'd spoiled things by starting the day with a stupidity. Forgetting where he was, thinking he was back in that town, feeling *pleased* at being back in that town, *pleased* at the notion of going to the movies with Edna. How perverse his mind was! The *one* time in all his life he didn't give a damn about, and that was the only part of his past his mind remembered. Not that it remembered much—the name of the town was gone, and the name of the tannery, and the names of his coworkers— but the little it did remember seemed to cling and cling. Only two items, all in all; Edna's first name and what she looked like, and Malloy, the name of the family he'd lived with there. Why he should remember those two things he didn't know, but there they were, always intruding, interrupting his thoughts. Especially Edna.

The apartment was getting a little messy, but he didn't

care. That part was finished, he had a better way to use his energy. He ate his breakfast now, and left the dishes unwashed in the sink, and then went back to the bedroom to get dressed. This afternoon he'd go to a movie, and tonight he'd go to the bar on 14th Street, see if Marty or Jack was around.

He'd just finished dressing when the knock sounded at the door. He went out to the living room, frowning, wondering who it could be, and when he opened the door Benny pushed his way in, looking belligerent and determined, saying, "Okay, man, enough is enough."

Cole remembered him, remembered his name and vaguely remembered the scene here the first night he'd come home, but he had no idea what Benny was talking about. He said, "What is this? What do you want?"

"You know what I want. Cough it up."

"Cough what up? Benny, I'm not ki—"

Benny made an angry gesture, saying, "Don't try that memory crap on me, man, I've had it up to here. Just pay me the twenty-five bucks you owe me and we'll forget about it."

Cole shook his head. "I don't remember," he said. "You loaned me—"

"I told you, don't pull that crap!"

"What crap? What's the matter with you?"

"You know who I am, don't try to kid me."

"Sure. You're Benny. You were staying here while I was gone."

"Beautiful. What an actor. I woulda brung an Oscar, but it slipped my mind. Pay me."

"Listen, I'm not acting. For God's sake, do you think I *want*—"

"I don't *care* what you want, man. What I want, I want that twenty-five *bucks*."

"If I owe you twen—"

"*If?*" Benny stared around the room as though looking for a weapon. His hands were clenched into fists, help up close to his chest, shaking.

"I'll pay you," Cole told him. "Just tell me why I owe it to you, that's all."

"Oh, you're a sweetheart, you are. I paid the December rent in this place, remember? You threw me out December twenty, am I right? Seventy-five bills a month for this crummy place, and I was only here two-thirds the month, so you owe me the other third, which is twenty-five bucks, and I waited now over a month, and today you pay me. I don't want no stall, no rough stuff, you try anything like last time I'll break your head, all I want's the twenty-five bills."

"Rough stuff? What—"

"I told you, cut it with that crap, I'm not interested. Big deal with the amnesia. Twenty-five bucks, that's all."

Cole took out his wallet. He had twenty-nine dollars left from last week's unemployment insurance check. He handed over twenty-five dollars to Benny, who made a big show of counting it before saying, "That's more like it. All you had to do was pay me right away, and we save ourselves all this noise and upset."

"Benny, I'm not lying about my memory, honest to God. You've got to believe I wouldn't do something like this on purpose."

"Who gives a shit?" Benny moved toward the door.

"Benny, please, listen to me. My memory really is bad."

"Who cares?" Benny stopped in the doorway, and spread his hands out wide. "Who gives a damn, huh? So get amnesia, so fall downstairs, so drop dead, who gives a fat rat's ass?" He turned away and went out.

Cole stared at the empty doorway a few seconds, hearing Benny going away toward the stairs. On sudden impulse, he shouted, "Hey!" and ran out after him.

Benny was at the top of the stairs. He turned his head, frowning, and looking a little wary. Cole ran up to him and grabbed him by the front of the jacket. "The square of shiny metal," he said. "Tell me about it, Benny."

Benny stared at him. "The what?"

"You know about it. You *all* know about it. Tell me about it. Benny, God damn you, tell me about it."

"Get your hands off me!"

"The square of shiny metal!"

They struggled a bit at the head of the stairs, and finally Benny broke loose and ran down the half-flight to the landing between floors. He turned and stared up at Cole, heaving for breath. "You're off your nut, man," he said, wonder in his voice. "Completely off your nut. You're a goddamn lunatic, you know that?"

Cole struggled for words—his chest was aching, a lead pillar was in there pressing outward—and he screamed, "You ought to care! You *ought* to care!"

"Drop *dead*."

Benny turned and ran on downstairs. A minute later Cole heard the front door slam.

He sat down wearily on the top step, and pressed his cheek against the cold metal of the banister post. He'd sat like this the very first night he was in New York, only one more flight up, up by the door to the roof.

"Edna," he said. His eyes burned, but he didn't cry.

31

The Sundays were the worst. There was nothing to do on Sunday, to begin with, no job to go to nor people to see. Marty and Jack were never around at the bar on Sunday, neither afternoon nor night; Cole had no idea how they spent their Sundays. Also, Sunday was the day he most often and most longingly thought of Edna; back in the town, he would be seeing her today.

During the week it wasn't so bad. He went to work at nine every morning, and quit any time from five to eight at night, depending on how much there was to do and when they finally got the truck back to the office. Two or three nights a week, either Marty or Jack or both would go along with him to the bar, and the other nights he usually went to the movies or sat alone in the bar watching television. He was getting between fifty and sixty dollars a week, depending on how many hours he worked, and he was spending it a little too rapidly, which bothered him from time to time.

The second Sunday, he returned in a way to the old routine of cleaning the apartment, but with one difference. Instead of just cleaning it, he'd made it over completely. The cooking utensils and clothing and records he'd been keeping in the bookcase all went back to their rightful places, and he took the bookcase apart and made ten or twelve trips downstairs, carrying bricks and planks, leaving them all in the little railed-in area next to the front door where the garbage cans were kept. Since he didn't listen to the records any more, he stored them away on the shelf in the closet, and dismantled the components of the record player, planning to try to sell them for enough to buy himself a radio. Eventually, he'd like to have a television set, too. Make the place seem more like home. But there wasn't any place open on Sunday where he might sell the phono-graph equipment, and so far he hadn't had any time away from work during the week, so the components were still sitting bunched together on the table in the living room, covered with dust, waiting for him to find a chance to take them away and sell them.

Only once since he'd started working had he run into anyone from the old life. That was the second Tuesday, when he'd gone out on a job in the station wagon. Most of the time he rode with Marty and Jack in the truck, but every once in a while the boss sent him out on a smaller job, in the station wagon, driven by a silent guy named Scotty. They went, that Tuesday afternoon, to an address on Christopher Street, not far from Cole's apartment. The party's name was Joseph Powers, which didn't ring a bell when he heard it, but when they got to the place and saw Powers Cole suddenly did remember him. Or recognize him, which wasn't exactly the same thing.

Powers recognized him, too, and seemed somewhat em-barrassed. After they said hi to one another there was nothing left for either to say; Cole busied himself with moving Powers' possessions feeling self conscious and ill at ease, while Powers watched him with a worried and uncomfort-able expression on his face. Cole was relieved when the job was finished and he said so long to Powers, and it seemed to him that Powers too was relieved.

Friday, the thirtieth of January, he'd taken time from work and gone back to see the doctor again. It was only a repetition of last time, with the same questions about his symptoms, to which he gave the same replies, and another session with the truth serum. This time, the doctor spent more time on the square of shiny metal, and Cole did manage to produce more information about it than he'd known he possessed.

Its size, for instance. Though it appeared in his dreams in various sizes, the 'right' size, it had seemed to him under narcosynthesis, was small, about a foot square, approximately the size of the piece in the mobile at Helen Arndt's place. And when it was small—he hadn't known this before, and couldn't guess what it meant—it was very often being held by a policeman. A tall, stern policeman in a blue uniform, with a badge shining almost as brightly as the metal square.

From the doctor's subsequent questions, it was obvious he felt he was on the trail of something important, some opposition to authority buried deep within Cole's mind. But when he'd asked Cole if the square of shiny metal were the most important element in his dreams, Cold had told him no; the most important thing was Edna.

Edna! Could nothing bleach her from his mind?

The doctor had seemed dissatisfied with his second session, and had urged Cole to come back shortly, but Cole had told him about the moving job and had claimed he couldn't get another afternoon off for a month. The truth was, he had no intention of going back at all; it only wasted time and stirred things up. The night after this last interview with the doctor was hell; the dreams came shrieking in at him, descending from the ceiling with jagged jaws, back again to their very worst. After a few such nights, the dreams eased somewhat, and permitted him uninterrupted sleep once more. He told himself his state was improving, soon everything would be all right.

But it would not. It was just no good. He could have made some sort of adjustment to his evolving life if it hadn't been for Edna, but with her so much in his mind it was just no good, and finally he had to admit it to himself.

He thought of Edna morning and night. Half the time, he awoke in the morning thinking he was back in that town, in the Malloys' house, and wondering if he was supposed to see Edna today. Half a dozen times a day he would see things or hear things that he would instinctively make an effort to remember, so he could tell Edna about them when next he saw her. These mistakes were always followed by periods of depression and loss, when he was silent and indrawn, not responding to anything said by Marty or Jack. All his feelings were brief and tenuous, and soon the depression would fade away, until the next time; but there always was the next time, and it was just no good.

The dam broke not on a Sunday after all, but on a Tuesday, the seventeenth of February, three and a half weeks after he'd started working for the moving company. He awoke with a confused jumble of impressions and ideas, thinking he was in the town, thinking also of the square of shiny metal and telling himself he would have to talk with Edna about that and see if *she* knew what it was.

The mistake lasted only a second or two, as it always did, and then he was straightened out again. If only he'd been able to work things out better with that old girlfriend of his, he thought idly, she might even be living here now with him, serving surely as a source of distraction, and he wouldn't spend so much time thinking of Edna.

He swung his legs over the side of the bed, sat up, and suddenly stopped motionless, his mouth open.

The girl's name.

His old girlfriend, the one he'd met during the holidays, she'd even been *up here*.

No.

He shook his head slowly, back and forth, back and forth. He couldn't remember it. The name had been in his head, on his tongue, not two months ago, but now he couldn't remember it. It was gone.

What else? God help him, what else?

The acting job. The man who'd gotten so mad at him, he remembered that, or at least that part of it, but what was that man's name? What had the acting job been? He'd done it wrong, he remembered being in the makeup room afterward with the man talking sarcastically at him, but what about before that, the acting job itself, what had that been?

Helen? What was Helen's last name? She was his agent, he really ought to know her last name. Sure, it was written in his little phone book over there, but it ought to be in his *head*.

It was all gone. There were probably other people, other places, other events, about which he'd forgotten so much he couldn't even ask himself questions about the details. Everything ran though his mind, dribbled through like sand in an hourglass. His mind was a sieve, in which some of the larger pieces of memory took longer to wash through, but everything washed through eventually, nothing was ever retained. Except, so far, Edna; so the memory of her must be, in some way, the largest piece of memory in his experience, for it to be taking so long to wash through.

It wasn't coming back, his memory just wasn't going to come back. It wasn't any better today than it had been the day he'd arrived in New York. It wasn't any better right this minute than it was the day after he'd had the accident that had caused this, whenever and wherever that accident had taken place; that fact was so far in the dim past that not a trace of it now remained in his mind.

It seemed to him now that he had known for a long while his memory wouldn't improve. It was so obvious, once he allowed himself to think of it, that he couldn't believe there had ever been a time when he hadn't known it as the truth.

He smiled, tentatively at first, reluctantly, but finally with full pleasure and relief. The memory wasn't coming back! No longer would he have to wait here, no longer struggle to be someone he wasn't, no longer expose himself to people who could feel for him only combinations of pity and impatience and disgust. If his memory was gone forever, he was *free*.

And Edna? What had kept Edna in his head after all this time, out of all the separate facts and elements that had entered his broken memory? *He* had kept her there, wasn't that obvious?

He was thinking thoughts now that had been trembling on the brink of consciousness for weeks, that he had been all unwittingly forcing down out of sight—because he'd been so mistaken about who and what and why he was—and which had finally become so strong that they *had* to force their way to the surface. The relief was incredible; he felt so *light*.

Edna. She isn't pretty, she isn't self-confident or self-assured, she'll never be very smart. But say all that and you have said nothing, nothing, nothing. She is mine if I want her, and I do want her, more than anything else in the world that it is possible for me to have, and that is all there is worth saying. Who cares if it's a feeling that can be called love, or if it's only a lot of smaller feelings in combination, the result is still the same.

It was so easy, once he started, once he began to look at himself. All he had to do was make the first small step, to acknowledge that his memory was never going to improve, and all the rest followed naturally and inevitably and beautifully. It seemed to him that he had trembled on the brink of that first small step time and time again, with Helen, with the doctor, with everybody, but it had taken a whole series of shocks—the acting job and all the other things he could no longer remember—and then some time for his mind to absorb their implications, before the first step could be taken.

Everything opened from there like a flower. He finally understood why Edna was still in his mind. He finally understood how he could get off this treadmill and find some tiny dance step of his own to perform in blessed peace and oblivion. He finally understood what there was still to do with his life.

He wouldn't be going to work today, that was the first thing. Not today, or tomorrow, or ever again, not with the moving company. No, and he wouldn't be living in this barren cold apartment any more, this apartment stripped of the old Paul Cole but not furnished with the new Paul Cole because the new one hadn't been born until just this minute.

He would go back to that town, that was the first thing. Now, today. He would go back there, and see Edna, and explain everything to her, and try to get her forgiveness, and he was sure she would forgive him. He'd live, for a while at least, with the Malloys, and he'd work again in the tannery. Instead of searching for someone to be, he would relax and be whoever he was.

If he managed to get a bus this morning, he should be there by tomorrow sometime. He no longer had his suitcase or canvas bag—he must have pawned them somewhere, he couldn't remember—but he could get another bag, and there wasn't that much he wanted to take with him anyway. He had over forty dollars, and if that wasn't enough to get him where he had to go he could always pawn something else.

Where he had to go. Startled, he realized he didn't remember the name of the town. How was he going to go there, if he didn't know the name of it?

He hurried over to the desk and started going through it, reading every scrap of paper he came across. Surely, somewhere, somewhere, somewhere he'd written down that name, a name as important as that.

Nothing. Nothing, and again nothing. One folded scrap of paper tucked away in a corner of a desk drawer read: *542 Charter St.* He frowned at it, and then recognized it; that was where he'd lived with the Malloys. The street address, but not the city. Why hadn't he written the name of the city? How stupid could he have been?

This scrap of paper had been with a few others in the same drawer, all obsolete notes he'd pulled from his trouser pockets at one time or another and stashed away here for some forgotten reason. None of the other notes made any sense to him, nor did any of them mention the name of the town.

What about the notes on the walls? He read them, but they all referred to matters here in New York. He went through the pockets of his clothing in the closet, but there was nothing in them either.

He went back to the desk, went through the whole territory again, desk and walls and pockets, went out to the living room and looked despairingly this way and that, looking for someplace more to search, and there was nothing. 542 Charter St., that was all.

On the third time through, searching the same places all

over again, he picked up a tax form, and saw Helen Arndt
referred to, and then he realized there was a way to find out.
Helen would know; it was as simple as that.

He phoned, but it was too early and no one answered.
Burning with impatience, he dressed, and put clothing out
on the bed to be packed, and made himself some breakfast.
Finally it was nine o'clock, and he called again, and this time
got a female voice that told him Miss Arndt hadn't come into
the office yet but was expected any minute. He said he'd call
back, and then sat at the desk, watching the clock, smoking
nervously, until it was nine-fifteen, and this time when he
phoned she was there and he was put through to her. He
told her who he was, and she said, "Oh. What's the problem?"
Her manner was cold and abrupt.

"I need some— There's a piece of information I need."

"Oh?"

"I want to know the name of the last town I was in with
that touring company. I was with a touring company, wasn't
I? When I got hurt?"

"The name of the town where you had the accident?"

"Yes. You'd have it there, wouldn't you?"

"What is it? Taxes?"

It was simpler to agree. "Yes."

"I'll look it up. It's Deerville, I know that much. Nebraska,
or Kansas, or Iowa, I'm not sure. Deerville. I'll look up the
state."

"Thank you."

She came back on the line a minute later and told him
the state, and he wrote it down and thanked her again. She
said, "Any time," brusquely, and broke the connection.

Next he phoned the Port Authority Bus Terminal, and
learned that a ticket to Deerville would cost him thirty-five
dollars and twenty cents. He wrote everything down, and
when the call was finished he counted all his money. Including a little change, he had forty-six dollars and fifty-five
cents. In addition, there were three dollars and change in
the checking account, which he could withdraw on the way

uptown, so he'd have almost fifty dollars. Fifteen dollars left over, after the bus ticket, to last him until he started working again. He could do it, he could leave here today.

But there was still a bag to buy. Well, why not take the record player out and pawn it? Then he could buy some sort of suitcase or bag in the same pawnshop. Yes, and stop off at the bank to close out the account. Then come back here and pack, and leave forever, and go off to catch his bus. By tomorrow night he'd be with Edna again.

He couldn't stop smiling.

32

There was snow everywhere along the route, so the bus was always behind schedule. Cole had to make changes at Chicago, and again at Lincoln. He missed his connection at Lincoln because his bus had run into a snowstorm through Iowa, and he had to wait six hours for the next bus to Deerville. Though he had no way of knowing it, this was a different bus company and a different route from the one he had taken when returning to New York and, despite the bad weather and the missed connection, it proved to be somewhat quicker.

To while away the time, he started a list of names, any name he could remember from the town. Edna, of course, and Malloy, and 542 Charter Street. Then other isolated names began to come to him, now he was trying to remember the town; someone named Black Jack, and someone named Bellman. A bar named Cole's Tavern? No, he must be making that up. Still, just in case, he wrote it down.

The thought of his coming meeting with Edna was somewhat embarrassing, because he could still remember how he'd treated her when he'd left the town. But the first meeting would be gotten through someway, and then everything would be good again.

Two days on the road. A little after three o'clock Thursday afternoon, the bus pulled to a stop at the storefront depot in Deerville. Cole got down from the bus and stood smiling at the depot, recognizing it. When he was waiting for his bag to be unloaded, he tried to decide whether to call the Malloys first or just go straight to the house and surprise them. It would be better to go straight there, Mrs. Malloy would get a kick out of it that way, opening the door and him just standing there.

But he knew he wouldn't be able to find his way around without help; he hadn't been able to find his way around too well while he was living here, and now he'd been gone a while. When he got his bag he went into the depot and asked directions to Charter Street.

"Charter Street? You go down here to the second traffic light, turn right. Fourth block up is Charter. It starts there and goes east. This side it's Raymor Street."

"Thank you."

It was a long walk. It wasn't snowing here now, though the sky was grey and overcast, but it had snowed heavily just recently; a hip-high ridge of snow separated the sidewalk from the street. Cole walked along, carrying his bag and repeating the directions over and over in a whisper, so he wouldn't forget them. He didn't recognize anything he passed, but that was only to be expected. He was surprised he'd recognized the bus depot. But he'd know the house when he came to it.

He found Charter Street, and the first house on the right was number 4, so he still had a long walk ahead of him. He rested a while in front of number 4, putting his bag down, flexing his fingers, and lighting a cigarette. Then he walked on.

516

518

520

522

524

It wasn't the right house.

He stood frowning at it, not understanding. The house was wrong, all wrong. It was a two-family gray clapboard, with porches upstairs and down, neither porch enclosed. It wasn't the right house at all.

He looked up and down the block, trying to figure out what had happened. He *knew* the address was right, 542 Charter Street. It was where the Malloys lived, he *knew* that.

Could he be wrong? Could it be somebody else's address?

Maybe Edna's. But this wasn't her house either. His memory of her house was so vague as to be almost non-existent, but he knew that this house wasn't it. Besides, he was *sure*. 542 Charter Street was *home*.

Why else would he have had it in a note? Why should he remember it as being the address of the Malloys' house if it wasn't? His memory lost things, but it didn't mix things up.

He went up the walk and stood by the stoop, staring up at the two doors. This just wasn't the right house, and he couldn't understand it, he couldn't begin to understand it, or think about what to do next.

The right-hand door opened and a woman stuck her head out "What do you want?" She was suspicious of him, ready to duck back inside and slam the door again if he made a wrong move.

He said, "I'm looking for the Malloys."

"Nobody here by that name."

"Did they—" He looked up and down the street, trying to understand. "Did they change the numbering on this street?"

"Not since I've been here."

"Did you just move?"

"Been here twelve years. You've got the wrong street."

"Is there another Charter Street in this town?"

"Of course not. Why should there be two Charter Streets in the same town?"

"They ought to be here," said Cole. He looked across the street, up and down in both directions, recognizing nothing, and while he was turned away the woman went back into her house and shut the door.

He had to find a phone book, that was all. He should have done that in the first place, called the house from the bus depot. He turned away and retraced his steps; three or four blocks back there'd been a small grocery store on a corner, and they might have a phone booth.

There was no phone booth in the grocery store, but the proprietor let Cole look at the directory. Cole held it in his hands, frightened, afraid of what he would find or what he wouldn't find, and then he turned to the M section and found the group of Malloys listed there.

There was no Malloy anywhere on Charter Street.

What was his first name, what was Mr. Malloy's first name? He'd remembered it last night, he'd written it down on the list. Matt! Matt Malloy, that would be Matthew Malloy, that would be Malloy, Matthew.

There was no Malloy, Matthew in the Deerville telephone directory.

"They're changing the set," he muttered. He could visualize the Malloy house now, with broad white X's painted on all the windows, and swarming around were the black machines and the men in yellow helmets.

The proprietor said, "What?"

"I don't know what's happening."

The proprietor watched him warily.

What next? The Malloys had disappeared, they'd never existed. He couldn't find Edna direct, he didn't know her last name. He didn't know anyone else's address.

The tannery. There'd be people there he knew, and they could tell him what had happened. He turned to the proprietor, saying, "How do I get to the tannery?"

"The what?"

"The tannery. The factory where they— The *leather* plant, the *tannery*!"

"Take it easy, will you? There ain't no tannery around here."

"Where, then? The other side of town?"

"There ain't any tannery in this town at all."

"But there *is*! I used to *work* there! God damn you, God *damn* you, what are you doing?"

"You back off there! I'll call the police, I swear to God. You get on out of here."

"I used to work in the tannery, I *know* I did."

"Not in Deerville, Mister. There ain't any tannery here and there never has been."

Cole stared at the man, but he was only the proprietor of a small grocery store, he had no reason to lie. He had to be telling the truth.

"Did I make it up?"

"You better get on out of here now."

"I *couldn't* have made it up."

"I'm not telling you again."

Cole went outside. Something was terribly wrong, terribly wrong, and he didn't know what to do, where to go, who to ask for help.

That man had mentioned the police. Could the police help him? He didn't like the idea of going to the police, but what else was there to try?

He stuck his head in the door, cautiously, and called, "Excuse me."

"Now, I *told* you—"

"I just want directions, that's all. How do I get to the police station?"

"The police station?" That seemed to shock him. He blinked, and looked helpless for a second, and then he waved an arm vaguely and said, "Downtown. You go on downtown and ask again there."

"Downtown is that way?"

"That's right. You go on downtown."

Cole retraced his steps, headed back in the direction of the bus depot again. When he came to the street with the stores on it, he stopped a man coming toward him and asked again where the police station was.

"Two blocks down, turn right. You can't miss it."

"Thank you."

Cole walked the two blocks, turned right, and there it was in front of him, a blunt brick building with green globes flanking the entrance. He went inside, and put his suitcase down, and walked over to the high desk behind which the uniformed policeman sat.

The policeman looked at him. "Can I help you?"

Cole opened his mouth to tell him everything, ask him

everything, but it couldn't be done. He said, "Could you tell me where the bus depot is?"

"Bus depot?" The policeman pointed with a pencil, giving Cole the directions. Cole thanked him, and picked up his suitcase, and left.

There was no place for him to go, so he went to the bus depot. Walking toward it, trying to think, he struggled with the problem of his memory and this town. He remembered almost nothing in the world but this town, and that memory turned out to be totally false.

Was there no Edna at all? Were there no Malloys, was there no tannery? Had he dreamed it all?

But he couldn't have, no, it was impossible. Edna was real, everything else was real.

He was in the wrong town, that's all. Somehow or other he'd gotten to the wrong town.

Helen must have told him wrong, must have looked at the wrong list or some such thing.

He reached the depot as he came to his decision, and went inside to ask the old woman behind the counter where he could find the Western Union office. He's send Helen a telegram, ask her to check again, she'd given him the wrong town to come to.

He stopped in front of the ticket window. "Excuse me."

The old woman looked at him. "Ticket?"

"No, thank you. I'd like to know—"

"Say! Aren't you that fellow—?"

He stopped, saw her frowning at him, said, "What?"

"That fellow the detective made leave town," she said. "Back last fall."

"Me?"

"You look like him," she said doubtfully. "Actor, he was."

"Yes!" Suddenly, there was light; this was the right town after all, for where he'd had the accident, but he hadn't *stayed* here! He said, "That's me, I'm an actor."

"Well, if you're the same fellow, you shouldn't have come back here."

"I shouldn't? Why not?"

"Well, you know why not just as well as I do." She was beginning to get indignant, apparently believing he was making fun of her.

He said, "No, wait. I had an accident, I don't remember things too well. You say a detective made me leave town?"

"Well, of course he did! Told you if you stuck your face back around here he'd put you in jail. The two of you sat right over there, waited for the bus."

"The bus. The bus to where?"

"The bus to where? How should *I* know? I give out a lot of tickets here, young man, you can't expect me to remember every last one of them."

"Well, you remember *me*."

"Of course I remember you! First time I ever saw anybody get run out of town, naturally I remember you."

"Then why," Cole asked desperately, "don't you remember where I went?"

"A ticket," she said, "is a ticket." Then her expression got more kindly. "I don't know what sort of trouble you're in, young fellow," she said, "but I do believe that was a very mean detective. I think you ought to clear out of town again."

"But where to? Where to?"

"I really don't know, just so you keep out of *that* man's way."

"Would *he* know?" Cole asked. "He threw me out, maybe he knows where I went."

"Why should he know? All he wanted was you out of town on the next bus, it didn't matter to *him* where that bus went."

Cole sagged against the counter. "Oh, God," he said. "Please."

"Are you going to faint, young fellow? You'd best sit down over there. Go on, you go over there and sit down."

He went over to the bench along the wall and sat down. He and the old woman were alone in the depot. He sat there, the canvas bag between his feet, and stared at the opposite wall.

He was so close, so close. He'd been here, in this room, and he'd bought a ticket—somewhere. Some other town. With a tannery, and people named Malloy at 542 Charter Street, and a girl named Edna. But where? He didn't even know which direction. If the detective had put him on the first bus through, it could have been in any direction at all. It could be fifty miles from here, or ten miles from here, or a hundred miles from here.

A tannery. People named Malloy at 542 Charter Street. A girl named Edna.

What was the name of that town?

He wasn't going to find it. He knew that as he sat there, knew it even as he fought his brain for the name of the town. How many towns would there be in a hundred mile radius around Deerville? And how did he know he hadn't traveled more than a hundred miles?

A name, that's all he needed. The name of the town. Or the name of the tannery. If only the Malloys had had a less common name, that might help. No, it wouldn't. How could it help, if he didn't know where to look? A million people there might be, or more, in a hundred towns or more in the area where he might have gone from here.

Damn this memory! If only it would give him this one name, just this one name, he'd never ask it for anything again, he could forget everything else, everything, just this one lousy stinking rotten name, one name!

The old woman came over and sat down on the bench beside him. "You're making awful noises, young fellow," she said. "You know that?"

He looked at her concerned face, and said, "No, I'm sorry, I didn't know it. I won't do it anymore."

"Should I call you a doctor?

"No. I don't need a doctor. Listen—do you know—is there someplace around here—some town—"

"Oh, easy! Easy!" She rested a hand on his trembling

forearm. "Be calm," she told him. "Just say it out calm and easy."

He inhaled deeply; it hurt his chest. "A tannery," he said. "I want a town with a tannery."

"Well," she said, "I suppose there's lots of those in this part of the country."

"Just one," he said. "Near here, that buses go to."

"There's Hammunk," she said. "That isn't very far."

"Hammunk." He touched the name, prodded it, but it gave off no echo of memory. Still, that wasn't any proof one way or the other. He said, "How much would a ticket cost me?"

"Three dollars and twenty-two cents."

"Then it isn't very far at all." Meaning it *might* be the place, it *could* be the place. If he'd been thrown out of town, and didn't have much money, he wouldn't have gone very far on the bus. He said, "Are there any other stops before Hammunk?"

"No, that's the first stop on that route."

"All right," he said. "I'll buy a ticket to Hammunk." It was a long chance, he had no real belief this town called Hammunk would turn out to be the right place, but anything was better than staying here. Besides, what the woman had told him about the detective had frightened him; maybe he was the policeman with the square of shiny metal, and if so Cole had no desire to meet him.

The old woman sold him a ticket to Hammunk, and told him the next bus for that town would be coming through in an hour and twenty minutes. Cole went to the lunch counter next door for something to eat while waiting.

Hammunk. No, it wouldn't be the right place. But he couldn't stop himself from wishing.

33

There was only an hour on the bus, crossing flat white land, and then the road curved into a low scattered town covered by a black smudge of smoke. Along the way, Cole had continued to grate his mind with the foolish fantasy in which it would turn out that this town of Hammunk was the right place after all, the place to which the detective had sent him last time and in which he would find Edna and the life he had stupidly abandoned, but when the town began to appear in the bus windows Cole knew at last it was the wrong place.

The bus sighed to a stop in front of the storefront depot that was the one standard inevitable similarity among all these towns. Cole stepped down onto the snow-packed sidewalk, carrying his canvas bag, and the bus went off again. He'd been the only passenger to alight, and no one had boarded here.

What now? In his pockets he had nine dollars and eight cents, and a dead man's identification, and a list of meaningless names, and half a pack of cigarettes, and half a pack of matches. He was in a place called Hammunk, a wrinkled town forming a little smudge on the flat table of the Plains States. In his canvas bag was some clothing. What now?

Next to the depot door was an iron newspaper rack, half filled with dogeared newspapers. In looking at it, Cole's eye was caught by a secondary headline over on the left:

STAR DEATH
SUICIDE?

"No," he said. He said it aloud, and immediately was embarrassed and looked around, but he was alone on the sidewalk.

Someone had mentioned suicide, not too long ago. The

doctor? Yes, the doctor, warning him against thinking of it for himself. But it would be silly for him to commit suicide, or think of it, particularly silly for him, sillier for him than for anyone else alive. Why should he kill himself? His problems could never be anything but temporary. Already, so much of that town had faded that he couldn't even remember its name. In a month or two the name Malloy would have lost its meaning. Sooner or later he would even forget Edna. It probably wouldn't even take a year. Maybe, now that there was no hope at all of ever finding her again, she would begin to fade right away. He'd forget her completely, name and face and place and person and meaning. Everything would be forgotten, everything smoothed out and silent and dark, in only a little while. What did he, of all people, what did he need with self-destruction?

He would continue to live. There was no particular reason to go on living, but on the other hand there was no particular reason to stop living, and of the two it was living that would take the least energy. So he was back to the question: What now?

A place to live, of course, that was number one. And a job. Some sort of life would gradually build up around him, inevitably, the way barnacles gradually build up on a keel. There was no point in going back to New York, no more point than there was in staying here in Hammunk. The two were the same, all in all; it just happened that Hammunk was where he was.

He went into the storefront bus depot, to ask about a hotel. There were always elderly people on duty in these places; in this instance, an old man, hunched over a copy of the newspaper Cole had seen outside. Cole asked him about an inexpensive hotel, and was told to try the Kent, three blocks down to the left. Cole thanked him and went outside again.

It was four-thirty in the afternoon, just beginning to get dark. There were practically no pedestrians on the sidewalks, and only an occasional Chevrolet or Plymouth passing with rattling chains on the street. Cole walked along, and in the middle of the second block he passed a building with green lights flanking the doorway, and POLICE STATION in gold letters on the glass of the doors. Cole glanced at it, and went on a few paces, and then stopped, remembering again the square of shiny metal. Something to do with police.

Not that it meant anything. He no longer believed that learning about the square of shiny metal would help him in any way—it wouldn't help him find Edna—but still it was nagging at him, unresolved, so after a moment of indecision he went back and climbed the police station steps and went inside.

There was a small room with a high counter across near the front, and a man in a gray uniform with blue chevrons on the sleeves sitting on a high stool behind the counter. He looked at Cole without interest and said, "Can I help you?"

"I don't know. I want to ask you about something." But then he didn't know how to go on, and he stopped, trying to arrange his thoughts.

The policeman waited, with disinterested patience.

Cole said, "I've got a memory problem. I was in a, in an accident one time, and now my memory's bad, and there's something I can't exactly remember, except it had something to do with the police."

The policeman was watching him with flat eyes. He said, "What's that?"

"A square of shiny metal. I guess it was about a foot square, and polished, so you could see yourself in it."

"A square of shiny metal? You mean a badge?" He pointed at his own.

"No, a thin square of metal, flat. No design on it or anything."

The policeman shook his head. "I wouldn't know what that might be," he said. "Not in connection with the police. Maybe something used in construction work somewhere, that's what it sounds like. You ever in construction work?"

"No. I don't think so."

The policeman shrugged. "Sorry," he said.

"Well...thank you."

"Quite all right."

Cole turned away, and started for the door, and the policeman said, "Wait a second."

Cole looked around at him.

The policeman said, "Your memory's bad, huh?"

"I guess so."

"You ever get picked up, maybe just wandering around not knowing where you were?"

Cole thought of the detective in Deerville. "I guess I was picked up one time, yes."

"Well, I never heard of anybody using a piece of shiny metal, but maybe so. I've seen it done with a glass, that's all. You know, a drinking glass, offer the suspect a glass of water."

"Why?"

"To get his fingerprints. You know, you don't want to book him, or you don't want to get him so worried he'll fly the coop if you're just checking him out, so instead of going through the whole rigmarole with the ink, you just get his fingerprints on something. A highly polished piece of smooth metal, now, that would do that trick."

"To get my fingerprints." Cole was holding his canvas bag in his left hand; he raised his right hand palm upward and looked at the tips of his fingers.

"Sure," said the policeman. "To find out who you are."

"To find out who I am." Cole smiled with one side of his face. "That's funny," he said.

"Is it?" The policeman was watching him with his flat eyes.

"Yes, it is. It's really very funny." Cole turned away, nodding, looking at his fingertips. "Very very funny," he murmured, and went outside, and turned left, and continued on to the hotel.

It was a small grimy hotel, and he could get a room without bath for three dollars a day. He paid for one night, left his canvas bag in the room, went back downstairs, and

asked the clerk did he know if the tannery was looking for
workers. The clerk said he thought Cole would have better
luck at the plastics plant, and gave him directions to get
there.

At the plant, a girl told him to sit on that bench over
there and wait. Sitting there, he patted his shirt pocket,
looking for his cigarettes, but on the bus he'd switched them
to his overcoat pocket. He reached in the wrong pocket of
the overcoat first, and pulled out a folded sheet of paper
which he at first didn't recognize. He put it down on the
bench beside him, and got his cigarettes out, and then
opened the sheet of paper to see what it was. It said:

Edna
Malloy
542 Charter St.
Black Jack
Bellman
Cole's Tavern

He put the paper down and tried to get a cigarette out of
the pack, but his hands were trembling and the pack spurted
away, cigarettes flying out and rolling around on the floor
like little white bodies. He got down on his knees and picked
them all up again, stuffing them back into the pack. Then he
took the piece of paper and wadded it up and carried it
across the room and dropped it in the wastebasket beside
the desk.

"I wouldn't have been happy there anyway," he said. He
could have cried then, at last, but the girl was coming back.